MW01641181

BLUESTREAM

A NOVEL OF HOUSTON
AT THE TURN OF THE MILLENNIUM

MICHAEL JUNGMAN

Print ISBN: 978-1-09831-022-6

eBook ISB: 978-1-09831-023-3

CHAPTER 1. MONDAY

CQC 49.33 0.77↑

Wheeler

On the fortieth floor of the granite and glass tower known as Conquest Plaza, Russ Wheeler stared into the vermilion light of a computer display. Numbers flitted across the screen and music poured from desktop speakers with enough volume to be heard far down the office hallways, if anyone else had been there to hear it. He changed the music from Eminem, whom he enjoyed, to Dylan, whom he revered, and rasped along with Bob as he continued crunching data.

It was four a.m. on Monday morning and he had worked through the entire weekend. His tie, a maroon silk knit, hung from a branch of the ficus tree in the corner of his office. Sweat stained his shirt and he sported several days' growth of beard. Remnants of carry-out meals littered the office carpet. He had studied the same file—headed *Bluestream*—for so long that his vision had gone fuzzy.

Leaning forward, he switched off the sound. "Christ," he said. "Jesus H." In silence, he put his feet on the desk and looked out the window at the lights of the refineries and chemical plants that lined the Houston Ship Channel. He imagined that somehow their noxious fumes had worked their way through the city's muggy air into his hermetically sealed downtown office.

He reached a decision. He inserted a blank diskette into the computer's data slot and instructed the computer to transfer the *Bluestream* file. When the first disk reached capacity, he replaced it with another and then another until he had copied the entire file. He dropped the disks into his briefcase and dumped a stack of files pulled from his desk drawer on top of them.

He composed and sent an email message:

> *To Norah Needham, Chief Financial Officer: I'll be out of pocket for a few days and since I have the only copy of the Bluestream financing plan, that leaves you in a bit of a bind, doesn't it? Don't worry. I'm willing to sell it back at a very reasonable price. I'll be in touch and in the meantime I'll keep it close—we don't want this good stuff falling into unfriendly hands. By the way, I quit. /s/ Russ Wheeler*

Wheeler jerked the computer's power plug from the floor socket and, with a screwdriver fished from the back of a desk drawer, removed one side of the computer's tower unit. A good hard yank on a gray ribbon cable broke the hard drive free from its mounting. He put the hard drive in his briefcase with everything else.

Jacket slung over one shoulder, he headed for the elevators. At ground level, a security guard looked up briefly as Wheeler hurried past and headed for the parking garage. Houston's perpetual drizzle spattered the back of his neck. He exited the garage and drove through downtown. It wasn't until he reached the on-ramp for I-10 that he remembered something important.

Dammit. He'd left his favorite tie hanging in the ficus.

Miranda

At five in the morning, Jesse fell out of bed. Miranda heard the thump almost before the boy hit the floor. She slipped from under the covers and crossed the hall into Jesse's room. His head and shoulders rested on the floor but his feet remained on the bed, tangled in the sheets. His eyes flickered open.

"Hi Mom. What's up?"

She touched his forehead with the back of her hand. "Not a thing, Jesse. You fell out of bed again."

The boy looked around, seemingly bewildered. "Is Dad up?"

"Nobody's up. It's too early."

Jesse climbed back into bed. Miranda pulled up his sheet and straightened his blanket. By the time she reached the doorway and turned around to check on him, he'd fallen asleep again. Miranda longed to go back to bed but now felt wide awake. She put on a pot of coffee and began a mental list of the things that needed attention when she got to the office. She was still adding items when the coffee maker gasped its final gurgle. She poured, slipped a cube of ice into the cup, took a sip and continued her list.

An hour later David, still half-asleep, emerged from their bedroom and made his way out the front door to retrieve the morning paper. Miranda put aside her list and turned to making breakfast. Icebox waffles in the microwave. Glass of milk for Jesse. Fresh coffee for David. When the microwave buzzed, she walked down the hall to wake her son.

David returned to the kitchen. Coffee cup in hand, he scanned the *Wall Street Journal*. "It says here that your CEO has called a press conference for this morning. Conquest is making another big acquisition."

Miranda shrugged. "I don't do big sexy deals," she said. "I count beans."

"Can I, Mom?" said Jesse, repeating a request she'd somehow missed the first time.

"Can you what?"

"Have breakfast in front of the TV?"

Miranda shook her head and mimed bringing a spoon to her mouth.

David read aloud, lowering his voice in imitation of a television news announcer. "Bluestream, a California firm, reportedly has developed a breakthrough telecommunications technology but needs capital to bring it into production. Analysts see the acquisition as a critical component of Conquest's broad-based diversification strategy."

"Jesse, time to go," Miranda said. "The bus will be here any minute."

Jesse went into a frenzy of sneaker-tying and backpack-stuffing. Before heading out the door, he turned to his mother, his face mock serious. "Have a good day at the office," he said gravely. "Make wise choices."

Minutes later, showered and dressed, she headed for the front door herself. David remained at the table, still in his pajamas, sipping his coffee.

"Aren't you going to be late for work?" she asked.

"Depends," he said.

"On what?"

"On what kind of mood my wife is in this beautiful morning."

As she kissed him goodbye, he took the opportunity to slide both hands under her skirt and up the backs of her thighs. "Maybe you could be late, too." He pulled her closer and rested his head against her chest.

"Oh David, please. Not now." She pushed away, but didn't mean it. With an eight-year-old in the house, they didn't get many chances.

He squeezed her rump pleasantly and nuzzled his face against the front of her blouse. Somehow he'd already undone the zipper at the side of her skirt and gotten his hands into the top of her panty hose. He worked them down far enough that she felt a draft from the air conditioner blowing against her bare backside.

Miranda faltered. She stood in her own kitchen, in medium heels, on the verge of being late for work. She was fully dressed for the office except that her skirt had fallen to her ankles and her pantyhose bunched uncomfortably around her thighs. Her husband had one blouse button between his teeth and had begun squiggling an inquisitive finger into the rapidly dampening space between her legs. Her knees trembled.

"Oh, for God's sake." She set down her purse, kicked away the skirt and headed for the bedroom. "Come on already," she called.

David followed at a saunter.

Jack

An ecru limousine with a license plate that read **CQC CEO** cruised eastward on Allen Parkway, ferrying Jack Burnam from his River Oaks mansion to his downtown office. Ahead, the 65-story silhouette of Conquest Plaza rose against the rest of the Houston skyline. Coffee and a warm Danish rested on a burled tray at Jack's side and neatly-folded copies of the day's newspapers lay on the limo's back seat.

He flipped open his cell phone and called his secretary to check Conquest's stock price. It was the Brownian motion of this number that, more than anything else, gave significance to Jack's earthly existence. When the stock price climbed, he felt fulfilled and his mood soared. When it fell, he grew querulous and cranky and doubted his purpose in life. Today, however, would be a good day. The market had responded positively to the early rumors about Bluestream. "Looks like we're up again today," he congratulated himself.

In less than an hour, Jack would walk into a press conference to announce the Bluestream deal, and the prospect triggered a jolt of adrenalin. So much so that he directed his driver Santo to open the limo's sunroof. Jack stood and lifted himself halfway out of the car, gripping the handholds that he'd installed on its roof for this very purpose. As Santo deftly navigated the winding curves of Allen Parkway, Jack shifted his weight from side to side like a boxer. Buffalo Bayou meandered through the parkland on his left and, to his right, a newly-completed luxury residential high-rise occupied the site of the old Gulf Publishing Building. The wind flattened his features and squeezed tears from the corners of his eyes. His hair slick with morning mist, Jack swelled with pride as the car roared into downtown. It was all he could do to stifle a triumphant bellow.

It wasn't until Santo brought the limo to a halt in front of Conquest Plaza and Jack stepped out onto the sidewalk that he spied the trailing police cruiser. The squad car pulled in behind the limo, red light bar flashing but sirens silent. Jack gave the cop at the wheel a friendly wave as he headed toward the building entrance.

"Santo, take care of this, will ya?" he yelled. "I got work to do."

Feo

The first time Feo saw Conquest Plaza, on a trip to Houston to interview for his job in the Security Department, he'd stood a block away and craned his neck upward. It wasn't the tallest building in the city, but almost certainly the shiniest. The chrome and white color scheme and the smooth rounded corners reminded him of the old-fashioned refrigerator in his mother's kitchen back in San Antonio, the one that on one sizzling summer day broke down beyond repair and let spoil a week's worth of groceries.

He'd taken the job with visions of snaring embezzlers and fending off corporate espionage. He'd expected to design systems to prevent executive kidnappings and write software to detect money launderers, the kind of things he'd learned in college. It hadn't turned out that way so far, not by a long shot. His daily assignment was to read the employees' Internet logs, for the purpose of enforcing company policy: *Internet use during office hours is permitted on a limited basis and only if such use does not interfere with job performance.* As if having instantaneous access to a million things infinitely more interesting than their work wouldn't hinder job performance.

Feo put his morning orange juice on his desk and set about scanning the logs from the previous day. It was the usual crap. A secretary on five who spent half of her workday shopping online for lingerie. A guy on twelve who day-traded on company time. The sad soul in HR who subscribed to seven different dating services and checked them all hourly. A VP who had spent most of the previous week analyzing his astrological compatibility with Jennifer Aniston. And the Senior VP whose fascination with certain forms of pornography left Feo so repulsed he hadn't had the nerve to report it.

After six months on the job, Feo had concluded that the great majority of the company's employees devoted at least a fourth of each workday to surfing the net. A pretty decent percentage of them seemed to come to the office for no other purpose. They weren't criminals or anything like that. They were ordinary people—well, except for the Senior VP—getting through a tedious corporate workday.

He wasn't sure what happened with the reports he gave the managers about the websites the employees visited on company time. More than a few times, he'd noticed, an offending website showed up a day later under the manager's name.

His phone rang.

"Duarte, hie yourself up to forty, okay? East side corridor, office of a guy named Wheeler. Check it out." It was the Deputy Chief of Security, an overweight, overstressed Anglo named Jenkins who used words like *hie* on a regular basis.

"Okay, boss. What's the story?"

"Not sure. This guy quit his job early this morning. Walked out."

Feo felt a surge of interest. Anything would beat another day in hot pursuit of Internet policy violators.

"What am I looking for?"

"What are you looking for?" Jenkins paused as if this hadn't occurred to him. "Good question. I guess you are looking for whatever's not there."

Miranda

Miranda, a bit sweaty and rattled at arriving late to the office, took the over-the-street passageway from the parking garage and descended the stairs to the Conquest auditorium. A sizeable crowd already awaited the press conference. She entered at the back and walked as inconspicuously as possible down the aisle. Norah Needham beckoned at her from the front row, motioning toward an empty seat. This is odd, thought Miranda. She'd had nothing to do with Bluestream, so why would Norah single her out now? Miranda felt her boss's appraising look as she slid into the seat.

Miranda had worked with Norah for the past six years and regarded that association as a decidedly mixed blessing. On the one hand, Norah had a near-legendary knack for crafting the innovative financial schemes that kept Conquest thriving through its ten-year acquisition binge. Her legerdemain had elevated her above all rivals to the position of Chief Financial Officer. Everyone knew that Jack Burnam didn't make a move of any consequence without getting Norah's buy-in. And though Miranda wasn't involved in that end of the business, it didn't hurt to be near the corridors of power. On the other hand, Miranda found Norah a remote supervisor with little sympathy for the messy business of juggling work and family. Past her 50th birthday, unmarried and single-mindedly devoted to her career, Norah seemed to Miranda the epitome of an anxious spinster.

"Good crowd, huh?" Norah took in the room with a quick wave of her hand.

"I guess this Bluestream thing is pretty big." Miranda offered, still wondering why she'd been called to the front row.

"Conquest will never be the same."

This jarred Miranda. Throughout Burnam's tenure as CEO, Conquest had bought and sold companies the way Jesse traded baseball cards with his friends. Geothermal energy. Coal gasification. Fiber optics. Robotic aquaculture. As far as she could tell, none of them had yet earned a profit, but that hadn't stopped Conquest's stock price from climbing. After an initial flurry of publicity, each one seemed to slip beneath the corporate waves. Conquest absorbed the companies and moved on to the next target. Why was Bluestream any different?

Applause rippled through the audience as Jack Burnam came on stage. Miranda saw him raise his hands as if to dampen the noise, but the crowd applauded all the more.

"Why is that?" Miranda whispered to Norah. "Why will Conquest never be the same?"

Norah seemed not to hear, her focus entirely on their CEO.

When Burnam finally lowered his hands and began his remarks, Norah turned back to Miranda. "You should be finished with the quarterly expenses by now."

"Of course." Miranda hadn't finished but she was close. She could wrap it up on her lunch hour.

"Stop by my office this afternoon. It's time I gave you an assignment with a little more upside."

Jack

As he waited for the applause to subside, Jack reflected on his highly congenial place in the corporate cosmos. Flags of the United States of America and the State of Texas flanked the podium. On the wall between them hung a huge silver corporate logo: **CQC**. Before him sat several hundred employees, stock analysts, financial reporters and, he would wager, more than a few corporate spies, all waiting on tenterhooks. He began.

"Welcome, everyone. As is our custom here at Conquest, we'll open with a silent prayer." He folded his hands and bowed his head. Most of the audience members followed his example. He waited a beat before lifting an eyelid to scan for those who didn't.

He spied Lulu Barker, from the *Houston Examiner*, on the aisle. The diminutive woman tapped her pencil against a notepad. Her short skirt rode up, revealing some aging but still-choice thigh. Jack had known Barker in college and, in fact, had dated her for a time. A college fling, it seemed to Jack, but once he became CEO it seemed she wouldn't let it go. She often showed up at press events with antagonistic questions designed to spoil the rosy scenarios that otherwise captivated his audiences.

He realized that she'd seen him looking at her. In fact, now she was holding the notepad with one hand to screen the obscene gesture she was making with the other. *Sonofabitch*, she was giving him the finger!

He lifted his head and looked out over the still-silent crowd. "Ladies and gentlemen, yesterday Conquest concluded negotiations to acquire Bluestream. Bluestream has achieved a technological breakthrough that represents a quantum leap forward in the telecommunications sector. Of course, I can't be specific in this setting, but I assure you that Bluestream's research capabilities, combined with Conquest's unparalleled financing, production and distribution platform, will catapult us into huge new markets."

The reporters wrote furiously and the stock analysts muttered knowingly. The employees exchanged gleeful smiles.

"The details are in the press release. If you have any follow-up questions when you get back to your offices, please direct them to our Chief Financial Officer, Norah Needham."

Norah rose stiffly and raised one arm.

Jack recaptured the room's attention. "But I'll take a question or two before we conclude."

For the next few minutes, reporters lobbed softballs and Jack enjoyed batting practice. Then, from the corner of his eye, he saw Barker with a hand in the air. He would have ignored her but the idiot handling the floor mic had already given it to her. He pointed in her direction.

"Mr. Burnam, does Bluestream's limited track record concern you? My sources tell me that they haven't had a single product make it past beta test."

Jack flashed irritation. "Do you really think..."

The woman had the temerity to interrupt. "At such a high price, aren't you putting your entire company at risk for some untested gimmick still in the think-tank stage?"

Enough already, thought Jack. He pushed a button under the lectern that cut off the floor mic. At the same moment, an enormous plasma TV at the side of the stage blossomed brilliant blue. "Let's let investors and stock traders be the judges of our corporate strategy. In other words, the *market*."

He gestured toward the screen. The Conquest logo dissolved and the real-time Conquest stock-price appeared: 49.25. Then, as if on cue, the number climbed until it stopped at 50.01. Jack beamed.

Sherry

Sherry Shipley squared her hips, centered her torso and crossed one wrist across the opposite forearm. She'd had no difficulty with the *Single Whip* or the *Repulse Monkey*, but the *Fist to Elbow* had unsettled the placid state of mind she needed for a satisfactory Set. She turned in a slow spiral, stretched her spine and started again. Gentle, continuous, circular. She did the *Wave Hand Through Clouds* four times before returning to the *Fist to Elbow*.

Sherry had learned the basics of T'ai Chi three years earlier while still living back home in Poteet. Of course, no one in Poteet could spell T'ai Chi, much less teach it, so she'd signed up for *Learn T'ai Chi Online* using her mother's iMac. Sherry started with the *Eight-Step Simplified Form* and zipped along until she'd taken every course offered. She'd framed all the certificates of completion that the Online Master sent in the mail and hung them on her bedroom wall.

Taco slipped out from under the sofa, mewing with insolence.

"Not now," Sherry answered, but the intrusion broke her concentration again.

Practice of the Set requires continuity, said the Master. On the other hand, T'ai Chi engenders elimination of self-centeredness. What could be less self-centered than to serve the needs of her pet? Spiritual dilemmas like these often preyed on Sherry's mind. She compromised by *Grasping the Sparrow's Tail* as she pushed open the apartment door. She did *Draw Bow to Shoot Tiger* on the way back to her practice mat. Taco, sprung, sprinted for daylight.

When the online offerings ran out, Sherry packed her clothes and took a bus to Houston. She knew not one of its nearly two million souls, but guessed that any city with so many people had to have someone who could teach her more about T'ai Chi. And she'd been right. Finding lessons proved no problem at all. Choosing the right class did. Taoist. Yang. Wu. Ch'uan. Zenobics. She hadn't known all those variations existed. She'd finally chosen a traditional program taught by a Master who'd studied with a Master who'd studied with Grandmaster Wong in China. More authentic, she'd figured.

With a real live Master, she had no need for a computer and enjoyed not owning one. Instead she bought a bio-magnetic mattress that gave her resonance therapy every night. In lieu of paying for Internet service, she enjoyed a monthly foot detox and bought all-natural, human-grade food for Taco. With no computer, no television, no microwave and a bare minimum of light bulbs, she'd reduced the radiation in her apartment to a tolerable level. And without all those distractions, she had plenty of time to practice T'ai Chi.

Taco wandered back in through the door, drizzle-damp, smack in the middle of *White Crane Spreads Its Wings*. The cat slouched into the bedroom and disappeared under the bed.

And as if Taco weren't enough distraction, her phone began chirping *Purple Bamboo Melody*, the ring she'd chosen to justify owning a cell phone. She tried never to put the device close to her head, instead holding it at arm's length and shouting into the speaker. A small price to pay to avoid a brain tumor.

She saw Wheeler's name in the phone's screen. "Russ," she said, "I've asked you not to call during my practice hour. The Master says..."

Sherry hung up when Wheeler responded with a crude remark about the Master. When the phone chirped again, she waited until *Purple Bamboo* had played through three times before answering.

"Listen, Sherry. Put your best bikinis in a suitcase. We're going to Mexico. The beach."

"Mexico? When?"

"This afternoon. Get a move on."

That's so typical, she thought. He'd made a plan to go to Mexico without so much as a *Maybe would you like to...?* She ought to tell him no and make a statement that he should treat her with more respect.

On the other hand, she loved Mexico. She *adored* Mexico, and might not get another chance to go any time soon. The last time she'd visited Puerto Vallarta she had soaked up enough *chi* to last a month. She paused and pictured herself on the beach, improving her tan and perfecting her *Fair Lady Weaves the Shuttle* all at the same time.

"You still there?" asked Wheeler.

"I'm still here," said Sherry. "What time are you picking me up?"

Miranda

Miranda breathed a sigh of relief. The expense numbers looked okay. She carried three copies of her report and handed over two of them as she stepped into Norah's office.

"One for you. One for Mr. Burnam."

Norah barely glanced at the expense binders. Instead, she passed Miranda a thick stack of files of her own. "I'm taking you off all of your regular work. I need you on another project. Very crash."

Miranda's stomach fluttered.

"You're going to run the securities filings for Bluestream. The 8-K. Mr. Burnam himself wants you on this."

Miranda hesitated, not sure how to respond. "Norah, I haven't been involved in acquisitions before. Are you sure?"

"Bluestream is big, but it's straightforward. Piece of cake for someone like you."

"What about Russ Wheeler? Wasn't he handling Bluestream?"

"Wheeler quit. Some kind of family emergency. Very short notice."

"Yes, but..." Miranda trailed off. She was flattered but uncertain. She wasn't sure she could do the job properly.

"I don't understand why you would hesitate," said Norah. "We're in a bind and this is a chance for you to pitch in and help. Why wouldn't you jump at it?"

The temperature in Norah's office seemed to have climbed as the early afternoon sun slanted across the carpet. She's right, Miranda thought. She should jump at it. She'd learn what she needed to learn on the fly. Maybe Wheeler's bad luck would be a big break for her.

She brightened. " Of course I'll do it. Thank you."

Norah reached across the desk and gave Miranda's hand a squeeze. Her grip was strong.

This must be important, thought Miranda. Norah never touched anyone.

"When do I start?"

"You have ten minutes to look over these files. Then come to the kickoff meeting in the Situation Room."

"Sure," said Miranda. "Who's running the meeting?"

Norah gave her a puzzled look. "You, of course."

Wheeler

Wheeler directed the cab driver into the departure lane at Terminal D of Houston Intercontinental. Remnants of the morning's rain stood in steamy puddles.

Sherry sat on the far side of the taxi's rear seat, chewing gum and staring out her window. "I still don't understand why we had to leave on such short notice," she said to the window.

"Aeromexico," Wheeler called to the driver.

"I told you," he said to the back of Sherry's head. "I thought we should take a vacation."

She turned to face him. "Right. You've been working day and night for weeks on this big project you can't talk about and all of a sudden today you decide we should take a vacation?"

Wheeler raised an index finger, kissed it and reached across the seat to touch it to Sherry's lips. "Later, okay?"

"This is it, sir." The taxi slowed to stop behind a Hertz bus. The driver stepped around to open the curbside door for his passengers and nearly tripped as he took in the white short-shorts, white sandals and lavender tank top that comprised Sherry's travel ensemble.

"How much?" Wheeler said loudly, breaking into the driver's reverie.

"Twenty-five, sir." Still watching Sherry, he began lifting bags from the trunk and placing them on a cart. When he finished, Wheeler handed him two twenties and told him to keep the change.

At the Aeromexico counter, Wheeler began negotiating with a mustachioed agent for two tickets to Zihuatanejo, his pronunciation so bad that it took the agent several minutes to figure out where Wheeler wanted to go. Sherry grabbed a stack of luggage tags from the counter and began filling them out assembly-line style—name-name-name, address-address-address, phone-phone-phone.

"How many bags?" asked the agent, a doubtful look on his face.

Wheeler waved vaguely at the array of leather luggage—his—and nylon bags—hers—stacked on the cart. He handed over his credit card to pay for the tickets and the extra baggage fees. "We may be there a while."

Sherry rolled her eyes. "I have a job, you know. Even if you don't care about yours."

Wheeler knew all about her job. Sherry taught holistic body conditioning to River Oaks matrons at an upscale fitness center on Kirby. In fact, she sometimes gave private instruction to Jack Burnam's wife Lacey, the contact that had enabled Wheeler to make the jump from bored VP at a mid-size oil drilling outfit to his hotshot finance job at Conquest. For a time he'd set his sights on someday moving up to the CFO spot, but then along came Bluestream. If he played it right, he thought, neither he nor Sherry would need jobs at all.

"I think the Ab-Salute can get along without you for a few days."

Sherry gave him a quizzical look and finished filling out luggage tags. With a fanfare of stamping and stapling, the ticket agent handed the paperwork to Wheeler and directed them to the first class lounge. Sherry remained ominously silent until they sat nursing their drinks—a margarita for him, fresh-squeezed papaya juice for her.

"All right," she said at last. "Spill it. I'm not getting on this airplane until you explain."

Wheeler sighed in surrender. "I promise. But first I gotta make a phone call."

Sherry made a face. "Who are you calling?"

Wheeler shrugged as if she should know. "I can't leave town without calling my wife."

Maggie

Maggie Wheeler turned from San Felipe onto Briar Oaks Lane where she spied the familiar columns of the Junior League building. A valet took her keys. Stepping inside, she scanned the Tea Room for her companions. She didn't think of herself as a Junior League kind of woman, but if a girl grows up in a certain neighborhood, and if her mother belonged to the League, then the girl might as well go along and be graceful about it.

"Hairyew, hairyew," someone shouted. Jolene.

"I'm good, I'm good," answered Maggie. "How 'bout your ownself?" Maggie had learned to switch her Texas accent on and off according to her surroundings. Jolene, on the other hand, was all Texas all the time. They traded air kisses.

A prim, blonde woman in her early twenties approached. Maggie checked her out: lime-green suit, muted paisley scarf, hose and heels. No visible body art. This must be their guest.

"Hidy," said Jolene. "You must be Sally."

When Sally offered her hand, Jolene pulled her into a hug lasting well beyond the time allowed for polite acquaintance in locales other than

Texas. It was her way, Maggie knew, of making prissy East Coast newcomers feel off balance right from the get-go.

"I understand your husband starts at the company next week," said Maggie when they were seated.

"That's right. He's just finished his MBA at Harvard," said Sally.

Maggie and Jolene belonged to a group of Conquest spouses that met and greeted the wives of new hires. Lately, it seemed that they all came from Harvard or Wharton or some other glitzy out-of-state MBA program. Conquest was hot.

"Har-vard," said Jolene, somehow making it rhyme with *barn-yard*. "No shit."

Maggie winked at Sally. "Don't mind her. Never been north of the Red River."

"No, Maggie here is the college girl," responded Jolene. "Went to *The University*."

"The university?" said Sally, puzzled. "Which university?"

"Down here," Maggie explained, "when people say *The University*, they mean the University of Texas campus over in Austin. I majored in suntan."

Jolene snorted. "Hell you say. Mags majored in pretty. She's the best-looking girl to come out of that school since Farrah Fawcett back in sixty-nine."

Maggie tried to shift the focus back to their guest. "Where did you go to school?"

"Mount Holyoke. Film Studies."

"Oh," said Maggie. "What kind of movies do you make?"

Sally looked abashed. "They don't teach you how to *make* movies. It's more, you know, film history and criticism."

"That must come in mighty handy," said Jolene. "Mighty."

A waiter set cups of tea in front of them and left, but Maggie called him back. "Bourbon okay?" she asked Sally. It took only a moment for three tumblers of Old Grandad to arrive, each diluted by a single ice cube. Maggie and Jolene offered toasts to Harvard and Mount Holyoke.

Maggie's cell phone interrupted.

"Tonight? Around seven?" said a man's voice into her ear.

"Yes, I think that will work." She said it brightly, as if scheduling a hair appointment. "That's right," she continued. "Just a cut and blow dry."

Maggie sipped her bourbon as they chatted. Although still shy of her 30th birthday, she didn't get along all that well with people right out of college. Older people were more to her liking. In particular, older men. Still, she was there on behalf of the company, so she steered the conversation back on track. "How do you like Houston so far?" she ventured.

"It's..." Sally began. Her face suggested that Maggie might have asked what she thought about last night's mud wrestling match on Spike TV. "We came here because my husband was excited about the job opportunity."

Maggie and Jolene chuckled. A job was the only reason anyone came to Houston. It was the largest city in the world with an almost complete absence of tourists.

"How's the weather?" Sally asked. "I hear it gets pretty hot."

"Calcutta," said Maggie.

"But it's humid, too," said Jolene. "Great for your complexion."

"And our apartment seems to have a lot of bugs," said Sally. "Is that normal?"

"Oh yeah, mosquitoes big as your hand," answered Jolene. "Cockroaches that fly. And fire ants."

"Fire ants?"

"Mean little bastards," said Jolene. "Burns like the clap if they bite ya."

Sally maintained a tenacious smile. "I'm confused. So do you like Houston or not?"

"You kiddin'?" Jolene looked genuinely shocked. "Wouldn't live anyplace else."

Maggie, although she might not use the same words, agreed completely.

Jolene rose and tapped her watch. "I'm afraid I'm due at the principal's office. My little girl got into some trouble again." She said goodbye to Sally and looked pointedly at Maggie.

"You be sure you don't get so drunk you miss that hair appointment."

In the silence that followed, Maggie studied Sally's hopeful face. She looked cheerful and optimistic, notwithstanding the bourbon flush in her cheeks. Maggie wondered what Sally would do with her Mount Holyoke self when the summer monsoons came and the streets flooded every afternoon and the mosquitoes rose in clouds like bats and she only saw her husband a few minutes each day because he was putting in 90-hour weeks at Conquest and when she did see him he'd be too tired to get it up. Perhaps, like Maggie, she'd have to find a little something on the side to preserve her sanity. A woman could sit through only so many films.

"Well," said Maggie, lapsing back into Texan. "Let's you'n me have another'n."

Miranda

After the kickoff meeting, Miranda sat in her office chair with a foot resting on an open lower file drawer. She considered calling David to tell him she'd be late for dinner, but decided to wait. Her head swam with all the new information about Bluestream and she needed a few minutes to synthesize. The woman at the press conference had a point. In its ten years of existence, Bluestream had developed a half dozen gizmos and sold the rights to big players like GE and Nokia, but none of them yet had gone into production. Not too impressive. But despite its failures, Bluestream had stayed in business and somehow raised enough venture capital money to pursue its next big thing. She wondered what new gadget the Bluestream people had dreamed up that Conquest wanted so badly? Her meeting had focused on the financial aspects of the acquisition, not the product itself.

There was another thing. The deal had a financing structure like nothing she'd ever seen.

Special purpose entity. Outside investors. She knew she was out of date on acquisition financing and had some serious catching up to do. It seemed sketchy.

She stopped herself. It wasn't her job to second-guess Jack and Norah. It was her job to get the 8-K filing ready and make certain all the right numbers were in the right places. She would push the lawyers and accountants and bankers and make sure the deal happened. Based on what Norah had said, this might be the biggest deal in the company's history, and Miranda would be a part of it.

She had begun a critical path analysis when her home number lit up the caller ID. "Mom, it's Jesse. I need help with my homework."

"You'll have to get your dad to help you. I've got a lot more to do here."

Jesse didn't answer for at least ten seconds. Then, "It's math."

Oh crap. They had a family agreement. David helped with English and social studies and Miranda handled science and math. "Okay," she said. "I'll be home in half an hour. If your Dad gets there before me tell him I'm picking up pizza."

Miranda gathered up the Bluestream files. She decided she would put in another hour or two of work at the kitchen table after dinner.

On the way to the elevator, she passed Wheeler's office and a thought came to her. If Wheeler quit on such short notice, he must have left behind his files and notes, and maybe she could find something useful. What she found instead struck her as excessively odd. Nothing but wastepaper littered Wheeler's desk and the credenza behind it. The desk drawer held only yellow stickies and paper clips. Norah had said he quit without notice early that morning so when did he have time to clean out his office? One more thing. She sat down to turn on his computer, but it was gone, at least the important part. In the spot where his CPU should have been she saw only a bunch of loose wires and bare plugs lying on the floor. She dialed the Tech Desk. "This is Miranda Sesno. Can you get me into Russ Wheeler's files on the shared drive? I'm taking over some of his work and I need everything there is on a deal called Bluestream."

"Sure thing," said a techie voice. "Gimme a sec."

Miranda gave him more than a sec. Five minutes later he came back on the line.

"This is weird. There's nothing."

"Nothing?"

"Sorry. Whatever he was doing, he did it on his local drive. There's nothing on the shared."

"Isn't that against company policy?"

"You bet. He could get fired."

Miranda hung up and glanced around Wheeler's office again. A flash of color in the far corner caught her eye—a necktie. On impulse she took it down from the ficus tree and slipped it into her purse.

Lulu

Lulu Barker kicked a file cabinet in her cubicle on the news floor of the *Houston Examiner*. Once. Twice. Three times. She fired a stapler at the wall. It sprang open, spewing staples and parts in all directions.

"Fuckall," she said to no one in particular.

Lulu's boss stepped out from the row of glass-walled offices that lined the news floor. "Bad day?"

"Fuck you, too." She was not about to tell him how Burnam had humiliated her at the press conference.

"Just a wild guess, but you seem annoyed." He took her by the arm and led her into his office, at the same time motioning at the other reporters to get back to work.

"Does your outburst have anything to do with the Conquest show this morning? My sources tell me you did your best imitation of a skunk at a cocktail party."

Lulu took a breath to calm her nerves. "Ed, I am positive that Burnam isn't telling the whole story about this deal. Bluestream shoots nothing but blanks."

"Lots of R&D firms shoot blanks. That's why they call it R&D."

"This is different."

"Different how? Different because it's Jack Burnam?"

Lulu felt herself flush. She turned away and looked out the glass partition, hoping that Ed wouldn't notice her unease.

Without explanation, he changed the subject. "Did you know I'm working on a screenplay? All newsmen...excuse me...all *newspersons* must write a bad novel or a lousy screenplay by the age of fifty."

Lulu said nothing.

"Sure, I'll tell you about it," said Ed. "Thanks for asking."

Lulu turned to face him, sat down in his guest chair and lifted her heels up to the edge of his desk. It ruffled her not in the least that he could see up her skirt all the way to her *Barelytheres*. Maybe she could distract him from where he seemed to be going.

"I'm all ears," she announced.

"Not entirely," he answered.

Lulu made an impatient circular hand motion that meant, *Get on with it.*

Ed forced his gaze to a spot over her shoulder and began. "It's about a college girl," he said. "J-school at Duke. Nice looking but smarter than she is pretty. Top of her class. Plans to make the world better, you know?"

Lulu grimaced.

"Meets a guy. Major crush. This is the movies, right? The guy is very political. Student body president. Save the planet, that sort of thing. The girl loves him so much she does his research, writes his papers, basically gets him through his last two years while he's being a hero."

Ed paused. Lulu swung her feet down from his desk.

"Glad you like it. Here's where it gets good. The happy couple decides to join the Peace Corps when they graduate. Go to Sri Lanka and teach. Very seventies. But when the girl gets to the airport to leave for Asia, guess what? The guy has changed his mind. Seems he's taken a job with some big bad corporation. Worse, he's engaged to another girl and this other girl's father is the one who got him the job."

Lulu finally spoke. "Okay. So she's pissed. How does it end?"

Ed waved a hand. "That's the hardest thing about a screenplay. The ending. I don't know for sure, but I think maybe the girl never gets over it. Maybe she carries a grudge for the next twenty or thirty years. Does that sound realistic to you?"

Lulu looked directly into Ed's eyes. "No. Not in the least."

Ed studied her for a long moment, then returned to their discussion about Bluestream as if nothing had interrupted. "So what's your next move?"

"Silicon Valley. Bluestream headquarters."

"You have a source?"

"I'll find a source. I'll go where the employees go for lunch. And after work."

"Long shot," Ed said, but he tapped his computer keyboard. "Continental has a flight at seven. You can make it if you leave in the next twenty minutes."

On her way out the door, Lulu hesitated. "One more thing," she said. "Your screenplay."

"Yeah?"

"Suppose, when the guy dumps the girl, it turns out she was pregnant. She gets rid of it and he never knows."

Ed rubbed his jaw thoughtfully. "That's pretty good. But I thought you said the girl doesn't carry a grudge."

It took far less than twenty minutes for Lulu to pack her briefcase, grab her travel kit and call an airport taxi.

Norah

"Good evening, Ms. Needham. A bit early for you." The concierge at Norah's apartment building handed her a stack of mail.

He's right, Norah thought. Six o'clock. She lived only a few minutes from her office but usually worked until nine or ten at night and ate take-out at her desk. Tonight, however, she had decided to give herself a treat. She had a stack of phone messages and could return the calls as readily from her own sofa as from the office. The Wall Street analysts would be at their desks for another hour or two. The West Coast reporters longer than that.

She slid a gourmet frozen dinner into the microwave. She poured a glass of *Llano Estacado* chenin blanc. The microwave signaled readiness and Norah dumped a steaming heap of chicken lasagna onto a plate. Her television lit as she clicked the remote and the *Gone With the Wind* DVD picked up exactly where she'd stopped it the night before. *As God is my witness, I'll never be hungry again.*

The telephone rang as Norah reached her sofa.

"Ms. Needham? This is Jenkins in Security. You asked me to report."

"So report." She forked a bite of lasagna.

"We staked out Wheeler's home, but he never showed. We're guessing that he'd already come and gone by the time we got there. There's been no unusual activity on his bank accounts, at least the ones we know about."

"Anything else?"

"We've got a tail on Mrs. Wheeler. If she knows anything, she's not giving any sign."

Norah hung up without saying goodbye. The Wheeler business was giving her a twitchy feeling. She walked down the hallway to her home office. She called it an office but it was more of a place to keep things than a place to work. She unlocked the office door and entered. File cabinets and shelves stacked with boxes lined the walls, and each file drawer and box bore a neatly-typed label. On a small desk Norah found a clutter of items she hadn't yet filed. An AmEx slip from dinner at Maxim's last Wednesday. Her December phone bill. A stack of newspapers. Half a dozen Good & Plenty candy wrappers. Her muscles began to loosen.

Throwing things away upset her. It felt much better to toss them into a spare room where she could organize them and then come back later for a visit. She opened a drawer at random and browsed a few old files. An electric bill from November of 1984. All of her expired Texas driver's licenses. A box of Dr. Pepper bottle caps. The twitchy feeling faded and her head began to clear.

Wheeler was a bright guy, very capable, but impatient, always lobbying for another promotion. He did his work well enough that she'd given him Bluestream, a plum assignment that might have earned him a six-figure bonus. But obviously he wanted more. Norah didn't blame him for that. Every man for himself. Or woman. What worried her most was the insinuation he might release some of his files into *unfriendly hands*. What the hell was that about? The press? The government? It gave her a chill. Conquest couldn't afford one iota of extra scrutiny right now.

She returned to the living room and took a sip of wine. The DVD had continued in her absence. *Oh Rhett, I always wanted to be calm and kind. I certainly have turned out disappointing.* Norah muted the television, picked up the stack of messages and began her evening's work.

Sherry

They had a one-hour layover at the Mexico City airport. Wheeler hadn't gotten through to his wife before they left Houston, so he was busy swapping dollars for pesos and swearing at the pay phone. Sherry strolled through an airport shop and found a nice *talavera* ceramic.

The fact that Wheeler was married had never bothered Sherry. She'd never met his wife and knew they didn't have any kids, so to her it didn't seem like a real marriage. Wheeler never complained about his wife, the way cheating husbands are supposed to do. He never talked about her at all. He took Sherry out all the time and the fact he had a wife never came up. Of course, it didn't hurt that he spent money like water, with no small amount splashing in Sherry's direction. What she made at the Ab-Salute barely covered her rent and car payment. Wheeler took her places like Mexico that she could never have afforded on her own.

He'd happened into the Ab-Salute one day, looking for a gift for his sister. Sherry sold him a spirit basket of poho oil and Dead Sea mud. He'd put the basket in his car and returned five minutes later to ask her out to dinner. Come to think of it, it wasn't much of an invitation. It was more like an announcement. *What would you like for dinner, Italian or Mexican?* He had simply assumed she would go with him and, truth be told, she liked that. She liked his bravado, though sometimes it seemed a bit put-on.

She'd fucked him twice that first night. Once, when they got back to her place after a dinner of spaghetti *alle vongole* and a bottle of Chianti, and once more in the middle of the night when he found her awake practicing the *Golden Rooster Stands on One Leg.* The wine had kept her awake.

He wanted it again the next morning, in the shower before dressing for work, and she'd had no objection. The sex seemed breathtakingly important to him, but it didn't do much for her one way or the other. The way she saw it, she could give him what he wanted so badly without it taking anything away from her. She would still have it to give away again the next day. Or later the same day, for that matter. It didn't take much effort on her part and with Wheeler it didn't take much time either.

The gift shop lady took Sherry's dollars and gave her back some pesos. As the woman bubble-wrapped the plate, Sherry looked out the shop window and down the airport corridor. She saw that Wheeler finally had managed to place his phone call. Through the glass, she saw him gesturing and talking into the pay phone.

Maggie

Maggie's cell phone buzzed again as she passed through the revolving door at the Hotel Magnolia. "Russ, I gotta put you on hold," she said. "I'm in the car."

Maggie checked the phone log as she stepped into the hotel elevator. She saw that he'd called several times while she'd been at the Tea Room with Sally and Jolene. Stepping off at the ninth floor, she looked both ways before proceeding to the suite. She slid a key from an inside pocket of her purse and opened the door. Dark and quiet, the place had a smell that reminded Maggie of the linen department at Nieman Marcus. She opened the curtains a few inches and took her husband off hold.

"Hi, honey. Sorry I missed you before. Where are you anyway?" She checked the phone's screen for a clue but the string of numbers told her nothing.

"California. Just landed. That's what I was calling to tell you before. Bluestream."

Bluestream. It was all Russ had talked about for months.

"For how long?" she asked. While she spoke, the suite's door opened and a man entered. She motioned to him to remain silent, pointing elaborately at her cell phone. The man moved noiselessly into the suite's kitchenette.

"I don't know," said Wheeler. "I may have to be here for a while." Russ's voice had a timorous edge that Maggie hadn't heard before. He sounded uncharacteristically nervous.

The man, drink in hand, sank down into an upholstered chair. Standing in the half-light of the partially-open curtain, Maggie stepped out of her shoes.

"I can't help it, Maggie. Burnam sent me out here himself."

Russ never missed a chance to drop Jack Burnam's name into a conversation.

"Hold on a minute," she said. "I'm at a stoplight now." Maggie set the cell phone down, reached under her Carolyn Herrera dress and wriggled out of her panty hose. She smoothed the dress and picked up the phone. The man in the chair watched.

"All right," she said. "So tell me about your day." Balancing the phone against one shoulder, she reached behind her back and unfastened her bra.

She shifted the phone to her other hand, snaked the bra out through the armhole of the dress and hung it over a chair. She was now naked underneath the dress.

She crossed the room and stood with her back to the man in the chair. He reached up to release the small clasp at the collar of her dress and slowly unfastened the row of tiny pearl buttons that extended from collar to waist. Maggie turned to face him and stepped back a pace. It took only the merest shrug of her shoulders to send the Carolyn Herrera to the floor. She did a slow turn, giving him the full treatment. On the phone, her husband said something about the importance of Bluestream to Conquest and of himself to Bluestream. His usual patter, but with an edge. She responded with an occasional, "Uh-huh."

The man reached out to touch her back. His finger traced the inky blue stem that emerged from the cleft of her buttocks and blossomed into an orchid at the base of her spine. She knew that he loved this view. Women his age didn't have tattoos, especially not *there*. She dropped to her knees and bent forward. "Uh-huh," she said again to her husband, while the man unfastened his belt and unzipped his zipper. He dropped his clothing indiscriminately to the carpet and onto her back and shoulders as he finished undressing. Pants. Shirt and tie. Boxers. One of his socks came to rest on the carpet beside her and she inhaled his foot-smell. She held the phone against her ear and glanced back over her shoulder to look at him. He was ready. No mistake about that.

She debated how much further to go before wrapping up the phone conversation. She knew the man behind her wouldn't mind one bit if she kept chatting with her husband while they went at it, but she had doubts. In the throes she could handle "Uh-huh," but anything beyond that could get tricky.

She interrupted her husband. "Honey, you're breaking up. I'm losing the connection."

"Okay," she heard him say. "I don't know where I'm staying yet. Call you soon."

Call Ended flashed a second later and she dropped the phone. The man placed his fingers once again on her tattoo. This time his moistened thumb pushed into the dark crevice below. His simultaneous pressure at multiple points of entry caused her to suck in her breath. She gasped, and gave each gasp a little extra fervor when she sensed how much he liked the sound effects. When she spoke again, after he'd pushed inside and settled into his familiar cadence, she asked the question that had stumped her for the past few minutes.

"Jack," she said. "Why the hell did you send my husband to California?"

Feo

Feo sat in a corner booth at the Magnolia Bar, a booth he'd chosen for its unrestricted view of the brass-trimmed elevator lobby. It was a nice bar. Dark wood, plush leather, dim lights. A waiter stopped by regularly to freshen his ginger ale. It occurred to Feo that he'd spent so much time at his desk he hadn't yet learned Conquest's expense reimbursement procedures. This was his fourth ginger ale since the Wheeler woman went upstairs, and his third since Jack Burnam followed shortly after. Coincidence? Maybe, maybe not. He'd know for sure if they got off the elevator as close in time as they got on it.

From the moment of Jenkins' call that morning, he'd thought about little besides Russ and Maggie Wheeler. He'd gone to Wheeler's office and found nearly everything gone except some trash and a busted computer CPU, which he carted downstairs to see if the Tech guys could do anything with it. He'd staked out the Wheelers' home, but hadn't seen anything amiss. If Wheeler was up to no good, he wouldn't return there, or he'd already come and gone by the time Feo arrived.

He'd devoted the rest of his day to tailing Maggie Wheeler and, he had to admit, he'd had worse duty. She had a late morning workout at Crunch wearing one of those shrink-wrap leotards. A visit to the Junior League with some girlfriends. A little shopping at the Galleria, followed by an early dinner with some other friends at a Cuban place. Nice life. Feo enjoyed following her, right up to the moment when he saw Jack Burnam step on the Hotel Magnolia's elevator.

His phone vibrated. Jenkins had called him on the hour all day long.

"After dinner, she drove straight to the Magnolia," said Feo. "Still here."

"Any sign of her husband?"

Feo knew, and he was sure that Jenkins knew, that Conquest maintained a corporate apartment at the Magnolia. But it was for use by the most senior executives, not medium-fry like Wheeler. Wheeler was about as likely to show up there as the Holy Ghost.

"No. Nothing."

"So who's she with?"

That was the question of the night, wasn't it? He'd been mulling over that one for the previous hour, and he couldn't come up with any scenario where it would be in his best interests to say anything about what he'd seen. Burnam, after all, was the man who allowed him to receive the generous monthly check that paid for his nice house in Montrose and his fancy new Saab convertible and the green-and-yellow riding mower that cut his lawn in less than fifteen minutes. And Jenkins—well, Feo hadn't worked for Jenkins for long enough to know what he was like, but Feo read him as a guy who didn't need another headache in his life.

So he lied. "It's not like that, boss. She's in the bar with some girlfriends. She's very sociable, this lady. Drinks like a fish."

Later that night, after he'd followed Maggie back to her house and his replacement had taken over surveillance for the night, Feo sat at home. He plugged his camera into his computer and brought up four photos on his monitor. Maggie, getting on the Magnolia elevator at 7:05. Burnam, boarding the same elevator four minutes later. Maggie stepping off the elevator at 8:57. Burnam at 9:02, looking, as they say in Texas, as happy as a gopher in soft dirt. Feo dismissed the possibility of coincidence. Then he deleted all four photos.

David

David heard Miranda call from the bedroom, "One down." Cripes, she was ready to start the game. He'd put Jesse to bed while Miranda finished some work. David stepped from the bathroom and found Miranda in her customary position, leaning back against the headboard, knees raised, the crossword book resting on one thigh. She wore cotton panties and one of his old tee-shirts, knotted at the midriff. She was a redhead, a singularity that David still found exotic. He wanted to have sex again but knew he'd already pushed his luck as far as it would go.

"Come on," she said. "Are you going to play or not?"

Their before-sleep game was a crossword competition. They would buy two copies of the same puzzle book and separately do the same puzzle to see who would finish first. He climbed into bed beside her and took up his book and pencil. "Okay, let's go."

After about fifteen minutes, he called, "Halftime." The rules of the game allowed either one of them to call a break. At halftime, they would kibitz about the day.

"Remember this morning when you asked me about Bluestream?" She didn't wait for an answer. "As of today, I'm smack in the middle of it. Norah took me off of everything else."

"Good for you," he said. "You deserve it." David could tell she was pretty enthused about the assignment but for some reason didn't want to show it.

"You seem uncertain," he added. "What's the problem?"

"I haven't done this kind of work before. I guess I'm not sure why Norah picked me."

"She picked you because she knows you'll do a great job. Don't worry so much."

"I hope you're right." She shrugged. "All right, halftime's over."

David still had ten words still to go when Miranda announced, "Done," and rolled onto her side. He wasn't surprised that she beat him. He'd found it impossible to concentrate after hearing her big news.

Miranda appeared to have dropped off immediately, but David couldn't sleep. He lay awake for nearly an hour, turning things over in his mind. Although he meant to be supportive, he felt a weird combination of jealousy and embarrassment. Jealousy, because he would have given anything to get a plum assignment like that at his law firm. Embarrassment, because it was becoming more clear every day that Miranda was far more successful in her career than he was in his. He knew that she was good at her job. Every year she got promotions and sizeable bonuses while he seemed to be running in place. Now she'd gotten onto the inside track at Conquest, and he seemed to be on no track at all.

She mumbled something in her sleep.

"Don't worry," David whispered. "You'll be fantastic."

What if she was fantastic? What if Bluestream was only the beginning? She might work her way into top management. She might get tapped as one of Jack Burnam's top people. He might never catch up.

He knew it was time for him to make a change. He would have to do something, something bold and impressive. But what?

CHAPTER 2. TUESDAY

CQC 50.01 0.68↑

Norah

Norah arrived at her desk on Tuesday morning in an upbeat mood. Falling asleep moments after Rhett threatened to squeeze Scarlett's skull between his palms like a walnut, she'd slept well and risen early. She had enjoyed a full breakfast at a restaurant close by her apartment before driving to work.

Wheeler's whereabouts remained the first order of business.

"Jenkins, this is Norah Needham. What's the latest?"

"Good morning, ma'am. Just a moment, please."

She heard him barking at his kids. He must have forwarded his office line to his home phone. Norah could ask his about his children, but she stifled the impulse. Too friendly.

He returned to the phone. "We have some information, but nothing conclusive."

"How so?"

"We think Wheeler called his wife yesterday evening. We confirmed that she received a call around seven-thirty, placed from the Mexico City airport."

"Okay. Sounds like you should send a man to Mexico."

"Maybe. But Mexico is a big place. He could have been connecting to South America or Europe or anywhere. Plus we don't know for certain it was him. It was a pay phone."

Norah clicked her tongue against the roof of her mouth. She was frustrated.

"Something else. Mrs. Wheeler seems to be following her normal routine. From what we can see, there's no unusual activities. It looks like he hasn't told her anything."

"So you think he's coming back."

"Yes, ma'am. Maybe. Probably."

Norah doubted that. Why would he keep his wife in the dark about his blackmail scheme if he was planning to come back to her? But she couldn't be sure of anything. Husbands and wives did strange things.

Feo

Feo yawned at his desk. He'd been up until nearly three a.m. tracing Maggie Wheeler's telephone calls. Then he had set his alarm for a halfway decent hour—six—and called Jenkins at home to tell him about the call from Mexico City.

"Nice work," Jenkins had said, managing to sound simultaneously impressed and sleepy.

Time-consuming, but not that hard. Feo had located Maggie's cell number in Wheeler's HR file and identified her service provider through the provider's website. Then he ran a program that generated random passwords without detection by the target site. In his line of work, Feo had become accustomed to the surprising choices that people make when selecting passwords, but he still did a double-take when Maggie's rolled up on the screen: *Jack4me*.

He called Jenkins at home. "You want me to go down there? *Se habla*, you know."

"No. We don't have enough yet. I don't want you out of pocket if Wheeler turns up somewhere else."

"What then?"

"Just sit tight for now."

Sit tight? Feo wanted to *do* something.

He considered his options. He could hack into Mexicana Airlines and Aeromexico and Continental and whoever else flew to Mexico City to see if Wheeler's travel record turned up. On the other hand, he could head up to the airport and look for a friendly ticket agent.

Feo looked outside. It was a rare day in Houston, dry with high clouds. He would put the top down on the drive to the airport.

David

David pulled his car into the parking area behind the offices of Marathon Trucking. He opened the car door and stepped out into a pothole filled with yesterday's rainfall.

Some lawyers make riveting arguments that save clients from undeserved prison sentences. Some lawyers meet with CEO's and CFO's to hand out advice that makes or breaks high-stakes corporate transactions. Other lawyers write compelling briefs that convince appellate judges to discover new rights for the greater good of society. Not David. David's job was *due diligence.* His law firm, Miller, Dunn & Parker, had a client that contracted to buy Marathon, and David had spent weeks poring over thousands of files—loan documents, insurance policies, traffic safety records—in search of anything that might pose an undue or inappropriate risk to their client. So far, David hadn't identified any undue or inappropriate risks and he wasn't sure he would know one if he saw it, but billable hours were billable hours. This type of work often fell to junior lawyers, and sometimes to paralegals, but somehow David's name always made it to the list when due diligence assignments came up.

David sat down next to Hamner, a fellow due diligence inmate. "Can I tell you something?"

Hamner studiously ignored him.

David continued, "I find this job tedious."

“Duh,” said Hamner. “Maybe that’s why you grind your teeth all day and fall asleep every afternoon. That is, on the afternoons that you don’t leave early.”

David folded a red-rope file folder into a hat and put it on his head, pirate-style. “Ay matey. I can’t help thinking I was meant for better things,” he said. “I just don’t know what.” He removed the hat and went face down on the conference room table.

David thought back to the day some anonymous asshole had left on his desk an article from *American Lawyer* entitled *Five Signs You Won’t Make Partner. 1. You’re often not busy.* Check. *2. You’re not getting assigned to any of the best cases*. Check again. *3. Your mentor doesn’t seem to like you.* What mentor? *4. The partners don’t trust you with important clients.* Or unimportant ones. *5. You don’t have any clients of your own.* Clean sweep. Later that year Miller-Dunn had made it official. They wouldn’t fire him, but they had relegated him to the never-never land of a permanent associate. He would receive work assignments, but they would be the jobs no one else wanted. He would be paid well enough but not as well as the associates still on partner track. He wouldn’t be considered for promotion, and barely-disguised pity would trail him throughout the firm’s halls, conference rooms and men’s rooms.

Hamner coughed. David reached for a stack of files and went to work.

In one respect, the Marathon assignment appealed mightily to David. The distance between Marathon’s office and his firm’s office downtown, combined with Houston’s wildly unpredictable traffic, made it possible for him to disappear for hours at a stretch. If downtown called, he’d left Marathon and I-45 was backed up all the way to Conroe. If someone from the Marathon team phoned, there was a truck on fire at Loop 610 and he had no idea when it might clear. David regularly visited his gym, located conveniently along the way, for a workout.

And so, after three-quarters of a day of desultory file rummaging, David stood and released a yawn. “I gotta check in downtown,” he said.

“Right,” Hamner snorted.

David exited the building, his gym bag on the front seat.

Wheeler

Wheeler banged open the door of the hotel's business center. The room was little more than an oversized closet with a desk and an ancient computer terminal. It wasn't much but the Villa del Sol was the only hotel in Zihuatanejo that advertised a business center. His laptop would handle most of the work he had in mind but he wanted some privacy and access to a printer and an Internet connection.

So much energy ran through his system that he dropped into a boxer's crouch and let go a flurry of punches. He set his laptop on the desk and turned it on. He had the room to himself so he played Dylan through the laptop's tinny speakers. That's when he noticed the handwritten note hanging from the monitor of the hotel's computer, a Pentium 386, or maybe a 286, saying that the Internet service was down. The faded paper on which the note was written and the yellowed tape holding it in place told him not to expect service any time soon. He would have to print out his message and send it to Norah by FedEx.

Since leaving Houston, he'd spent some time thinking about the right number. Ten million? Fifty million? He'd finally decided on twenty-five million. It was enough to set him up for life, but not so much that Norah would put up much of a fight. He typed:

> *Dear Norah. $25 million will get you the Bluestream files. A big number on its face, yes, but not a lot to assure the success of the most important deal in the company's history. Wiring instructions attached. All the best. /s/ Russ Wheeler*

Wheeler connected his laptop to the hotel printer but when he clicked *Print*, it gave him only a groan and an error message. With a curse, he clicked *Save*. He'd have to figure out the printer later.

Next, he began duplicating all the Bluestream data disks so that he would have a set to ship to his lawyer in Houston for safekeeping. Near the end of the process the laptop surprised him with a low battery signal. Shutting down the music and dimming the screen to save power, he finished the data disks only seconds before the battery expired. In the now dead quiet room, peering at the blank screens of both his laptop and the hotel's desktop, he felt his spirits flag. The overhead lights and the printer's on-light both had gone out. *Shit!* It wasn't the battery. There was a power outage.

Wheeler sighed. This blackmail thing might be harder than he'd thought.

Norah

At half past noon, Norah entered the dining room of the Houstonian Club. She knew nearly everyone there, but said only a few hellos.

The maitre d' greeted her. "Mr. Cooper is at your table. Please follow me."

Pete Cooper served as the partner-in-charge of the Conquest account at Dudley & Dudley, Houston's largest and most prestigious accounting firm. Tall, white-haired and nearly as angular as Norah herself, he stood as she approached the table. They must look, Norah thought, like two storks on a pond.

Norah rarely socialized but nevertheless had lunch with Pete Cooper nearly every Tuesday. That's how important D&D was to her company's business. Everyone—the shareholders, the bondholders, the banks, the regulators—relied on the auditor to keep a public company honest. Every quarter, the firm wrote a letter to Conquest expressing D&D's opinion that the company's financial statements fairly presented its financial status. Every time Conquest closed a major transaction, D&D delivered another letter saying that the company had booked the deal properly. Those letters were crucial to Conquest's continued success. Therefore, the management of D&D and Pete Cooper was fundamental to Norah's job.

"Congratulations on Bluestream," Cooper said as Norah sat down. "Is it as big as Jack says?"

"This is the one we've been waiting for. No doubt in my mind."

Cooper lowered his voice a notch. "I have to warn you. My standards committee isn't all that comfortable with the financing structure."

Norah's success in securing D&D's blessing on a decade's worth of unconventional financing schemes and problematic accounting treatments had played no small part in her rise at Conquest. Increasingly, though, Pete had been getting static from his internal standards committee, a group set up to make sure its accountants adhered to the rules in the face of pressure from a major client.

"Nothing you can't handle, I'm sure." She meant it. When push came to shove, Cooper would explain the facts of life—goodbye to Conquest and to its millions of dollars in audit and consulting fees—to any members of the standards committee so foolish as to actually insist on standards. Norah and Cooper sat while the waiter announced the daily specials. Cooper ordered a salad and Norah asked for a lunchtime filet mignon.

Cooper looked unusually troubled. "I mean it, Norah," he said. "We have some new people on the committee. There could be trouble this time."

"Bluestream isn't any different from a lot of the deals we've already done. It's just bigger," Norah responded.

"It isn't so much any one deal, but when you pile them all up, at some point you have to wonder if the shareholders are getting a true picture. You know what I'm saying?"

Norah regarded Cooper as the closest thing to a friend she had in the business world, but business was business and Bluestream was too important to Conquest's future for her to take any chances.

"Not a problem, Pete. You know it's funny. I got a call yesterday from Burns-Whiteside saying they've come up with some new wrinkles in acquisition financing. Something that might be a good fit for Bluestream.

I wasn't going to take the meeting, but maybe I should. I don't want you to get crossways with your committee."

The Burns firm was Houston's second largest and D&D's principal rival for big-money clients like Conquest. Norah had received no such call, but she knew that the merest suggestion that she might entertain such a meeting would send Cooper into near-apoplexy.

Cooper's face turned as white as his hair. "No need for that, Norah." He sighed in defeat. "I'm sure we can find a solution. We always do."

"So true," said Norah. "There's always a solution."

Miranda

Miranda returned to her desk carrying a Souper Salad bag soggy at the bottom with leaking barley soup. She planned to eat at her desk every day until she felt up to speed on her new assignment. Her door was closed and her secretary had instructions to hold all calls. She needed time to think about Bluestream.

Conquest had agreed to pay $2 billion for Bluestream. Where would it get the money? The company had made so many acquisitions that the customary sources of funds were tapped out. Issuing more stock would dilute the current shareholders and drive down the price. Selling bonds was out of the question because the future earnings stream from Bluestream was, to put it mildly, speculative. Any additional debt might cause the credit rating agencies to downgrade their ratings on Conquest, which could trigger lawsuits by the existing bondholders. Nor did Conquest have any non-core assets that it could sell on short notice to raise funds.

The solution, according to the file Norah had given her, was an *indirect* borrowing. Conquest would set up a new company—Miranda decided to call it Blueco, for the sake of discussion—that would take ownership of the assets of Bluestream. A syndicate of banks would lend the amount needed to Blueco, not Conquest. The banks, much like the credit rating agencies, wouldn't be satisfied with Blueco alone as the source of repayment, so they would require Conquest to write a backup guaranty. Under normal circumstances, the backup guaranty would cause the auditors and rating agencies to put the bank borrowings on Conquest's balance sheet, the same as bonds any other direct borrowings. In the case of Blueco, however, they would make an exception. And what an exception.

Miranda shifted in her chair and stretched her spine. This is where it got tricky. Norah's file included some accounting rules that were nothing like the rules Miranda had studied in college. If Blueco had an independent outside investor that contributed at least three percent of the equity, the auditors and the rating agencies would forget all about the Conquest guaranty. They would view it as *off-balance sheet*. That was good.

But there was one more thing. The outside investor, not Conquest, would have full control over Blueco. And the outside investor had to be fully independent of Conquest. That was bad.

She rubbed her forehead with both hands. She knew that off-balance sheet financing schemes had become all the rage, and that plenty of big companies used them. In addition, Norah had said that the Bluestream deal was the same as many deals that Conquest had done in the past, just bigger.

She scraped the bottom of the soup carton with her plastic spoon. It had been excellent soup. So why did she have such an empty feeling?

Sherry

Sherry emerged golden and dripping from the pool at the Villa del Sol. With one hand she squeezed the water from her hair and with the other reached out into empty space for a towel. An attendant bolted from his poolside booth to oblige. Three men occupying underwater stools at the pool bar turned in unison to watch her.

The reason for this trip remained a mystery to Sherry, as did Wheeler's choice of hotels. She liked the Villa del Sol, but would have preferred to sleep in a thatched cabin on the beach. She wanted to step from her room onto warm sand and hang her macramé bikini from a palm frond. Wheeler, however, had insisted that they stay in a hotel with a *business center.*

"I thought this was a vacation," she said. "I thought you wanted to get away."

"It is. I do. But I have to finish a couple of things."

Something wasn't right with him. He'd gotten out of bed early and done push-ups on the floor, as if trying to burn up excess energy. Then he spent most of the morning in the business center working on something. Now he'd finally arrived at the pool, scowling and cursing and carrying his computer in a beach bag. It was embarrassing.

"What gives?" she asked.

"I can't leave it in the room. Someone might steal it."

Sherry picked up her sunglasses and reached for her tube of sunscreen. She smeared the lotion on her shoulders and legs.

"*Una mas, seňorita*?" A waiter motioned toward her empty glass.

She held up two fingers. "*Dos.*" She intended to have a good time regardless of whatever problems Wheeler had brought along. The pool bartender made a frozen fruit and yogurt concoction so fantastic that she wanted two more.

Despite her preference for the beach, this swimming pool was the most elegant she'd ever seen. Azure water lapped against the edges of several mid-pool islands overgrown with tropical vegetation. A handsome *antiquario* tile formed an umber-shaded pool border. The constant susurration of an unseen fountain, like white noise, created a nice sense of privacy in a public space.

Wheeler rose so suddenly from his lounge chair that he nearly fell into the pool. "I'm sorry," he said. "I can't sit still. Gonna go for a run." He pointed to the beach bag. "Will you watch this for me?"

Sherry watched him disappear down a stone walkway that led down to the beach. She wanted to know what had him acting so strange, so she pulled his laptop from his beach bag, booted up and scanned the list of files last closed. The most recent one was headed *Bluestream.* It was an enormous file comprised of memos and spreadsheets. She skimmed it but saw almost nothing she understood. To her, the question was why Wheeler was so anxious to get out of Houston if he still had work to do on Bluestream.

She opened the next file, headed *Dear Norah*. This one was tiny, a one-page note. She squinted to read in the bright sunlight. Omigod! Bluestream. Twenty-five million dollars. He was trying to blackmail Conquest! Her hands shook and her heart pounded as she shut off the laptop and put it back in Wheeler's bag. He could get arrested! What if someone thought she was an *accomplice*?

T'ai chi would help her calm down. Sherry assumed a standing position at the edge of the pool, placing her feet flat on the *antiquario* tile she liked so much. She tucked in her chin and tailbone and put her heels close together. Her head, she imagined, hung from a thread that extended down from the sky. She was a puppet on a string. She moved through the warm-up exercises, lifting her arms toward the sky, gathering *chi*. She placed her hands one over the other against the flat expanse of flesh between her navel and her bikini bottom, the lower *tan tien*, where the body stores *chi*.

Gentle, continuous, circular. She moved through the Set. *Holds the Ball. Single Whip. Embraces Tiger. Steps Back to Repulse Monkey.* She began to calm. It was starting to work. There seemed to be a lot of *chi* down here in Zihuatenajo, way more than in Houston. The hot midday Mexican sun glinted off the shimmering surface of the swimming pool. It warmed her back and the twin hemispheres of her buttocks as she flexed and stretched through the Set.

Sherry began *Steps Up to Seven Stars*, a move that required her to extend her fists in opposite directions while simultaneously sliding her left knee forward and dipping down on her right knee. In the final pose, her body looked like the stars that make up the Big Dipper. As she reached maximum extension, she felt her glutes become as smooth and hard as the dark tile beneath her toes.

The three men at the poolside bar broke into applause.

Jack

A group called Houston Tomorrow wanted Jack's ideas for a new city slogan. Apparently the old slogan had petered out. Jack had been a fixture of the city's business and social scene for so long that most people thought he was born and raised in Houston, a misapprehension he did nothing to correct. He never mentioned his origins in Parsippany, New Jersey, and the company's media relations people had strict instructions never to include that damning bit of information in their endless stream of bios, news releases and puff pieces.

Without question, his adopted home had been good to him. He had arrived in the late seventies as a mid-level manager and now he sat atop a colossus of a company. He lived in a veritable palace and earned more money than he had ever dreamed possible.

A local boast had it that Houston offered more freedom and opportunity than any other place in America, and Jack would not disagree. Houston remained the Wild West of great American cities, an unapologetic bastion of free enterprise, a place that welcomed risk-takers of every stripe and dispensed only mild condemnation to those who turned out to be liars or frauds. It was the place God made for people who think there can be no higher calling in life than making money, and who don't mind cutting a few corners along the way. People like Jack.

* * * * *

THE PROMOTERS

HOUSTON CITY, 1839

John Allen stood on the rough planks of the new dock, pushed his pince-nez higher on his nose and peered into the morning fog. He could see little other than the tangle of scrub pine and blue magnolia that scrapped for space and light along Buffalo Bayou. Something dark and scaly—an alligator, possibly—raised its snout above the surface of the water for a moment and then submerged. John wondered, not for the first time, how he and his brother Gus had come to bet their entire stake on this particular patch of swampland.

Most of the few remaining citizens of Houston City had gathered at the dock to greet the steamship *Laura M*, now three days overdue. Should the *Laura M* in fact arrive, she would be the first steamship to navigate the fifty-mile stretch of bayou that meandered from Houston City to the Gulf of Mexico. A successful transit would demonstrate Houston City's viability as a commercial port of entry to whatever modest portion of the world might give a damn. If the trip failed, John planned to abandon Texas altogether and go back east.

"I don't believe she's coming," he said to Gus.

Gus clapped John on the back of his waistcoat. "Let's take a walk." He turned on his heel and headed across town toward their office.

The brothers had traveled from New York to Galveston seven years earlier with one simple objective. They would make a fortune in real estate speculation in the inchoate nation known as the Republic of Texas. Shortly after Texas won its independence from Mexico at the Battle of San Jacinto, the brothers paid $9,000 for 6,600 acres of vacant prairie and slough centered at the headwaters of Buffalo Bayou. Gus named the place after General Sam Houston, the hero of the Texans' war for independence, although in truth the brothers had never met Sam Houston and the General had nothing at all to do with their project. Nevertheless, *Houston City* it was.

John had placed announcements written by Gus in newspapers all over the United States: *Nature seems to have designated this place for the future seat of government.* And sure enough, at the end of 1836, the fledgling Republic of Texas designated Houston City as its new capital. In John's view, however, *nature* had less to do with it than the five hundred dollars he'd spent on whiskey and whores for the newly-elected legislators. People flocked to the new capital and the population shot upwards. They laid out a plan of avenues named after Texas heroes—Travis, Milam and Fannin—intersecting with streets appropriate for a center of government—Texas, Capitol and Congress. A capitol building and an executive residence rose beside the bayou.

Then, as they'd begun to turn a profit from lot sales, things fell apart. Daily downpours turned the streets into an impassable bog. Mosquitoes carried yellow fever that decimated the population. Alligators maimed a few drunks and, worse, the Karankawa raided and carried away a score of terrified victims. After less than two years, the government loaded its furniture and records onto wagons and shipped everything west to Waterloo. Many of Houston City's residents packed up and followed.

Gus remained equable. John had to give him credit for that, and for the speed with which he adapted to catastrophe. Gus devised a new boast: *Destiny has marked Houston City to become the great interior commercial emporium of Texas.* Overnight, Congress Square became Market Square and before long the government buildings became warehouses. That was when Gus had lured the captain of the *Laura M* into piloting his boat upstream from the Gulf with the promise of a $1,000 bonus.

As John and Gus reached their office doorway, shouts went up from the landing. The *Laura M* had docked! Word came that the boat had passed the dock three days prior but in the fog the crew had completely missed the sparse community. The *Laura M* had continued upstream until debris and logjams forced a turnaround. Gus unlocked a desk drawer and rummaged through their cashbox until he found enough Texas redback dollars to pay the captain.

He held up a draft of new advertising copy. "What do you think of this?"

> *There is no place in Texas more healthy, having an abundance of spring water, and enjoying the sea breeze in all its freshness. Vessels from New Orleans or New York can sail without obstacle to this place.*

John swallowed hard. The rock-bottom falseness of it pained him. People already had perished of malaria and worse. Natural springs were scarce. Nearly fifty miles of hard travel stood between their property and the faintest whiff of sea air.

On the other hand, suppose Gus in his damnable optimism had it right. Maybe buildings would rise along the bayou and Houston City would become the commercial center of Texas. Maybe ocean-going ships would arrive to bring manufactured goods to the frontier republic and carry back grain and cotton and timber. Maybe tens of thousands—hell, hundreds of thousands—of people would come to seek their fortunes and would live and work and sleep and die here by the bayou. Maybe great companies would form and transact business and sell bonds and issue shares.

If Gus had it right, then what would a few falsehoods along the way matter? What would it mean in one hundred years or two hundred that Houston City owed its very existence to a pack of preposterous lies offered up by a pair of ambitious hucksters?

John looked across the desk. "Not bad," he said. "I'll put it in the usual papers."

* * * * *

CHAPTER 3. WEDNESDAY

CQC 50.88 0.87↑

Norah

Norah left Conquest Plaza via the Tunnel for a mid-morning stroll. She liked to prowl the six-plus miles of underground walkways that linked Houston's downtown buildings and protected pedestrians from the city's stifling summers and clammy winters. She could buy clothing, groceries and art. She could get cash and take in a movie. She could have dinner, anything from McDonald's to fine French cuisine. She could see her gynecologist or get a massage. All in a steady-state year-round seventy-two degrees without ever having to venture above ground.

Her phone chimed. It was Jenkins again.

"I think we've got something this time," he said. "Wheeler bought a ticket to Zihuatanejo the day he quit. It's way down there, on the Pacific side."

"How'd you find out?"

"I had a man snoop around the airlines. He paid a couple of ticket agents to look the other way while he ran a search."

"Okay, so you send a man to Mexico. Who's good?" She had reached one of her favorite sections of the Tunnel. Seven pillars bore murals of the cartoon Jetson family. Norah especially liked George Jetson, shown in beleaguered conversation with his tyrannical boss, Cosmo Spacely.

"Feo Duarte. One of our best. Former CIA."

Ex-CIA? That seemed a bit strong to bring back Russ Wheeler and his hard drive. But it wasn't her call.

"Ms. Needham, one more thing. Wheeler isn't traveling alone. He's with a woman."

"Girlfriend?"

"Excuse me for saying so, ma'am, but have you ever gotten a good look at Maggie Wheeler? A man would have to be crazy."

As it happened, Norah had once gotten several good looks at Maggie Wheeler, including a full frontal in the changing room when Conquest had its annual holiday party at Memorial Tennis. Jenkins was right.

"All right. Not a girlfriend. Then what?"

"Honestly, I don't know. I guess we'll find that out when we find them."

Norah signed off and dropped her phone into a pocket. Up ahead, she saw the escalator that led up to the offices of Payton-Mosel, the city's most prominent investment banking firm.

Feo

Feo handed Jenkins his action plan. Timing, strategies, locations, options. A good agent doesn't take the field without a plan. He had his ticket and he was ready to go, but Jenkins wanted a sit-down. The plan listed the twenty-seven hotels in the vicinity of Zihuatanejo and its sister city Ixtapa. Feo would start with the bigger beach hotels and see what turned up. If he found nothing, then he'd move on to the smaller places secluded in the trees and up on the mountainsides.

Jenkins scanned Feo's proposal. "They teach you this at the CIA?"

The CIA wisecrack hit Feo in a tender spot. He'd put on his job application that he'd worked there. One hundred percent true. During his last two years at George Mason, he had parked cars part-time at Langley. He'd met a lot of the big shots, including Tenet and Deutsch and Woolsey. And plenty of deputies, assistant deputies and deputy assistants. All right, so maybe he'd stretched things a bit, wanting them to think he was more than a modem jockey. He couldn't have known that these Conquest guys would have such a hair trigger. On the day of his interviews, all they wanted to talk about was *the Agency*, so he'd told them a few stories. They got pretty worked up and before Feo knew what was happening the Chief of Security took him up to sixty-five to meet Mr. Burnam himself. After that, he couldn't back down, but whenever anyone mentioned his CIA training, Feo ignored it, like they should know it was something that he couldn't talk about.

"The systems guys find anything on Wheeler's computer?" he asked.

"No," said Jenkins. "He removed the hard drive. It had the only copy of whatever he was working on and nobody else seems to know how to reconstruct it. In fact, I can't find anybody who admits to knowing exactly what it is."

"Suppose I find Wheeler," Feo said. "What do you want me to do?"

"He stole company property. Bring it back. Bring him back, if you can."

"What if he doesn't want to come back?"

"If that happens, call me. We'll decide then."

Jenkins gave Feo a hard look, as if realizing what they might be up against. "Where'd you grow up?" he asked quietly.

"San Antonio. South side."

"Big family?"

Feo suspected that Jenkins, like most Anglos, believed that every Hispanic family had enough little *niños* and *niñas* to overflow its broken-down station wagon. "Only child," he said.

"What kind of a name is Feo, anyway?"

Feo swallowed. He had a feeling that Jenkins already knew the answer. "Ugly," he said. "Feo means ugly in Spanish."

"Your mother named you *ugly*?"

"She didn't name me. My mother's husband did. My stepfather."

Jenkins took a moment to sort this out. "Ah," was all he said.

"That was his condition for letting her keep me. Otherwise she'd of had to put me up for adoption."

"What about your real father?"

"Beats me," said Feo. "I never met him."

"Well, it suits you. Feo, I mean."

"So I've been told."

Norah

Norah stepped into the reception area of Payton-Mosel. She studied three enormous paintings by Frederic Remington and a sculpture of men standing around an oil derrick in poses reminiscent of the famous flag raising at Iwo Jima.

"May I help you?" asked the receptionist.

"I'm Norah Needham, from Conquest. I don't have an appointment. I finished a meeting nearby and I thought I'd take a chance that Mr. Payton might be in the office."

The receptionist pointed toward the heavy oak and glass door leading to the elevator lobby. At that moment, Franklin Payton exited the elevator. He did a double-take when he saw Norah.

"What a treat," he said, pushing through the entrance. "You've never visited our offices before, have you?"

In fact, no one from Conquest had graced Payton-Mosel's offices, although the firm had chased the company's business for years. Norah found it hard to justify giving work to the smaller Houston-based investment banks, no matter how well connected, when the giant New York securities houses fell all over themselves to get her attention. But today she had a special need.

"Hello, Franklin, it's nice to see you." She got right to the point. "I want to talk to you about helping out on Bluestream. I'd like to add a few private equity investors to the mix."

"We pride ourselves on private equity here at Payton-Mosel."

An understatement, Norah thought. She already knew that the firm's investor prospects included every person in Texas with a net worth above $15 million and a long list of Middle Eastern investors as well.

Payton waited for Norah to offer some details. When she said nothing further, he shifted into investment banker mode and began firing questions. Norah handed him a one-pager from her briefcase.

Payton studied it for several minutes. "We can do this. No doubt about it."

"I know you can, Franklin. That's why I stopped by."

"When would you like our proposal?"

"No need for that."

Greed and suspicion competed for control of Payton's facial muscles. Norah enjoyed watching the struggle. "Conquest strives to operate as a good corporate citizen," she said. "From now on, whenever possible, I want to direct our investment banking business to firms here in Houston."

Payton's handsome face threatened to split wide open. "I guess I don't have to tell you I agree with that philosophy. I wish more of our local brethren and...uh..."

He stumbled to a halt and Norah realized he was searching, unsuccessfully, for the female equivalent of *brethren*. She suspected he was about to say *cistern*.

"I do need a favor from you, Franklin. Nothing big." She handed him another sheet of paper. "This is the background of a fellow named David Sesno." Norah had pulled together some basic information from things Miranda had told her. "He works at the Miller-Dunn law firm here in town and he's bored, of course. Wants to get into investment banking."

Payton was wary. "Drugs? Boss's daughter?"

"Nothing like that. He's married to a woman who works for me and I'm helping out. Give him a little push."

Payton seemed satisfied. "Fine, then. We'll bring him in for an interview."

"Do that. Then call me and let me know what you think. Don't make him an offer until we talk. I wouldn't want you to be stuck with someone who isn't up to your standards."

"Of course," said Payton. "What else?"

"That's it, Franklin. A pleasure." Payton extended his hand, but he was obviously unsure of the gesture. Norah guessed he'd never done business with a female CFO before. He seemed relieved when she didn't hug him.

"Thanks," they said, in uncomfortable unison.

Sherry

Time to turn over. Sherry reached back to retie her bikini top and sat up. She waved at the poolside waiter and ordered a glass of ginseng tea and a plate of vegetarian nachos. Wheeler had kept her awake much of the night shuttling between bedroom and bathroom. His nerves seemed to have gotten the best of him. By morning he'd looked like death and skipped breakfast altogether. When Sherry gathered her things and headed to the pool, he'd taken his laptop and disappeared, presumably to the business center.

Just then, Wheeler returned and fell into the chaise lounge next to her. "They got the electricity on, but the Internet is still down," he said and followed up with several curses.

Sherry wondered why he seemed surprised. He'd brought them to a beach resort in a remote part of Mexico. Sometimes it took hours to place an ordinary phone call.

"I need to send an e-mail to Houston and they have no clue when it might be fixed."

Sherry sucked in her cheeks, savoring the last few ice cubes from her glass of ginseng. "Can you send a message by courier? There's a FedEx office in town."

"There is, but it's in Ixtapa. That's a thirty-minute taxi ride." He grimaced. "I'm not sure my stomach can handle it."

A waiter appeared. On the small tiled table between Sherry and Wheeler he set a tray bearing a tall glass of tea and a platter of nachos. Sherry initialed the check and handed it to the waiter. Wheeler stared at the nachos for perhaps a minute, apparently transfixed. Wisps of steam rose from the *frijoles* and *jalapeños.* He knocked over Sherry's iced tea glass as he rose and ran for the poolside bathroom.

She called after him, "I don't mind going into town for you." She didn't mind at all.

Lulu

Lulu steered her rental car onto Calaveras Boulevard, which would take her to Highway 101, which would take her to the town of Mountain View and Bluestream's headquarters deep in the heart of Silicon Valley. On arrival, she scanned the Bluestream building, three stories of metal and glass in a prototypical California office park.

She had a simple plan. Bluestream had only a few hundred employees. Of these, she guessed that fewer than two dozen knew for certain whether Bluestream had a hot new product or another dud. She would meet people until she found one that told her something useful.

At five o'clock employees began to exit in ones and twos. The men wore jeans and open-necked shirts and sported well-trimmed beards. The women favored khaki pants and casual tops. Lulu wanted a group of at least four, preferably six, figuring they would be headed out for drinks. She would follow and make their acquaintance. If they knew anything worth knowing, there was a better chance they would spill it after knocking back a few.

A group emerged that fit the bill. Five men and a woman, gossiping and cracking jokes. They clustered around a lean blond man about six feet tall. Lulu pegged him as a project leader taking his employees out for a few team-building beers. As they piled into their cars, Lulu cranked up her rent car.

She followed them to a place called *The Back Yard.* Lulu waited in the parking lot long enough for them to finish a first round or drinks. Pulling down the visor mirror, she refreshed her lipstick and loosened the third button of her blouse. Minutes later, passing through the doorway into the interior of *The Back Yard*, she had an only-in-California moment. Picnic tables and chairs stood on artificial grass surrounded by plastic shrubs and a tall cedar fence. Food sizzled on charcoal grills and waitresses dressed like June Cleaver served drinks and food to a cheerful crowd. An adult-sized swing set and teeter-totter filled one corner and an in-ground Jacuzzi occupied the other. As she watched, a young woman in a mini-skirt and tank top stepped into the Jacuzzi and performed an underwater headstand for the entertainment of her drunken friends. Her smooth bare legs pointed to the ceiling until she collapsed and came up for air.

Lulu spied her quarry. She walked to their table and introduced herself. "I'm Lulu Barker from the Houston Examiner. Mind if I join you?"

"Barker?" said one of the men. "Do you?"

Lulu had heard this one more than a few times. "Actually," she said, "I'm more of a growler."

Appreciative sniggers and an invitation to sit down. This was her opening.

"I'm writing a story on the Conquest deal. Would you be willing to talk to me?"

The tall blond one moved to the empty chair beside Lulu. He was, she thought, pretty good looking.

"I'm Josh," he said, and then went around the table introducing the others, much too rapidly for Lulu to get their names.

She opened with a question about corporate culture, a topic on which, in Lulu's experience, most corporate managers would hold forth *ad nauseam*. It served as her surefire interview starter. When this group tired of corporate culture, Lulu narrowed the focus. "What about this big breakthrough technology that Jack Burnam is touting? Is it for real?"

The group fell silent and Josh gave her an appraising look. She may have shown her cards too quickly. There would be a price for the information she wanted.

"I could answer that," he said, "but we'd have to become a little better acquainted first."

Lulu shifted in her seat. At forty, she was no great beauty but she had a good healthy body and a rough-and-tumble look that seemed to attract men of all ages and stations. She uncrossed and re-crossed her legs.

The woman in the group departed for the ladies' room. Two of the men said they needed to get home and the other two left without explanation.

Lulu had long known that her profession sometimes imposed unfair demands on women. You traveled to strange cities, you forced yourself upon people, usually men, that you didn't know and might never meet again, and you asked them intrusive questions about things they might or might not want to discuss. They saw your need and weighed it against their own.

It wouldn't be the first time Lulu had slept with a man for a story and it wouldn't be the last. Besides, Josh was young and handsome. She might have slept with him anyway, story or not.

She placed the fingers of her right hand on the back of Josh's wrist.

Sherry

Two envelopes, one fat and one thin, lay beside her on the seat of the battered taxi. Wheeler had addressed the thin one to Norah Needham at Conquest Plaza. That must be the blackmail note. The other envelope bore the name of a lawyer and a Post Oak address back in Houston. Wheeler's personal lawyer, Sherry guessed. He was sending a duplicate of the Bluestream files to his attorney for safekeeping, in case something happened to his laptop. Or to him.

The taxi made its way along a two-lane highway that tracked the mountainous water's-edge between Zihuatanejo and Ixtapa. Her driver gave her a running commentary on a series of ocean vistas that left Sherry nearly breathless. *Playa la Madera. Playa Principal. Playa la Ropa.* Each *playa* more *bonita* than the last. He told her that Zihuatanejo had existed for over a century as a tiny fishing village but that Ixtapa had been built as a tourist destination within the past twenty years on what had been a stretch of magnificent virgin beach. When the highway crested, he pointed out in the distance the string of beachside hotels comprising Ixtapa.

The road descended into tall trees and the driver resumed his commentary. "This was a coconut plantation. Used to be all that was here was coconuts and fish. *Cocos y pescado.*"

Sherry tried to imagine the place before the tourists arrived. Oddly, into her head came a vision of a white stucco *hacienda*, hidden away among the coconut palms, but within easy walking distance of the beach. It had a well-tended garden and a modest servants' quarters out back. She pictured herself on the front porch in a simple cotton dress. A gardener pushed a wheelbarrow filled with manure and potted shrubs. He set about digging holes and dropping plants into them, one by one. The pungent stink of the manure somehow blended with the scent of coconut. A darkly attractive man brought her a sweating glass of papaya juice and sat down alongside to enjoy the sunset over *Bahia de Zihuatanejo*. She didn't recognize the man. He didn't look like Wheeler, though. Not at all.

The taxi rattled to a halt, ending Sherry's daydream. She sighed. *Dreams are very comfortable*, said the Master, *and waking is bitter*. The driver deposited Sherry in front of a low adobe structure housing a variety of shops—beachwear, arts and crafts, leather goods. "*Plaza Los Mangos*," he announced. Sherry spied a small but familiar Federal Express sign at the far end.

Entering the dusty FedEx office, Sherry handed the two envelopes to the man on duty. She filled out the customs forms and gave the man a stack of peso notes. He counted out the proper amount and returned most of the notes to her. "Is there anything else, *senorita*?"

Sherry paused. "*Si, señor*. I made a mistake." The vision of the white *hacienda* at sunset returned. She squinted at the man in the vision. No, she decided. It definitely wasn't Wheeler.

She reached for the two envelopes. "Do you have another address label?"

To the bulkier envelope, the one containing the computer disks, she carefully attached a new label, addressing the package to herself back in Houston. She wasn't entirely sure what she would do with the package, but if something happened to Wheeler, why shouldn't she have it instead of some stuffy lawyer?

The FedEx man tossed both envelopes into a canvas bin marked *Estados Unidos*. "*Gracias*," she said happily. She stepped from the dusty office into a brilliant mid-afternoon Mexican sunshine. Her shopping bag was empty and she still had thousands of pesos. The shops of *Plaza Los Mangos* beckoned.

Lulu

When they reached Lulu's hotel room, Josh wasted little time. She had barely closed the door before he'd undone her blouse and unhooked her bra. He was very adept.

"Whoa," she said. "Aren't you forgetting something?"

"I've got it in my pocket. Don't worry."

His breathing was ragged. Maybe he was younger than she'd thought.

"That's not what I meant." She turned her face up toward his and pulled him into a kiss. "I'm old-fashioned."

He acquiesced in the kiss, but at the same time snaked one hand down to grasp for the zipper and clasp at the side of her pants, seemingly determined to remove her clothes before she changed her mind. As if. He maneuvered her into the bedroom and onto the brocade comforter that adorned the king mattress. Lulu fluffed the pillows and offered up her best imitation of Manet's *Olympia*. Naked but for a necklace and silver watchband, she kept her face blank and composed.

Josh peeled off his shirt and knelt at the foot of the bed. He nudged her legs apart and put his face in a place that left no doubt as to his intentions. "You're gonna love this," he told her.

Pretty sure of himself, Lulu thought. That was good. He might let something slip.

Josh's whiskers scratched against her inner thighs. He breathed in puffs and snorts that made her think of deer in the woods on a winter day.

Her mind wandered. A tiny computer screen appeared in her head and within seconds she had her lead:

> Has Jack Burnam Lost His Touch?
>
> Sources inside Bluestream have confirmed industry suspicions that its highly-touted next-generation Internet technology remains very much in the experimental stage. Earlier this week, Conquest CEO Jack Burnam cited Bluestream's telecom products as the principal factor justifying a whopping acquisition price of $2 billion. But a Bluestream engineer, speaking on condition of anonymity, said...

Josh adjusted his position and Lulu emitted an appropriate "Mmmm" and an "Oh yeah." He picked up his tempo and she wondered if he did some kind of tongue exercises. It felt like a moray eel poking around down there.

> "This gadget might work, or it might not. The design shows promise, but we're still early in the game." Another Bluestream source expressed doubts regarding the cost factor. "We can make this thing work eventually, but the question is whether we can get production costs down to a realistic price point."

He raised his head and looked up at her, quizzical. Lulu arched her back and moaned again.

> At least one industry analyst thinks Conquest may have overpaid for Bluestream. "Two billion dollars is a ridiculous

> premium for a company with such a spotty track record. Jack Burnam is way out over his skis on this one."

Lulu heard noises of frustration from down below. Josh raised his head again, his face slick with her juices and red with exertion. He wiped his chin with the back of his hand. That's enough of that, Lulu thought. She rolled over onto all fours and stretched out her arms to brace herself against the headboard, her face pressed flat against the comforter. He scrambled up behind, grabbed her by the hips and pushed into her.

> Moreover, market observers report that at least one investor has begun shorting Conquest stock in anticipation of a steep and rapid decline. Additional short sellers could put further downward pressure on the company's stock price.

She felt Josh pick up his pace. Better, she thought. Much better. This time a part of her mind stayed with him. But only a part.

> These events combine to create perhaps the greatest challenge Jack Burnam has faced during his time at Conquest. As the Bluestream story plays out, the next few weeks will tell whether golden-boy Burnam pulls another rabbit from his hat or finally loses his Midas touch.

Now he was going at her like a jackhammer. She was getting worked up in spite of herself. She hadn't been pounded like this since college.

The jackhammer motion ceased. "Lulu, did you...uh...you know?"

She was nowhere near getting off, but surmised that Josh was done. On the computer screen inside her head, she clicked *Save.*

"Oh yeah," she said. "That was unbelievable." She manufactured a sigh of satisfaction and rolled out from underneath him. "That was great, Jack."

He corrected her. "It's Josh."

"Josh. Of course."

Jack

Jack reclined in his leather desk chair, taking in a yellow sunset behind the Spindletop restaurant as it revolved atop the Hyatt Regency and thinking happy thoughts about the fine, firm flanks of Maggie Wheeler. Quite a find, that one. Legs like palm trees and breasts like those big Ruby Red grapefruit they grow in the Rio Grande Valley. Eager as a month-old spaniel but old enough to know the score. And a soft Texas accent that Jack found irresistible: *Sure, Jay-ack.*

He'd met her at one of those company holiday functions where the employees and their spouses flock around the brass hoping to make an impression right before bonus season. Maggie had impressed Jack when, after five minutes of banter and innuendo, she'd touched his arm and slipped her cell phone number into his pocket.

He thought about how times had changed. In the old days, he'd had his pick of the good-looking secretaries. Then came women's liberation and then sexual harassment. It had gotten so a man could get sued for nothing more than having a hard-on in the office. Then came Generation X or neo-feminism or whatever they called it and now he had his pick of the best-looking young wives, all wanting to do something to advance their husbands' careers. The Lord giveth, and the Lord taketh away.

There was nothing quite like fucking another man's wife, Jack thought, unless maybe it was buying his company right out from under him. Come to think of it, most of the men Jack knew would sooner give up their wives than their companies. Jack certainly would.

Maggie, he'd concluded, had no conscience whatsoever. That's why he'd let her have a key to the suite at the Magnolia and had planned to give her husband a promotion and a six-figure bonus. Too bad the kid had messed it up. He was puzzled. Wheeler had quit his job but told his wife some crazy lie about going to California on business. Was he dumping Maggie? That didn't seem likely. He started to get hard again, thinking about her. So what the hell was Wheeler up to?

His intercom buzzed. "Mr. Burnam, your package has arrived. The one from Senator Logan's office."

Jack felt a ripple of excitement that pushed Maggie Wheeler and everything else out of his mind. His secretary brought the package in and put it on his desk. It was two inches thick and bore the seal of the U.S. Senate. Jack sliced it open with a silver letter opener. Inside a layer of bubble wrap, he found a framed photograph and a note that was signed by the Senator's wife but read more like a form letter prepared by a staff member.

> *Jack, the Senator and I appreciate your support and all the fine things you and others in the business community are doing for America. /s/ Lorelei Logan*

He'd hoped for something a little more intimate, something that would have marked the special nature of the evening. Taken on the occasion of a White House reception honoring the Business Roundtable, the photo showed Senator Logan and Lorelei, with Jack in between, standing in the Blue Room in front of a white marble fireplace. The Senator's look seemed to say, *This is my kind of guy*. Lorelei wore a smile that, to Jack's eye, said much the same thing.

Jack had run into Lorelei Logan at a number of political functions and he admired her. A former Miss Texas and a Miss America semi-finalist, she'd had small parts in a few movies and for a few years had hosted a morning show on television. After getting married, she'd worked at her husband's side at thousands of campaign events but also carved out her own role as an advocate for the arts. Jack respected her dedication and the way she represented the best of Texas womanhood in Washington and all over the world. For that matter, he liked the way she filled out those designer dresses she always wore. Christ, there was no other way to put it. She was a damn fine-looking woman. Ripe, full-figured and classy.

Lorelei had flirted with him shamelessly at the Business Roundtable reception. Initially he'd chalked it up to her husband's need for contributions to help launch his incipient run for the presidency, but when the three of them moved into position for the commemorative photo, he began to suspect there might be more to it. The Senator had rested his arm over Jack's shoulder and Jack had wrapped his arm casually about Lorelei's waist. Jostled by a passing staffer, Jack's hand had come to rest—inadvertently, of course—on the pleasant swell of Lorelei's rump. She neither objected nor moved away. Instead, when the same passing staffer distracted the Senator with some type of confidential message, she'd pressed against him and whispered, "Why Jack, aren't you fresh?" *Fresh?* He hadn't heard that in years. And when the photographer said he had finished, Lorelei instead insisted on several additional takes. By the time they finally broke out of their poses, Jack's hand had enjoyed a thorough exploration of her backside and he'd worked up a sweat.

He examined the photograph more closely. This was no secretary, no bored wife of a junior executive. This was a recognized beauty, a woman of intellect and charm. Moreover, she was married to a U.S. Senator, a man who had achieved as much in his own sphere of influence as Jack had in his, a man who had a fair shot at someday occupying the Oval Office. Jack didn't like to think that any woman was out of his league, but Lorelei Logan might be a stretch. He studied her face, searching for clues. What exactly did she have in mind?

CHAPTER 4. THURSDAY

CQC 49.75 1.13↓

Miranda

Miranda dialed the number of Willa Bates, her college roommate. Willa had gone to law school and made her way to a New York law firm that specialized in corporate finance. Miranda hoped that Willa would serve as an off-the-record sounding board. She knew that financing structures like the Bluestream deal had become commonplace, but she hadn't kept up with the details. It was embarrassing to have to ask Willa for a remedial lesson, but she had to move quickly to meet the filing deadline.

She summarized what she knew about Bluestream and asked point-blank, "Do companies do this kind of thing nowadays?"

Willa laughed. "Every day of the week," she answered. "All major companies use some form of off-balance-sheet debt. Standard."

Miranda didn't want to seem out of touch, but her common sense told her that a company obligated to repay $2 billion should report that fact in bold type on its balance sheet and not in an obscure footnote. And she didn't understand how management could tell the public that Conquest owned and operated Bluestream if it was managed by some outside investors who put up only a tiny fraction of its cost.

"Isn't this different? How can Conquest give up control over such an important acquisition?"

"That's a formality," said Willa. "The interests are aligned. There's no reason to think the third party won't operate in Conquest's best interests. Companies do it all the time."

Miranda's assistant spoke to her from the office doorway. "Jesse has a basketball game this afternoon. You asked me to remind you."

Miranda rubbed her forehead. She needed to spend every possible minute at the office, but she'd missed Jesse's last two games and had given him an unconditional promise to make it today.

She refocused on Willa. "So where do companies get the magic three percent? Who are these outside investors?"

"I don't know for sure about Conquest, of course, but I would guess they would raise the money in-house."

"In-house?" How could independent investors be in-house?

"Why not? Senior management brings in the investors. Golfing buddies. Big shots. People they can trust. A club deal."

Miranda frowned but said nothing.

"I gotta go," said Willa. "But I can tell you this deal is nothing out of the ordinary. This train left the station a long time ago."

She's right, thought Miranda. Not only had the Bluestream train left the station, it was hurtling down the track at breakneck speed. Did she want to step in front of it? Norah had put her on Bluestream to get the deal done, not to raise questions that someone else had already answered. She should relax and go with the flow.

Maggie

Maggie hadn't visited the Rice campus in years. She found a parking space on a side street off Bissonet and walked to Fondren Court, a great expanse of lawn encircled by sprawling azaleas and ancient oak. On the far edge of campus hulked the football stadium, a 70,000-seat behemoth. She recalled a concert at the stadium during her high school years when she danced in the aisle as Pink Floyd played *Money, it's a gas*. Still one of her all-time favorite songs.

A friendly coed directed her to the Office of Continuing Studies where she found the current class listings. She needed something that met on Tuesday nights. If she was going to see Jack on a regular basis, she would need some serious cover. Like a weekly seminar that met for three hours. The first half-hour of each class would give her enough bits of information to sprinkle into conversations with her husband. Then she would head to the Magnolia for her rendezvous with Jack. She could read the assignments on nights when Jack was late.

She perused the list. *Studio Art. Creative Writing.* Maggie wrinkled her nose. She wasn't all that creative, except in the bedroom. *Software Development.* Too technical. Wait, there was something promising: *Fundraising for Nonprofit Organizations.* Tuesday evenings, seven to ten. Perfect. Not only would it give the cover she needed, she might learn something about charities and nonprofit fundraising. It could come in handy after she and Jack got married.

She froze. Where did *that* come from? He was already married. She was already married. What she and Jack were engaged in was sport-fucking, wasn't it? Good, clean fun. Besides, seeing Jack gave her plenty of chances to remind him of how hard Russ worked. In a way, she was doing this for her husband. Marriage to Jack was totally out of the question. Wasn't it?

Maggie filled out an enrollment form and paid the tuition. A secretary gave her a copy of the syllabus and told her where to buy books.

Back outdoors, a wave of memory enveloped Maggie as she spied the red tile roof of Baker College, one of the campus's student residence buildings. She had attended Baker's annual Shakespeare fest one year dressed as a serving wench, and her date had gotten upset because she'd spent most of the night in a lip lock with another guy that she met at the party. The other guy came dressed as a jester, complete with pointy-toed shoes, tights and a ridiculous red-and-yellow tunic. They'd necked and petted for hours without exchanging names. Finally, she'd let him remove her wench outfit and make love to her in someone's empty upstairs dorm room. Ten years later, she remembered that jester as one of the best lays of her life.

Almost as good as Jack.

Jack

In Jack's view, Conquest's most important product was *change*. Instead of making better or cheaper widgets, he drove his company to generate new products and find virgin markets. As a rule of thumb, he wanted at least twenty percent of corporate revenue to flow from lines of business that didn't exist two years earlier. That way, every five years or so, Conquest would completely reinvent itself.

To that end, a few years earlier Jack had set up an in-house committee, informally called the Shapeshifters, to help him evaluate new business proposals submitted by Conquest employees. It was the old-fashioned corporate suggestion box writ large. Sometimes a proposal related to the making of a new product. Other times it was the acquisition of a company, like Bluestream. It might involve an entirely new venture or a novel way of marketing an existing service to a new customer base. If an idea got the committee's okay, its sponsor, whether a senior executive or a messenger, got a spot on the project team and a percentage interest in the profits. It was, Jack thought, corporate meritocracy at its best.

The Shapeshifters hadn't met for a while, and Jack looked forward to today's session. "What have you got?" he said to the room.

Chase Colvin, whom Jack knew as one of the hotshots in the marketing department, stepped forward. He wore a three-piece suit and sported trendy wire-rim glasses that Jack suspected he'd bought to make himself look especially serious for this meeting. Colvin clicked a remote control and a screen dropped showing a map of the United States festooned with arrows emanating from Houston. "Step One," he began. "Conquest forms partnerships with every major electric utility in the country. Our target is coverage of seventy-five million households."

Colvin had Jack's attention. He was thinking big.

"Step Two, Conquest launches a media blitz to advance awareness of the company's commitment to renewable energy." He clicked to a new slide. On this one, arrows pointed from the Conquest logo to images of the sun, wind turbines, a hydroelectric dam, and a herd of cattle. Then a single line of text: *Greenquest. We're doing our part. Are you?*

"Chase," said Jack. "What do cows have to do with electricity?"

"Anaerobic digestion," Colvin shot back, "produces flammable bio-gas."

Jack nodded. Bio-gas.

Colvin's next slide showed a blowup of a post card. "Step Three. Our utility partners include this card in every customer's monthly bill. Recycled paper, of course."

Choose Conquest for renewable energy, read the card, above the same images of the sun, wind farm, dam and cowherd. *One simple fact*, it continued accusingly. *Each year, more than thirty billion pounds of carbon dioxide can be kept from entering the Earth's atmosphere if as few as ten percent of Americans choose renewable energy sources.* Nice, thought Jack. Who could resist that?

The card's fine print noted that a *Greenquest* customer would pay, in addition to their regular utility bill, a modest override of five dollars per month because, unfortunately, renewable power didn't yet have the economies of scale enjoyed by traditional sources.

"We project," said Colvin, "that at least ten percent of the households that receive this card will choose *Greenquest*. That's thirty-seven million five hundred thousand dollars per year. Ten percent of that goes back to our utility partners, leaving Conquest with..." He paused for dramatic effect. "... more than thirty million dollars each year for as far into the future as you can imagine."

Jack didn't disagree with Colvin's projections. The United Nations had put out a report on climate change, and more and more people were believing that claptrap. This would make them feel good about themselves. Ten percent of households might be on the low side.

"Okay," he said. "You're onto something as far as the revenue side goes, but where do we get all this renewable power? Conquest has a few wind farms, but that wouldn't be near enough."

Colvin adjusted his reading glasses. "Begging your pardon, Mr. Burnam, but it doesn't say anywhere that we actually deliver the power to the customer. On the contrary..." He brought up his final slide, an image of a document printed in type so small that everyone in the room began to squint. "The customer service agreement will provide that *Greenquest* would acquire electricity from renewable sources and deliver that power into the appropriate regional grid. The consumer draws down power from the grid, but of course there's no way of knowing which electricity reaches any given consumer."

A committee member coughed. "It seems to me," he said, "that your proposal poses some serious accounting challenges. With so many customers and grids and sources of power, it's going to be a bitch for anyone to figure out whether the amount of electricity that *Greenquest* delivers bears any relationship at all to what we get paid. In fact, I suspect it can't be done."

Colvin removed his glasses, shut off the projector and turned on the lights. "Yes, sir," he said. "You could be right."

A silence descended as the committee took in the genius of Colvin's proposal. Several of them walked over to Colvin to shake his hand. Jack wiped away a tear. He wouldn't need his lucky silver dollar to decide this one.

Miranda

Jesse grabbed the rebound, pivoted and dribbled toward the opposite end of the gym. Nine other third-grade boys, four wearing white jerseys and five wearing red, swarmed after him like bees around a hive.

"Protect the ball," called a voice behind Miranda. She turned and recognized the mother of one of Jesse's teammates. Nice woman, Rhoda something.

Jesse crossed the free throw line and shifted the dribble from one hand to the other, shielding the ball from the red shirt coming up behind him. The red shirt careened past and Jesse went in for a layup. Two points flashed on the electric scoreboard and the dozen or so parents watching the game burst into applause. Jesse gave his mom a sidelong glance to make sure she'd seen.

"Nice basket," Rhoda said.

"I had no idea he could do that," said Miranda.

"He's gotten to be one of the best players." Rhoda patted the empty space beside her and Miranda moved up one row.

The ball moved back and forth until a buzzer signaled halftime. Jesse's team led six-to-four and Jesse had scored two of his team's three baskets.

"I won't be seeing you much the rest of the season," Rhoda said abruptly.

This surprised Miranda. Rhoda was a stay-at-home mom who never missed a game. "Why not?" Miranda asked.

"I took a job." Rhoda mentioned the name of a well-known advertising agency.

"Congratulations. That's great."

"Not really." Rhoda looked around to make sure no one else was listening. "My husband got fired. I had no choice."

Miranda made a show of looking for Jesse on the basketball court. She didn't know Rhoda all that well and wasn't sure she wanted to hear a confessional.

"Tell you the truth," Rhoda continued, "I'm all for women who want careers, but what I want is to be a mom. I never wanted to be the breadwinner."

Miranda thought about that. She'd always assumed that someday David would make partner at his law firm and she'd at least have the option to stay home and take care of Jesse and maybe have another baby. It wasn't looking that way now, with David having been passed over and her own career on the rise. At least David wasn't in danger of being fired.

"It's getting to be more and more common," Rhoda said. "Women support their families while their husbands stay home. It's trendy, but I don't much like it."

The buzzer erupted and the boys streamed back to the center of the court.

"Get to your spots," Rhoda shouted.

Miranda checked her watch, hoping the game would end in time for her to get in a few more hours at the office.

Norah

Driving home from work, Norah succumbed to an impulse to pull over at the Medical Arts Building. The Wheeler business had her on edge again. Not to mention Bluestream. Jack had bet the farm.

She didn't expect Dr. Frost to be in his office at this hour. More likely, by now he'd be on a tennis court at River Oaks. Maybe she would sit in the car and reconstruct one of their sessions in her head. It would be cheaper that way, and she never much liked what he had to say anyway.

Norah had first gone to see Dr. Frost several years earlier complaining of depression and wanting a prescription for one of the wonder medicines, like Prozac or Zoloft. But Dr. Frost had insisted on several months of disagreeable talk therapy and, when that was done, he'd gone down a wholly different track.

"You may be a *hoarder*," he'd said.

"Excuse me?"

"Hoarding. It's a form of OCD. For example, people with an unreasonable fear of germs wash their hands over and over. People with an irrational fear of intruders check and recheck their doors and windows dozens of times."

Then she'd asked him what do *hoarders* fear. Actually, she found the terminology repugnant so she didn't say *hoarders*. She said *people like me*. What do they fear?

Dr. Frost's answer was succinct. "Loss, Norah. They fear loss."

Norah thought that Dr. Frost, like all shrinks, was interested mainly in making a buck off the latest psycho-craze. He'd wanted to visit her home and assess her living space to complete his diagnosis. He couldn't have been more wrong. It simply made her feel good to keep things. That was all there was to it. If she needed more space, she would buy a bigger house.

A rap at the window startled her. "Norah, are you okay?"

It was him, in tennis whites, perspiring. She guessed that he was returning from River Oaks for an evening consultation. He walked to the passenger side, opened the door, and climbed inside. "Norah, what are you doing here?"

It struck Norah that he didn't look at all like a psychiatrist. He looked more like a tennis pro. "Fine, doctor, fine. I stopped here to make a phone call."

"I haven't seen you for quite a while. We've developed some new behavioral therapies. You might want to reconsider."

Norah heard, *We could work on your backhand.* "Really, Doctor, no."

"It isn't talk therapy. I know you don't like that. We'd work together to refine certain skills, like classifying your possessions, separating the important from the unimportant. And discarding. You would practice discarding things and I would coach you."

To Norah, it sounded like this: *Your return of service is weak. I can help you.*

"Doctor, really, this isn't a problem. I told you before."

He wrote a day and time on the back of a business card and handed it to her. She seemed to have agreed to an appointment in spite of herself. It was pointless, though. She didn't want therapy.

"Fine, then," said Dr. Frost. "See you next week."

"Sure, Doctor. Next week."

She made a mental note to call and cancel. Then she thought about where she would file his business card when she got home.

CHAPTER 5. FRIDAY

CQC 49.81 0.06↑

Norah

When she arrived at her office on Friday morning, Jenkins stood in the doorway, FedEx envelope in hand. "Our wayward ex-employee has surfaced," he said. "This is addressed to you." He ripped open the envelope and handed to Norah the single sheet of paper inside.

Norah read Wheeler's note twice. Twenty-five million. He was an audacious bastard, but smart. He knew she couldn't quibble over price. Besides, if her plan worked, the price wouldn't matter.

"Ms. Needham?"

She'd forgotten about Jenkins. "Where's your spook?" she asked.

"He's in Ixtapa. That's where the package originated."

"Tell him to get his CIA ass in gear. I want that hard drive back and anything else Wheeler has with him."

"He's working on it, but I can't make any promises. It's been over twenty-four hours since Wheeler sent this package. He could be long gone."

Norah gave him a half-smile. "Tell your man to keep his eyes and ears open. I have a feeling that some time later today Russ Wheeler will come looking for us."

Miranda

Miranda saw David's number in her caller ID. She was happy to take a break.

"Miranda, you won't believe this." David's voice quivered with excitement. She wondered what could have him so worked up.

"I got a call from Franklin Payton. You know who he is, right?"

Of course. Everyone in Houston knew Franklin Payton. But how did Franklin Payton know David?

"He asked me to come in for an interview."

Miranda was mystified. "What kind of interview?"

"For a *job*. At Payton-Mosel."

"So when is the interview?" She strained to match David's level of excitement, feeling guilty that possibility hadn't occurred to her.

"This morning. I already did it. I spent an hour with Franklin and I met the other senior partners. Then I met two junior partners and a couple of associates."

"David, what's this all about?"

"They offered me a job. I'm going to take it. I'll be an investment banker."

"What?" She paused to collect her thoughts. She knew David was going nowhere at Miller-Dunn. Maybe the firm had helped to outplace him. This could be a godsend.

"I thought you'd be pleased for me."

"I am. I'm in shock. It's so sudden. What does the offer letter say?"

"Well," he said. "I didn't get an offer letter. Everything was verbal. But that's a formality. This is an investment bank, you know. They like to move fast."

A warning light went off in Miranda's head. "David, this could be the break you've been waiting for, but..."

"But?"

"But, promise me one thing. Don't resign until you have an offer letter in hand. You never know what could happen."

She could hear David breathing at the other end of the line.

"Promise?"

"All right, I promise." He sounded deflated. She'd ruined his big moment.

The connection went dead. Miranda said a silent prayer.

Lulu

Since her Wednesday night roll in the hay with Josh, Lulu had lolled around her hotel, waiting for him to call as promised. She'd visited *The Back Yard* again, trolling for another source, but she caught a few of the Bluestream employees staring and got the impression that someone had warned them not to talk to her. Then came a handwritten note:

> *Lulu, come by my apartment this afternoon. I'll show you what you want to see. /s/ Josh*

The reverse side gave her an address in nearby Alviso.

She checked out of her hotel and drove to the address, where she found a complex of luxury apartment buildings hugging the side of a hill. Lulu parked her car and climbed a stone walkway, searching for his unit. She took her time, enjoying the mild California sunshine. Finding the apartment, she knocked. Josh opened the door and held out a gadget like nothing she had ever seen. Blue aluminum and a polished silver bezel embraced a five-inch screen. There was no keypad to mar the smooth design, no pull-out antenna.

"Hi, Lulu. This is Bluebox."

Lulu looked at the thing. It was simple and elegant, and it made her old Nokia with its tiny buttons and miniscule grey-scale screen and stubby antenna seem like an artifact.

"Looks good, I give you that, but how do you dial? How do you send a message?"

Josh pressed the single button on the side of the gadget and the screen came to life. A virtual keypad appeared and he tapped out a text message that popped up on her phone a moment later: *It's called a touchscreen.*

Lulu had seen touchscreens before, although she had to admit not as stylish as this one. "That's worth two billion dollars?"

Josh responded by speaking to the device rather than to Lulu. "Bluebox," he said, "Internet." The virtual keyboard disappeared and an Internet search box—*AskJeeves*—replaced it.

That, Lulu had to admit, was something her cell phone couldn't do. She had to use a computer to access the Internet. She thought about using this gadget to read news reports, anytime, anywhere. It would change the news business beyond recognition.

Josh spoke again. "Bluebox, Oprah." The screen shifted again and came to life in color with a sharpness that rivaled the best televisions she'd ever seen. Oprah appeared in mid-interview with Naomi and Wynona Judd regarding their next final tour. Lulu studied the streaks of mascara running down Naomi's face.

"Impressive," said Lulu, "but Sony already makes a little-bitty television. A portable television isn't worth that much money, no matter how fancy it is."

Josh looked at her as if she were a stubborn child. "You're not getting it." Then, to the gadget, he said, "HBO. Oscar winner." The screen changed and Lulu recognized the previous year's Best Picture winner. "Disney Channel," said Josh, and the screen shifted again. "Discovery Channel."

It dawned on Lulu that he wasn't showing her broadcast TV channels. He was showing her cable TV with no apparent cable hookup. Wireless cable, for lack of a better term. "How are you doing that?" she asked.

"It's called *streaming.* Bluebox connects to the Internet, of course, and can stream all these channels over the Internet. Bluebox will make cable TV obsolete."

Holy shit. She felt her reportorial skepticism slipping.

"There's more." Josh handed her a pair of miniscule ear buds and something that looked like wraparound sunglasses. He called more instructions and Bluebox swiftly transported Lulu to another time and place altogether. The inside lens of the wraparounds located her in a first-tier seat at

Carnegie Hall. Yo-Yo Ma, alone at center stage, eyes closed in concentration, swayed at his cello. A Bach sonata reverberated in her head with bass notes so deep and powerful they nearly brought tears to her eyes.

"My God," she said. "That's incredible."

Josh lifted the wraparounds from her face. She plucked out the ear buds and handed them over with a sigh.

"Bluebox, RAM." Yo-Yo evaporated and the Bluebox screen displayed a menu of tiny icons.

"RAM?"

"Remote Appliance Management. Each icon represents an appliance here in my apartment. Want coffee?" He tapped the screen and Lulu heard the coffee maker in his kitchen begin to heat up.

"Say you're on a trip and you forgot to lock the front door." He tapped the screen and Lulu heard a deadbolt turn in the apartment's front door. "You can turn on your oven on the way home from work. Or program your DVD from the office."

Bluebox began to vibrate, then shifted to a pleasant buzz. "It's an e-mail from my boss," Josh said. "Hold on a sec."

Lulu watched as he tapped out an answering e-mail. That was something else her phone didn't have.

Josh smiled. "Are you getting it now? It isn't just Bluebox, it's the content delivery technology behind it. Giga-capacity Internet, streaming, voice recognition, e-mail, voicemail, texting, everything. It's all tied together in this little box."

Lulu drew a breath. She knew something like this had been Silicon Valley's wet dream for nearly a decade. The next big, big thing. But she found it hard to believe that Conquest would be in the middle of it. She bit her lip. Goddamit. If she wrote about what Josh had shown her, the story would send Conquest's stock price over the moon, and she certainly didn't want to make Jack Burnam any richer than he already was. On the other hand, if she didn't write about it, she'd be playing along with whatever strategy was causing Burnam to keep this thing under wraps.

And there was always a chance that this was some kind of hoax. Josh had shown her a fancy gizmo that worked in his apartment, but it might not be ready for the rest of the world. She had no reason to trust him.

"One last question," she said. "Why are you telling me all this? What's in it for you?"

With a smile he showed her the menu of RAM icons on the Bluebox screen. He tapped the one that looked like a tiny spa with clouds of steam rising out of it.

Lulu thought for a moment. "I get it," she said, taking the gadget from him and simultaneously stepping out of her shoes. "How do you turn on the bubbles?"

Wheeler

Wheeler reclined on his private sundeck at the Vista del Sol, staring at the ocean and waiting for the room telephone to ring its jingly, old-fashioned Mexican ring. *Ting. Ting.* For a while, Sherry had waited with him, but she had abandoned the sundeck for the beach an hour earlier. He wasn't certain, but he thought he could make out her lime green thong bikini down near the thatched hut where the hotel rented snorkels and sailboats. *Ting.* He grabbed it before the second *ting.* The caller, as expected, was his contact at the Bank of Montserrat. Wheeler had checked in every thirty minutes since the opening of business to see if Norah had sent the money. "Can you confirm the transfer of funds?"

The man from the bank wouldn't allow Wheeler to shortcut the process. He insisted on all the required identifiers. Account number. Tax ID. Mainland mailing address. The two pass codes required for an offshore account. Wheeler had everything at hand.

"Yes, Mr. Wheeler. There has been a transfer."

Wheeler let out a long breath. The tension that had plagued his stomach and bowels for the last few days eased. Conquest had paid him the money. *Twenty-five million!* He glanced down at the beach. The woman in the lime green bikini had climbed into some kind of harness. She stood at the water's edge holding a rope that stretched out to a powerboat bobbing in the surf. The boat surged forward and the woman rose into the air underneath a rainbow-colored parasail.

The man from the bank continued in an exceedingly formal tone. "In addition," he said, "we've completed the investment purchases you directed. There were a great many securities. That is why I could not return your call until now."

Wheeler's excitement froze in his chest. He hadn't given any investment instructions.

"Walk me through the investments, okay?"

The man seemed offended. "We purchased exactly what you told us to purchase. I have your instruction letter right here."

The powerboat towing Sherry, if it was Sherry, made a broad U-turn and headed back toward the beach. It looked as if she could let go the rope and sail right over Wheeler's head.

"Do me a favor, okay? I want to double-check."

"Yes, Mr. Wheeler. As instructed, we've credited your account with certificates representing shares in a large number of private investment partnerships."

"What partnerships?" Wheeler asked warily. His tongue felt like sand.

"Rogue Ventures. One thousand units. Stryker LP. One thousand units. Booster Ventures One through Four. One thousand units each."

Wheeler interrupted. "That's enough." He knew all the names and grasped in an instant what Norah had done to him. She'd paid him $25 million and simultaneously put the money into an array of Conquest's funky financing vehicles.

"There are quite a few more."

"There's been a mistake."

Papers shuffled at the other end of the line. "I don't think so, Mr. Wheeler. The paperwork is fully in order."

"When did you receive these investment instructions?"

“This morning. By fax from your personal fax machine in Houston. We have your signature on file and confirmed its authenticity.”

Christ. Conquest had his signature on a hundred documents. Norah had copied it onto the instruction letter and sent it from the machine in his office.

“I want to reverse the investments. Send everything back.”

“I don’t understand.”

Norah had outsmarted him. He couldn’t turn the investments into cash unless Conquest wanted to close them down and distribute the earnings, which could take months or years. And he couldn’t sell a private partnership interest without Conquest’s signoff. So he had his twenty-five million, but he was still under Norah’s thumb. To make matters worse, she’d nullified his blackmail threat. With his name on all those partnerships, any investigation would lead directly to him. And she’d made sure to create a paper trail showing lots of money going into his offshore account and back again.

“I don’t want them. I refuse delivery.”

“I’m sorry Mr. Wheeler, but there’s nothing I can do. The bank has already taken delivery, as per your instructions. Reversing the purchases would involve a great deal of paperwork and attention. We’d have to file reports.”

Was the man mocking him? Maybe Norah had gotten to him.

The powerboat crunched through the surf as Sherry sailed over the beach. She was near enough to wave at him. Wheeler’s arm lifted in automatic response.

“Reports? With who?”

“With the American tax authorities, of course.”

Of course. Wheeler was certain now that the man was laughing at him. The dishonest creep might have Norah holding on another line. He banged the phone down.

The boat made another turn and headed out to sea. The lime green bikini became a tiny green dot in the sky, sailing away toward the horizon.

David

David couldn't get his bearings after the conversation with Miranda. He thought she would congratulate him on his big score. Instead, she seemed to think it was some kind of mistake, like he wasn't good enough for a job at Payton-Mosel. Of course, he didn't tell her that he had already prepared his letter of resignation. It lay on his desk, ready to go.

His desk phone buzzed. "David, Mr. Howell would like to see you," said his assistant.

David was surprised. Howell was a senior partner, a long-time power within the firm due to his tenacious grip on several major oil and gas clients. Also a major hard-ass. Why would he want to see David? Maybe the partners had gotten wind of his interview with Payton-Mosel. Maybe they had set it in motion to ease him out. On the other hand, oil and gas was booming. Maybe Howell needed more lawyers in his group.

David folded the letter of resignation and put it in his jacket pocket. He didn't want anyone to come across it while he was talking to Howell.

A short elevator ride took David up three floors. Howell occupied a corner office with a view to the south. A landscape painting with cactus and bluebonnets hung behind Howell's desk.

"David, good news. We're taking you off the Marathon job."

That was good news, but David was wary. "Yes, sir," he said. "There's something else you want me to do?"

"Exactly. One of my clients has put in a bid for a drilling company. I need somebody to go through their files with fine-tooth comb. Make sure we don't get any surprises."

David squirmed in his seat. Another due diligence assignment. It wasn't what he was hoping for, but it had to be better than Marathon. And maybe since he'd be out of the office he could sneak in some time to study for the securities exams that the guys at Payton-Mosel had told him he would need to take.

“Okay, sure. Where are they located?” David hope he wouldn’t have to drive as far as he did for the Marathon job.

“Alaska,” said Howell. “Prudhoe Bay, to be exact. This company operates on the North Slope. The offices are in Deadhorse.”

“Deadhorse?”

“Yeah. It’s of those towns that got built to support the oil operations in the area. Three thousand people or so. Man-camp. That sort of thing.”

David couldn’t keep the dismay from showing on his face.

“It isn’t that bad, David. They have Internet. A movie theater.” He paused. “I’m told they even have a gym.”

David flinched slightly. Maybe Hamner had ratted him out. He couldn’t tell from Howell’s bland expression whether this was an innocent remark or a jab.

“It is pretty remote, but this deal is very important to my client. Gotta be done fast and gotta be done right. Shouldn’t take you more than a month.”

“A month?”

“Maybe three weeks, if you work through the weekends.”

David had a fleeting vision of himself in snowshoes and an anorak, slogging across the frozen tundra, and wondered momentarily if Howell for some unknown reason was pulling his leg. “Sir, are you serious?”

“As serious as an owl. Are you?”

“Sir?”

“Serious, David. Are you serious?”

Now he was sure Hamner had ratted him out. He decided to try a Hail Mary.

“Mr. Howell, if I do a good job on this, is there any chance it would put me back on partner track?”

Howell guffawed, then lowered his voice. “There’s more than one track around here, David. There’s the partner track, but there’s also the having-an-office-to-sit-in track and the getting-a-paycheck-at-the-end-of-the-month track. Those are the tracks I’d be thinking about if I were you.”

David did as Howell had suggested. He thought about spending three or four weeks living in a man-camp in Deadhorse, Alaska. He thought about what it said for his future prospects at Miller-Dunn that a senior partner had singled him out for this particularly miserable piece of work. He thought about Franklin Payton's genial, friendly face as they shook hands after David's interview. And, briefly, he thought about the promise he'd made to Miranda not to resign until he had received Payton-Mosel's written job offer.

He reached into his pocket and handed over his letter of resignation.

Jack

Santo parked the limo in front of a newly-renovated two-story house at the corner of San Jacinto and Rosedale. He left the engine running and stepped around to open the rear door for Jack. He held an umbrella to protect his boss from a light evening drizzle.

Jack emerged talking. "Santo, have the car in the alley at eight headed that way." He pointed a finger toward the far end of the block. "Be ready to go."

"Yes, Mr. Burnam."

The limo pulled around the corner and blended into the evening traffic on San Jacinto. Jack stepped onto the front porch and paused to examine an oval medallion hanging near the door. It declared the house, in raised black and aluminum letters, a City of Houston landmark. One of the few, thought Jack. He passed through the door into a living room half-filled with people milling about and drinking cocktails. A pianist played Chopin. The twenty-five or thirty people in the room represented, Jack guessed, nearly a quarter of the city's collective wealth.

"Welcome, Jack. It's going to be quite a night, isn't it?"

Jack looked at the elderly, bird-like woman who had spoken to him. Her name escaped him, but he knew that she was the matriarch of an old Houston family and presided with an iron fist over the Houston Historic

Preservation Alliance, one of the many civic groups to which Jack devoted his time and Conquest's money. Jack admired Houston's heritage, but he drew the line at old buildings. He thought Houston needed historic preservation as much as it needed ski lifts.

"Yes, ma'am, yes ma'am." Maybe a heavy dose of hearty would cover up the fact that her name hadn't come back to him yet. "Yes, ma'am. Quite a night."

Jack eased into the kitchen and gave a nod to the crew of waiters and waitresses. He peered through a rear window to make sure it was as he expected. A high fence screened the back yard from the alley and from the front of the house. When the time came, they would be able to slip relatively unnoticed out the back door and into the waiting limousine.

A brochure lying on an antique table in the front room told Jack the story of the house. Alfred C. Finn had designed and built it in 1920 and lived in it until 1956. Finn's many other designs included the Gulf Building, a Depression-era Art Deco skyscraper in downtown Houston. Jack recalled visiting the city in the early seventies when the Gulf Building still featured a fifty-foot rotating orange neon sign known locally as the *Lollipop.*

"Thanks so much for helping out with our little project." Bird-woman had found him.

Courtesy of a half-million dollar donation from Conquest, the Preservation Alliance had saved the Finn House from destruction by a condominium developer and converted it into the Texas Museum for Women in the Arts, the only museum in the state devoted exclusively to paintings and sculpture by, for and about persons of the female persuasion. Jack, of course, didn't give a damn about the Finn House. His idea of a place worth keeping around was the *U-Tote-Em* over on Park Place, the world's first drive-up convenience store, opened in 1949 and the great-granddaddy of every *Kwik-Stop* and *7-Eleven* in the country.

"I see you're being modest," she said when he didn't respond. "If you don't mind my asking, what was it about the Finn House that caught your attention?"

A commotion at the front door drew the attention of the small crowd and saved Jack from having to answer. Two Secret Service agents with visible hearing devices entered the room. One took a sentry position near the entrance and the other began an ostentatious inspection of the house. Bird-woman smiled with anticipation. "The Senator's wife must be on her way. We'll begin the dedication as soon as she arrives." She whispered, "You know, this museum is one of her pet projects."

Jack tried to act surprised. He'd come upon this fact months earlier and within twenty-four hours had delivered a Conquest check into the eager hands of the preservationists. The donation assured him a prominent position at the dedication ceremony, an event certain to draw Lorelei Logan back to Texas from Washington, D.C.

"Really?" he said mildly. His phone vibrated and he excused himself.

"Mr. Burnam, it's Security. The protesters are in position. About twenty. We've got 'em on a bus about two blocks away. We'll move in on your go-ahead."

"What did you tell them?"

"They think they are part of a protest against the Senator's position on..." He faltered. "You know the type."

"That's fine," said Jack. Wait until you see the Senator's wife enter the house, then be ready."

"She's going in now, Mr. Burnam."

Jack returned to the main room to find an appreciative but shy semi-circle surrounding Lorelei. He watched as she made her way across the room shaking hands and making small talk. Her auburn hair angled across her forehead and down to her shoulders in a manner that, for a politician's wife, seemed positively rakish. She wore pearl earrings and a fuschia-colored suit over a paisley silk blouse. Studying her, it struck Jack that the preservationists had a point. Sometimes older is better.

She approached the end of the semi-circle where Jack waited. He sensed that her awareness of his presence was as keen as his own consciousness of hers. A modest blush mottled her throat.

"The Senator is out of the country. He won't be returning for several more days." She was answering a question put by the person standing next to Jack, but her manner of speaking seemed intended to assure that Jack overheard. His hopes rose like a child's kite in a hurricane.

She reached the end of the line and stopped. "Good evening, Jack," she said in a low voice. "So nice to see you again. I've been thinking about our time together at the White House." Her tone was warm and, once again, flirtatious. They bantered. She placed her hand on his arm. Jack flexed.

He directed her attention to a huge painting in an adjacent room, and they moved away from the crowd. A stunningly naked Psyche gazed from the canvas, iridescent wings unfolding from her shoulders as a beam of sunlight drew the observer's eye to an unmistakably erect pair of nipples. A muscular and equally nude Cupid pulled her in for a kiss. The painting captured the empyreal moment when, in legend, Psyche ascended to Mt. Olympus, became immortal and embarked upon an eternal love. It was giving Jack a hard-on like a fence post.

"Painted by Annie Swynnerton in 1891," he told Lorelei. "On loan from the Oldham Gallery in London." Conquest had donated another quarter-million to secure it.

"Mmmm," said Lorelei. She dropped her hand from his arm but stood close to him as she studied the extraordinary painting. So close, in fact, that he could feel the warmth rising from her skin. Her perfume smelled of sweet grass. People had begun to look in their direction, but Jack paid no attention. She drew back and looked Jack full in the face. "Jack," she said. "Is there something you wanted to ask me?"

Jack had to take several deep breaths to calm himself down.

"You know," she continued. "I never wanted a life in politics. All those nasty reporters and unpleasant little Congressmen. I was much happier back in Texas, before my husband became a senator." Her voice trailed off momentarily. "And now he's thinking about running for president."

Jack put on a sympathetic face. "It must be a lonely life," he said. "So many people around, but no one you can trust."

"Exactly," she said. "It's impossible to find someone to confide in. You know, someone who has experience in the world but doesn't have a political axe to grind." She sighed. "I always expected I'd marry a businessman."

This was going far better than Jack ever dreamed possible. The time was right. Momentarily oblivious to their surroundings, he reached for her.

"Not here," she whispered.

Not here? Not *here*? That meant...*somewhere.*

"Shall we begin the dedication now?" said Bird-woman.

She led Lorelei away, leaving Jack grasping at empty air. In the heat of the moment, he'd almost forgotten his elaborate plan. As Lorelei delivered gracious remarks on the many contributions of women to the arts and culture of Texas, he speed-dialed his flip phone.

"Now," he said. "Hurry up, dammit."

Within minutes, a clamor outside interrupted Lorelei's speech. Through a front window Jack saw a gaggle of protesters streaming off the bus and into the front yard.

"Jesus," said one of the Secret Service agents. "This is trouble."

The protestors began to chant something unintelligible but clearly truculent. Most carried signs. Some of them surged onto the front porch. One pounded on the door. Another rapped on a window. The agents looked jittery.

Jack took charge. "Come with me," he said to Lorelei.

One of the agents blocked their way. "Wait a minute, sir. You can't..."

Lorelei cut him off. "It's okay." She tilted her head toward Jack. "I'll be fine."

The agent didn't move. "I'm sorry ma'am, but it's not allowed."

At that moment, the sound of breaking glass startled the crowd. A demonstrator's elbow appeared through a broken window and withdrew. The chants revved up in volume. In the split-second when both of the Secret Service men turned their attention to the shattered window, Jack grasped Lorelei's arm and led her in the opposite direction. He quick-stepped her through the kitchen and the back yard and into the alley where

Santo stood, umbrella in hand, waiting beside the car. Jack swept her onto the warm leather of the limo's back seat and climbed in after.

"Where are you taking me?" Her voice was curious, but calm.

"Santo's going to take us for a drive. Maybe out to the Ship Channel. Don't you love the lights out there?"

She eyed him. "Let me get this straight. You're asking me to go cruising? I haven't been cruising since high school."

Jack motioned at Santo to get moving. A push of a button raised a privacy panel and Santo disappeared from sight. Another button opened a small bar. Jack held up two glasses and a chilled bottle. He poured and handed her a glass. "To us," he said. "And to cruising."

Sherry

Sherry, slathered in aloe gel, couldn't decide between room service and a solo dinner in the hotel restaurant. While she pondered, a knock sounded. She opened the door. A man stood looking at her. He was nearly the same height as her, but she might have a half-inch on him. His complexion was dark. She fought an impulse to press her hand against the side of his face. It wasn't that the man was so handsome. In fact, this man was downright plain. But he had a sturdy build and something else that made him attractive that she couldn't quite figure out.

"Sorry to intrude," he said. "Are you acquainted with someone named Russ Wheeler?"

"Who wants to know?"

He had a way of smiling that crinkled his forehead and made him look happy and perplexed at the same time.

"I'm Feo Duarte. I work for Conquest Corporation, in the Security Department. Mr. Wheeler is a former employee of Conquest and his former employer would like him to return to Houston."

His voice was low and full of self-confidence. It reminded her of the way the Master's voice sounded when he was giving a lesson.

"You're in luck," she said. "Mr. Wheeler left for Houston a couple of hours ago."

Feo looked more perplexed than before. "The last flight to Houston was at one o'clock. That's more than a couple of hours ago."

Still the smile. Still the calm voice.

"He's on some kind of charter to LA and he's planning to catch a redeye from LA back to Houston."

Feo said nothing.

"Really," she said. "He was in quite a state."

"A state of what?"

Sherry thought about this. "He was very agitated. Panic. I'd have to say he was in a state of panic."

He seemed to believe her.

"Did he take all of his belongings with him?"

"Yes. Why?"

"You said he was in a rush. Maybe he left some things behind."

"No. He took everything."

He didn't say anything for at least thirty seconds. She thought he was about to leave, but then he asked another question.

"Do you mind if I ask your name?"

She didn't mind. "I'm Sherry Shipley. A friend of Russ. Well, a *former* friend." With her hip she nudged the door open wider.

The smile faded and he seemed to be trying to interpret her intentions. For the first time, he looked at *her*, as opposed to looking at Wheeler's girlfriend. She wished she wasn't covered in aloe vera goo.

"I've got some other things I have to do right now," he said.

Sherry rested her shoulder against the door jamb. What he'd said didn't sound like a complete sentence.

"But maybe you'd like to meet for dinner? Half an hour? At the hotel restaurant?"

"Maybe," she said.

He waited while she thought about it. He had said he works in security. Sherry wondered how much money people made in jobs like that. Maybe not as much as Wheeler, but then again, Wheeler was gone. And security sounded like steady work.

There was something else. She liked the way that since she opened the door he'd remained standing in exactly the same spot. He hadn't stepped forward or back and he didn't lean to either side. He hadn't raised or lowered his voice. She'd never seen someone who seemed so much at ease and so perfectly balanced in one place. He seemed...dependable.

"You're not married or anything, are you?"

He laughed. "No. I'm not married. Or anything."

"Okay, then," said Sherry. "I'd like to have dinner with you, but not at the hotel. I know a place down the beach. Right on the water. *Playa De Los Amantes*."

"Lovers Beach," said Feo. "Perfect."

Jack

On the drive from the Finn House, Jack reflected on Lorelei's distaste for the political life. Ironically, during his college years he'd had an all-consuming passion for politics. Student government. Voter registration drives. Community action organizations. A turning came when Jack met Lacey Winston or, more to the point, Lacey's father. Jack's own father, a New Jersey store owner, seemed puny and small in comparison to J.D. Winston, then a Senior Vice President at American Oil & Gas and widely viewed as the power behind the AO&G throne.

One Christmas vacation, Jack, Lacey and J.D. had enjoyed the sun room of the Winston estate in New Canaan, Connecticut, overlooking a private skating pond shared by Lacey's family with three neighbors, a network news anchor, the managing partner of the third most prominent securities firm on Wall Street, and a former U.S. Secretary of State. The

Winston family enjoyed a level of opulence and sophistication that Jack hadn't known existed.

For J.D.'s benefit, Jack laid out his career plan. He'd begin working for a public interest research group. Environmental protection or consumer advocacy, most likely. Then he'd spend several years at a nonprofit corporation where he could hone in on one issue and pick up some financial management skills at the same time. Before turning thirty, he'd run for public office. State representative, maybe. He'd get some experience in campaigning and fund-raising. After that he'd grow his base of support by...

The look on J.D.'s face brought Jack up short. It was a look that Jack might have expected if he'd voiced a burning desire to become a dog groomer or a radio disk jockey.

"Hell, Jack, you seem bright enough. Why would you take a government job if you didn't have to?"

Jack had never thought of it as a job. He thought of it as a career, a career in public service. He wouldn't work for the government, he'd work for the people.

"What about...?" Jack said the name of J.D.'s neighbor, the former Secretary of State. Surely he believed in the merits of public service.

"That's different. He didn't want to do it. The President asked him to help out, so his company sent him down to Washington for a few years. He helped out like he was asked, then he came home and went back to his real job."

Jack wasn't sure what to say. The thought that serious people might scorn, rather than applaud, his ambitions had never entered his mind. And he'd never met anyone more serious than J.D.

Lacey elbowed her father.

J.D. sighed "Let me put it differently. Any jackass can run for public office, and a lot of them do. All you need is good hair and a thousand bucks for the filing fee."

Jack looked out at the skating pond where a young girl led a boy her own age onto the ice. She'd already learned to skate, it appeared, but the boy hadn't. Grandchildren of the neighbors, Jack surmised. Kids who start life already rich.

J.D.'s arguments began to make sense to Jack. He saw himself as smart, energetic and fiercely ambitious. It wouldn't make sense to throw all that away on the wrong kind of work.

Lacey nudged her father again. "Daddy, I don't think you understand. Jack wants to do big things. Good things."

J.D. sighed again. "There's lots of ways to do good things. My company provides jobs for thousands of people. What's more important than a job? We donate millions to worthwhile causes. Got a whole department that does nothing but give money away. I'm on more charity boards than I have time for."

Lacey moved behind Jack and rested a hand on his shoulder. Outside, the young girl and the young boy skated uneasily, side-by-side, hand-in-hand. They circled about an island at the center of the pond and turned back, their perfect teeth apparent even at this considerable distance.

Two months later, Jack flew from North Carolina to New York to interview at the Rockefeller Center headquarters of AO&G and four months after that he entered its executive training program, taking the first step of the business career that eventually led him to the helm of Conquest. He spent the afternoon of his scheduled departure for a Peace Corps tour in Sri Lanka in the satin-curtained bedroom of Lacey's Raleigh apartment, celebrating their decision to marry and begin post-college life together.

J.D.'s words had stayed with Jack. *There's lots of ways to do good things.* At Jack's behest, Conquest allocated a percentage of corporate earnings each year for charitable giving. Jack himself participated in endeavors ranging from the Food Bank to Businessmen for Better Schools. Jack felt sure that if there were a way to measure units of good brought into the world, he'd rank near the top of the list.

J.D. had been right about politicians, too. Over the years Jack had come to regard them as a form of life ranking not much higher than carnival barkers. Actually, no higher at all. Still, as the limo glided through the Houston night and the streetlamps intermittently flashed across the features of Lorelei Logan, the wife of a man who had spent his life on the course that Jack had abandoned, he couldn't help but think about the path not taken.

Wheeler

Wheeler stuffed his travel bag into the cramped overhead bin and slid into a seat. If the flights went well, he would be in Norah's office by nine o'clock Saturday morning. Norah almost always worked on Saturdays and there would be few others around to witness his humiliating return. After the call from Montserrat, he had spent the rest of the afternoon stewing over what to do and alternating Margaritas with slugs of medicine. His nervous stomach had metastasized into a full-fledged case of the runs. The hotel concierge had given him something called Lomotillo that he promised would work better than Kaopectate. *Muy fuerte*, he'd said. By the time Sherry came in from the beach—it *was* her parasailing in the lime bikini—sand-spackled and sunburned, he'd already packed his bags. She shouted and cried when he told her he had to go back to Houston, but then seemed preternaturally calm when he said he could get only one seat on the charter flight. He could still see her face as he said good-bye, almost as if she were the one doing the leaving.

His stomach rumbled and he had the taste of bile in the back of his throat. He prayed they would take off soon so he could get to the toilet. The airplane had only eight passenger seats, all of them filled. Several Mexican businessmen occupied the rows ahead of him, their coats and ties seeming out of place on a flight returning from a vacation paradise. A fat flight attendant passed toward the back of the plane and the businessmen jostled each other and laughed. Wheeler didn't have to understand Spanish to understand they were admiring the sheer scale of her ass.

He had a straightforward plan for his return to Houston. First, he'd make sure his lawyer destroyed the data disks in the package that Sherry sent up from Mexico. Next, he'd take a shower and clean himself up. Third, he'd go to Norah's office to return the Bluestream files. Then he'd get down on his knees and beg for his old job back. If that went well, he'd check in with Maggie and see how much trouble he faced on the home front.

The plane lifted off and Wheeler felt it bank into a left turn that made him dizzy. The pilot headed out to sea to gain altitude before turning to fly back over the mountains surrounding Ixtapa. Looking down, he could see the contours of the hotels lining the beach and the running lights of a score of boats in the bay.

He was fully prepared to grovel. His scheme had fallen into a shambles, so he would try to worm his way back into Norah's good graces. After all, Conquest couldn't report him for blackmail any more than he could turn in Conquest for the information in the stolen files. The way he saw it, it was a draw. Return to Go and start over.

His stomach churned and he rose abruptly to make his way to the toilet in the rear, grabbing the bottle of Lomotillo to take with him. The flight attendant blocked his way. He did his best to indicate to her that he couldn't wait. She shouted at him in Spanish and gestured angrily, pointing at his seat. At last she let him squeeze by so he could get to the miniscule toilet closet. It measured not more than twenty-four inches square and he had to hunch his shoulders to fit inside. Worse, the lid of the toilet stood only about a foot off the floor. Jesus, he thought, only a child or a contortionist could do their business in here.

He unbuckled and unzipped and let his pants fall. He banged head, elbow and knee while working his boxers down to his ankles. Then he pressed his back against the rear wall and lowered his body toward the commode like a flag moving down a flagpole. He stuck, unfortunately, at half-staff. His knees refused to bend any further but his butt still hung a good ten inches above the lid. With a groan, Wheeler released the death grip that he'd maintained on his bowels since boarding the plane. Four days of tension and frustration made their way out of his system with a repellant noise that he was convinced could be heard throughout the cabin.

He slugged down more Lomotillo. He'd been drinking it for hours, with no discernible improvement in his condition. Between the Margaritas and his inability to understand Spanish, he no longer had any idea of the correct dosage. Two teaspoons every four hours? Four teaspoons every two hours? Hell, he didn't have a teaspoon anyway. Now that he'd wedged himself into this closet, he planned to keep drinking the stuff until he got his money's worth.

Some time later, an insistent knock at the door startled Wheeler awake. He was incredulous that he could have dozed off in such an ungainly position. He pushed the door open and found himself eye-to-angry-eye with the flight attendant. He could see that she wore a name tag: *Loida*. What a lovely name, he thought, until she unleashed a torrent of furious Spanish and gestured at him to get up. He attempted to stand—his gastric system finally had achieved a condition of at least temporary quiescence—but found himself unable to rise. He could move his head and arms, but his legs and butt seemed to have fallen dead asleep. He couldn't feel anything below the waist.

He was painfully woozy. He couldn't recall ever being this woozy. He thought of a joke about a fat woman and a revolving door and told it, but Loida didn't get it. She got angrier instead. She yanked the door fully open and extended a hand to pull Wheeler into a standing position, but slammed the door shut again after only a moment, nose wrinkling in disgust. Wheeler could well imagine that the sight of his pale gringo nether region was more than she could take. No matter. The plane would land pretty soon. He would stay in here until then.

Oddly enough, the toilet had a window. Why hadn't he seen it before? Craning his neck, he looked down at the freeway traffic as the jet made its long approach to LAX. He enjoyed watching the cars and imagining where they might be headed on a Friday night in Los Angeles. He looked forward to returning to his normal life in Houston.

Something dug into his thigh. He reached for it and found the Lomotillo bottle trapped between his leg and the wall. Empty. Wheeler stared at the strange words on the label. *Alertar. Peligrosa. Sobredosis.* The words made his head hurt worse. *Sobredosis?* Jesus, that sounded like... *overdose.*

He was still puzzling over the meaning of *sobredosis* when he slumped against the toilet wall and everything went blank.

Jack

It had taken less than an hour for the champagne and the amber lights of the Ship Channel to work their magic. Jack sat back against the car door and looked at Lorelei, who seemed not at all discomfited at the notion of having had unruly sex in the back seat of a car with a man not her husband.

"So," Jack mused, "how about that?"

"This is classified," she said. "Top secret."

He studied her, enjoying the ease with which she carried her post-coital self. She neither flaunted nor covered her nakedness, and she didn't fiddle with her hair or reapply her lipstick. She sat with legs akimbo, one foot on the floor and the other on the car seat, affording Jack an unobstructed view of her full, but neatly trimmed, pubic hair. It was hard to tell because of the poor light, but Jack was pretty sure he saw no sign of gray. Her breasts looked like extra-plush inflatable pillows from which a little of the air had escaped.

As they chatted, she extended one leg across the car seat, pointed her toes like a ballet dancer and inserted them into the space beneath Jack's scrotum. When she wiggled her toes, it felt like mice playing volleyball with his testicles. It was not at all unpleasant and Jack's erection began to revive.

There was a tap on the window of her side of the limo. She pushed the button to lower it an inch. Jack recognized one of the Secret Service agents and saw a government-issue Ford parked a discreet distance away. The agent scrupulously avoided looking at Lorelei as he spoke. "Everything okay, ma'am?"

"Couldn't be better. Thanks for asking."

She raised the window again. “Senator’s wives don’t get much chance to be naked in cars.” She pronounced it *nekkid,* as Jack imagined she had said it back in high school. He found on the carpeted floor of the limo several crumpled items of lingerie and held them up for inspection.

“Sexy, huh?” said Lorelei, reaching for them, as if the time allotted for their tryst had come to an end.

Jack tossed the lingerie back to the floor. “Again,” he said.

CHAPTER 6. FRIDAY ONE WEEK LATER

CQC 50.93 0.33↑

Feo

"Wheeler's dead? From what?" Jenkins had been out sick. He was incredulous when Feo rehashed the Wheeler situation for him.

"The active ingredient is diphenoxylate hydrochloride," said Feo. He translated a Lomotillo label for Jenkins' benefit. "*Sobredosis*—overdosage—may result in severe respiratory depression and coma, possibly leading to brain damage or death."

Jenkins still looked dubious.

"He drank the whole bottle. Enough to plug up a dinosaur. Plus a lot of alcohol, plus the altitude. Very bad combination."

"You think it was accidental? Any chance somebody poisoned him?"

"If you were going to poison somebody, would you do it with a Mexican diarrhea medicine?"

When Feo returned to Houston from Ixtapa, he had expected to find Wheeler back at his desk. What he found instead was a message to follow up on an inquiry from the Los Angeles Police Department. They had found a dead guy in an airplane toilet. The dead guy's wallet contained a Conquest employee ID card. Did anyone want to come out and have a look? He'd flown to LA on the first flight out in order to get there before Wheeler's wife, hoping that Wheeler would have had the Bluestream files with him when he died.

"Any sign of the hard drive?" asked Jenkins.

"I'm guessing he junked it. We found the laptop, though, with all the files he stole. I gave it to Ms. Needham."

"Couldn't he have made another copy?"

"Sure," said Feo. "If he did, and if another blackmailer has it, I think we would have heard something by now."

"What about the girl?"

Good question, thought Feo. What about the girl?

After dinner they had walked barefoot on the *Playa De Los Amantes*, the moon hanging over them in a blue-black sky. Sherry wore some kind of see-through peasant dress over a white unitard. She talked of her devotion to T'ai Chi and the Master and a dozen other things from her holistic life-style, most of which made no sense to Feo, but her voice carried so much intensity and enthusiasm he couldn't help being drawn along.

"Watch this," she had said, as they walked past a ramshackle beach café. She pulled the peasant dress over her head and tossed it on the sand. "Part the Wild Horse's Mane," she announced, straddling an invisible steed and running her hands over the horse's neck. Her triceps and quads elongated gracefully and her hamstrings drew taut. The sounds of Mexican music and Anglo merriment drifted to them from the café as she demonstrated more T'ai Chi postures.

When they reached the part of the beach below her hotel, she kissed him and whispered into his ear something that got lost in the ocean's roar and before he could ask her to say it again she turned away and walked toward her room. He watched until she turned again. She waved good-night standing in the light of a bare electric light bulb hanging from a beachside lamppost.

"I don't think so," Feo told Jenkins. "There was no sign of her. She must have checked out as soon as Wheeler decided to come back to Houston." Feo couldn't think of any way he could get caught on this lie or any reason why Jenkins wouldn't believe him. And he felt certain that Sherry had no inkling of the blackmail scheme. There was no reason to draw her any further into Wheeler's mess.

“Really, boss. She wouldn’t have a clue what to do with the stuff he stole. I checked her out. Some kind of holistic fitness teacher. I doubt she knows a debit from a credit.”

Jenkins had run out of questions, so Feo returned to his desk. He’d gotten way behind on his Internet logs.

David

In the week since resigning from his law firm, David had learned a lot about day trading. He’d learned the difference between a trumpet and a whisper and which way to trade on both. He could tap the squawk at three different securities firms and he knew what to do when the spoo goes south. He’d learned how to skim the cream from a dead cat bounce and, not least, he was now on a first-name basis with most of the guys who hung at Velotrade. It wasn’t a bad way to pass the time while he waited to hear about his new job at Payton-Mosel.

“David, my man. I got one word for you. Mirage Optics.” This from Fib, the guy at the next trading station. Fib had worn the same paisley print jeans and burnt orange *Longhorn Track* jacket every day since David had arrived. His real name was Morris Fibitz, but everyone called him Fib instead of Morris or Mo and there was no point in telling him that Mirage Optics was two words.

“Not sure if I’m ready yet, Fib.” David had advanced the $10,000 required for a seat at Velotrade, but so far had done only small lots, getting a feel for things. With the leverage provided by the Pro Trader package, eventually he could jump in for a lot more. But not until he was sure he was ready.

The $10,000 came from his joint account with Miranda. What he’d taken represented most of their rainy day fund, but David felt sure he could make enough in the stock market to put the money back long before his wife noticed its absence.

Velotrade occupied most of the third floor of a former savings and loan building on Westheimer. In fact, traces of the old savings and loan logo remained on the glass door that opened from the hallway onto the thirty-station trading floor. Every spot offered real-time quotes and one-click order execution for stocks, options, currencies, commodities and e-minis, as well as enough analytic capability to support a moon landing.

David logged on. He checked all of his regular market information sources. He reviewed yesterday's tape and the Level II numbers on the stocks he had chosen to follow for practice, including Citrix, Espeed, Leapfrog, Red Hat and five others. He wanted to read the *Wall Street Journal* but worried that one of the guys would see it on his screen and peg him for an investor. He wasn't an investor. He wasn't an investor. He was a day trader.

"Look at this, Davey! What'd I tell you?"

He rolled his chair back to look at Fib's screen. A graph that tracked Mirage Optics for the past twelve days looked as regular as the teeth of a power saw. Then Fib overlaid a second graph that almost precisely matched the ups and downs of Mirage.

"What's that?" David asked.

"*Sex and the City*," said Fib. "I watch the reruns. Every time Samantha bangs a new guy, the stock goes up. Otherwise, the stock goes down." His expression said, *I rest my case.*

David recalled that Samantha once had tried it with a woman and wondered where that would show up on Fib's graph.

"So, you gonna buy? Last night she did it with a new guy. Go long."

"Sure, Fib. I'll do a hundred."

Fib blew air through his lips. "I must have made a mistake. I thought you came here to make some money." He reached over and felt between David's legs. "Huh," said Fib, shaking his head. "Feels like balls."

David remained unfazed. He was developing his own system and following his own discipline. He wouldn't trade until he was ready, and he wouldn't doubt himself, no matter what Fib said. He wheeled back to his own terminal and entered the order for Mirage. One hundred units at twelve and an eighth. He looked at Fib, who gave him a limp wristed wave. Hell's bells. *Two* hundred units

At first, David had thought he'd rather trade from home. Sleep late, work in his pajamas. He only signed up at Velotrade so Miranda wouldn't find out that he was day trading, but he had decided he liked seeing Fib and the others every day. He enjoyed the noise and camaraderie. The guys wanted to see each other succeed and they passed around all kinds of information. Some was crazy, like Fib's tip, but some of it was good.

He pasted a monitor in the corner of his screen. Mirage moved to thirteen like a cricket jumping out of a sleeping bag.

One thing David hadn't learned in the past week was whether or not he had a job at Payton-Mosel. He called every day, but the bitchy English receptionist put him on perma-hold. When she came back on the line, it was always the same. *Mr. Senso, we've nothing new to tell you. Mr. Payton requests you call back tomorrow.*

He had once read the anecdote in *Liar's Poker* about how the old Salomon Brothers never offered anyone a job. After the interviews, if you had enough self-confidence, you were supposed to assume that you got the job and show up for work. So two days ago, he'd put on his best suit and tie and reported to Payton-Mosel bright and early.

Payton put an arm around David's shoulders and maneuvered him back to the elevators. "That's a nice effort, son, but how about you give me another call tomorrow. This isn't Salomon Brothers, you know."

Mirage climbed some more. Nearly fifteen.

Another thing David didn't know was when Miranda might start speaking to him again. The morning he told her about quitting Miller-Dunn, she had set her mouth in a tight line and looked at him as if she'd never seen him before. When he brought up the due diligence assignment in Alaska, she either didn't believe him or didn't care.

"I've got problems, too, David," she'd said, and gone off to work. Since then, she hadn't said a single word that wasn't necessary to get through their daily routine. It made him angry that she couldn't see his side of it.

She was working on the hottest deal at the hottest company in town. What problems could she have?

When he screwed up in the past, he'd always managed to jolly her out of her snit, but this time something had changed. No amount of coaxing, cajoling or wheedling worked. And forget about sex. He didn't have the nerve to ask.

Fib let out a whoop that brought the trading room to a standstill. David checked his screen. Mirage was at sixteen. Up *thirty* percent in half a day.

David closed out his position. Less commissions, he'd made about $750. He wished he'd plunked for more than a chicken-shit two hundred lot.

He brought up the HBO website on his computer screen. It looked like he could catch *Sex and the City* at nine that night. If he begged, maybe Miranda would watch it with him.

Jack

Jack shared a conference table with a management consultant and a contingent from his Human Resources Department. The consultant placed on the table a stack of presentations: *Conquest's Core Values: What Are They? What Should They Be?* Jack stifled a yawn. Needless to say, sitting through a meeting with a bunch of HR flunkies didn't make his list of the top ten things to do at the office. He liked to spend his time buying companies or making speeches. Or taking the Lear to New York to pitch the securities analysts. Or going to Washington to explain free market economics to those idiots.

"Mr. Burnam," said the head of HR, "you asked my department to develop a statement of core values for Conquest, a corporate credo that articulates the company's organizational morals."

Jack recalled no such request, but wasn't about to admit it. Wait a sec. It was coming back. The U.S. Chamber of Commerce meeting last year. Jack recalled a very leggy blonde in the hotel bar—Millie? Billie?—some kind of freelance management consultant who had explained to him that GE and General Motors and Amazon all had statements of core values. She had said Conquest was way behind. That's the consultant they were supposed to hire, not this pinstriped dweeb.

"A corporate value statement can serve as a powerful management tool," offered the consultant. "It can help guide the aspirations of the employees and make them feel part of something bigger than themselves."

That's what paychecks are for, thought Jack. And stock options.

The consultant hadn't stopped talking. "These days, every major company has a value statement. It's something the institutional shareholders look for as part of the corporate governance package."

So that was it. The shareholders wanted something enobling to read while they calculated their capital gains.

The consultant opened the flipbook. "*Ethics*," he intoned, as if reading from the Bhagavad-Gita. "Conquest insists on the highest standards of personal and professional conduct. *Teamwork*. Conquest employees work collaboratively to achieve greater success. *Excellence*. Conquest strives for excellence in everything it does."

This guy belongs in the greeting card business, thought Jack.

"Of course, this is only our Basic Value Module," said the consultant. "You may want to look at some of our more advanced modules."

Jack was appalled. He'd be damned if his company would get its core values from a pre-packaged *module*.

The HR Director stepped in. "Of course, the values already exist within Conquest. We all know that. Our consultant is here to facilitate the value articulation process."

The *value articulation process*. That was a good one.

"For example," said the consultant, "we have one called *Values for Socially Conscious Companies*. Conquest embraces the triple bottom line of economic, social and environmental success."

Jack looked around the table. Even the HR Director looked embarrassed. With a barely perceptible motion of his head, Jack took a pass on the triple bottom line.

He flipped to the back of the presentation book. "How about this one?" he asked. "*We are committed to the delivery of innovative, proven solutions that enable customers to achieve their potential and do business in new and exciting ways*. It's short. Pithy."

"It's also taken," sniffed the consultant. "It belongs to Microsoft."

"Fuck," said Jack.

Some of the HR staffers offered up suggestions. *Accountability. Integrity. Commitment.* For each value, the consultant had a ready-made platitude.

Jack cut in. "Let's suppose you guys agree on all this. Then what?"

The consultant flipped pages so fast Jack could feel a breeze on the other side of the table. "That brings us to our *Values Delivery Module*," he announced. "You post your values on the company website. Put them in the annual report. Incorporate them into the employee evaluation forms."

An HR staffer raised her hand. "I have an idea. What if we gave every employee a mouse pad with the core values printed right on it? That way, everybody would think about the values all day long."

A moment's silence ensued before the consultant's nose turned up. "Please," he said. "Let's not be trivial."

Jack had sort of liked the mouse pad idea. He rubbed his chin. "How about some stone tablets in the plaza out front? Like Stonehenge."

Silence returned, and Jack could tell they couldn't decide whether or not he was serious. He wondered if anyone would have the balls to laugh.

"I have another meeting," he said.

Miranda

Miranda didn't like confrontation, but she didn't like to be bulldozed either. If she was responsible for the Bluestream deal, she wanted to have a full understanding of it and she couldn't seem to get there. So she had scheduled another meeting with Norah.

After more than a week of looking, she hadn't come up with any information about Bluestream's outside investors or, for that matter, the outside investors for any of Conquest's off-balance-sheet acquisitions. What she had learned was that Conquest had more than *two hundred* of these companies. She was beginning to think that Conquest did more business off balance sheet than on. Yet she couldn't find a trace of what should have been hundreds of outside investors and many millions of dollars of outside capital.

It would help if she had the benefit of Wheeler's work product up to the point of his resignation. She had hoped to have a chance to ask him some questions at some point, after his family emergency was over, of course, but now he was dead. So odd. He'd resigned, destroyed his work files, dropped out of sight and then died on an airplane. The rumor around the building was that he had a severe drug problem.

She rapped on Norah's office door, and Norah waved her inside. "Fill me in on Bluestream," she said.

Miranda led her boss through a discussion of completed work items followed by a shorter discussion of items still in process. "We're ready for the securities filing. Right on schedule."

"That's excellent. Terrific work. I'll tell Mr. Burnam." Norah began rummaging for something in her desk drawer, as if she expected Miranda to leave.

Miranda sucked up her courage. "Norah, there's an aspect of this deal I don't get."

Norah looked up. "What's that?" She continued to rummage.

"The third-party investors."

"What's not to understand? We've done this many times before." She finally stopped rummaging. Whatever it was she was looking for, she'd come up empty. "Okay. Tell me what's on your mind."

Miranda stood and paced in front of Norah's desk. "We don't want this deal to screw up Conquest's balance sheet. So we put Bluestream into a new company—we've named it Blueco—and Blueco borrows the money."

"So far, so good," said Norah. "What's the problem?"

"Blueco has to have some outside investors who put in at least three percent of the equity, and the outside investors have to have control. Otherwise we consolidate Blueco back onto Conquest's balance sheet and we're back to where we started."

"Your point?" said Norah mildly. She was unusually patient, as if she regularly spent her afternoons debating the niceties of arcane accounting rules.

"If Bluestream is as important as you said, and if Conquest's entire future depends on it, how can we let someone else have control? What if they botch it?"

Miranda watched Norah's face for a glimmer of recognition of the question she'd put, but Norah's face betrayed nothing.

"Do you like to ride? Horses, I mean."

Miranda's head swam. What did horseback riding have to do with Bluestream?

"Sure. I haven't ridden in years, but I love it."

"You know the Somerset Equestrian Center? It's in Memorial, out past the cemetery."

Miranda knew of Somerset, but she'd never been there. What was this all about?

Norah jotted an address on a piece of paper and handed it to Miranda. "I'm going to the analysts' luncheon in a few minutes. How about we meet at two o'clock. We can talk more there."

"Norah, I don't have any..."

"You can pick up pants and boots at the tack shop. Put it on the company account."

Miranda stared. For the first time since she came into the room, she seemed to have Norah's full focus. In nearly a decade, she'd never known her boss to leave work in the middle of the day, and never before had Norah invited Miranda for so much as a lunchtime sandwich.

"There's no problem with the outside investors," she said. "Trust me."

Miranda continued to stare.

"We'll go riding," said Norah. "It'll be fun."

Fun?

Norah

After the analysts' luncheon, on the way out to Somerset, Norah took Memorial Drive through the Park instead of I-10. It gave her a little more time to think. Overall, she was optimistic. The CIA guy had brought back the files Wheeler had stolen. When she looked at the entire file, Norah got a queasy feeling deep in the pit of her stomach. The way Wheeler had arranged the information was, to her taste, way too direct. Although Miranda had gotten the filings for Bluestream ready in record time, Norah remained dubious about her attitude. The woman always did a thorough job, and this wasn't the first time she had driven Norah crazy with niggling questions, but her questions about Bluestream had a sharper edge. It was time to step up the pressure.

She had dangled a nice carrot—Somerset. Now it was time for some stick. She dialed Franklin Payton.

"Norah, I'm glad you called. We're a little confused about the investor list. You crossed off some of our best prospects."

Payton-Mosel had sent her a list of ninety potential buyers of shares in Blueco and she had eliminated two-thirds of them.

"I told you, Franklin. We're very selective regarding our partners."

Payton huffed out a string of investment banker aphorisms intended to convince her to undertake a much broader marketing effort. Maximum exposure. More favorable pricing. Norah let him huff until she saw the Loop 610 stoplight ahead. It was only another ten minutes to Somerset.

"I understand all that, Franklin. Conquest doesn't mind paying up a bit to make certain we have investors we are familiar with." She didn't mention that Conquest already had all the investors identified and didn't need his marketing effort at all, other than for putting on a show.

"You're the client," he said finally.

She spent another few minutes on other aspects of the transaction before getting to the real purpose of the call. "By the way," she said. "What's the status of David Sesno?"

Payton's voice became wary. "That would be up to you, wouldn't it?"

"Has he filled out all the forms? Taken all the tests?"

"Of course. That was a week ago. Poor bastard calls every day to find out if he has a job or not. Just like I've been calling you. I heard he resigned from Miller-Dunn already."

Norah also had heard that bit of information. "That was rash," she said. "Does that raise a question in your mind about his judgment?"

A city block went by before Payton responded. "You think I should reconsider? That's pretty harsh."

Norah drove through the gate of the equestrian center and parked. She could see that the grooms already had saddled and tacked Charley, a big American Saddlebred, for her to ride.

"Yes, I do think you should reconsider. I wouldn't want to be the cause of you taking on a hothead." Norah figured they could revisit the matter once Miranda had fully acquiesced to her new role. Having an unemployed husband might incline her to ease up on the accounting issues.

"Whatever you say," said Payton.

Norah watched from the car as Charley flicked his tail.

Sherry

Sherry waited until the Kinko's guy returned to his post at the front of the store before she reached into Wheeler's bag for the first data disk. She had paid $25 for an hour's rental of a computer, and the guy used the first fifteen minutes peering down the front of her shirt while pretending to demonstrate the machine. She finally bent forward and gave him an unimpeded look-see to get it over with.

She loaded the disk onto the tray and nudged the tray into the tower unit. The computer digested the disk and displayed a matrix of dozens of rows and at least one hundred columns. The columns had unintelligible headings and nearly every cell contained at least seven digits. The only things that made any sense at all were the tabs near the bottom with titles like *Investor 1 Returns, Investor 2 Returns,* and so forth. And there was one headed *Investor Index* in a special bold typeface. She hadn't expected to understand the numbers but she was curious to find out if, as she suspected, the disks contained the Bluestream material that she had seen briefly by the pool in Mexico. She wanted a longer look at what Wheeler had thought would be worth so much money.

Her minded drifted while she waited for the computer to read the second disk. In spite of the bad things that happened, she had enjoyed the trip to Zihuatanejo. A person could live a simple, uncomplicated life in a place like that. She thought again of her vision of the *hacienda* set among the coconut palms, and how real the vision had seemed to her. And although she didn't like to admit it, the truth was that Wheeler's death didn't bother her much. Whatever appeal he once had held for her had run its course on the dusty road to the FedEx office in Ixtapa.

And then there was Feo. The memory of their walk on the beach returned again and again. He hadn't called yet, but she thought it wouldn't be much longer. She liked Feo. He might be the one for her. Of course, she hadn't let on that she knew about Wheeler's scheme or that she had taken a copy of the blackmail package. On that score, she had played dumb.

The computer seemed to have frozen. Sherry arched her back and waved at the Kinko's guy for help. He clicked the mouse a few times and the disk's content menu popped onto the screen. She bent forward again to show her appreciation.

Wheeler's disappearance from her life had one major drawback. Financially, she was in trouble. What she earned at the Ab-Salute barely covered her expenses, and taking a week of unpaid vacation had left her woefully short of funds.

Her hour was nearly over. She had made it through only three disks, but she'd seen enough. She gathered her things and mulled over what to do with Wheeler's package, which she had taken without necessarily having a clear plan. Over the past week, the notion had grown slowly that she might pick up where Wheeler left off. Not for $25 million, of course. That was ridiculous. But maybe for five. Or one. After all, she lived a holistic life with simple needs. A huge company like Conquest might pay her a million dollars without stopping to quarrel.

When she had a break in her work schedule, Sherry sometimes drove her used Prius up and down the streets of nearby River Oaks to gape at the mansions and trees and gardens and fountains. It was like nothing she had ever seen, certainly not like anything back in Poteet. She knew that Jack and Lacey Burnam lived in River Oaks, and people who lived in a place like that could overlook a million dollars two or three times a year.

Why not? A rich girl could get as much *chi* as a poor one.

Miranda

The Somerset setup included two horse barns, two jumping rings, a dressage area and a tack shop, all ringed by thirty or forty acres of pine trees and bridle trails. A dozen horses grazed in white fenced paddocks adjacent to the barns.

Miranda had chosen tan cotton jodhpurs, a Charles Owen riding helmet and a pair of dark brown leather boots. She tried to pay cash but the woman at the counter insisted on putting the charge on the Conquest account. Private club, no cash accepted.

When the groom led her into the barn, Miranda gasped with surprise. Teak paneling covered the walls and the floor consisted of a rubberized material rather than dirt or concrete. Small brass plaques identified the horses by name and a sound system piped music into the stalls. "They mostly like classical," explained the groom.

Norah arrived and the two women rode side-by-side, Norah on a big black named Charley and Miranda on a paint called Fanny, to a place where the trail entered piney woods. Norah, Miranda couldn't help noticing, rode awkwardly, as if she feared that Charley might toss her off at any moment.

Miranda felt immensely guilty. It was mid-afternoon on a weekday and she had left piles of undone work stacked on her desk. And if she had an afternoon off from work, she should spend it with Jesse. She had half a mind to leave, but only half.

Though she hadn't sat on a horse for years, Miranda rested comfortably on Fanny. The mare moved at a smooth trot and before long Miranda rose and fell in the saddle in perfect time with Fanny's gait. Rays of sunlight pierced the loblolly canopy and a dense accumulation of pine needles covered the muddy trail bed. When the path narrowed, Norah moved into the lead and Charley began to canter.

Miranda followed on Fanny. A feeling of exhilaration rose inside her until she had to choke back a shout. She was glad that Norah, riding ahead, couldn't see the idiotic look on her face. Ages had passed since she felt so irresponsible, since she didn't have to spend every minute thinking about her job, or looking after her son, or fretting over her husband's failing career. The shout came again and she couldn't keep it down. It erupted as a growl of pleasure and she prayed that Norah hadn't heard her.

The path beneath the trees gave way to an open area. She saw Norah pull up, her horse breathing hard. Miranda came alongside and leaned down to press her cheek against the coarse hair of Fanny's neck.

"You've done this before," said Norah.

"Not since college. It comes back, though." In high school, she had entered shows and won a few ribbons, and she often rode for pleasure during her college years. She had hoped to own a horse after graduation, but it had long since become an unaffordable luxury.

“The company keeps these horses and a few others,” said Norah. “Some of the senior execs like to bring clients here. They take a trail ride and eat Mexican food at those picnic tables behind the barns. Sometimes they hire a *mariachi* band. Clients love it, especially the New Yorkers. They think this is the real Texas.”

Miranda couldn’t absorb the notion of owning and stabling horses solely for the purpose of entertaining clients. “But who rides them?” she asked. Horses, like humans, need regular exercise to stay in shape.

“Mostly the grooms, I guess. I learned enough to be able to ride with clients,” she added with a shrug. Charley let loose a whinny and Norah pulled back on the reins.

She looked thoughtful. “I’ll add you to the membership list. Why not?”

“Oh my God,” said Miranda. She pictured herself of a Saturday morning, taking jumps in the big ring while Jesse enjoyed a lesson in the smaller one.

“The horses are already here,” Norah continued. “It isn’t going to cost the company anything to let you ride them.” She jabbed a heel into Charley’s side and trotted toward the other side of the clearing where the trail entered the woods.

An hour later the two women re-emerged from the pine forest. They dismounted and handed the reins to waiting grooms, who led the horses to the barn. Miranda thanked Norah and walked toward her car. Her ass hurt, her clothing was soaked with sweat and a blister had sprung up beneath the stiff leather of the new boots. She hadn’t felt this good in years.

It was much later in the evening, as she looked over Jesse’s geography homework, that she realized that Norah had never gotten around to answering her questions about Bluestream.

Or had she?

Lulu

"Ladies and gentlemen, last week we lost a beloved member of the Conquest family."

From her customary seat on the aisle, Lulu saw Burnam at the podium, looking determinedly solemn. Behind him, the stock price monitor flickered. Conquest had continued to climb despite a general market malaise.

"Russ Wheeler, one of our finest young employees, died in a tragic accident in California. A moment of silence, please, for Russ and his valiant young widow, Maggie."

A hush descended. Lulu fidgeted and waited for Burnam to come out of his phony trance. Once the press conference got under way, it followed the customary pattern. Burnam read the earnings announcement. The analysts in the audience jotted notes. Reporters asked Burnam a few questions that he answered with false humility.

She still hadn't worked out what to do with the Bluebox story. She had written it twenty times in twenty different ways, and each time had torn it up. She had talked to dozens of people who knew the sector, but none had helped. What Josh had shown her was what everybody in Silicon Valley was after, but it wasn't possible that anyone had it yet, they said. Whoever got there first would make more money than Bill Gates and J.K. Rowling put together. The other problem was that Ed insisted on more than one source and she had only Josh.

So she had come to an ordinary quarterly press conference at which Conquest would present its earnings guidance. The previous evening Conquest had treated the female reporters to a fashion show at Neiman Marcus and the males to a tour of Houston's gentlemen's clubs. Lulu had tagged along with the men to see the strippers, hoping she might pick up some useful information. In her experience, guys getting smashed were prone to giving up secrets, and this was doubly true if they were busy stuffing twenties into a dancer's sweaty g-string. On this occasion, however, she hadn't learned much. All she heard was a third-hand rumor about Burnam having an affair with another man's wife. That was hardly news.

Lulu heard a burst of noise from the back of the room. Turning around, she saw Rona Fairbanks, a reporter for one of the television celebrity news shows, leaving the press conference early. Then she saw that Burnam's eyes followed the woman as she made her exit. Odd, thought Lulu. Why would an entertainment reporter attend a routine press conference on earnings?

When Burnam starting taking questions from the floor, Lulu decided to fish around on Bluestream just for the hell of it. He surprised her by calling on her almost immediately..

"Mr. Burnam, rumors have circulated that Bluestream's technology hasn't come as far as you thought. Can you comment?"

"I'm glad you asked about that, Ms. Barker. Those rumors are completely false."

"So you remain on schedule for getting it into production?"

Jack waved a hand as if shooing away an insect. "Honestly, there are some technical issues that might set us back a few months, but I remain completely confident in the wisdom of our decision to buy Bluestream."

Lulu was puzzled. The mildness and directness of Burnam's response made Lulu think maybe he was telling the truth. And that Josh had told her the truth. She checked the stock price monitor. The number on the screen wavered and dropped slightly. Sixty and change.

Moreover, Burnam had an expression on his face that Lulu had never seen. He looked distracted, as if there were something else more pressing on his mind. What could be more pressing than the biggest deal of his life?

Maggie

Maggie, wearing black leather stretch pants and a Dior jacket, scanned the back room at Bo's Barbeque in search of Jolene. Bo's was upscale as far as Texas barbeque restaurants went, having a bartender serving mixed drinks in addition to the same scarred linoleum floors, ripped vinyl upholstery and Melamine dishware as most barbeque places.

Heads turned as she crossed the room. Bo himself pulled out a chair and expressed the condolences of the management and staff for her untimely loss. It would be their honor if she and her friend would accept a complimentary platter of ribs and sausage. And perhaps a drink or two as well. Maggie smiled in appreciation. Jolene ordered a Tidal Wave for Maggie and a Gulf Breeze for herself.

"You poor thing," said Jolene. "Your husband dead and all."

Maggie did her best to put on an appearance of grief. Not for Jolene's benefit, but in case someone else she knew happened into the restaurant. The waiter arrived with their drinks, and Maggie asked him to bring an extra side of potato salad.

"At least your terrible grief hasn't hurt your appetite," said Jolene.

Maggie took a sip of her Tidal Wave. "I admit it threw me for a loop at first. Made me do some serious thinking."

"And?"

"Jo, I'm not cut out to be a junior executive's wife. Going to the company holiday party and kissin' up to the boss's wife. Givin' hubby some extra nookie every time he gets a promotion."

She paused while the waiter set more food on the table. "And it's not as if Russ didn't have his shortcomings. If you know what I mean. Short. Comings."

"Oh, my," said Jolene.

"Fact is, we hadn't had sex in months."

Jolene took in this information as she savored the brisket. "That ain't like you," she said.

"No," said Maggie. "It ain't like me one damn bit." She poked around at her plate of ribs, then beckoned at the waiter again. "Have you got a hotter sauce than this one?"

For several minutes, they ate and drank in comfortable non-judgmental silence. The restaurant filled up with construction workers, businessmen and housewives. The waiter returned with a bottle labeled *Pappy's Wild Ride* and Maggie splashed it over her barbeque.

"So what's your plan?" asked Jolene.

"Get married again, but to an older man, one who can take good care of me the way my daddy did. Take me to parties and show me off."

"You want to be a trophy wife."

"Bingo."

Jolene meditated on this disclosure. "It's good to have an ambition in life. I guess this particular ambition runs in the family."

Maggie smiled. "You could be right about that." She was descended on her mother's side from Bud Higgins, the man who brought in the Spindletop gusher in 1901. Family lore held that the forty-year-old Higgins had adopted a teenage girl from a local orphanage and, after a few years, made her his wife. Polite society frowned, of course, but Maggie thought it sexy in the extreme. She wasn't sure she could blame her penchant for older men on heredity, but that wasn't going to stop her from trying.

The waiter brought pecan pie with ice cream for dessert and, without being asked, another round of drinks.

"My," said Maggie. "Aren't we gonna be drunk?"

"Skunks," agreed Jolene. "What about money? You got enough to tide you over?"

"Oh, sure, my family will help out. But it's funny you should mention that. I had a meeting with Russ's lawyer about the estate. He told me Russ had an account at a bank in the Caribbean. I didn't know anything about it."

"That sounds interesting. What's in it?"

"I'm not sure yet. The lawyer said the account has some investment partnerships with funny names. He thinks somehow they are connected to Conquest, maybe something Russ got as part of his bonus. Profit-sharing, maybe." Maggie pushed away from the table and arched her back. The stretchy leather fabric felt good against her skin. "Whatever they are, they're mine now."

Jolene asked another question but, for Maggie, the room had begun to spin. The third Tidal Wave had swamped her. She cradled her head in her arms, conscious but unable to sit up. Her hair spilled over the checkered tablecloth and a busboy scrambled to move dishes out of the way. Maggie felt Jolene stroking her back.

A childhood memory flitted into Maggie's dim consciousness. She was seven, wearing a blue-and-white striped dress with blue Keds, holding her father's hand at a huge outdoor party at Hermann Park. Tall and athletic, he wanted to join a softball game, but Maggie didn't know any of the other children at the party and wouldn't let go of his hand. With reluctance, he abandoned softball and hoisted her up on his lap. He sipped beer from a paper cup and chatted with two other men about grown-up things. The afternoon sun warmed her face and arms. Her father smelled of after-shave. She held onto a button on his shirt and listened to him talk and basked in his off-handed attention.

The room turned back upright and held steady, at least briefly. Maggie thought about Jack. With the funeral and lawyers and all, she had had to cancel on him last Tuesday. She would make it up to him. Soon.

"You'll have to excuse my friend," she heard Jolene say to the busboy. "She's recently lost a loved one. All broke up, you know."

* * * * *

THE PROPHET OF SPINDLETOP

EAST TEXAS, 1901

Annie Jay found her underclothes on the chair next to the big four-poster bed. She waved both hands to cool the blush in her face. Then she stepped into her corset and began lacing. Bud remained in bed, breathing hard. He propped himself up on his one good arm.

"Why aren't you getting dressed?" she asked. "I thought you wanted me to go out to Spindletop with you."

"I do," he said, "but first I want to ask you something."

She didn't wait for him to ask the question.

"We can't get married, Bud. You know that."

Bud's expression went from earnest to plaintive. It seemed to Annie Jay hardly fair that she, a girl of seventeen, had to remain sensible while Bud, a grown man, went on and on with foolish talk of marriage.

"Okay," he said. "We'll talk some more on the way."

Fifteen minutes later, they climbed into a buckboard and Bud snapped the reins. The horses knew the way on their own. For years they had pulled the buckboard out to the small rise south of town called Spindletop. Everyone in east Texas thought Bud Higgins was daft, and Annie Jay wasn't so sure they were wrong, but Bud had convinced himself that Spindletop's salt dome lay atop a pocket of oil pushing its way to the surface. No one else had shown the slightest interest in wildcatting out there, but Bud had sunk three wells in eight years. He had nothing to show for his efforts, but he did have a new partner, Captain Lucas, and together they had raised more money and hired a crew to drill again. He swore that he would strike oil this time and when he did it would be God's doing. Annie Jay wished he would tend to his brick factory and his other businesses and forget all about oil.

They passed out of town and headed south. The land was flat and hot but a bit of a breeze cooled her neck.

"Why won't you marry me, Annie? Give me one good reason."

She could give him a bushel. For starters, though there was a slender chance that people in town might look past the age difference, there was no way in hell they would approve of a woman marrying the man who adopted her. It was one thing to be an orphan. Nobody could blame a child for losing her parents, but this was different. She would be a social outcast in a way that would make being an orphan seem like an honor.

Not that she didn't have a soft spot for Bud. The day he had come to the County Home and chosen her from among all the girls there to bring home to live with him was the happiest of her life. Living in his big house on Jefferson Street was nice. Warm in winter and cool in summer, and Bud's mother set a fine table. Annie Jay enjoyed the nice clothes that Bud let her buy, not to mention attending a regular school in town with boys and girls from real families.

She didn't mind it all that much when he tiptoed up the stairs late at night and slipped into her bed and rolled on top of her. A girl doesn't come of age in an orphanage without learning plenty about that sort of business. It didn't seem like a high price to pay for a decent life away from the orphanage, but that didn't mean she wanted to spend the rest of her life with him. In five months she would turn eighteen and finish school. She had plans and they didn't include marriage to an old lecher like Bud Higgins. He wouldn't allow singing or dancing or drinking alcohol and he forbade her from swimming or going to shows. It seemed to her that he disapproved of every kind of fun except, of course, his own fun of sneaking into her room at night when no one was looking.

Then there was the matter of his right arm. She felt bad that he'd lost it. The rumor was that a sheriff's deputy had shot it off in a gunfight, but the stump gave her a peculiar feeling when they were in bed together. Sometimes he would topple over and she'd have to help him get back aboard. Annie Jay wasn't about to spend a lifetime with a man who did a thing like that.

"Bud, I..."

The clatter of hooves of an approaching horse saved her from having to say more. Captain Lucas pulled to a stop in front of the buckboard, his horse lathered and twitching and stamping. A gooey greenish-black substance clung to the horse's legs and hindquarters. Captain Lucas was red-faced and so out of breath he could barely speak.

"Higgins," he finally shouted. "Higgins, come and see!"

He spun his horse and headed back toward Spindletop at a gallop. Bud snapped the reins and shouted at the horses to step it up.

Annie Jay suspected a terrible accident, but when they reached the drilling site, it was more like the end of the world. Sections of broken drill pipe lay scattered around the wellhead like matchsticks. The drilling crew stood at a distance, seemingly stunned, their clothing spattered with the same goo as Captain Lucas's horse. A geyser of oil spurted up from the wellhead like pictures she had seen of Old Faithful, except this was black and green. It shot up more than twice as high as the derrick, with mud and oil and sulphur gas and a stench as awful as anything she had ever smelled.

Bud seemed unable to comprehend what he saw. He turned to Captain Lucas. "It's a good well then? Fifty barrels a day?"

"Fifty?" Lucas laughed like a crazy man. "More like fifty *thousand*."

Annie Jay moved closer to Bud. As she watched a lake of oil forming around the well, and growing deeper by the minute, and as she listened to the whoops of glee of the Captain and his crew, she realized that she might have been a bit hasty earlier in the day.

Annie Jay Higgins, she said to herself. It didn't sound so bad after all.

* * * * *

CHAPTER 7. SATURDAY

MARKET CLOSED

David

David sat at the breakfast table in his pajamas, coffee mug in hand, while Miranda bustled around the house doing weekend things. She came into the kitchen and freshened his coffee. Jesse had his face plastered to the monitor of the family computer. Then Miranda set about packing what looked like a picnic lunch for herself and Jesse. She told him to log off the computer and to put on a sweatshirt and comb his hair.

Miranda had put on riding gear. Boots, sweater, riding pants. The jodhpurs framed her butt in a way that he hadn't seen for some time. She was a small woman, a size two petite, but her rear end went a half-size larger. He'd always liked that. "Nice pants," he said.

She tilted her head in his direction and gave him a *Not now* shake of the head, but she was smiling. He could tell she liked the compliment.

"Where are you going, anyway?"

"I told you last night. Did you drink so much you don't remember?"

"That's possible." He searched his mind, but found nothing. "It's a blank."

"I'm going horseback riding this morning and I'm taking Jesse with me."

David looked at her in mock desolation. She moved behind him and tousled his hair.

"Don't worry. We'll do something tonight to celebrate your new job. Something nice."

She told Jesse to go on out to the car and followed him to the doorway. Then she stopped and turned about to look at her husband. "David, I'm sorry. I should have had more faith in you."

He offered up a look of wounded insouciance. "Not to worry," he said.

Miranda

She climbed up on the wooden stool and threw a leg over Fanny's back. The horse skittered to one side. She pulled back on the reins while fitting her boots into the stirrups. Two-day old blisters burned. She got her balance as Fanny launched into a brisk walk.

Jesse hung over a fence but had proven unenthusiastic about their outing. He rejected the offer of a riding lesson and asked twice if they would be doing something with Dad later in the day. He clearly hadn't forgotten the stresses of the past week. He wanted more evidence that things were back to normal.

Miranda intended to put Fanny through her paces to test both the horse and herself. She wanted to see how well Fanny could jump, but also how much of her own riding skill remained. Twenty or thirty minutes of flatwork would make a good start. If that went well, she would try some low jumps toward the end of the session.

It was a glorious morning, one of those fragrant early spring days that made it possible to forget the gray monotony of Houston's winters. The scent of pine mingled with the smells of hay, manure and horse sweat. The sun had pushed the temperature up into the fifties. Fanny seemed ready to canter and Miranda loved it.

Now that David's job situation was settled, she felt bad about giving him such a hard time. A week of the cold shoulder was pretty severe. Not that he didn't deserve it. He never should have walked out on Miller-Dunn, especially after promising her that he wouldn't. But all's well that ends well, and he seemed extraordinarily pleased at the prospect of his new career at

Payton-Mosel. Maybe it would be the change of scenery that he'd needed all along.

"Mom, watch out," called Jesse.

He was whiny and nervous. She could see the tightness in his face as she urged Fanny into a faster gait. It dawned on her that Jesse might never have seen his mother doing something purely for pleasure. She spent eight to ten hours at the office every day and when not at work took care of the family. Those parameters defined her life as precisely as the white fence on her right circumscribed the jumping ring.

Not that she minded, not at all, but maybe things were about to change. Investment bankers could make piles of money. Big piles. She wasn't going to get carried away, but if David did well at Payton-Mosel, then after a while—quite a while—she might be able to quit her job and stay at home. Despite her current success, it wasn't as if she had set out to be a career woman. If she quit, she could attend all of Jesse's school events and help him with his homework and have dinner on the table every evening and go horseback riding as often as she liked and...

"Mom, please."

He'd gone past plaintive. He dropped to the ground and crouched on one knee, watching her through the boards of the fence. It was as if he had a premonition of disaster—Mom tumbling head over heels onto hard ground—and he desperately wanted her to stop before it happened.

The workout had gone well enough, but Miranda decided to cut it short and save the jumps for the following weekend. She let her son lead Fanny back to the barn and encouraged him to help the groom remove the saddle and bridle. He calmed a bit as they passed through the barn and Miranda told him about the different breeds of horses.

Miranda slipped into the changing room, leaving Jesse to browse in the tack shop. She removed her helmet and washed her hands and face. She dug into her purse for a clip to put up her hair but found nothing. She dumped the purse's contents onto a bench. An item she'd forgotten all about fell on top of the resulting pile of keys, pocketbook, tissues and pens. A square of folded silk.

It was a man's tie, the one she had taken from the tree in Russ Wheeler's office on the day he quit. A strange empty feeling came over her. He had gone and died before she could give it back to him.

David

It wasn't much of a lie. In fact, in David's mind, it hardly qualified as a lie at all. What he had told Miranda was the absolute truth. The way he saw it, he had merely advanced the truth's effective date by a day or so. After all, what else could the smooth Friday afternoon voice-mail from Franklin Payton have meant? *David, I'm sorry I've been so difficult to reach all week.* That sounded to David like an apology. *I want to talk with you as soon as possible, but I'm tied up tonight at a fundraiser and tomorrow morning with a client. You know how it is.*

David did indeed know how it is. Investment bankers are busy men, and Franklin Payton was one of the busiest. It wouldn't be long now until David joined their ranks, the ranks of busy, wealthy investment bankers. He wished that he hadn't been at the gym with his phone in his gym bag when Payton called, but no matter. Payton's intentions couldn't have been any clearer.

I'll call you over the weekend. Sunday latest. Take care, buddy.

Buddy! David had felt a sudden surge of warmth for the old pirate. He pictured himself several weeks hence, sitting at the huge antique table in the Payton-Mosel conference room, surrounded by colleagues. Payton would turn and say, *Nice work, buddy!*

As soon as he picked up the message, David had decided there was no point in letting Miranda fret any longer. She'd been so worked up since he quit Miller-Dunn that the whole family had been upset. This way was better. She could relax and they all could enjoy the weekend.

Maybe he had stretched the truth a tad, but it wasn't for his own benefit. It was for the good of the family. And it had worked. As soon as he told her the good news, the tension in the house dissipated like morning fog. Miranda became her old companionable self in no time.

He couldn't wait for Franklin Payton's call.

Feo

Feo cranked the wheel of the riding mower and backed into the corner of the yard where the leaves piled up. There was no need to cut the grass, but Feo liked the way the riding mower sucked up the winter detritus and made the lawn as neat and clean as his living room rug.

He finished the lawn work and maneuvered the mower into the metal-sided garage at the back of his property. After killing the engine, he sat listening to the *tick-tick* of cooling metal. He felt frustrated and sluggish.

It was lunchtime, so he drove over to the Pig Stand on Washington Avenue. The waitress brought a pork sandwich with fries and a milkshake out to his car where he sat and ate alone.

He decided to go see Sherry. He'd dialed her number again and again, but each time he put the phone down before pushing the *Send* button. What if she was in the middle of something and promised to call back? Then he'd be frozen, waiting for her to call, and he didn't think he could stand that. Worse, what if she took his call and talked to him like the near-stranger that he was? Their few hours together now seemed like a dream. To learn what he wanted to know, Feo needed to see her face and smell her hair and feel the touch of her fingers on his skin. He needed to know if she would look at him and talk to him the way she did in Mexico.

Even in the light weekend traffic, it took Feo nearly twenty minutes on the Katy Freeway to reach the place where she lived. It was one of Houston's ubiquitous cheap garden-style apartment complexes: a parking lot surrounding a flat-roofed, three-story rectangular building with a patio, a swimming pool and a cluster of cheap aluminum furniture. The city had

10,000 structures like this one, Feo thought, and it made him appreciate the crooked streets and singular shapes of old San Antonio where he'd grown up.

He nosed the Saab into a vacant space, turned off the ignition and waited. He had no clue what he would say. In Mexico, he'd hardly said anything and that seemed to work fine, but he didn't expect it to work again. This time he'd have to make a move. There are rules. Beads of sweat dripped from the back of his neck into the collar of his shirt.

Concrete steps led to Sherry's second-floor apartment. Maybe something would come to him when she opened the door and saw him standing there. He knocked, hoping a look at her face would give him inspiration. He knocked again, but there was no answer and no sign that she was at home. Feo deflated like a blow-up Christmas yard decoration.

Squinting between the slats of the front window mini-blinds, he peered into a darkened apartment. Posters decorated the walls and some cat paraphernalia stood in one corner of the living room. Then he saw scrap of blue paper sticking out from under the bottom of the door. *Overdue Rent—Second Notice*. Why was Sherry off vacationing at an expensive resort if she couldn't afford to pay her rent?

"Can I help you, mister?"

Feo turned, embarrassed at having been caught looking through the window. The neighbor, a middle-aged women with a beehive hairdo, clearly regarded him as a peeping Tomás. She carried two sacks of groceries.

"I'm looking for Sherry Shipley," he said. "Do you happen to know if she's around?"

The woman's didn't respond and her expression didn't change.

"My name's Feo Duarte." He put out his hand. "I'm a friend of hers."

Shifting the groceries, the woman extended a reluctant hand. "You missed her."

"Do you know when she might be back?"

"She's out of town. Only reason I know is that she left me a note to feed Taco."

"Taco?"

"Her cat." She lifted one of the grocery bags in his direction and Feo saw multiple tins of Holistic Blend All-Natural cat food.

"Trouble is," said the woman, "I got to get down to Victoria myself. My sister's in the hospital."

Feo put on a sympathetic face.

"Pneumonia," she said.

Suddenly a gleam came into her eye. "You're Sherry's friend, you say?"

Feo tried to look as unthreatening as might be humanly possible.

The woman set both grocery bags on the cement walkway floor and set about rearranging their contents. Eventually one bag contained nothing but cat food and the other bag contained everything else. She withdrew a key from her pants pocket, tossed it in with the cat food and handed the bag to Feo.

"If you're Sherry's friend, you must like cats."

Norah

Since when did Dr. Frost make house calls? And on a Saturday?

"What are you doing here?" Norah asked.

"You didn't show up for your session last week. I was alarmed."

Oh that. Norah had intended to cancel the appointment but it had slipped her mind. She wasn't sure what to think about her former shrink showing up unannounced, except that she was plenty annoyed. She never socialized at home and rarely allowed anyone to come inside.

"May I come in?"

She didn't answer. She didn't want to let him in, but she couldn't think of a way to refuse. If she turned him away without a believable excuse, he would think she was hiding something.

Dr. Frost apparently took her silence for acquiescence and edged inside. "You were quite discomposed that day I saw you in the parking lot. I wanted to see how you are getting on."

Now she recollected their encounter more clearly. It had been the day after Burnam announced the Bluestream deal and shortly after Wheeler disappeared. Dr. Frost had been dressed for tennis that day also. She recalled that he'd given her a business card for the appointment. She'd forgotten the appointment but knew exactly where she had put the card.

He looked around the apartment. Then he looked around again. It wasn't the informal once-over of a friend wondering what kind of furniture Norah liked. He had on his face the same troubled, patronizing expression that he'd worn when she visited his office for therapy. Norah bristled with a mixture of irritation and embarrassment.

"How are you feeling about things?" he asked.

It hit her that this was no casual visit. This was some kind of *intervention*. She laughed bitterly. He didn't mean *things*, as in life. He meant *things*, as in *possessions*. How did she feel about her *possessions*?

"Dr. Frost, I'm not one of those weirdo hoarders."

He looked around a third time. Unfortunately, his gaze came to rest on the hallway leading to her home office. She had piled a few things in the hall recently, too busy to file them away. Bills. Newspapers. A broken puppet she had seen at an estate sale and couldn't resist. She gave herself a psychic kick in the rear, wishing she had put all this crap behind closed doors.

He inclined his head toward the end of the hallway. "What's in there?"

"It's my home office."

"May I see it?"

"It's an office."

"Uh-huh." He took an old newspaper from the hallway and tucked it under one arm. He picked up the puppet.

"Fine," he said. "I could get rid of these things for you on my way out."

Norah's pulse raced and she felt as if someone had pushed her from the deck of a ship. She flailed in heavy seas, watching the ship's silhouette recede. Dr. Frost stood high above at the ship's railing, looking down at her. The bastard. He knew exactly what he was doing. A deep, abiding fear gripped her and wouldn't let go.

“All right,” she said, reaching for the puppet. “All right.” She unlocked the door of her home office and flipped the light switch. She stepped inside and turned to watch his face.

An involuntary curse escaped his lips as he took it in. An entire room jammed with her trove, and every inch of space covered with overflow. “Norah, you need help.”

She smiled politely.

“There are therapies. You're not alone. Millions of Americans suffer from hoarding disorder.”

“I know, I know. You explained all that to me before.” She imitated his earnest tones. “Hoarders sometimes replace normal social relationships with an unhealthy attachment to possessions. They come to feel more intensely about things than they do about people.”

Dr. Frost gestured at the room. “Including things that have no real value.”

Norah stepped gingerly across the items littering the floor. She thought of all the bits and pieces of her collection. Some holiday cards she had bought in 1986 came to mind. They had funny penguins on the front. There were twenty extras and she had saved them to send out another year. The cards were in the third cabinet, top drawer, about a half-inch from the back. The tightness inside her eased a bit as she thought about those penguins.

Norah opened her eyes to find Dr. Frost staring open-mouthed. She had forgotten he was there. She motioned for him to come closer.

“Really, Dr. Frost. I have no idea what you're talking about.”

Lulu

Lulu propped both feet up on her desk. She printed two photographs and pinned them to the wall of her newsroom cubicle. One picture showed Jack in a three-piece suit riding a stallion onto an auditorium stage at some kind of corporate pep rally a few years earlier. The other picture showed

Lorelei Logan speaking to a group of schoolchildren. The genuineness of her smile impressed Lulu. They made an attractive couple, if indeed they were a couple.

A bowl of black bean soup sat on her desk. With a plastic spoon, she fished out a bean and flicked it at Jack's picture. "He loves her," said Lulu. She fished out another bean and flicked it at the Senator's wife. "He loves her not." She continued until all the beans were gone. By the end, the photographs had turned into soggy pulp and the beans accumulated in a mound on the carpet beneath. She wished she had bought the large carton of soup.

Ed, wearing a hideous plaid golf shirt, peered over the wall of the cubicle. "Saw your car," he said. "What are you doing here?"

"This," said Lulu, scraping one final bean from the bottom of the soup carton and smacking it into Burnam's head.

"Nice shot," said Ed. "If that rumor is true, there's a story that has legs like a supermodel."

Lulu couldn't decide what frustrated her more. That she didn't know what to do with Josh's information on Bluestream. That she'd gone to California and missed the biggest story in years breaking in her own back yard. Or that Jack might be cheating on his wife with someone near his own age, and it wasn't her.

"Whereas my story..." began Lulu.

"...isn't a story. It's the ruminations of an oversexed engineer in a hot tub."

To convince Ed of the validity of what Josh had shown her, she'd had to reveal some of the more unorthodox aspects of her reportorial technique.

"But I saw it work. I heard it. It's astonishing."

"You saw something work, but you don't know whether it works out in the world or if it's something he ginned up in his apartment to snow you. And if it does work, you don't know if it belongs to Conquest. Your friend might be freelancing. And if it works and Conquest owns it, you still don't know what Conquest plans to do with it." He nudged the pile of beans on the floor with the toe of his golf shoe. "You need more."

At first she thought he'd read her mind about getting the larger carton of soup, but then it clicked that he was still talking about Bluestream. She needed more for her story. She tore a length of paper towel from a roll in her desk drawer, scooped up the beans and dumped the mess into her wastebasket. She unpinned the remains of the photos and dropped the scraps in on top of the beans. "Okay," she said. "What do you suggest?"

"Take a break from Bluestream. I want you to go in a different direction."

Lulu groaned. She didn't want to write another story on NAFTA.

"See if you can get an interview with Lacey Burnam," Ed said.

Lulu's head whipped around. "Lacey doesn't do interviews."

"She might do one now. If she's heard this rumor about the Senator's wife she has to be embarrassed. Give her a chance to tell her side. She can stand by her man and blame the whole thing on the media." He paused. "Or not." He smiled. "She might open up. You two have so much in common."

Lulu gritted her teeth. "Whatever you say."

She heard his golf cleats tearing the carpet as he walked away.

Miranda

The woman who answered Miranda's knock looked as if she had stepped off the cover of *Shape* magazine. She wore pink running shorts and tank top. A pink band barely held in check an abundance of wavy hair. Miranda couldn't help but notice the woman's nipples pressing against the thin fabric of the tank top. She certainly didn't look like a grieving widow.

"Maggie?" she asked.

"Miranda?"

They shared an awkward two-handed squeeze.

"It was nice of you to call," said Maggie. "I don't know many of Russ's work colleagues."

Miranda stepped into a pleasant living room furnished much like her own, except for the absence of any sign of children. Where her own house had video games and sports equipment, Maggie's had fashion magazines and antique glassware.

"This is a little odd, I know, but I thought you might want Russ's tie." She handed it to Maggie, neatly folded. "I'm so sorry for your loss."

Maggie accepted the tie and put it aside. She said nothing. Maybe she was wondering how Miranda happened to have an article of her husband's clothing.

"I was asked to take over some of Russ's work, so I went into his office looking for the files. I didn't find any files, but I did find this tie, hanging in a tree. It look as if Russ had accidentally left it behind when he emptied out his office."

Maggie cocked her head. "Why would he empty out his office?"

Miranda hesitated. "Well, this was on the day he quit. When he resigned."

"Quit?" Maggie looked baffled. "Russ didn't quit."

Miranda recalled her confusion that day in Wheeler's office. She hadn't been able to figure out how he emptied his office if, as Norah had said, he resigned that very morning. And now it sounded as if he hadn't resigned at all. Uncertain, she decided to play along. "I'm sorry. I meant when he left for California."

Maggie gave her a quizzical look. "How about I pour us some wine? You like cabernet?"

Miranda took a seat in a bentwood rocker. Maggie returned from the kitchen with two classes of red wine and placed them on the coffee table.

"You're telling me that Russ resigned from Conquest?"

"Well, I didn't talk to him myself, but that's what Norah Needham told me. And it did look like he had cleared out his office. I couldn't find anything to help me out."

"I've talked to Norah three times in the past week about Russ's affairs and she didn't say anything about that. Did she happen to tell you why he quit?"

"She said Russ had a family emergency."

Maggie blinked. "There was no family emergency. Russ told me Mr. Burnam sent him to California to work on Bluestream."

"That's the project I took over from Russ. He wasn't on the deal team anymore." Miranda tucked both feet underneath the rocker. "Something doesn't make sense."

Maggie sipped her wine. "You're right about that."

Miranda hadn't touched the cabernet. She felt awful and wished she hadn't come. It was bad enough the woman lost her husband. Now this.

"Unless," Maggie said, "he did resign, but he didn't tell me about it."

"Why would he do that?"

Maggie walked about the room, wineglass in hand. "Maybe he had a girlfriend. Maybe he had some money stashed away in an offshore account. Maybe he was planning to leave me."

Miranda stood. "I'm sorry. This isn't any of my business."

"That plane was coming back from Mexico, you know. A resort town called Ixtapa. It's supposed to be very romantic. The bastard."

Miranda felt her face redden. The funny thing was that Maggie didn't seem embarrassed or flustered at all. In fact, she had a crazy half-smile on her face.

"Miserable bastard," Maggie repeated. All at once she seemed to notice Miranda's discomfort and waved a hand. "I guess our marriage was a little rocky."

Jeez, thought Miranda. I guess so.

"Could you do me a favor?" Maggie asked.

Miranda shrugged assent.

"Russ apparently had some investments that I didn't know about and I don't understand. Some kind of partnerships connected to Conquest."

"What would you like to know?"

"I'm assuming the company gave these to Russ as part of his bonus. Don't some companies do that?"

Miranda said yes. She wasn't aware of anything like at Conquest, but that didn't mean it didn't happen. There seemed to be more and more things at Conquest that she didn't know about.

"Could you help me figure out how much these are worth? I could ask the company, of course, but if you work in Russ's department, maybe you would know off the top of your head."

Miranda looked over the typed list that Maggie had put in front of her. She saw familiar names like Rogue and Cyclops and Booster and Iceman. "Off the top of my head, I have no idea. But I can look into it for you."

Maggie raised her empty glass, as if offering a toast.

Lulu

"Lulu," said the voice on the phone. "It's Josh Morris."

"Hooray," she said.

"Why didn't you go with the story? Didn't I give you what you needed?"

He was trying awfully hard to sound casual, it seemed to Lulu. "Why do you care?"

"It was such a big story. You saw everything work. What else do you need?"

He definitely was trying too hard, Lulu thought. She flashed on what it might be. "You bought options, didn't you?"

"No, of course not. I..." He didn't finish.

"You thought Conquest stock would shoot the moon, so you bought options."

He uttered more denials, but finally confessed. "The options expired yesterday. I took quite a bath."

Lulu said nothing, weighing the information. He'd had an ulterior motive. That didn't prove his story was false, but it certainly didn't help.

"I was hoping to get out. You know, before Conquest takes over."

Again, she said nothing. Did he expect an apology? He'd been lying all along, Lulu concluded. No doubt about it.

"So, anyway, I'm coming to Houston next week for a meeting with some Conquest people. Would you like to get together?"

"You mean, would I like to fuck you again?"

"That's not..."

"No thanks," said Lulu. "My editor took me off that story."

Miranda

Driving home from her meeting with Maggie, Miranda's head buzzed with questions. She turned into the empty lot of an office building on Woodway. She drove to the back and parked beside a dumpster. Make a list, she told herself. Sort it all out.

She started with Wheeler. The story of a family emergency was a lie. There was something that Norah had found necessary to cover up. And there wasn't much point in confronting Norah. Her answer was...*let's go horseback riding.* Miranda felt a flush of embarrassment at letting herself be sidetracked.

What about Wheeler's investments? The comic book names made it clear that the investments involved some of the fancy transactions that Miranda had learned about over the past few weeks. She had promised Maggie that she would take a closer look, but she had lost the desire to find out where all this led.

She rolled down the car window, but the nearby dumpster reeked of garbage. She raised the window, but her nostrils remained full of the stench.

Miranda wasn't one to make snap decisions, but it hit her that she wanted no more of Conquest or Norah or Bluestream. She didn't want to think about Maggie or Wheeler's investments or any of it.

A strange feeling of release came over her. David had a new job that would pay a lot of money. She could quit Conquest. The investment banking thing might not work out in the long run, but surely David would stay with it for at least a few years. That would give her plenty of time to look around. Houston was booming. She could find something at another company. There wasn't a doubt in her mind. She would resign first thing Monday morning, before she learned any more things she didn't want to know.

She thought again about her visit with Maggie. What if Maggie was right about her husband and his girlfriend and his offshore bank account? What kind of a man had he been that he could do things like that? And why didn't his widow seem to give a damn?

She had an unexpected urge to talk about all this with David. Maybe he screwed up sometimes, but at least she knew where he was at night. He loved her. He wasn't down in Mexico spending secret money on some kind of home-wrecker.

Miranda started the car, idled it back to the street and opened the moon roof. The odor of trash receded as a few deep drafts of fresh air helped clear her head. Everything would be fine.

She gunned the engine and raced back onto Woodway, heading home.

David

"David, this is Franklin Payton."

David clicked off the television. Finally, the job offer.

"Sorry to call you on a Saturday."

"No problem. None at all." Payton presumably wanted David to report for work first thing Monday morning. He would miss the guys at Velotrade.

"Like I said, I'm sorry to disturb you, but I'm afraid I've got some unhappy news."

David sucked in his breath. "Is there a problem with the job? Some kind of delay?"

Payton didn't answer immediately. David heard him clear his throat several times.

"No, it's not a delay."

David relaxed.

"There is no job. I mean, Payton-Mosel won't be able to offer you a job. I'm sorry, David, but I thought I should let you know right away."

David said nothing. The call somehow ended. He walked down the hall and peeked into Jesse's bedroom. His son snored softly.

David clicked the television back on, but muted the sound. The automatic jump button made it change every few seconds, and David watched it jump through every channel. He enjoyed five-second glimpses of programs that he didn't know existed. The Swedish Home and Garden Channel. The Chick Flick Channel. If he never turned it off, he guessed that the television would keep jumping all night long and into the next day.

He watched in silence and waited for his wife to come home.

CHAPTER 8. SUNDAY

MARKET CLOSED

Jack

Jack chose a weathered bench on a hillside and sat down to take in the view at Glenwood Cemetery. In the vast flatness that comprised metropolitan Houston, only Glenwood's sixty acres boasted a terrain to which the term *rolling hills* fairly applied. Nestled into a southward bend of Buffalo Bayou only a third of a mile west of Conquest Plaza, the cemetery served as the final resting place for an eclectic grouping of business tycoons, Confederate soldiers, movie stars, and politicos.

Maggie slipped onto the bench beside him. Although it had been less than two weeks since their last rendezvous, a lot had happened and he had forgotten how attractive she was.

"Goddam, you look good," he said.

"Jack, why are we meeting here? I've been to enough graveyards lately."

Jack hadn't attended Wheeler's funeral. He had made certain, however, that Conquest paid for it and that any of Wheeler's co-workers who wanted to attend got the afternoon off.

He stood and offered Maggie his arm. They had the place to themselves on a beautiful Sunday afternoon. He'd seen only one other car and it passed out of sight heading toward the cheap water-logged plots at the back. They strolled like tourists along winding stone pathways while Jack told her some of the history of the place. Dating from 1871, an ancient date by Houston standards, Glenwood boasted more than a century's accumulation of crepe myrtle and Spanish oak, and its grave markers ranged from nineteenth century scrolled stonework to twentieth century modern sculpture.

He pointed out the grave of Gene Tierney, the actress, and Maria Gable, the one-time wife of Clark Gable. They passed Anson Jones, the final President of the Republic of Texas, and former Houston mayor H.B. Rice.

"See that one over there?" He pointed at a heart-shaped gravestone with a large hole in the center. "Denton Cooley. He pioneered open-heart surgery." He shifted his attention to another grave. "That one there, Dr. Thomas Cronin. He invented silicone implants. He performed the world's first breast augmentation, right here in Houston. Nineteen-sixty-two."

"How do you know that?" asked Maggie. "*Why* do you know that?"

They walked on. Jacked paused deferentially before the markers belonging to Joseph Cullinan, founder of Texaco, and Ross Sterling, a co-founder of Exxon. Soon they passed the graves of Glenwood's most notorious residents: Glenn McCarthy, the legendary oil wildcatter, and Howard Hughes, the infamous aviator, movie producer and businessman.

"I like it here," Jack told Maggie. "It's peaceful. I feel like some of the great men of history are talking to me."

Maggie stopped in the middle of the path. "You worry me, Jack. Glenn McCarthy died flat broke. Howard Hughes spent the last twenty years of his life watching spy movies and letting his nails grow."

Jack ignored her. They completed the circuit of Glenwood and returned to his bench. Nothing broke the silence other than a single lonely cicada. From time to time, high cirrus blocked the sun's rays, but only briefly.

Jack knew what was coming next and it was a conversation he didn't want to have. He'd already had it with his wife and it wasn't fair he should have to have it again with his mistress.

"What's on your mind, sweetheart?"

"The rumors, Jack. The Senator's wife. It's all over Houston."

He mustered up his most earnest expression. The same one he used with his Board of Directors when presenting the next year's business plan.

"There's nothing to it, Maggie. I give you my word. It's terrible how people gossip." He hitched a shoulder as if to demonstrate how much pain the whole situation caused him.

"If there's nothing to it, why is everybody in town talking about the scene you and her made at the museum dedication?"

"That was a security situation."

Her face told him he wasn't close to making a sale.

"She could have gotten hurt if I hadn't gotten her out of there. The Secret Service guys gave me an honorary badge." This wasn't exactly true. Lorelei had asked one of the security men for it and given it to Jack as a remembrance of that night at the Ship Channel.

Maggie's face softened. He decided not to say any more. Lacey had bought it. Maybe Maggie would, too.

She said nothing, but pretty soon slid an inch or two closer on the bench. Jack relaxed and almost immediately felt an erection begin to stir.

"Nothing's changed between us," he told her. "Nothing at all."

Maggie put her head on his shoulder and sighed. Sunlight glinted off a window in a nearby mausoleum.

"Jack, there's something else."

He softened immediately and put on a look of concentration, guessing she was going to talk about her dead husband and about her guilty feelings now that he'd passed on.

"It's a financial thing. Russ owned some investments I don't understand. Partnerships held in a secret offshore account."

Jack shelved the sympathetic expression and gave her a businesslike *go-ahead* nod.

"They have funny names. Russ's lawyer thinks they might be something Russ got from Conquest as a performance bonus."

Jack had almost forgotten. The hush money that Norah gave Wheeler. Twenty-five million. "I can check into it for you," he said. "They might be worth a hundred thou. Maybe more."

Maggie's fingers tweaked the front of his pants where his rekindling erection made a tent.

"Tell you what," he said. "I can arrange for the company to cash you out. How does a quarter-million sound?"

She blew hot breath against his ear. She got his belt buckle undone and his zipper down with only one hand. Pretty impressive. She slipped warm, moist fingers deep inside his pants. He'd never gotten a hand job in a cemetery before, and he found the weirdness of it more than a little potent. Maggie's hand went up and down as if working a bicycle pump.

"All right," he said. "A half million. Tragic widow."

She slid off the bench onto her knees. Her mouth replaced her hand. He barely had time to say, "Okay already, a million," before he spurted like an uncapped fire hydrant.

Maggie reached into her purse for a tissue and dabbed the corner of her mouth.

"That was fantastic," he said. "Tuesday nights still good for you?"

She refastened his pants and, still in a kneeling position, looked him straight in the face. Something in the nature of her pause gave him the distinct impression that he'd miscalculated. When she finally spoke, it was with a soft but unmistakable edge he'd never before heard in her voice. The edge told him that not only was the meeting not over, but she was only now getting to the most important item on her agenda.

"You know, Jack, now that I am a *tragic widow* and all, I might need a little more consolin' than you can handle in one night a week."

That hadn't occurred to Jack. With Wheeler out of the way, he could have Maggie as often as he wanted. "Sure," he said. "What are you thinking? Two nights? Three?"

She tossed away the tissue and raised her hand up to his cheek. "Seven, Jack. I reckon I was thinkin' seven."

Norah

Norah circled about the showroom floor of Bronco Dave's Ford dealership. She admired the best-selling lines and sumptuous interior of the F-150 SuperCrewCab, but avoided conversation with any of the salespeople. She had no use for a pickup truck and didn't particularly want to explain why she'd spent the last forty-five minutes studying this one.

It was Wally Day, and Wally had loved trucks. Back when Wally was alive, Ford didn't sell the F-150. The F-150 didn't come out until 1984, the year after Wally died. He couldn't have afforded a new truck anyway. During the years that Norah had been with him, he drove a dented 1971 two-tone F-100 that he inherited when his uncle went to the rest home.

Every so often, according to no particular schedule, Norah had Wally Day. She avoided Conquest and Jack Burnam and everything else in her life and for a full day, give or take, visited places that Wally loved to visit and did things that Wally loved to do. Like looking at pickup trucks. Mostly Fords and Dodges. Wally would no more have considered a Chevy than he would a Peugot or Fiat, and he refused to acknowledge the existence of the crappy little trucks the Japanese began selling in the seventies.

Norah slid onto the passenger seat of the showroom truck and a rush of remembrance rolled over her. The slick leather seat felt the way the nylon seat covers in Wally's F-100 felt against the backs of her bare legs on the sweltering nights when they cruised out the Gulf Freeway for a weekend at one of Galveston's ramshackle beach motels.

"Take 'em off," Wally would say.

She would make a ritual fuss and then wriggle her panties out from under her sundress and hand them over. He would hang them from the rear view mirror for the rest of the drive for the sheer fun of knowing that she would let him do it. The white cotton underwear would blow about in the swampy tidal air pouring in through the truck's open windows, signaling Norah's easy acquiescence to passing drivers. She still couldn't understand how, with no more than a glance, Wally could get her to do things that, at any other time of her life and with any other person, she would dismiss without a moment's consideration.

A salesman gave her a funny look and Norah realized she was sitting in Bronco Dave's show truck smiling like a fool. She may have laughed out loud. She climbed out and perused the rack of glossy brochures near the door long enough to snag the one on the F-150.

Lunch, on Wally Day, meant Roznovsky's, Wally's favorite beer and burger joint. The cheeseburgers came on lightly toasted buns with mayo, mustard, diced onions, ribbons of shredded lettuce and plenty of grease. Norah ordered two burgers loaded, plus fries and a couple of longneck Pearls. It was what Wally had ordered for them on the night he proposed.

The marriage lasted two years, four months, twelve days. Every one of them happy, as far as Norah could recall, but she wasn't completely sure. Maybe her memory played tricks on her. She had been scrawny and flat-chested and, most of the time, morose. In retrospect, it seemed impossible that he loved her the way she remembered it, and she wondered how Wally would recall their time together. *Cherished flower*, he had called her, something he found in a book of bad Rod McKuen poems. He would intone the words solemnly every time he wanted to have sex, which was pretty nearly every night. But maybe her memory played tricks about that, too. Wally was the only man ever to see her naked, the only man ever to make love to her. There had been no one else before and no one since. Unless she had missed it, no one else had asked.

The food arrived, neatly arranged on a brown platter, everything wrapped in thin waxed paper. The waitress had tucked a handwritten check underneath the napkins. Three dollars each for the burgers and a buck-fifty apiece for the beers and fries. Barely twelve dollars total. Norah put a twenty on the table and thought about how much money twenty dollars seemed like when she and Wally ate together at Roznovsky's and how little it seemed to her now.

After lunch, she drove east on Washington and turned right into Glenwood Cemetery. The sign read, as it had for as long as she had been coming to this place, *Gates Close at Five, Lots Available.* She drove to the back and parked. She wondered what a Glenwood plot cost now. When she had buried Wally, the best she could afford was a small single within a stone's throw of the noisy thoroughfare that ran by the southern boundary. Wally had never complained about Houston's inordinate traffic, so he wouldn't mind the incessant rush of cars passing overhead on Allen Parkway. For over ten years Norah had made modest monthly payments on the plot, and the headstone and casket, too, until the year that Conquest bought the company that she worked for and she had enough to pay all her debts with a considerable sum left over.

Her shoes sank into the soggy ground as she made her way to the grave. *Walter Edward Harvey*, it read, with the dates of his birth and death and nothing more. At the time, addled by grief, she couldn't think of a suitable epitaph. It would have cost extra, anyway.

She knelt in the damp grass and pressed her forehead against the cold granite. The drone of distant lawn mowers and leaf blowers competed with the buzz of passing traffic. An unseen dog barked. Dead leaves from the previous fall clustered around the base of the headstone. It seemed that the Glenwood caretakers didn't often make it this far back. Norah pushed aside some of the leaves and placed on Wally's grave the Ford brochure, a bottle of Pearl beer and one of the cheeseburgers, now gone cold. The birds and squirrels would eat the cheeseburger and she hoped the caretakers eventually would come by and cart away the rest.

That evening, well after dark, she drove over to Crawdaddy, took a table near the stage and ordered more beer. She planned to drink enough for herself and Wally both. After the customary wait, the lean and wrinkled Texas Johnny Brown came on stage wearing a white shirt and creased blue suit. He strapped on his guitar and tuned it as the three other members of his Quality Blues Band joined him onstage. They all wore matching widebrim hats, except for the drummer.

Norah guessed that Texas Johnny had advanced well into his seventies, although he sported the same plastic-framed glasses and pencil-thin moustache that he had when Norah and Wally first saw him in 1979. He gave the band a sign to begin and they did and his Les Paul spit out sad and tender sounds. The band played *Moanin' and Groanin'* and *Strange Situation* and *Blue and Lonesome* and *Stand the Pain* and a half-dozen others that Norah had heard so many times she knew every snarl and swell of the music before it happened. The style of playing and singing the blues was understated and very personal and made Norah ache with memories and longing.

At the break, she stood in line for the ladies room, and the giggly twenty-year-olds in their crop tops and skin-tight denims with their flat bellies and gorgeous hair gave her pitying looks, as if to question what a woman like her was doing alone in a place like this. One of them tapped Norah on the arm and asked if she was okay. A sharp retort rose in Norah's throat but she cut it off. Her face somehow had become wet with tears, and the girl was only trying to be nice to a lonely old scarecrow of a woman.

She peed in the bathroom's toilet stall and splashed cold water from the bathroom sink on her face and went back to her table at the side of the room. She ordered more beer, staying with Pearl. The band started up again and Texas Johnny picked his way through *In the Dark* and *Rained Out* and *Just Can't Do It*. Then he paused for an unusually long time, fiddling with the strings on his guitar and trying to get them right. When he was ready to go, Texas Johnny mumbled a dedication but Norah didn't catch the name and then he ripped into *Cheatin' and Stealin'* and *Did You Lose Your Way?* and when those were finished he played his traditional closing song *Nothin' But the Truth*. Through these last songs it seemed to Norah that he was looking through the thick lenses of his horn rimmed glasses right at her. The deep and certain comprehension in his eyes scared her a little.

The audience called for more, but Texas Johnny never played encores. He and his band delivered two hours of quality blues and that should be enough. Johnny, Norah understood, sold an honest product and disdained artifice.

She stood and walked unsteadily toward the exit, where a bouncer she recognized from a previous visit steered her to a line of drunks out front. She gave him $200, a business card and a key to her car, and he gave her a promise to deliver the car to her office by noon the next day.

As it worked out, the number of waiting drunks exceeded the number of waiting taxis and Norah had to share a ride. The crumple-faced stranger that piled onto the seat beside her smelled of sweat and wore a gimme cap and a brown corduroy sport coat over a black tee shirt and exuded an air of inebriated melancholy scarcely less desperate than her own. The man slumped toward her in the dark of the back seat of the taxicab. Their hips pressed together and their forearms touched briefly and his head fell against her shoulder.

For the duration of the trip, with the benefit of five or six bottles of beer, Norah found it not at all hard to convince herself that the beefy body warming her own, and the heavy hand on her thigh, and the alcoholic breath fogging the air, belonged not to a stranger at all but rather to her beloved husband Wally, with whom she was riding home after a night out on the town and who, by the look of him, had enjoyed one helluva good time.

CHAPTER 9. MONDAY

CQC 51.77 0.84↑

Miranda

Monday morning. Miranda woke, early and alone. The clock read six-fifteen a.m. Cold radiated from the side of the bed where David usually slept. She had banished him to the sofa Saturday night but his snore assaulted her ears as if he were right beside her. She needed coffee.

While it brewed, she looked into the living room and examined her still-sleeping husband with as much objectivity as she could muster. He lay flat on his back. A strand of drool fell from a corner of his mouth. His tee shirt rode up exposing his soft belly. His legs looked sallow and hairy in the dead morning air. When had he started looking like this? Miranda punched his shoulder until she saw his eyes flicker. When she was sure he was awake, she punched him again to let him know she was still mad as hell. "You can move now," she said. She wanted him off the sofa before Jesse woke up. David rose and stumbled off to the bedroom. Miranda folded his blanket and returned it to the linen closet. She opened the morning newspaper and pressed the warm coffee cup against her cheek.

Fifteen minutes later, Jesse padded into the kitchen wearing a glassy expression. "Morning, Mom. TV?"

Normally Miranda didn't let him watch television in the morning, but she felt her willpower giving way. She was tired, ready to let go the rope. "Why not?" she said, as he turned on *SpongeBob SquarePants.*

She scanned the business section of the newspaper, which recently had begun to carry a bizarre mixture of high society and crime news. Speculation about corporate profits alternated with photos of major executives being led away in handcuffs. The *perp walk*, they now called it. Coverage of the romantic endeavors of celebrity CEO's ran close by stories of corporate mergers. A disgraced former corporate chief serving time for stock fraud wrote a weekly column called *Live From Club Fed*. A market analyst predicted that a story about a CEO checking into rehab would boost his company's stock price. Strange, thought Miranda. People seemed to buy stocks because they recognized a famous name or it might give them something to talk about at a party.

"Turn it down," she shouted at Jesse. Abashed, he pushed the mute button.

Her Saturday night resolve to resign from Conquest had evaporated with barely a trace. Not only did David not have a job with Payton-Mosel, for all she knew he might never work again. She thought about the conversation she'd had at Jesse's basketball game. Like her friend Rhoda, she was the breadwinner now.

It was time to make sure Jesse was dressed and packed for school. It was her day for this chore, even though her husband had nowhere to go, nothing to do. Even though he was asleep in bed, snoring like a hefalump. Even though she needed to go in early to catch up on the work that now provided their sole means of support. The coffee tasted bitter and she pushed it away.

Miranda carried the cup to the kitchen sink. Sliding down beside Jesse, she wrapped both arms around him and inhaled his drowsy boy-smell. *SpongeBob* normally offered up a tone of relentless cheer, but this episode struck a darker note. SpongeBob's friend Sandy Cheeks was homesick and depressed and had decided to leave Bikini Bottom and return to her home in Texas. Miranda sympathized. Everything around her seemed different. She longed for life to go back to normal.

Miranda began counting the bubbles that rose from SpongeBob's undersea pineapple home. Pretty soon she forgot the morning news, the files waiting on her desk, and her husband's many failings. She reached for the remote and raised the volume to a level that drowned out everything else in the world. Together, in their pajamas, mother and son watched *SpongeBob SquarePants* until Jesse had missed the school bus and Miranda was way late for work.

Norah

Norah nursed a ponderous hangover but at the same time felt remarkably refreshed. Wally Day sometimes had that effect on her. A bottle of Evian sat on her desk. She downed four Advil, along with a smidge of Xanax.

She summoned up the mental focus necessary to deal with the issues of the day. First, Wheeler's widow. She needed to get those partnership shares in the Montserrat bank account back into friendly hands, and fast. Presumably, Maggie Wheeler would inherit everything and Norah didn't want Maggie having rights to the information that went along with those shares. She composed and sent an e-mail to Burnam asking for his okay to contact Maggie. Normally, she would walk around to Jack's office, but her head hurt and she didn't want to go out into the light of the hallway.

Next, there was the Senator's wife or, rather, Jack's rumored infatuation with the Senator's wife. Over the years, Jack's propensity for adultery had become the stuff of legend. Secretaries, executives, employees' wives, marketing reps seeking Conquest's business, they were all the same to Jack. Somehow he'd managed to stay married to Lacey, though God only knew how she put up with him. This one was different. Never before had he put the company at risk, but trifling with a Senator's wife seemed a quantum leap. How might the Senator respond? The more Norah thought about it, the more ticked off she got.

A knock sounded at her office door and Norah waved Miranda inside, wondering if the combination of carrot and stick had had the desired effect. The Bluestream filing would have Miranda's fingerprints on it. Miranda's husband had no job and few prospects of finding a job any time soon given the way he had walked out on his law firm. And the Somerset setup should have given Miranda a healthy taste of life in the inner circle. Only a schoolgirl would throw it away because of some picayune accounting rules.

"Norah," said Miranda, "I think I have everything lined up for the filing. I wanted to go over the drill for signatures and document distribution. You know I haven't done this before."

Miranda had a look of resignation on her face, but Norah liked what she heard. No more irksome questions about outside investors and three percent equity and the like. Only some nuts and bolts needed to get the deal done.

Norah handed Miranda a key.

"What's this?"

"Go down to the basement. File Room B is where we keep the documents for all the structured deals. Wheeler used to call it the Batcave. You'll find everything you need in there."

Miranda took the key and left. Norah couldn't tell for certain if the earnest redhead had decided to get with the program, but she seemed pointed in the right direction. And a few days of file immersion in the Batcave conceivably would keep her going that way.

Now that Norah thought about it, Miranda had come through in the clutch. She deserved a promotion and a raise and maybe a mid-year bonus. Norah jotted some figures and fired off an email to the head of HR to set the process in motion. Then she thought again of the look of resignation on Miranda's face. She made a note to herself to call Franklin Payton in a few weeks. If Miranda continued to play ball, she would have Payton resurrect his job offer to Miranda's husband. They would be fine in the end.

"Jesus, Norah, who died?" Jack, without knocking, had come in and flicked on the lights.

A rare look of embarrassment passed over his face. "Besides Wheeler, I mean." He stood by the office window looking out but talking to her at the same time.

"I got your e-mail," he said. "I'm way ahead of you. I talked to Mrs. Wheeler over the weekend, to offer my condolences. She's happy to return the investments. She already signed them over."

"Happy?" asked Norah. "Why would she be happy to give back twenty-five million dollars worth of securities?"

"I told her we would pay a remembrance bonus, of course, out of respect for her husband's fine work."

A remembrance bonus. Nice. "How much?" Norah asked.

"Not a lot. A million dollars."

A headline flashed through Norah's mind: *Conquest Widow Alleges Fraud.*

"That's great, but what if she finds out they're worth twenty-five times that much? She'll know you duped her."

"Not likely," he said. "I can't imagine any way she could get access to that information. Can you?"

David

David slumped into his seat at Velotrade. He had intended to come in earlier, but Miranda had dawdled around the house far longer than normal. He'd pretended to be asleep so he wouldn't have to face her.

"Where you been?" asked Fib, his voice heavy with disapproval. "Day trading is a job." He took a closer look at David and made a face. "You do look a bit worn."

David barely had the energy to respond. He gave Fib a weak wave and began scanning the morning's market information. He read over his trading log from the previous week and looked at the data on his practice stocks. It all seemed like it had happened ages ago.

Another click brought up additional analytics. He saw that he had prepared candlesticks on the practice stocks showing price movements in fifteen-minute increments. One of the stocks, Keystone, looked modestly interesting. For some reason, every afternoon between one-thirty and three-thirty, Keystone's price fell about a dollar. The price level didn't seem to matter nor did any price movements earlier or later in the day. Sometimes it climbed for a while, but at the end of that two-hour window, every day, Keystone had fallen nearly a buck. He had no idea what caused the pattern. Maybe an institutional trader sold off a few lots every day. Maybe it was a program trade by one of the big hedge funds. In any case, it was a verifiable market event, not a bizarre concoction like Fib's *Sex and the City* trade.

The negative was that a one-dollar price movement wouldn't generate much profit. He would have to short several thousand shares to make the trade worthwhile. If he used $10,000 of his own money, Velotrade would match that on margin. Keystone currently sold for about eleven bucks a share, so $20,000 would let him short around 1,800 shares. Not as much as he would have liked, but enough to do some damage. He could make a profit of $1,800 or so in a day and then repeat it the next day and the day after, if the pattern held. He set the analytics to track back several months.

While the program ran, he couldn't help wondering what had happened with Payton-Mosel. They had fallen all over him at the interview, but then...nothing. It was as if some unseen hand had dangled the opportunity within his reach and then snatched it away.

A chart popped up on his screen. The Keystone pattern held for the preceding three months. His interest level stepped up a notch. He decided to run a test. He would short a hundred shares to learn the drill. If all went well, then tomorrow he might step it up.

He placed his order. One hundred shares, short sell at 10.97. Execute immediately.

Two hours to kill while he waited for the window to close. He surfed, checking the sports news for tidbits to talk about with Jesse. David was in the middle of an Astros update when a popup ad enticed him to *Bling.com*. He browsed the offerings until he came across a simple and tasteful bracelet that he thought would look great on Miranda's wrist. It cost almost a thousand bucks, but if his trading strategy worked out... He put it in his shopping cart for future reference and logged off.

At three-thirty, a timer clicked and Keystone's price came on the screen—10.02. Right where it was supposed to be. He logged an order to buy enough shares to cover his short. Ninety-five cents per share on one hundred shares. After costs, he had made next to nothing, but that wasn't the point. His test was a success. David chuckled loudly enough that he got a sidelong *What's with you?* from Fib.

Maybe he wouldn't need a job. He was a day trader!

Lulu

To Lulu's surprise, Lacey Burnam agreed to an interview. No objections and no conditions.

"Come by the house around eleven," she'd said breezily. "We'll talk." As if answering a reporter's questions about her husband's public philanderings were an everyday occurrence. As if meeting her husband's old college girlfriend...well, it occurred to Lulu that Lacey conceivably didn't know about that. Lulu herself was curious to finally meet the woman for whom Jack had dumped her two decades earlier. Lulu wasn't at all unhappy with the life she had led, but she couldn't deny her interest in meeting the woman who had the husband Lulu once thought would be her own.

She parked in a circular cobblestone driveway off Willowick Drive, not far from the River Oaks Country Club. The Burnam house was as big as a hotel, built in the style of a Mediterranean villa. The neighboring homes were barely visible through the surrounding pine forest. Lacey met her at the door and showed her into what she called the sun room, a glass-enclosed space toward the back of the house filled with plants, white wicker and floral cushions. While Lacey brewed tea, Lulu admired an eye-popping arrangement of flowering cactuses.

"They're called zygocacti," Lacey explained. "A type of cactus but from the rain forest, not the desert. Perfect for Houston." She wore perfectly-tailored but comfortable-looking corduroy pants and a red cashmere sweater. Lacey poured the tea and pushed several varieties of scones in Lulu's direction. Despite the enormous house and all the trappings, Lulu thought, Lacey had an agreeable way about her.

Having an excuse to meet Lacey Burnam for old time's sake was fine, but Lulu had no expectation that the exercise would produce a story. After Ed ordered her to do the interview, Lulu had dutifully spent a half-day reading up on Kathie Lee Gifford, Hillary Clinton and other wives who had found themselves in similarly humiliating circumstances. The research confirmed her instincts. Lacey almost certainly would reject the rumors and profess faith in her husband's fidelity. Then, after the media storm ran its course, she would cut his nuts into tiny pieces and stir them into his morning cereal.

"Mrs. Burnam," Lulu began, "I suppose we should get right to business."

"Lacey. Please call me Lacey."

"Lacey, can you comment on the rumors regarding your husband and a certain Senator's wife?"

Lacey laughed. "You don't seem like the kind of a woman who wants to write for the *National Enquirer*. You cover business news, don't you?"

Apparently Lacey had done some background research of her own. Moreover, her blithe answers made it quite apparent that she had no intention of saying anything about her husband's extramarital activities.

Lulu was puzzled. "If you don't want to talk about the affair—the *alleged* affair—then why did you invite me here?"

Lacey reached for the teapot and made a pouring motion. "More?"

She handed Lulu a handwritten note addressed to *Jack Burnam, CEO*. The note said, in the simplest of terms, that its sender had known Russ Wheeler, had a copy of certain confidential Conquest files and would return same to Conquest for one million dollars. Otherwise, the files would be released to the news media. It was signed by someone named Sherry Shipley. The yellow paper, purple ink and loopy handwriting suggested that

Sherry might not be particularly well versed in matters of high finance. But no matter, thought Lulu. She didn't need to understand Wheeler's files to believe that Conquest would pay for their return.

"How'd you get this, if you don't mind my asking?" said Lulu.

"Sherry Shipley was my personal trainer. She left this note for me over the weekend. She knew Russ Wheeler, who..."

Lulu completed the sentence. "...used to work for Conquest but died in an accident two weeks ago." Lulu thought out loud. "So Wheeler had some dirt on Conquest, Sherry found out about it and now she wants to blackmail the company. Do you have any idea what the dirt is?"

"Not really. Jack and I don't talk about his business. I do know that Wheeler was a rising star at the company. He certainly was in a position to know things that might cause a flap."

Lulu evaluated the possibilities. According to the news reports, Wheeler died in California, where he had been working on the Bluestream transaction. A domino fell. Lulu's first instincts had been right on target. Bluestream's technology was a dud and Wheeler's files would prove it. No other explanation made sense. Josh's demonstration was a hoax, given at Burnam's direction in the hope of a story that would throw the stock market into a buying frenzy. Sherry, who must have been Wheeler's mistress or girlfriend, somehow got into the files. After he died, she looked at them and figured out that her gold digging ass sat atop a mother lode.

"Why are you showing me this?" Lulu asked.

Lacey's face tightened. "I don't know exactly what this is about, but it sounds bad. A little rumpus at the company might help Jack keep his mind on business." She sipped her tea. "It's possible Jack has had too much time on his hands lately."

This made sense of a sort. A dose of bad news about a blackmail scheme, coming hard on the heels of the rumors about Lorelei Logan, might suggest a CEO not fully in control. It could trigger rumblings that at least would force Jack to stay close to home for a while. Even when things are quiet, Lulu figured, the logistics of diddling a Senator's wife must be pretty daunting.

Lacey handed over another piece of notepaper. It contained the name, address and telephone number of the Ab-Salute Holistic Fitness Center and Spa.

"This is where Sherry works. If she isn't there, they'll know where she lives." Lacey reached for the first piece of paper. "I need the blackmail note back, of course. Jack hasn't seen it yet. I expect I'll give it to him in a day or two. Does that give you enough time?"

"Sure," Lulu said. She reached for one of the scones and took a bite. Mmm, there was a hint of orange in with the cinnamon. She saw Lacey watching her.

"I understand you went to Duke," Lacey said brightly. "I was Alpha Phi. Too bad we never met. I think we might have been friends."

Lulu, who had loathed sororities in her college years and regarded grown women who still talked about their sorority days as cases of arrested development, strangely found herself agreeing. She savored the last of a second scone before answering. "Better late than never."

Miranda

Miranda stood in a large windowless basement room stacked with bound volumes, red rope folders and loose documents. File Room B, aka the Batcave. She had worked at Conquest for years, but hadn't learned of its existence until now.

After spending the morning on the sofa with Jesse watching *SpongeBob*, she felt her attitude adjusting. All those bubbles. Just as Sandy Cheeks eventually decided that Bikini Bottom wasn't so bad, Miranda would make the best of her new situation. If she couldn't leave Conquest behind, she would do the job to the best of her abilities. She would learn everything she could about these mysterious off-balance-sheet deals and more. The lawyers and auditors, not to mention Norah, had approved everything. Who was she to question what they had been doing for years? She would become the new Wheeler.

She picked up a file at random, one labeled *Boiler*. She recalled that two years earlier Conquest had announced a joint venture with a company called O-Power that had a new design for ocean thermal energy conversion. At the time, it had seemed to Miranda like one of Conquest's more promising new undertakings, but Burnam had called it off after six months, blaming technical problems with the O-Power design. Miranda assumed that Conquest had written off a sizeable loss.

Not so, according to the deal file. Conquest had set up Boiler as a long-term joint venture with O-Power. An independent energy consultant had signed off on a projection of revenues, sales and expenses. Fifty thousand megawatt-hours the first year. A hundred thousand the second year. And so on for twenty years, right up to full capacity. Then, using mark-to-market accounting, Conquest had calculated a present value of the projected profit and booked it as a gain, all in the year the joint venture had been formed. A profit of $210 million. Miranda thought about the analysis. Mark-to-market was a standard accounting treatment for stocks and bonds and other assets with visible pricing. She hadn't seen it used for something like this, but they did have the energy consultant's independent valuation. D&D had signed off as did Conquest's outside lawyers, but O-Power's accountants had balked. Hmmm.

She had come to work late, and the work day wasn't yet over, but Miranda decided to go home. She felt her attitude adjustment wavering.

CHAPTER 10. TUESDAY

CQC 50.44 1.33↓

Lulu

Lulu banged away at her story. She was sure this one would cause a cave-in at Conquest Plaza. She didn't usually suggest headlines—that was the editor's job—but this time she couldn't resist: *Bluestream Only a Trickle?*.

> Confidential documents reveal that Conquest's pending acquisition of Bluestream has begun to unravel. The documents confirm the suspicions of many industry insiders that Conquest misstepped badly when it committed $2 billion to buy the tiny California research and development shop...

Lulu paused, wondering exactly what Wheeler's files contained. There was no question in her mind she had the big picture right. It was only a matter of fleshing out some details.

She would feel better if she could track down Sherry Shipley. She had gotten Sherry's home address at the Ab-Salute and camped out there for most of a day, until a neighbor told her that Sherry had gone away. No one would say where she'd gone or when she might return. If Lulu were in Sherry's shoes, she would do the same thing, but Lulu's story simply couldn't wait any longer.

> Conquest acquired Bluestream to gain access to a highly ambitious project known as Bluebox. Bluebox seeks to meld into a single hand-held device a variety of highly

> innovative telecommunications and entertainment technologies. The *Examiner* has learned, however, that design and development flaws plague the project. 'Unfortunately,' said a source inside Bluestream, 'it's a great idea whose time hasn't yet arrived.'

Lulu saw it like this. Burnam had pushed his financial people to strike a deal to buy Bluestream. Then his technical people took a harder look at Bluebox and put up red flags. Burnam sent Wheeler to California to get a handle on the situation and his report said that Bluebox was a bust. When Wheeler went down, his girlfriend Sherry Shipley had waylaid his files. Sherry didn't have to understand the technology to know Conquest would pay to keep the report under wraps. Now Burnam had called Josh to Houston for a showdown. It all fit.

> In light of this startling new information, the Bluestream deal looms as a fatal mistake for Conquest CEO Jack Burnam, who already is mired in a scandal regarding an alleged romantic relationship with Lorelei Logan, wife of Senator Thomas Logan. The prospect of such a prodigious mistake made while the CEO's tumultuous personal life dominates the company's attention must have the members of Conquest's Board of Directors scratching their collective heads.

Pretty good, thought Lulu, but there was a problem. She still didn't have a hard on-the-record source and without one Ed wasn't going to let her story go to press. She looked away from the computer and thought about how badly she needed this story. She knew the story was right. She *knew* it.

If Ed needed another source, she would make damn sure she got one. She resumed typing.

Miranda

Although Miranda, like every Conquest employee, knew of the legendary Shapeshifters, never before had she watched the committee in action. Norah had insisted she attend. *Face time with the boss,* she'd said. *Good for your profile.* Sure enough, shortly after Miranda got settled, Burnam entered and sat down at the opposite end of the conference table.

To Miranda's surprise, Winston Loomis entered the room next and took the hot seat. She had assumed that most of the new product ideas were pitched by young hot-shots on the way up, but Loomis didn't fit that mold at all. About sixty years old, Loomis worked in corporate compliance and affected an absent-minded-professor personae.

He began his pitch in a roundabout fashion. "The Greek philosopher Diogenes," he said, "carried a lamp through Athens in broad daylight in search of an honest man." With a nervous flourish, he removed a device from a case and held it up for the committee to see. "This is a modern-day Diogenes lamp."

To Miranda, the device looked like Jesse's Super-Soaker water rifle, except it had an array of wires and lights.

"A few years ago," Loomis continued, "scientists determined that magnetic resonance imaging, known commonly as MRI, can detect a neuro-physiological difference between a true statement and a lie. MRI tracks blood flow to groups of neurons as they fire. As with many brain functions, one particular group of neurons fires when a person tells a lie. To a trained observer, it's as obvious as Pinocchio's nose."

Loomis picked up the Lamp and pointed it at Burnam. A small circle of light appeared above his right eye.

"Point that damn thing somewhere else," Burnam snapped.

Loomis swung around and pointed it at Miranda. "If you don't mind," he said, "tell me where you are at this moment."

Startled at first, Miranda recovered quickly. "I'm in a conference room at Conquest Plaza in Houston, Texas," she said.

The Lamp flashed green.

"Let's try that again," said Loomis. "Where are you?"

Miranda smiled, getting the idea. "I am in the Metropolitan Museum of Art in New York City."

The Lamp flashed yellow.

"Would you tell us your name, please?"

She was beginning to enjoy this. "Madame Curie," she said.

Loomis went back and forth with Miranda—green, yellow, yellow, green—asking her progressively more difficult questions, until the committee members began shifting in their chairs. Although the Lamp unerringly distinguished Miranda's fabrications from the truth, the Shapeshifters didn't seem to find the Lamp nearly as impressive as she did.

Loomis shifted gears. "Old fashioned polygraph machines measure pulse rate and heartbeat, but good liars can control these indicators, and sometimes extraneous factors cause false readings. That's why most courts don't admit polygraph evidence. Diogenes Lamp, however, is one hundred percent accurate. No one can manipulate their neurons."

Miranda thought about the potential market for the device. Police departments, of course, for prisoner interrogation. And the entire judicial system. She decided to offer Loomis a little help. "Schools and colleges could use this," she blurted, "to keep students from cheating. And how about airport security? And right here at Conquest, we could use it to screen job applicants."

She saw Burnam staring at her and broke off. One of the committee members yawned and another excused herself to take a call.

"Are there any questions?" Loomis asked gamely.

In the ensuing silence, as he swung the Lamp around in preparation for returning it to its case, the Lamp's small circle of light swept fleetingly across Burnam's forehead.

Just at that moment, bringing the meeting to a close, Burnam said, "This looks very promising. We'll give it serious consideration."

Yellow.

David

At one-fifteen, David placed the order. Keystone, *two* hundred shares. Short sell at 11.02. Hmm, it was up a smidge from the day before. Execute immediately. He was tempted to increase his bet. Maybe *five* hundred shares.

He stopped. Stick to the plan. Whether it was two hundred or five hundred didn't matter. What mattered was whether the pattern would hold for another day.

Congratulating himself on his self-discipline, he logged onto CNN and browsed the day's events. If he saw something interesting, he might bring it to Miranda's attention. Of course, for that to happen they would have to be on speaking terms, which they weren't. It was lonely on the living room sofa.

Fib tried to convince him to try another trade, something he called a correlated forex pair. It sounded interesting and pretty exotic, but David passed. Stick to the plan, he told himself.

At three-twenty-eight, David checked Keystone and found it at 10.12, right on the mark. He put in his buy order and calculated a profit of $180. Fib, passing behind him on his way to the coffee machine, snickered into his hand.

David felt a pang of regret. If he'd had the nerve, he could have made some real money.

No matter. Tomorrow was another day. The *Bling* package hadn't arrived yet anyway.

Miranda

Miranda was at her desk preparing the final paperwork on the Bluestream filing when her assistant buzzed. "Miranda, your friend Willa is on the phone. Do you want to take it?"

Miranda remembered calling Willa for a reality check nearly two weeks earlier when she had first been assigned to work on Bluestream. She picked up the line.

"I've got someone you might want to talk to," said Willa. "He's on hold."

"Who is it?" Miranda asked.

"He's a friend of mine, but he won't tell you his name because he doesn't want this traced back to him. He works at a bank in New York that has done some deals with Conquest over the past few years. If you're still interested in learning more about this kind of business."

Was she? At this point, Miranda wasn't sure if she wanted to know more, especially from an anonymous source. It seemed a bit too clandestine, but before she could answer another voice came on the line. Very aggressive, very Wall Street.

"The deal was called Booster," said the voice. "Five hundred million dollars. Closed about two months ago."

"Are you sure?" said Miranda. "Conquest hasn't closed any acquisitions in the past couple of months."

"This is different."

"Okay," said Miranda. "Walk me through it."

"In this deal, Conquest sold bandwidth capacity—you know, basically space on the Internet—to a shell company called Booster. A billion units a year for the next five years. Booster made one upfront payment for forward deliveries of bandwidth. They call it a *prepaid forward*."

"But if Booster is a shell company, where did it get the money?"

"That's the next step. Booster signed a mirror contract to sell all the bandwidth it bought from Conquest to a group of banks. My bank organized the syndicate."

He didn't sound proud of his role in the deal.

"Why does a group of banks need that much bandwidth?" Miranda asked.

"They don't. They sell it back to Conquest."

"So what's the point?"

"The banks paid for the bandwidth in one up-front payment, same as Booster. Five hundred million. But when Conquest bought it back, it agreed to make payments over time. One hundred million a year for five years. Plus some extra for the banks' transaction fees."

Miranda's eyes widened. "That sounds a lot like a loan."

Willa interrupted. "The lawyers and accountants don't treat it like a loan. There's enough window dressing to give it a different economic substance. That way Conquest doesn't have to report this to the rating agencies."

"That's part of it," said the voice, "but that's not all. Conquest reported the half billion dollars up front as revenue. It was booked as a payment for sale of bandwidth."

Miranda stood and walked in a slow circle around her desk. With Bluestream at least there was some genuine business activity underneath the fancy footwork. Likewise Boiler, which had started as an effort to build an ocean thermal power plant. But this deal seemed like nothing more than musical chairs. Conquest supposedly had earned $500 million by signing a bunch of legal documents. The bandwidth in the deal might as well have been potatoes, or cupcakes.

"Okay," she said, sitting back down. "I can imagine that last quarter the company needed some extra revenue to hit its earnings target. Maybe that's why they called it Booster. So Norah and the accountants decided to bend the rules, just once. Then the next quarter the earnings would bounce back and they wouldn't have to do it again."

"That's exactly how this got started, except it wasn't last quarter. We closed the first Booster deal eleven quarters ago."

Miranda's voice rose. "You're telling me that Conquest has done one of these deals every quarter for nearly three years?"

"Oh no. Sometimes, they did two or three in the same quarter."

Sherry

Precious things may lead one astray, the Master had said. *She who stands on tiptoe cannot maintain the pace.*

Sherry had moved into the spare room at the Master's studio after dropping off her blackmail note at the Ab-Salute. It would be nicer if she could stay in her own cozy apartment with Taco, but Sherry knew the manager would come by asking for the rent money she didn't have. Besides, Wheeler had thought it smart to go all the way to Mexico to hide out. She couldn't afford to leave the country, but at least she could avoid her apartment for a few days.

At first it was fantastic staying with the Master. She'd taken T'ai Chi lessons twice daily and he had let her teach a beginner class. Better yet, on the wall he hung a poster made with a photo he'd taken of her several months earlier. In it she wore a stretch cotton tube top and workout pants, the kind with a roll-down waist that showed about an acre of abdomen. The camera had caught her in the midst of a *Snake Sticks Out Its Tongue* so perfect he had asked if he could use it in his advertising materials. She said yes, of course, considering all he had done for her. When she noticed some of the students in the beginner class studying the poster, she replicated the pose and got a nice round of applause.

But after class, right out of the blue, the Master had jabbed her about *precious things*. And then he insisted on analyzing her aura. *A tint of greed discolors your emanations. Greed plagues all beings but greed unchecked leads to imbalance.*

Uh-oh. He seemed to know all about Conquest, although she hadn't breathed a word to him or anybody. In truth, she had already begun to have second thoughts about asking for so much money. *Underneath the color of greed lies that of lust, like a red sun shining behind a yellow moon during an eclipse.* Excessive lust? Wow, he knew about Feo, too. Her feelings for Feo must be pretty strong. *You are wise to seek help at an early stage. Your aura contains no hue of grey or black, which means that appropriate therapies may heal your malady.*

Sherry heaved a sigh of relief. She could be healed.The Master would give her guidance.

He prescribed something called the *Cosmic Beam*. He gave her instructions for faster healing. *Be with nature. Be cheerful. Drink plenty of water. Wash hands and feet at regular intervals. Go barefoot. Practice the Set three times every day.* When the Master sensed that she was ready, the Sadhak would direct to her a beam of universal energy, supplemented by magnetic waves from the earth's gravitational field. With luck, the *Beam* would rebalance her personal energy centers.

"Who's the Sadhak?" Sherry asked. She had hoped to keep things a little more private.

The Master showed her into a small office where, to her surprise, he had a computer, complete with Internet access. Apparently he wasn't as holistic as she thought. He clicked the mouse and brought up the Sadhak's website: *The Cosmic Beam*.

"The Sadhak is a very wise healer and teacher. He lives in a small village in the mountains in India. He is very pure. That is what makes him able to direct the universal energy to heal people." The Master paused. "I sent him a copy of your photo to help me analyze your aura."

Sherry considered all this a stroke of good fortune, but wondered what she would be able to do to repay the Sadhak for his services. She knew that the universal energy wasn't free, and she didn't have any cash. "How will I make payment to him?" she asked.

"The Sadhak does not refuse healing merely on the ground that one cannot pay in cash. If a sufferer has no money, then the sufferer may offer payment in kind."

"Payment in kind? What could I offer that might be of use to the Sadhak?"

The Master typed a quick e-mail and hit *Send*. The answer came back with startling speed, almost as if the Sadhak were sitting and waiting at his own computer terminal over in his mountain village.

"You're in luck," said the Master. "The Sadhak says to send more photos."

Jack

"So where are you taking me this time? Is it a drive-in movie or the senior prom?"

Jack and Lorelei again occupied the back of his limo. She wore an overcoat, medium heels, sunglasses and a head scarf. Very Jackie Kennedy.

"Let's go, Santo," Jack said, at the same time raising the privacy panel.

Lorelei at first seemed a bit distant to Jack, but his disquiet vanished when she took off the head scarf and opened her overcoat. Underneath it she wore a velvet gown with a plunging neckline that gave him a nearly unobstructed view of the most fantastic fifty-year-old rack he had ever seen. The tops of her breasts undulated with the motions of the limo as it wove through traffic. It took every bit of Jack's self-control not to jump her right there. "Godamighty," was all he could think of to say, but it seemed to be plenty. She closed the coat with a satisfied smirk and sunk down into the soft leather seat.

Since their first encounter, Jack had felt himself changing. Usually, his interest in a woman waned as soon as he got her into bed. Once they had done it, he would disentangle himself and begin the pursuit of his next quarry. It took a rare woman to hold his interest for more than a few weeks.

Lorelei, needless to say, fell into a different class altogether. He'd never felt such an attraction. He thought about her constantly and, instead of wondering how to extricate himself from the relationship, found himself planning their future together. He was convinced that he was in the throes of genuine adult love. The fact that the crinkle of her tiny crow's feet and the modest sag of her breasts didn't repulse him stood as a signal of his new-found maturity. And the thought of another man's hands on those still-excellent breasts made him savage with jealousy, notwithstanding that those hands belonged to her husband and might rightfully deserve some connubial distraction from time to time.

Moreover, he was sure that she felt the same way that he did. They had burned up the telephone wires since their night at the Ship Channel. Every day she spoke to him with open scorn of life in Washington and with palpable dread of her husband's upcoming run for the presidency. National affairs and electoral calculations left the Senator exhausted, with no time or energy for her or his family. She wanted to get off the political merry-go-round and come home to Texas.

Twice in ten days he had commandeered the company jet for jaunts to see her. At a fundraiser, when they got a private moment, she had hinted that she might be doing the Senator a favor if she left him before he announced his candidacy, so that he could go about campaigning without any personal distractions. The other time she invited Jack on a private tour at the Hirshhorn Museum and somehow arranged for their elevator to get stuck between floors for an exhilarating fifteen minutes.

It was plain to Jack that he faced the greatest merger opportunity of his lifetime. And, as with any merger, certain assets would become redundant. Like Lacey. And Maggie. And the Senator.

"So where *are* you taking me?"

Her voice jolted him back into the moment. "You like museums, right?" he said.

Santo parked the limo in front of a large Spanish Revival house in the Broadacres subdivision, not far from the Rice Campus and the Houston Museum District. He walked around and opened the rear door. Jack took Lorelei's arm and she clasped her overcoat's lapels modestly as they walked up the front walk and passed through the front door.

The main hallway contained a row of life-sized marble busts standing on oaken plinths, each with a brass nameplate. Rockefeller. Morgan. Vanderbilt. Gould. Mellon.

“I give up,” said Lorelei. “What are these things for?”

“This is going to be the Museum of American Business,” Jack answered. “We'll have audio-visuals to tell the story of the great CEO's down through the years. Exhibits to teach the kids about capitalism and free markets. Lectures by some of today's prominent business leaders. It'll be the only one of its kind.”

Lorelei chuckled. “And I thought politicians have big egos.”

“Of course,” continued Jack, “all these busts are from the nineteenth century. When it's finished, the series will go all the way up to the present day, if you get what I mean.”

“There's one of you?”

Jack led her down a hallway. They stepped over a canvas floor tarp to the center of a side room where an unfinished sculpture stood on a wooden table surrounded by sculptor's tools. It seemed to be about a quarter-size larger than all the others and there was no doubt about who it represented.

Jack dropped to one knee and took Lorelei's hand in his own.

“Jack, what the hell are you doing?”

Words began to spew out of him. He told her of his plans for the future and how he wanted her to join him. He talked of how he had made Conquest into one of the leading companies of the world, but that wasn't enough. He wanted more, much more, and he wanted her at his side, here in Texas, to help him do it. He popped the question.

Lorelei withdrew her hand and removed her sunglasses. “Let me make sure I understand,” she said. “You want me to divorce the Senator and leave Washington. You're going to divorce your wife. You want us to get married. Is that it?”

“Exactly. Right away. As soon as possible.”

At precisely that moment the rays of the setting sun burst through the windows. A portion of the room was plunged into darkening shadows, shadows that he felt sure would remind Lorelei of her husband and her unhappy life in Washington. At the same time, the sun's final yellow beams shone like a spotlight on his unfinished, oversized likeness.

For an agonizingly long time, Lorelei turned away. Then she turned back to Jack. "You've got some big balls," she said. "I like that. I'll give it some serious thought. Very serious."

In Jack's world, when a woman didn't say *no*, she had said *yes*. He stood happily and spread his arms. Lorelei stepped into his embrace.

Sherry

Sherry spent the evening browsing at Bayou Bygones. After two days at the Master's studio waiting to hear from Conquest, she needed to get out for at least a few hours. The shop carried a tempting mixture of vintage clothing, antiques and curios, and Sherry had passed more than a few lunch breaks in its narrow aisles as if she had money to spend on such things. Maybe one day soon she would.

On this visit it wasn't clothing or jewelry that captured her attention, but rather an old black-and-white photograph in a frosted glass frame that brought her up short. In the picture, a slim young woman in a white ruffled dress, tights and white shoes stood on a low stage maintaining an absolutely flawless *Part the Clouds*.

Wait, thought Sherry, looking more closely and laughing at herself. The woman wasn't doing Tai Chi. She wore a tutu and ballet shoes. A small orchestra played at the side of the stage. The young woman was a ballerina.

Sherry showed the photograph to the owner of the store, herself something of an antique. "Do you know who this is?" Sherry asked.

The old woman nodded. "That's Belle Rivard. She had a ballet academy near here."

"Had?"

"Belle passed, quite a while back. She was married to a man in the oil business." She paused, as if reminiscing. "In those days everyone in Houston was in the oil business. He died and Belle pretty much lost interest in things after that."

The woman turned the photograph over and showed Sherry the handwritten note on the back. *Emerald Room, Shamrock Hotel, August, 1949.*

"Belle came here from San Francisco and never went back. This picture must be from one of her first performances."

"Where is the Shamrock? I've never seen it."

"They tore it down about twenty years ago. Where the Medical Center is now."

The image of the this young dancer in the Houston of fifty years earlier fascinated Sherry, and she wanted to know more. "What was she like?"

* * * * *

A BALLERINA IN THE LAND OF THE BIG RICH

HOUSTON, 1949

"Welcome to the Shamrock Hotel."

The man who had spoken to Arabella was skinny and looked about sixty years old. He didn't wear cowboy boots or a cowboy hat and didn't look at all the way she expected someone from Texas to look.

"Do you work for Mr. McCarthy?" she asked.

The man laughed. "Sure. I was in the oil patch until I ruined my arm, then he gave me this job. Mr. McCarthy owns this place. This was all his idea, every bit of it." Eddie gestured at the immense Art Deco lobby with a wave that took in capacious green walls framed by burled mahogany woodwork. "My name's Eddie. I'm an Assistant Manager."

Arabella gasped quietly. She had never seen such a seamless blend of extravagance and dubious taste, and couldn't find the right words to respond. At that moment, Arabella's traveling companion, Christophe, made his way through the entrance, looking as if he might collapse. Although they had flown from San Francisco in relative comfort on the private airplane sent by the Shamrock, the shock of arriving in Houston's sweltering August heat appeared to have put Christophe in a near-coma. Arabella, on the other hand, felt strangely energetic and full of curiosity.

"Would you like a tour of the hotel, or do you want to go to your rooms first?" Eddie asked.

"Tour," said Arabella.

"Room," gasped Christophe. He staggered behind a bell boy pushing a luggage cart.

"Don't worry about him," Arabella told Eddie. "He's French."

Eddie nodded as if that explained everything. "Come with me, please," he said as he began walking. "The Shamrock is eighteen stories tall and has eleven hundred rooms. It cost twenty-one million dollars and is the largest hotel built in the United States in the last ten years. Mr. McCarthy's goal was to build the finest hotel in America, better than the Waldorf Astoria. Every room has a television, a telephone, a push-button music system and at least one item of original art. In the basement we freeze all the garbage before they take it away." He gave her a sideways glance. "The heat, you know."

They had reached the front desk and Eddie handed her a fountain pen to sign the registration book.

"Green ink?"

"Mr. McCarthy is Irish. The hotel roof is made of green tile, all the inside walls are painted green, the tablecloths and napkins are green, and all the employees wear green uniforms. Sixty-three different shades, though, so it doesn't get monotonous."

Arabella raised an eyebrow.

Eddie led Arabella to the entrance of a lovely glass-enclosed cafe called the Pine Grill that looked out on a fan-shaped swimming pool as big as a lake. Lush rows of palms, bamboo and other tropicals lined the pool apron and created narrow shafts of shade.

Eddie followed her gaze. "Ah yes, our famous pool. The largest outdoor swimming pool in the world. Three-story diving tower. Gardens designed by Ralph Ellis Gunn. I can get you a ticket to tomorrow's exhibition if you like."

"Exhibition?"

"Water skiing. Twice each week. Very popular."

Arabella saw a tiny but powerful-looking motorboat tied up in the deep end. They had water skiing on a swimming pool. Shaking her head, she turned back to Eddie. "Can you show me where we will dance?"

They walked down a wide hallway until Eddie stopped and pushed open a set of heavy wooden double-doors. "This is the Emerald Room," he said. "We've already had Sophie Tucker, Dinah Shore and Dorothy Lamour on this stage. Next year Frank Sinatra is coming. But you'll be our first ballet dancers." Eddie's tone suggested he wouldn't be surprised if they were also the last.

Months earlier, someone from the Shamrock had contacted the San Francisco Ballet, where Arabella and Christophe were members of the troupe, with an offer of an extremely generous donation as well as a royalty in something called the New Ulm oil field, if the company could arrange for two dancers to perform a week of recitals at the hotel's cabaret. Arabella volunteered immediately, having listened with amused fascination to the radio broadcast of the Shamrock's raucous grand opening a few months' earlier, when a crowd of 50,000, including 150 Hollywood celebrities flown in for the occasion, somehow descended into such chaos that the broadcast had shut off in midstream. She couldn't wait to see the Shamrock, but none of other dancers in the troupe expressed the slightest interest in the trip. The company director finally had coerced Christophe with the promise of a more prominent role the first ballet to be presented upon their return.

She studied the Emerald Room, noting the plush leather seating, the gold strands somehow woven into the floor, and the intimately low stage. The room would seat, she guessed, an audience of about eight hundred, and she wondered how many their performances would draw to this peculiar venue. "This will do just fine," she said to herself as much as to Eddie.

The tour concluded, Eddie delivered Arabella to her room on the tenth floor.

"Thank you," she said, a tone of mild disappointment in her voice.

"Was there something else?" Eddie asked.

She had decided she liked Eddie well enough. "I'm going to be here about ten days altogether," she said, "and I've never been to Houston before. Would you be willing to show me around the city?"

A grin creased Eddie's face. "Of course. My instructions are to take care of anything you need."

"And one more thing," said Arabella. "From what I've heard, every third person in this town is an oilman. A wildcatter. Will I be able to meet one?"

"Not to worry," said Eddie, as he closed the door to her room. "At last count, there's 284 millionaires in Houston and I know quite a few of them. Not to worry."

After several afternoon rehearsals with a small contingent from the Houston Symphony Orchestra, Arabella and Christophe began their week of performances before a middling Tuesday evening audience. They opened with a series of popular *pas de deux* from *Giselle*, *Sleeping Beauty* and *Flower Festival at Genzano*. After an intermission, they performed the *grand pas de deux* from *Don Quixote*, a choice Arabella thought particularly appropriate for this city of dream-chasers. Allowing time for costume changes and intermission, the show lasted a little over an hour. Arabella speculated that many in the audience had never before seen a ballet performance, but they nevertheless applauded fiercely at each break. Christophe's dancing was perfunctory, but the audience seemed much more focused on her anyway. As the week progressed, the number of empty seats in the Emerald Room diminished a bit each evening.

As Eddie put it, "People here want to do a little culture now and then."

True to his word, Eddie drove her around the city for a few hours every morning, always with a bit of Texas brag thrown in. "Texas has two-thirds of the nation's oil reserves, you know, and refines ninety percent of the oil pumped in the whole country." She visited the newly-completed San Jacinto Monument, "the world's tallest war memorial." They drove past a working oil field where she saw a forest of iron derricks and an army of roughnecks, and Eddie boasted that Texas wildcatters drilled more than ten thousand wells a year. At the Ship Channel, the fumes of the refineries and petrochemical plants forced her to hold her nose and roll up the car's windows. Eddie took her to shop at The Fashion, a store that rivaled any place in San Francisco, and he took her for lunch at a place called Swayze's that advertised "the best BBQ in the world or any other place." She saw a rodeo and the Pin Oak Charity Horse Show, and one rainy day Eddie took her to the Houston Museum of Fine Arts where she saw paintings by Van Gogh, Braque, Derain and O'Keefe. "You ain't the only culture in town," he said with a gentle poke in the ribs. Every day she invited Christophe to join them, but he remained in his room complaining of the heat and general vulgarity of the place. He was right, thought Arabella, everything was *gauche* beyond words, but she liked it anyway.

On Saturday night, they presented their final performance to a full house. Christophe finally seemed energized, possibly buoyed by the prospect of a speedy return to San Francisco, and Arabella felt that their dancing was truly exceptional. For an encore, they performed the *Black Swan pas de deux*, and received a thunderous standing ovation. Hands clapped, boots stomped, and Texas-accented shouts of *bravo* and *brava* resounded. "You're a smash," said Eddie. "I couldn't have been more wrong."

Eddie brought to her dressing room an invitation for her and Christophe to join a small group of oilmen and their wives for drinks at the Cork Club on the hotel's top floor. "You wanted to meet an oilman," he said. "They don't let you join the Cork Club unless you're worth at least a million dollars."

She expected Christophe to beg off, but he opted to join the group. They sat at a table with three jovial men and their pampered wives. The wives reminded her of some of the patrons' wives she had met in San Francisco, but the men seemed a breed of their own. The wives peppered her and Christophe with questions about their training and life as professional dancers. The men told them anecdotes of careers spent in the oil patch and million-dollar deals done on a handshake, and argued among themselves about who had the best Cadillac. After the third round of drinks, one of them made a good-natured offer to buy Christophe a regular pair of men's pants so he wouldn't have to dance in his underwear, and even Christophe laughed at that one. At the end of the evening, she headed back to her room feeling that the trip had been a thorough success.

The next morning, Arabella took a final breakfast alone at the Pine Grill before the drive to the airport. She was nibbling a pastry and sipping coffee when one of wives she'd met the evening before stopped at her table.

"Do you mind if I join you? I'm Bonnie, in case you don't recognize me. I was part of your adoring crowd last night."

"Thank you." Arabella hadn't remembered the woman's name, but recalled that she had a warm laugh and a straightforward way about her. "Of course, Bonnie. Please sit down."

"I'll get right to the point," Bonnie began. "A few of us ladies have been talking and we have a proposition. It's a long shot, but we were wondering if you might like to stay here in Houston and open a ballet academy. We don't have anything like that and I know dozens of mothers that would love to send their daughters to you. And a few sons, too."

Arabella gazed at her in surprise.

"Could you at least think it over?" Bonnie asked.

Arabella did think it over. She was twenty-seven years old. She might have another five years with the troupe, but she knew by now that she wasn't going to dance the lead roles. She would never be a *prima ballerina*, but only a member of the troupe. And Houston, despite its coarseness, had become agreeable to her. She liked its enthusiasm and its lack of airs.

"I'm very flattered," she said haltingly, "but I don't have money to start a ballet school."

"Oh, we suspected that might be the case. We would be prepared to double whatever you're earning now. We've already picked out a nice apartment for you over by River Oaks. We'll pay all the expenses of the starting the academy and when it's a success, which I know it will be, we'll sell you half our interest at cost so you'll be an owner as well as the director."

Now in a state of shock, Arabella looked away, out the windows toward the sensational swimming pool.

Bonnie took it as a hint. "Yes, that, too. We could arrange a membership for you at the pool club. It's become the social center for the younger set. Café society, they like to call it."

"That's very generous, Bonnie, but it's so much. I can't imagine."

"Belle," Bonnie began. "I hope you don't mind if call you Belle. It's a little less formal and our town isn't all that formal."

Arabella nodded her concurrence. Her mother had called her Belle as a child and it pleased her to hear the name on this woman's lips.

"Belle, you simply needn't worry about the money. This is Houston."

* * * * *

CHAPTER 11. WEDNESDAY

CQC 51.76 1.32↑

Lulu

Lulu watched Ed's face as he read the draft of her story. His elbows rested on his desk and he flicked his gaze from side to side and occasionally upwards to meet her own. Whatever he was thinking didn't show.

"So now you're convinced that Bluebox doesn't work?" he asked.

"Exactly."

"But before you were convinced that it was for real."

"That was a hoax. That's why Josh showed it to me at his apartment and not at the Bluestream offices. He bought options on Conquest stock, expecting it to jump when I wrote the story." She did her best to look contrite. "We were wise not to go with that story."

"We were wise, weren't we?" said Ed. "Tell me again why we've changed our minds."

She had covered this already, but she couldn't blame Ed for his caution. She went over it again in detail. "Russ Wheeler worked for Conquest. On Jack Burnam's personal say-so, Wheeler went to California to iron out some details of the Bluestream deal. He died accidentally before he could report back. His files from that trip fell into the hands of his girlfriend who, coincidentally, was Lacey Burnam's personal trainer. Via Lacey, this girl delivered a blackmail note to Burnam. She wants one million dollars or she'll make the files public."

"You've seen the files?"

Lulu tread carefully. She already told Ed she hadn't seen the files. "No," she said. "The girl is in hiding, but I saw the blackmail note. She believes those files are a big problem for Conquest. I think Wheeler was going to report back that Bluebox is a bust. Why else would it be worth a million dollars to keep the files confidential?"

She stopped herself, trying not to seem desperate or pushy. After a pause, she went ahead in a quieter voice. "If Bluebox is a bust, the Bluestream deal comes apart. Conquest may be paying two billion dollars for nothing."

Ed squeezed his lower lip between thumb and forefinger. "I'm with you so far, but what you have so far isn't enough. You're probably on the right track, but *probably* doesn't make the front page."

She felt a hint of a favorable breeze. He wanted to believe. Another stab at contrition might help. "Believe me, I've learned my lesson. That's why I didn't bring this to you until I got the call yesterday, the one I told you about."

Ed released his lower lip long enough to make a circular motion with his hand. *Go on*, it said. *Tell me again.*

Lulu shifted in her seat. Reporters, she thought, do what she was about to do every day of every week. If they didn't, most of the junk that people call *news* would never see the light of day. Daily newspapers would run only a few pages and half-hour television news programs would be cut back to ten minutes. It was only the unlucky ones and a few nutcases that get caught. Like Janet Cooke of the *Washington Post,* who won a Pulitzer and a movie contract for a totally fabricated tear-jerker about an eight-year-old heroin addict. And Jayson Blair, the *New York Times* reporter who wrote *I lied and I lied and I lied and then I lied some more*, as the opening line of his autobiography. And Stephen Glass, who attended law school after being fired by the *New Republic* for years of prodigious falsifications. At least, Lulu figured, his experience in misrepresentation would come in handy in his new profession.

So, having reached her own moment of untruth, Lulu looked Ed right in the eyes, forced herself to remain composed and steady and, without blinking, looking away or drawing an incriminating *here-goes-nothing* breath, uttered what was undoubtedly the most extravagant prevarication of her professional life. "My source was an engineer at Bluestream. He quit last week because he doesn't want to be a drone at a big corporation like Conquest."

"He worked on Bluebox?"

"Up until three months ago. He said that's when the company shut it down."

"Why's that?"

"I don't know the technical reasons, but Bluestream's management gave up on it. They only brought it back to life when Conquest came calling."

"And your source told this to Wheeler?"

"That's what he said."

"And he called you why?"

"I talked with fifteen or twenty Bluestream employees when I was out there. I passed out a lot of business cards. It wasn't hard for someone who wants to air a grudge to find me."

"If he quit his job, why does he want anonymity?"

"He's looking for a new job. He's worried that Conquest will retaliate." Lulu handed Ed a fax. "He sent this and asked me to pass it on if I heard of any openings."

This was the clincher. Lulu had assembled a composite resumé from information she picked up on *monster.com*, including college, grad school, prior jobs and family. She had e-mailed it to the concierge at the hotel in Milpitas and then convinced the concierge to fax it back so it would have marks showing transmission from the area code where her source would live if he really did live somewhere. It wouldn't hold up if Ed did any checking, but that wasn't likely.

Ed fiddled with his tie, studied the resumé for a moment and handed it back to her. "Okay," he said. "Let's go with it."

It wasn't until Lulu had walked out of Ed's office, down the hallway, past all the reporters' cubicles, through the reception lobby and into the vacant ladies' room that she let loose a shriek of victory that echoed and then faded into the chilly bathroom air.

Norah

"Look at this," said Jack, handing Norah a note handwritten in purple on yellow paper.

Norah read the note. "Where did you get this?"

"From Lacey. This girl was Lacey's personal trainer. She left the note on Saturday."

"Saturday? That was four days ago."

"Lacey passed it on to me this morning. She didn't read it. She thought the girl was looking for a new job or something."

Norah returned the note to Jack. "I believe her. We know that Wheeler was traveling with a girl. It isn't unlikely that she got a copy of his files. She might have known that he was trying to blackmail us before he died." She paused. "We should pay," she said, "and the sooner the better. Why take a chance over a million bucks?"

"Let's get Jenkins on it right away."

"Jenkins is out sick again, and I don't think we can wait for him to get back."

"Who then?"

"Duarte. He's the one who went to Mexico looking for Wheeler."

"The CIA guy?" said Jack. "I like him."

Jack

Tranquility Park comprised a sunny city block of trees and pools and a crisscross of walkways in downtown Houston. Abstract towers of stainless steel jutted upwards among grassy mounds. Kids rode skateboards over the walkways and water cascaded down the sides of several immense cylindrical fountains. The fountains operated only intermittently and after each interval of quiet a wave of water gushed from the top and burbled down the sides of the towers into reflecting pools.

The idea of a park honoring the first lunar landing, one of the most electrifying achievements of the twentieth century, pleased Jack no end. Jack sometimes would stroll to the park from his office to get some time to himself. Notwithstanding a few stares, he would climb atop a picnic table and lay down, flat on his back, and think about his daily challenges. From his spot on the picnic table he could glimpse Conquest Plaza's upper floors high above the trees.

On this occasion, he'd come to the park for a different reason. He sat at a table across from Josh Morris, the Bluestream engineer who had served as the team leader on the Bluebox project. Morris had come to Houston on Jack's instructions and brought with him a dozen prototypes. A demonstration of the gadget for a group of very senior executives was scheduled for later that afternoon and a public unveiling for Friday. But Jack wanted to see the thing first for himself with no one else around.

The Bluebox on the table between them buzzed. Josh picked it up and moved around to Jack's side of the table so they both could see the screen. "Watch this," he said. "Someone is at my apartment."

On the screen, Jack could see the brown uniform and impatient face of a deliveryman, waiting for someone to come to the door.

"Hello," said Josh. "You were supposed to deliver yesterday."

The deliveryman looked around to see where the voice was coming from. He answered when he located Josh's face in the view screen on the front door. "Where do you want it?"

"Leave it inside the door." Josh touched an icon that unlocked the door. They watched as the deliveryman reached in and set down the package.

"You want me to lock up?"

"No need," said Josh. "I'll do it." He clicked the remote lock icon a second time.

Jack and Josh watched as the delivery man turned away shaking his head.

"I'm impressed," said Jack. "My flip phone sure won't do that. What else?"

Jack watched in silence as Josh ran through the functions of Bluebox. Voice control. Touch screen. Internet access. Camera. Streaming. Satellite positioning. As the device performed each task, Jack became more and more excited. "This thing beats Sony, HTC, Nokia, Motorola, all of them. Sonofabitch!"

"One more thing, Mr. Burnam. "When I got the message about where to meet you, I downloaded something I thought you might like. It's from the NASA video library."

He handed Jack the Bluebox visor to put over his eyes and the ear buds to put into his ears. Within seconds, Jack was watching a grainy image of Neil Armstrong stepping down from the spindly ladder of the Apollo 11 lunar module. The camera zoomed in on the grooved footprints left in the moon's dust by Armstrong's boots. Buzz Aldrin climbed down the ladder and joined Armstrong. The two astronauts cavorted on the surface of the moon as President Nixon's call came through.

> *Hello, Neil and Buzz. I'm talking to you by telephone from the Oval Room at the White House, and this certainly has to be the most historic telephone call ever made...*

Jack issued his judgment on Bluebox in the louder-than-necessary voice used by people wearing headphones. "Houston, Tranquility Base here. Bluebox has landed."

Miranda

Miranda unlocked the door to the Batcave, entered and closed the door. She re-read the list of names that Maggie pressed into her hand on Saturday. She had almost forgotten her promise to look into the value of the woman's inherited investments, but it seemed a small enough favor.

In addition to the names she had seen before, like Rogue, Cyclops, Booster, and Iceman, there was a slew of other names along the same lines. Wheeler must have had some kind of comic book fixation.

Scanning the shelves, she found the files and bound volumes that matched the names on the list. She created a handwritten table with a row for each investment partnership and columns for net asset value and other key data items. She jotted down numbers for all of them. When finished, she returned everything to the shelves.

Back in her office, Miranda set about calculating the value of the investments, starting with one called *Mystique*. Net asset value of $329,272,880. Divide by 132,000 total outstanding units equals $2,494.49 per unit. So Maggie's one thousand units were worth...$2.5 million? Something was way out of kilter. Miranda had expected to see a number on the order of $50,000 or $100,000. And this was only one of the investments.

She rechecked her data and calculations but couldn't find a mistake. After working her way through all the names on Maggie's list, her calculations showed that the eleven investments ranged in value from a low of $1.4 million to a high of $3.9 million. The total was right at $25 million.

Miranda stretched her hands toward the ceiling and cracked her spine. She stood, bent over and touched her toes several times. She popped a breath mint.

She had prepared herself for the idea that Norah might have paid Wheeler some outlandish bonuses, like the other hot-shot employees that she had heard about, but $25 million was way too much for a guy at Wheeler's level. Only the top brass made that kind of money. And she didn't know for sure that the investments represented bonus money or possibly something else.

Outside her office window, the horizon had turned nearly black, signaling the onset of a blue norther. She watched a sparrow beating its wings against the oncoming wind. What the hell was a sparrow doing forty stories up in downtown Houston?

David

A weird buzz rose from the trading floor. It went beyond the customary raucous bravado and instead sounded edgy and crazed. He raised a quizzical eyebrow at Fib.

"It's Jannsen. He made his number this morning."

Jannsen was a heavy hitter on the back row, a guy who had day traded for years.

"What do you mean?"

Fib lowered his voice. "He set a target years ago when he started day trading. He hit the target and now he's done. No more trading." Fib paused, scowling. "He's putting all his money into municipal bonds."

This, to David, was incredible news. He knew a guy who made enough money in day trading to *retire*, as if he'd had a regular career.

"So what have you been working on?" asked Fib. "You've been quiet lately."

It was true. David had spent so much time obsessing over his Keystone strategy that he had largely withdrawn from the trading floor give-and-take.

"Nothing really," he said. "Just more research."

"Suit yourself," said Fib, turning back to his monitor. "Big fucking secret."

David checked the ticker and found Keystone at 11.3. It had climbed again since the day before, but no matter. He reviewed his graphs to confirm one more time what he already knew. The daily pattern had held for months. It was fantastic. If it kept up, he would soon start making a profit and he'd replace the money he had borrowed from savings.

Then why were his palms so sweaty?

He checked his *Bling* account. The package had shipped and would arrive that afternoon. He imagined the pleased look on Miranda's face when he told her he'd made thousands of dollars in only a few days. She would forgive him for quitting his job and they would put the Payton-Mosel snafu behind them. Before long their lives would return to normal.

One-fifteen. Time to act. He checked the current price and found that Keystone had dropped a few cents. As he'd done the past two days, he entered the information for an order to short shares of Keystone, except this time for a manly 1,800 shares instead of a pusillanimous two hundred. All the data appeared on his screen. His finger hovered over the enter key. David hesitated, having a moment of doubt. What if the pattern broke? Maybe he should run more tests. Maybe he should call it quits and move on to another trade.

A commotion on the floor interrupted his worrying. It was Jannsen, heading for the door carrying two cardboard boxes. Every trader in the room looked up and, one by one, they stood and clapped. Jannsen stopped at the doorway, set down the boxes and raised his arms over his head like a boxing champion. The traders continued applauding until Jannsen closed the Velotrade door behind him.

The time was one-twenty-two. David sat back down, ready to go. Jannsen didn't make his number by getting cold feet on his first big trade. "Here goes," he muttered under his breath. "Wish me luck." He touched the *Enter* key.

He must have spoken louder than intended because Fib came right back. "Good luck, buddy."

Now that it was done, David's misgivings assaulted him like a cloud of bats. A small, quiet voice in his head told him that, notwithstanding Fib's best wishes, he had gone beyond the point where luck could help him.

Miranda

"You look a little down," said Norah, catching Miranda by surprise. "Maybe this will brighten your day." She handed Miranda a letter signed by Jack Burnam.

What Miranda read in the letter flabbergasted her. She was to get a thirty percent increase in her base salary, a mid-year bonus of half a year's salary, another bonus of equal size at year end, and a share in the executive investment pool. Overnight her comp had more than doubled. Three days earlier, she had planned to resign and let David support the family. Now it didn't matter whether David worked or not.

"Mr. Burnam thinks you did a superb job getting the Bluestream filing ready," said Norah. "He mentioned it again this morning and specifically asked me to tell you so."

True enough. She had taken charge of Bluestream and driven her team to meet a nearly impossible deadline.

"You're on the inside track now. Mr. Burnam takes care of people who take care of the company."

Miranda gave her boss a tentative smile. She couldn't think of anything to say.

"Oh, there's something else," said Norah. "I need your signature. Strictly routine."

She handed Miranda a document headed Deal Approval Sheet. In the box asking for a description of the corporate action in question, someone had penned *SEC Filing—Bluestream Acquisition*. Another box specified value at risk: *$2 billion*. Significance to Conquest: *Tier One*. Timing: *Critical.* Below that a set of signature blocks and names that comprised a roll call of the people regarded as the company's movers and shaker. Miranda felt almost embarrassed to be included among them.

"I haven't seen one of these before," she said.

"Welcome to the big leagues. Mr. Burnam requires one in the file for every major corporate action. He says it helps him keep track of the people that get things done."

Miranda's head spun. Bluestream. Boiler. Booster. Maggie's $25 million. Now this. Things were happening too quickly for her to know the right thing to do. She thought of what Jesse told her every morning. *Make wise choices.* Easier said than done.

Norah nudged the DASH an inch closer to Miranda. She obviously was getting impatient.

Miranda reached a decision. For now at least she would get in the boat with Norah and Burnam and everyone else. Later, when she had more time to think and didn't feel so pressured, she could always jump out again. At least, she hoped so. Miranda pulled the DASH to her, signed it and handed it back to Norah.

"One more thing," said Norah. "Mr. Burnam asked me to invite you and David to the opera tomorrow night."

"The opera?"

"Mr. Burnam is on the board of the Houston Grand Opera. Every so often, he arranges a private performance for a group of Conquest people. If you like opera, it's a treat. If you don't, it's more like a rite of passage."

Miranda nodded dumbly.

"Do you?" Norah asked. "Like opera?"

DASH. Movers and shakers. Rite of passage. *Get in the boat.*

Miranda paused hardly at all. "You bet," she said. "I love opera."

Maggie

Maggie's pants caused whiplash as she entered the lobby of the Magnolia, as she had fully expected when she ordered the $300 crack-huggers from a London designer. A ribbon of panty lace emerged from underneath the back of the jeans and made a T-shape that hung high on her hips, giving additional emphasis to the inordinately low cut of the pants.

Jack had called earlier in the week and asked if they could reschedule their regular Tuesday night rendezvous for Wednesday. Then Wednesday to Thursday, and then Thursday back to Wednesday. She'd said yes all three times. It wasn't as if she had a husband to hide things from any longer. Besides, if she read the tone of his voice correctly, he had something important to discuss.

She sensed the crowd in the Magnolia Bar staring as she waited for her drink. Let them look. She felt sure events were breaking in her favor. For one thing, Lacey Burnam wouldn't tolerate the rumors going around for much longer. She would have to file for divorce. For another, before long this silliness about the Senator's wife would run its course to a dead end. What Senator's wife would leave her husband? The door to Jack's affections would swing wide open for her, and she planned to stroll right through it.

Maggie had another cause for her good spirits. Earlier in the day she had deposited Conquest's check for $1 million into her bank account. She hadn't imagined that her husband's investments were worth anywhere near that much, and she couldn't have been more pleased that Jack had come through with it. She took it as a sign of his growing fondness.

Her drink arrived. Maggie climbed off the barstool, hitched her pants up a fraction and carried the drink across the lobby and into the elevator. On the ninth floor, she used her key to open the Conquest suite and made herself comfortable while she waited for Jack.

Maggie looked forward to her new life. The more she thought about it, the more she thought this was the role for which she was born. She was a good twenty years younger than Jack and would look exquisite on his arm at all those parties and fundraisers. They would become one of Houston's most talked-about couples. Not that she didn't see challenges ahead. She already had identified a place in Dallas that gave courses in subjects of particular interest to young women married to older men. It was a kind of finishing school for trophy wives.

An hour later, Maggie found herself still alone, with no word from Jack. This hadn't happened before, and she wasn't sure what to do. She wanted to dial his cell number, but held off. He might be in the middle of something crucial, like discussing divorce terms with Lacey.

The suite's mini-bar had five single-serving bottles of Scotch when she arrived and she had already gone through three of them. It was a joke, she thought, to call those tiny bottles a serving. Not by her standards. She poured the last two into a tumbler partially filled with ice and splashed in some water.

Her cell phone rang and she grabbed for it with relief. She already had decided not to give Jack a hard time about being late. It was way too early to start bitching at him.

"Maggie, this is Miranda. Miranda Sesno."

Why was Miranda Sesno calling her?

"I have some information for you. About your husband's investments."

"Oh. Sure." Maggie had nearly forgotten that she asked Miranda to look up their value.

"I know this might not be what you are expecting, but I've gone over it several times. I'm sure it's right."

"Okay." Maggie wondered what Miranda was going to tell her. A few hundred thousand?

"By my calculation, the investments on the list you gave me are worth approximately twenty-five million dollars."

It seemed as if Miranda's voice was coming from a distance, like an old-fashioned radio broadcast with lots of static. She wanted to adjust the tuning dial for better reception. "You're mistaken. Russ didn't have that kind of money."

"I know it's very odd. That's why I double- and triple-checked. There's no doubt in my mind."

Maggie put the cell phone on a table and tried to think. She wished she hadn't drunk so much whiskey. Jack had tricked her. He had paid her only a fraction of the real value of the investments. And she thought he'd done her a favor.

"Maggie, are you still there?"

She picked up the phone again. "Yes, I'm here. I don't know what to say. Thanks, I guess, for checking on it."

"I'm sorry I didn't call sooner. I'm still at the office."

Maggie wanted to get off the phone, but Miranda sounded chatty. God almighty, $25 million.

"A few of us were on call here to finish up a speech that Mr. Burnam is giving tomorrow. They were holding his plane at the airport until we finished."

Maggie tried to keep her voice calm. "He's out of town?"

"He's giving a speech in Washington tomorrow. His plane took off about an hour ago."

"Washington?"

"Maggie, are you okay? You don't sound so good."

Maggie struggled to respond. "Thank you, Miranda," she choked out. "I have to go now."

Maggie shut off her phone and put it in her purse. She may have majored in suntan but she was smart enough to know that these were not the actions of a man thinking of spending the rest of his life with her. She had misjudged Jack by a few light-years.

She opened the mini-bar. Since there was no more Scotch, Maggie removed all the other little bottles and lined them up on the coffee table. The bourbon on the left, the gin, vodka and cognac on the right. She didn't drink clear liquors and she didn't want anything sticky or sweet. Besides, she was right-handed. She picked up the first little bottle of gin and hurled it across the room and through the bathroom door where it made a satisfying smash against the Tuscany wall tile that surrounded the over-sized whirlpool tub. Then she hurled another and another until only the bourbon remained. Someone would clean up the mess in the tub, she knew, but glass is tricky. There was a decent chance that a few shards would remain to work their way into Jack's butt the next time he stayed in the room. That was as much revenge as she could hope for. She was a flea flailing at a man as powerful as Jack Burnam. Better to take the one million and move on. After all, it wasn't as if she loved *him*. She loved the idea of being a trophy wife.

Drawing open the room curtains, she opened a sliding glass door and stepped out onto a small balcony. She rested her hands on a railing and looked across downtown. Cars and taxis filled the damp streets with noise and movement. All around her, Houston's lambent skyscrapers illuminated the night. Chevron. Allen Center. Reliant. Pennzoil. Brown & Root. Conquest. She loved this part of the city. So much activity. So much wealth.

She walked back into the room and, as if Jack were watching from his chair, methodically removed her pants, top, bra and lace ribbon panties. She intended to don a hotel robe but paused first to examine the image of her body reflected in the glass of the sliding door. What she saw, she liked. At not quite thirty, she had years before age would diminish her looks. Plenty of time. She was newly widowed and had money in the bank.

A room light flashed on in the opposite wing of the Magnolia and Maggie peered through the sliding glass door at a man visible in a room one level above. Middle-aged and graying, he wore an expensive-looking business suit. The bellboy bowed, showing his appreciation for the bills the man handed him as a tip. After the bellboy departed, the man loosened his tie and hung his coat over the back of a chair. He mixed a drink and looked out his own window.

Maggie enjoyed the expression of bemused arousal that came over his face when he caught sight of her. He stared shamelessly. She resisted the impulse to cover her nakedness and, instead, remained still as a mannequin. When the man raised his glass in her direction, she smiled and took another measured sip of bourbon.

12. THURSDAY

CQC 52.22 0.46↑

David

David rubbed away grits of sleep, trying to figure out where he had spent the night. His head ached and his mouth tasted of yesterday's liquor. He lay in a bed, not a sofa, so he knew he wasn't at home. He saw a new beige carpet and freshly-painted white walls. He was in someone's apartment and whoever it was hadn't lived there long.

He sat up, astonished to find himself naked. He spied his clothes in a rumpled pile beside the bed and reached for them but the level of pain in his head ratcheted up. He lay back and closed his eyes against a wave of nausea. His arm brushed against something warm and smooth. A shoulder. A female shoulder.

When the vertigo receded he pried his eyes open again. Beside him were ropes of dark hair splayed out over a woman's bare back. She was nearly as naked as he was, wearing a pair of black panties so small she might have stolen them from a Barbie doll. She snored softly into a wrinkled pillow, her face slack with sleep. David glimpsed one smallish, well-tanned breast pressing against the white bed sheet. The nipple reminded him of an acorn, hard and brown. She seemed a total stranger, except for one troubling fact. She wore on her left wrist the bracelet he had ordered from *Bling*. David groaned.

The previous day began to come back in hazy fragments, like whitecaps floating toward shore atop waves of remorse. He tried to ignore the throbbing in his head and to piece together what he had done. He knew that after his Keystone order went into the system, he suffered a case of the nerves that forced him to the men's room for half an hour. He should have watched his screen but he feared if he did that he might back out of the trade. He'd gone outside and paced the parking lot. Thirteen times around, two minutes per lap. A couple of unwanted marketing calls and another visit to the men's room soaked up the rest of the time. At 3:29 he returned to his computer, praying he would find a tidy profit waiting for him.

What he found instead made his stomach heave. Keystone's pattern had shattered. It hadn't fallen the expected dollar but instead had spiked to nearly 16, like a spider scurrying up a web. At first, he simply didn't believe it. Fib, he guessed, somehow had gotten into the system and altered the price as a practical joke. A sidelong glance told David otherwise. Fib showed not the slightest interest.

"Fib," he called in desperation. "You ever hear of a stock called Keystone?"

Fib snorted. "'Stone's in play. Hit the wires this morning."

David sank further into his chair. A tremor ran through him.

Fib looked puzzled at David's obvious distress. "Don't you read?"

In truth, he'd been so nervous that morning that he skipped his customary sweep of the business news. Someone had launched a takeover bid and he missed it.

The office door of the Velotrade floor manager swung open. The floor manager headed directly for David's station, a look of mortal consternation on his face.

"Sesno," he said. "Margin call. You have to post more margin or cover your short."

Cover? To cover at this point meant a loss of nearly his entire $10,000. David did the only thing that seemed appropriate under the circumstances. He begged. "Can't we wait? It's gonna fade back any minute now."

"Absolutely. We can wait. As long as you do it on your own money, not mine."

"Look," David began, but the floor manager cut him off.

"Can you post more money or not?"

David shook his head and the floor manager went back to his office at a trot. Within ninety seconds, David received three e-messages. The first one advised him that Velotrade purchased shares for his account and covered the short. The second advised him of his remaining margin account balance: $217. The third one asked him to vacate the premises. He had fallen miles below Velotrade's minimum equity balance.

Tears welled up and his insides churned. He felt he would either cry or puke, or both. He picked up the nearest heavy object, a metal paperweight, took aim and launched it across the room. It thunked harmlessly against the door to the floor manager's office. Inside, the floor manager didn't bother to look up, but David's computer screen immediately went dark.

After that came a blur of half-remembered images: the pitying faces of two dozen day traders as he made his disgraceful exit. Margaritas served in quart-sized glasses in the sunless cool interior of a Mexican restaurant. A small, darkly pretty woman materializing from the gloom with her own Margarita in hand. The square tail lights of the woman's car as he followed her through the early evening traffic. Sex with an angry tone that didn't leave him feeling any better. Sleep like a coma.

He didn't know how the woman came to wear the bracelet he'd intended for Miranda, but there it was on her arm. What words, he wondered, could he use to ask her to give it back.

She shifted and lifted a sleepy eyelid. "Good morning. Can't recall if we got around to names yesterday." She yawned comfortably. "I'm Jane."

"David," he said, immediately wishing he'd thought to tell her a different name.

Jane climbed out of bed and stretched, arching her back in a way that gave emphasis to her undersized breasts. The tiny black panties looked fantastic on her compact body. David felt his semi stiffen into a genuine hard-on.

Jane saw the effect she was having and laughed appreciatively. "I'll be damned. Thought we wore it out last night." She shucked off the panties and climbed back on the bed.

David slumped, wondering exactly what had gone on the night before. He had never cheated on Miranda but nearly two weeks of the cold shoulder had left him with plenty of pent-up demand.

He needed to leave. Right away.

"Do you know where my cell phone is?" He made a show of searching through the pile of clothes on the floor.

Jane pointed to the top of a cheap Danish dresser. "I turned it off about midnight. Right after you passed out."

David picked up the phone and gave her a questioning look.

"It rang but I couldn't wake you up. Didn't know what else to do."

Unmitigated panic rose in David's chest.

"What's the matter?" asked Jane. "You have a wife or something?" Her voice was filled with disappointment, but not surprise.

"Yeah," said David. "I have a wife."

Jane stood and walked into the bathroom. She sat on the toilet without closing the door. Presently David heard the low burble of her urination into the bowl. She continued peeing for far longer than seemed possible for a girl her size.

Norah

Norah's phones had chirped, beeped and buzzed all morning. The onslaught started at home well before seven and hadn't let up since she reached the office. The lights on all four lines on her desk had blinked nonstop since she arrived. Everyone wanted to ask about the Bluestream story in the morning's *Examiner*.

She checked the stock price monitor. Conquest had opened at 52, plummeted to 44 in the first few hours of trading and continued drifting downward. It was already the biggest one-day nosedive in the company's history and Norah expected it to continue for as long as the story remained unchallenged.

She dialed the number of one of the members of the Board of Directors. "No basis whatsoever," she said. "I have no idea where the *Examiner* got its so-called facts, but the story is dead wrong."

A big institutional shareholder came on the line. "It isn't true," she repeated.

And, as far as she knew, it wasn't true. Like all of Conquest's senior management, Norah had attended the Bluebox demonstration the afternoon before and the thing impressed the hell out of her. The guy from California put on a terrific show, including a great bit with Yo-Yo Ma at Carnegie Hall. He'd handed out prototypes for people to use over the next few days. Hers rested on the corner of her desk, something she planned to look at more closely in the afternoon.

Her assistant handed her a message from a reporter at the *Wall Street Journal*. "No comment at this time," Norah told her.

Burnam intended to make a full public rebuttal, complete with a Bluebox prototype in hand, and she didn't want to jump the gun with any particular reporter. Half the conference rooms in the building had an emergency meeting in progress to pull together every last bit of information on Bluebox. Norah wanted to make certain that her boss had every relevant fact at his fingertips.

"Oh, Ms. Barker," said Norah. "I'll be right with you. Let me wrap up this other call." Norah put Barker's call on hold, as she had done four times already, and watched with satisfaction as the light blinked away through the next seven calls that Norah returned. Was it her imagination, or was the light blinking more and more quickly as time passed? Norah couldn't imagine how Barker cooked up her story, but she knew the little sawed-off bitch deserved to sweat.

One loose end troubled her. She hadn't yet heard back from Duarte. After the Bluebox story, every financial reporter in the country would be digging for more dirt on Conquest. It wasn't out of the question that one of them might stumble onto Wheeler's girlfriend and get a look at those files. If that happened, Lulu Barker's wanna-be exposé would look feeble by comparison.

Norah reached to dial Duarte's number when she heard a sound that differed from all the other chirps, beeps and buzzes. This one sounded more like a sea captain's whistle. She looked around in puzzlement until she focused on the Bluebox on her desk. She hadn't known it was turned on.

"Norah?" she heard. It was Jack's voice. She picked up the Bluebox and saw a nose filling the screen. The picture was so clear and sharp she could count the hairs protruding from the nostrils.

"Norah?" again. And then, to someone else. "How do you work this thing?"

The image on the screen backed away from Jack's nose until she saw his entire ruddy and clean-shaven face. Someone's finger intruded, there was a moment of static and then the picture resolved again. Jack stood on a practice green at River Oaks Country Club. He wore a rain jacket, held a golf club in one hand and an umbrella in the other. The California guy—she assumed that the intruding finger belonged to him—seemed to be holding the Bluebox while Jack posed. Norah marveled at the color and clarity of the scene. She could almost smell the rain and damp grass.

"Norah," Jack shouted again, gesturing toward the Bluebox. "Isn't this the greatest goddam gadget you've ever seen?"

Feo

"Yes, ma'am. Yes ma'am. Yes ma'am." Norah Needham intimidated Feo, no doubt about it. Although no one had said a word since his last *Yes, ma'am*, he said it again for good measure. "Yes ma'am."

The Wheeler fiasco had sprung to life again in the worst possible way. Sherry, whom he'd told Jenkins wouldn't have the brains to carry out an extortion scam, had done exactly that. To top it off, this morning's paper had some kind of crazy story about Bluestream that sent the company's stock reeling and had everyone in the building buzzing like wasps around an overturned nest. Norah was incensed that Feo hadn't already handled the payoff, and made it abundantly clear she didn't want to wait around to see if Wheeler's girlfriend got spooked by all this publicity and did something foolish. The phrase *Wheeler's girlfriend* gave Feo an unpleasant twinge, in spite of Wheeler's being dead.

He had instructions. Take $100,000 in cash from the corporate treasurer's office. Meet with the girl and deliver the cash as a show of good faith. Make sure he got every last copy of Wheeler's files, although how he was supposed to be sure of that he didn't know. Take care of it all on the double-quick. As soon as he gave a signal, Norah would wire the balance of the money to the girl's bank account.

Conquest's corporate treasury moved hundreds of millions of dollars every day, sometimes a billion or more, so his request for $100,000 of cash caused not a ripple. He found in one of the Security Department's closets a heavy-duty canvas satchel perfect for making deliveries of stacks of cash, and couldn't help but wonder if this sort of thing had come up before.

Then he called Sherry's cell and that's where he hit a wall. *I'm preparing for the arrival of the Cosmic Beam and can't be interrupted*, said her voicemail. *Please call back later*. He shook his head. What kind of blackmailer was this?

He wished her scheme would fall through. If it didn't, she would be living under a cloud, always looking back over her shoulder. And what about the tax authorities? What if they got wind of a millionaire personal trainer? Worse, with a million dollars to her name, Sherry wasn't exactly going to swoon over his house in Montrose or his slick new convertible. Despite their time together in Zihuatenajo, the notion that she would want to see him again now seemed laughable.

On an impulse, he dialed Jenkins' number. "Boss, how are ya?" He summarized his discussions with Norah and went over the payoff arrangements. "This might be a little over my head, boss. Maybe you want to handle the operation?"

Feo wasn't telling the truth. A monkey could have handled the operation, but he thought if someone else delivered the money, he might have a better chance of convincing Sherry to give it back.

"Sorry, Feo. No can do."

"I've been seeing some weird stuff on the Internet logs. I don't want to lose focus on that."

"Christ, you must be desperate."

Feo considered his last resort—telling Jenkins the truth—when Jenkins cut him off.

"I'm retiring," he said. "I've retired."

"You've retired?"

"This might be a case of getting out while the getting is good. The company isn't like it was a few years ago, if you know what I'm saying."

Feo wasn't the least bit sure what Jenkins was saying. "What do you mean?"

Before Jenkins could answer, a secretary put a message slip in front of Feo.

"Stay there, will you?" he said to Jenkins. "Ms. Needham's on the other line."

Norah, when he switched, demanded a progress report. He told her that he had the cash, making this first step sound more time-consuming that it was.

"The wire for the rest of the money is ready to go," she said. "And I'm going into nonstop meetings beginning at four o'clock. I need to hear from you by then."

Chingada! She'd given him a deadline. He had to wrap it up by four o'clock at the latest.

He picked up Jenkins' line, but it had already gone dead.

Miranda

A knock sounded at the conference room door and fourteen people looked up as one from a table strewn with laptops, coffee cups and documents. "Miranda, I'm sorry to interrupt," said her assistant. "Your husband is downstairs. He said it's urgent."

Miranda was mortified. She had assembled this crisis team on short notice and nearly everyone in the room had dropped other work to attend. Now she had an interruption for personal reasons? Her colleagues gave her looks of concern, probably suspecting something to do with their son. Miranda knew better. This wasn't about a child. It was about a man who, for the first time in their marriage, hadn't come home at night. She was relieved that he had turned up safe, but by the time the elevator reached the ground floor, her feeling of relief had dissipated.

"So you're alive?" she said. "What are you doing here?"

David looked like death, unshaven and pathetically hangdog. She yanked him into a hallway off the main lobby. The last thing she wanted was for her colleagues to see him in this condition.

"About last night," he began. "I want to explain..."

She made certain that nothing in her eyes contained a smidgen of sympathy.

"What I need to tell you..." He trailed off again.

"I'm waiting."

"I lost some money," David finally blurted out.

Money? That wasn't what Miranda was expecting. What did losing money have to do with staying out all night? "Come again?"

A woman who Miranda recognized as one of Mr. Burnam's schedulers passed them in the hall. "Miranda," she said sweetly. "I'm so glad you're able to attend the opera tonight." She gave David a dubious look. "Will your husband be coming also?" she asked, less sweetly.

Miranda tried to speak quickly, but David was quicker.

"Wouldn't miss it," he said. "Thanks for including me."

Miranda forced a smile. "We're looking forward to it."

There was a row of telephone closets near the end of the hall. As the woman moved away, Miranda hustled her husband into one of the closets and shut the door.

"What do you mean you lost some money?"

"I started day trading," he said. "I made a mistake."

The closet was tight, a space meant for only one person at a time. They were forced to stand closer together than they had been in a week. David smelled as bad as he looked.

"How big a mistake?"

Another long pause. "Ten thousand."

Miranda dropped into the closet's single chair. She found herself staring at David's belt buckle. "Ten thousand dollars. And this money came from...?"

"Our savings account." David spoke in a whisper.

She stood up again. His face contorted with tears but the idea that he might cry made her more furious. "David, that money belonged to both of us. You know that."

He sniffled. It hit her that he thought she would feel sorry for him.

"What gave you the right?" she began to say, but stopped herself. A pointless question. Nothing gave him the right.

Her new pay package more than made up for the loss, but that didn't make her any less upset. If anything, she felt angrier and more trapped.

She hesitated, then asked the big question. "So where were you last night?"

He muttered the name of a cheap highway motel not far from their home. "I was drunk. I was too embarrassed to face you."

Miranda couldn't come up with a single reason why she should believe him. Funny, she thought. Her marriage was blowing apart and she felt little more than a pressing need to get back to work.

"I hope you kept the motel room," she said. "You'll be needing it."

Feo

Feo, with Taco under one arm, once again peered through the front window of Sherry's darkened apartment. The cat seemed to recognize his erstwhile home and tried to squirm free. Feo squeezed him more tightly, suffering several scratches as he bent to pick up the *Eviction Notice* tucked under the front door. It was early afternoon and he had no better plan than to visit Sherry's apartment looking for a clue as to her whereabouts. He did not relish the idea of facing Norah Needham empty-handed at the end of the day.

Feo inserted the key that Sherry's neighbor had given him on his first visit. He stood in the open doorway as Taco disappeared with a disgruntled yowl into the bedroom. The cat was his cover if another neighbor happened by. He would say he was expecting to meet Sherry to return her pet.

Her apartment was strangely devoid of electrical devices. From what he could see, she had no television, telephone, or computer and only a few lamps. He flipped some wall switches with no result. She had a futon sofa, a Shoji screen, several silk paintings and a handful of Japanese candle lanterns. The spare décor created an effect of stillness and serenity that made Feo want to lay down on the floor and close his eyes. He recalled the astounding degree of body control that Sherry had exhibited on the beach in Mexico. It wasn't hard to imagine her bending and stretching in this tiny dim room with incense burning.

Taco returned from the bedroom with a stuffed mouse clutched in his jaws. Feo studied a wall poster that he'd seen through the window once before. It was an advertisement for the Taoist Arts Center of Houston where someone called Master Cheng taught yoga and T'ai Chi. A photograph of a woman in a pose that mixed astonishing grace and sensuality dominated the poster. He recognized the pose as the one that Sherry, in her white unitard, had demonstrated for him in Zihuatanejo. The woman in the photograph, Feo comprehended at last, was Sherry.

There was an address for Master Cheng's studio at the bottom of the poster. Feo scooped up Taco and bolted for his car.

Sherry

The Cosmic Beam, Sherry thought, might be bogus. The Sadhak had more or less taken over her treatment from the Master, and she had followed his instructions to the letter. *Refrain from strenuous activity, including all forms of sex. Get at least twelve hours of sleep. Bathe with eucalyptus and camphor oil. Drink purified water and eat whole-grain bread. Relax with stretching exercises in a quiet place. Clear the mind of all distractions and await the Beam's healing force.*

After a further and deeper analysis of her aura, the Sadhak had stipulated a sequence of three treatments of the *Beam* at three in the afternoon on three consecutive days. The number three, Sherry knew, represents eternal balance. The first two days she had made all the requisite preparations and waited calmly until the appointed hour. She had felt...nothing.

Nothing, except a fleeting sensation of strolling on the sands of the *Playa De Los Amantes* with the ocean roaring in her ears. So real was the feeling that she had reached down to flick the sand from her feet, but found only the worn floorboards of the Master's spare room. The first time she dismissed it as a fluke. The second time she asked the Master for his opinion. *The song of the lark rings true, but false spirituality has the odor of old shoes.* She had no idea what that meant. Maybe the Master and the Sadhak had unresolved issues from a prior lifetime.

She sent the Sadhak a quizzical e-mail.

The Beam takes many forms, he'd responded. *The Beam could arrive as a startling thought, a comforting feeling, a fragment of beautiful music, or the reappearance of an old friend. It could be as bold as thunder or as subtle as a firefly at dusk. The seeker must remain open to all possibilities.*

Maybe so, Sherry thought, but *sand?* Ridiculous.

Maybe the fault lay with her. Each time she felt the sensation of being on the beach, it was all but impossible to keep her mind free of some highly distracting thoughts. The sand under her toes and the pounding ocean waves blended with the yellow moon over the *Bahia de Zihuatanejo* and the blare of mariachis and the feeling of Feo's hand in her own. She recalled the solid feeling of his body when she pressed against him. She'd gone a little damp between the legs, something that almost never happened to her. Maybe the *Beam* came and went while she was daydreaming about the bulge in Feo's pants.

The more she thought about the Sadhak's diagnosis of her aura—greed, tinged with lust—the more troubled she felt. Not the part about lust. Lust was something she'd missed out on much of her life, and she was more than happy to give it a try. But if the part about lust was right, then the part about greed could be right, too. *Precious things may lead one astray.*

It was nearly three o'clock on the third day. She had made all the requisite preparations and this time was absolutely certain she would be ready. At five before the hour she began a deep breathing routine that worked like a charm. Her body felt as relaxed as a palm frond swaying in an ocean breeze and her mind had the crystalline clarity of the warm azure waters of the *Bahia de Zihuatanejo*. The waves slapped against the sand and she watched Feo's expression as she hiked her peasant dress up over her...*cripes*, she'd done it again. She strained to empty her mind and hoped like hell she hadn't missed the *Beam* for the third time running.

A tentative knock at the door broke her already shaky concentration. For God's sake, except for the Master and the Sadhak, no one knew where she was, so who on earth could be knocking?

She rose from her Lotus position and walked resignedly to the spare room's door. It was exactly three o'clock and she was going to miss it again.

Sherry opened the door and her breath caught in her throat. It was Feo, with a stricken look on his face, Taco under one arm and a big canvas satchel under the other.

"Oh my God," she said.

"Don't do it," he answered.

Three o'clock on the nose. Feo. *The Beam!*

David

"Looking for a handgun, sir?" David looked up at a cheerful fellow in a yellow shirt.

His name tag read *Buzz* and he had a haircut to match.

David wasn't planning to hurt anyone. He simply intended to go over to Velotrade, push his way into the office of that asshole floor manager and scare the living bejeesus out of him. Keystone, after vaulting upward on yesterday's news of a buyout, had dropped back below 11. If he could have waited a day, he wouldn't have lost a nickel. He wanted to force the floor manager to admit his mistake. That's why he had driven over to the Academy Sporting Goods store on the Southwest Freeway and asked where they kept the guns.

These were not, David knew, the thoughts of someone in total control of his emotions. He could see that the misfortunes of the past few weeks might have loosened his hinges a tad. He doubted he could explain how buying a gun and using it to frighten the life out of the floor manager would make anything better. He thought maybe it went back to confidence. If he could do this, it might break his run of bad luck. And if that happened, he could get on a roll and turn everything around.

David motioned at a Smith & Wesson Model 22A. At $200, it had the lowest price of anything in the case. Buzz handed him the gun, but his frown left no doubt that it didn't come with his recommendation. Sure enough, it felt like a cheap toy in David's hand.

"May I make a suggestion?" Buzz lifted a Rossi 357 magnum revolver from the case. "Simple and reliable," he said. "Perfect for self-protection. Big bore, too. One little squeeze blows a hell of a hole in anything that gets in front of it."

David checked the price tag. It was only a few dollars more than the Smith & Wesson. He took the Rossi in his hand and pointed it at the wall. The stubby barrel made him feel like a fledgling gangster.

"I don't know," he said. "What's that?" He pointed at a small black pistol near the back.

Buzz's face lit up. "It's a Glock, sir."

"A Glock," said David. He loved the sound of it.

"That's right, sir. A Glock."

He placed the gun in David's hand and delivered his sales pitch. "It's a forty-caliber sub-compact semi-automatic. Perfect for a back holster or your nightstand drawer. Excellent stopping power. Frankly, sir, it's a fucking hand cannon."

David didn't need to be sold. Even though it cost twice as much as the other guns, he found the name compelling. He said it once more, out loud. "Glock."

"That's right, sir," said Buzz.

David came in closer until he was nearly touching Buzz's forehead. He lowered his voice to a near-whisper. "I'll take it."

Feo

Feo couldn't have been more pleased. With himself. With Sherry. With life and all its enchanting prospects. He drove north on Main at breakneck speed and reached the stretch where the Rice University campus faced across the street toward the greenery of Hermann Park. A red light at Sunset forced him to stop and, while he waited, the sun broke through the clouds. He lowered the Saab's top.

When Sherry opened the door to her quiet back room at Master Cheng's studio, Feo had dropped both Taco and the money bag on the floor and, with as much passion and persuasion as he'd ever mustered in his life, pled with her to abandon the blackmail scheme. He'd explained to her all the risks and problems and it had worked—or at least something worked—because right before he got to the part about his enviable career prospects, she held up her hands for him to stop.

"Aren't you just the nicest man?" she said, only it wasn't a question. She reached into her overnight bag, withdrew a well-worn manila envelope and handed it to him.

"This is Wheeler's stuff. Take it."

And that was that.

The envelope now occupied the passenger seat beside him. He planned to deliver it directly to Norah as soon as he reached the office. In the trunk was the canvas satchel of cash, which he would return to the corporate treasurer.

Better yet, he carried with him Sherry's promise to meet him later in the evening at her apartment, where they would pick up her belongings and move them to Feo's house. She couldn't stay in the apartment and, since he had talked her out of a million dollars, the least he could do was give her a place to stay for a few days. Or longer.

It was a few minutes past four o'clock, so he'd missed Norah's deadline, but not by much. He imagined how astonished she would be when she heard that he had saved the company the payoff money. Once Jenkins' retirement became official, Feo felt sure he would have a better-than-even shot at getting a promotion.

He dialed Norah's number. He wanted to let her know there was no need to send the money to Sherry's account.

An assistant answered. "She's in a meeting with Mr. Burnam, but she told me to interrupt if you call." The assistant's voice dripped with disapproval, as if she thought there could be no way on earth that Feo Duarte should intrude on a meeting with Jack Burnam.

"You're late," said Norah when she came on the line. "Do you have the files?" Her voice was tight with impatience.

"Yes, ma'am, but there's something else."

She cut him off. "Listen, I'm sending the money right now. Anything else will have to wait until tomorrow."

"I have the files," Feo repeated, "but you don't..."

"I'm completely tied up tonight. Keep the files and don't let them out of your sight. Bring them to my office first thing in the morning."

"Ms. Needham, wait..."

A burst of static erupted. *Call Ended*, read the screen of his phone.

He redialed and the same assistant answered, several degrees frostier than before.

"Can you put me through again to Ms. Needham. We lost our connection."

"She went back into the meeting. She said to tell you that she wired the money."

"You don't understand. She doesn't need..."

"Really, Mr. Duarte. You expect me to interrupt Mr. Burnam *again*?"

Feo paused. He didn't want to break into Norah's meeting a second time. On the other hand, there was a million dollars at stake, "Yes," he said. "It's important."

"It's your funeral," he heard the assistant say before another blast of static broke the connection. This time, when he redialed, he got nothing but dead air.

Feo reached the place where Main goes under one of the interstate highways that passes by downtown Houston. Clouds now obscured the sunlight of a few minutes earlier and he felt a chill. He decided to put the Saab's top back up and with a grunt of frustration nosed the car into the nearest parking area, which turned out to be the lot of a shabby place called Jimmy's Nudie Bar. *Destiny Dances Tonight*, read the marquee.

While he waited for the top to close, Feo thought about electrons. Before Destiny's dance was over, some electrons representing a shitload of extorted money would have hurtled over some wires and come screeching to a halt among a much smaller gathering of electrons representing Sherry's bank account.

Oh well. They would send the electrons back. How hard could it be?

Miranda

Miranda had on the black silk Tadashi gown that she'd bought at Neiman's years earlier. Since this was a business event, she had pinned the side slit so as to show as little leg as possible and covered the already conservative neckline with a pearl-trim tweed jacket.

She arrived alone and hoped that David would have the good sense not to come at all. She hadn't spoken to him since the mid-morning sob session in the telephone closet, but she had made it clear that his attendance at the opera would be about as welcome to her as a cervical exam. This was going to be hard enough without him.

Mr. Burnam approached, with his wife at his side. Lacey Burnam wore a gown that made Miranda wish she'd left the Tadashi at home and sprung for something new.

"Norah tells me you like opera," said Mr. Burnam. "I'm more of a rodeo guy myself."

She laughed in embarrassment, partly because she'd never had occasion to make small talk with her CEO and partly because she couldn't imagine him getting worked up over a bulldogging competition. They stood in the center of the Grand Foyer of the Wortham Theater Center, home of the Houston Grand Opera. Millions of rose-colored bricks formed an atrium that soared overhead and dwarfed the assemblage of Conquest big shots and spouses awaiting the night's performance. Miranda, in truth, liked opera a great deal, and not only the old warhorses like *Don Giovanni* and *La Boheme*. She also enjoyed the totally un-hummable modern operas for which the HGO was famous. She got a kick out of living in a city that turned out for contemporary opera in cowboy boots and Texas big hair.

"Guilty," she said to Mr. Burnam. "Season tickets for the past five years. In five more I'll have the seats I want." She had methodically worked her way down from the balcony to the rear orchestra. When she reached the premium orchestra seats, she planned to keep them for life.

Burnam raised his eyebrows, as if wondering why anyone would be willing to wait five years for anything.

"Where's that? The seats you want, I mean."

Miranda's embarrassment deepened but, after all, he had asked. She specified section, row and seat numbers.

"No reason you should have to wait five years," he said. "My assistant will get those for you for next season."

Lacey excused herself as a group of men and women that Miranda took for HGO board members called for her attention.

Burnam stood there, looking at her sociably as if he had nothing else in the world to do. She was sure that the time he'd already allotted to her was far more than someone of her rank merited, but he seemed in no hurry to move on. She couldn't quite think of what to say, but he rescued her.

"So tell me about tonight's performance. All I know is that it has a racy title."

She laughed again. The HGO had mounted a production of a piece called *The Golden Ass*. To help set the mood, the stage designer had transformed one corner of the Grand Foyer into a replica of a marketplace in ancient Carthage. Cast members dressed in tunics and togas mingled with the Conquest crowd.

"It's a contemporary work," Miranda said, "but it's based on a second-century story by Apuleius, the Roman philosopher." She paused, wanting to make certain she wasn't boring him, but he seemed fully focused. "It's about a man named Lucius. He's a wealthy man who dabbles in magic and accidentally turns himself into a donkey. It's a bit silly. Like most opera stories, completely unbelievable."

Burnam's amiable countenance turned serious. "People will believe anything, Miranda." He gestured toward the faux-Roman marketplace across the foyer. "But sometimes you have to dress it up a little."

Miranda suspected that Burnam had changed the subject without exactly saying so. He had succinctly enunciated his business ethos and at the same time, without taking his hands from his pockets, he'd somehow given her the secret handshake.

He began a barely perceptible toe-bounce signaling that her allotted time had come to an end. On cue, Norah slipped between them. "Sorry to interrupt," she said, "but you're needed in the Donors' Room, Jack. A couple of the Bluestream investors want to talk to you."

"Duty calls," Burnam said to Miranda. "Have a wonderful evening."

Miranda exhaled deeply. She dearly wanted to follow him across the room and have a look at these Bluestream investors. Norah, however, positioned herself at Miranda's side like a bony anchor.

"Nice visit?" she asked.

"I'm sure I bored him with opera talk."

"It doesn't matter what you talked about. The only thing that matters is that he stood in the center of the foyer with you long enough that everyone here couldn't help but notice."

Sure enough, no sooner had Burnam departed than Miranda found herself at the center of a small swarm of people. In her years at the company, she had never spoken to so many vice chairmen and department heads, every one of whom offered congratulations for her work on Bluestream. Norah apparently had put out the word that Miranda had single-handedly pulled the deal back from the brink of disaster after Wheeler's untimely death. She appreciated the recognition of her work, but it gave her a bit of a queasy feeling.

Eventually, to her relief, the lights flickered to signal the start of the performance. She took a step toward the concert hall when a scene unfolding near its entrance brought her up short. *What in blazes?* David stood on the other side of the foyer engaged in animated conversation with Jack and Lacey Burnam. He should be sitting in his seedy motel room counting his sins and wondering how to get back in her good graces. Instead, against her express wishes, he'd thrust himself into an evening that belonged only to her. Not only that, he was chatting it up with her CEO and having a fine old time.

At least he did look better than he had that morning. He was clean-shaven and tuxedo-clad, thank God, but there was something odd about his behavior. He twirled an empty wine glass so dangerously close to Lacey that she stepped away and headed for her seat. Miranda heard his unnaturally loud voice echoing off the foyer walls. He was drunk.

At exactly the moment that she had thought of a plausible course of action—she would hide in the ladies room until the lights went down and hope like hell that he would take a seat without waiting for her—both David and Jack Burnam turned and from halfway across the room gave her nearly identical smiles, one affectionate and one paternal, but both saying, *Miranda, why in hell are you riveted to the floor way out there when the curtain is going up?*

Miranda steeled herself for the remainder of the evening. She forced the corners of her mouth into a smile and willed her feet to move one before the other until she reached the place where the two men stood staring at her like affable bookends. After choking out a pleasantry, she entwined with her own the arms offered by both men. To the opening strains of the overture to *The Golden Ass*, Miranda allowed them to escort her down the aisle of the now pitch-dark concert hall.

CHAPTER 13. FRIDAY

CQC 41.01 11.21↓

Miranda

Miranda spread the morning paper out on the kitchen table and scanned the headlines. *France to Build Fusion Reactor. Car Salesmen Surpass Business Executives in Gallup Ethics Poll. Conquest Shares Plunge 20%.* She had reached home not much before midnight. After paying the babysitter and checking on Jesse, she fell into a restless sleep that lasted until five in the morning. At that point, the kitchen and a pot of coffee won out over continued tossing and turning in the bedroom.

A few weeks earlier David would have been reading the headlines aloud, cracking wise and patting her on the rear whenever she passed within reach. She missed the familiarity of their morning routine, but not nearly enough to consider forgiving him. Drunk. Boorish. Belligerent. She couldn't come up with words that would adequately describe the wretchedness of his behavior at the opera. The well-wishers who had crowded around her before the show kept a polite distance during intermission, and she caught more than a few pitying glances thrown in her direction.

A new thought had come to her during the final act, a thought that had kept her awake much of the night. It wasn't, she knew, particularly original. It surely came to millions of women every year, but never before had it come to Miranda. The thought was that she could not continue to have this man as her husband. A husband who had no job was one thing. A husband who wasted her hard-earned money was quite another. He was day trading, in Miranda's estimation the functional equivalent of tossing thousand dollar bills into Buffalo Bayou. Not to mention that she didn't for one second believe his fabrication that he'd spent Wednesday night alone in a hotel room. On her personal balance sheet, he had moved from asset to liability.

Jesse padded into the kitchen, logy with sleep, and climbed onto her lap. He unwittingly brought her crashing to earth, a living reminder of the complicated reality of her situation. She had a child. *They* had a child, one who loved both parents boundlessly and who had no comprehension of jobs, paychecks, day trading or nights spent in the company of unknown strangers.

Most likely, the weekend would bring a showdown. David wasn't going to stay at the motel forever, but it wasn't the weekend yet. For the time being, she pushed away all thoughts of her husband. She distracted herself as best she could with caffeine and newsprint.

"Mom, something's broken." Jesse pointed at her coffee cup.

He was right. Miranda turned the mug to one side and saw a hairline fracture in the white porcelain. It was small, barely visible, but coffee already had begun to seep through and collect in a murky puddle around the mug's base.

Feo

Feo watched as Sherry stood on tiptoe in the corner of his bedroom, arms above her head. A perfectly straight vertical line ran from her toes through her legs, back, head and arms, all the way to her fingertips. She appeared not to breathe. She was stark naked.

"What's that one?" he asked.

"Splinter at Sea Bottom."

Sherry, he had learned, practiced T'ai Chi the way that children watch television. Any time that nothing else was happening, she would run through the Set. *Elm Sways in the Wind* followed by *Hand Strums the Lute* followed by *Blue Fades to Green*. He watched spellbound until he risked being late for work.

"Sorry," he forced himself to say at last. "I have to go."

Sherry broke out of her stance, pulled on one of his old *Los Lobos* tee-shirts, and offered him a sweaty good-bye hug. He felt the warm weight of her breasts mash against him. It was the kind of hug that said those breasts would be there waiting when he got home from work.

After the previous night it seemed clear that Sherry would be staying for a while. They'd gone to her apartment and packed her clothes, some books, a few candle lanterns and her portable steam bath. He wasn't entirely clear about the importance of the steam bath but by the time she finished explaining all of its holistic benefits he'd already put the thing into the trunk of his car and gone back inside for the next load. When they reached his house, Feo circumspectly stowed her things in his small guest bedroom. After a glance at his kitchen, stocked primarily with beer and frozen burritos, Sherry insisted on going back out to buy supplies at *Sprout*. The notion of enchiladas filled with fresh tuna and butternut squash at first made him nauseous, but it took only a bite or two to turn him around.

They'd sat on his front porch drinking wine until long after dark. When yawns replaced conversation, he waited for Sherry to go into the guest bedroom but, instead, she led him into his own bedroom, doffed her clothes and slid into his bed as lightly as if she'd been there many times before. Then she had showed him some positions he was pretty sure she didn't learn from the Master.

He needed to leave for work, but hesitated. "You'll go to the bank today?"

No answer.

"We agreed on this, didn't we? The money has to go back."

"We agreed," said Sherry. She made a sighing sound. "But you didn't say today."

Feo studied her face. "Meaning?"

"Just for a day or two, I'd like to know what it feels like to have all that money. That's all. I've never been rich."

Feo started to object, but didn't. He liked having Sherry in his house. She was gorgeous and sexy and for the evening dinner had promised to fix macrobiotic tamales with mushrooms on the side. He didn't want to quarrel.

"I'll do it on Monday," Sherry said. "Tuesday latest. I promise."

Taco slipped from underneath a dresser and gave Feo an appraising look as if waiting to see how he would handle the situation. Feo wished that he knew Sherry as well as Taco knew her.

"Fine," he said mildly. "Plenty of time."

Sherry

Sherry adored Feo's house. It was a modest two-level brick with a slate roof, located in a quiet part of Montrose she had never seen before. An old-fashioned front porch swing looked out on a neighborhood where moms pushed strollers and kids rode bikes in the street. Taco had already chosen a favorite napping spot beside the living room window.

It was apparent that Feo didn't know the first thing about Feng Shui. The *chi* had to do acrobatics to make it from one room to the next. As soon as he left, Sherry started on a nine-square *Bagua* map. Carrying a rough sketch, she ambled from room to room, soaking up the undertones and deciding where to assign each *Bagua* category. Once she finished the map and did a little redecorating, she had no doubt the *chi* would flow like the Gulf Stream.

Sherry peeked into Feo's tiny office. He had explained to her that he was more than a security guard. He had a degree in information security and he owned a high-end computer and a raft of peripherals. She wrote *Knowledge* on the floor plan. She unpacked her books on T'ai Chi and put them on the shelves next to his books on spyware and database protection.

Health was an easy one. Feo's kitchen with its ancient appliances and cute breakfast nook was perfect. She reminded herself to go back to *Sprout* to restock the pantry top to bottom.

She walked into the guest bedroom where, for the Bagua map, *Wealth* came to mind. She fully intended to return the Conquest money then residing as a guest in her bank account, but she couldn't help feeling there might be a reason why Feo couldn't stop it from coming to visit her in the first place. *We attract forces according to our being*, said the Master. *The crooked stick cannot be made straight*. Still, she had made a promise to Feo and intended to keep it.

A side door from the guest room led to a back yard graced by the high-arching branches and gnarled roots of an ancient live oak. She looked forward to practicing the Set in the tree's luxurious shade. The back yard unquestionably represented the *Center*, the place that harmonized all the other areas, where the *chi* would gather and recharge. She would keep the *Center* quiet and uncluttered to promote meditation and calm thoughts. She picked up several lawn chairs and moved them to the garage, where she saw Feo's riding mower. *This* was a problem, she thought. She wondered how he would take it when she sold the green-and-yellow smoke-belcher and replaced it with a nice planet-friendly push mower. The Master used one on the small patch of grass out front of his studio and it made only a pleasant swishing sound.

Sherry went back inside and for the master bedroom wrote *Love*. It was the one room in the house that Feo had arranged so perfectly that the *chi* nearly knocked her over every time she went in there. The night before, when the time came for bed, she'd seen no reason to delay the inevitable. The Cosmic Beam may have cured her *greed*, but it hadn't made a dent in her *excessive lust*. There was no way she could have known that when they reached for each other under those clean white sheets that he would prove as tender and solicitous a lover as Wheeler had been hasty and selfish. She had come long before he did and her orgasm was like a burst and then another burst before she finished the first one. And this when she could count on less than all of her fingers the number of times she had gotten off in her whole life. Afterward, as she lay against his chest listening to the whir of the bedside clock, she couldn't keep from weeping. Feo, troubled, asked if somehow he had hurt her. *Hurt?* She hadn't felt that good since the time...well, to be honest, she couldn't remember ever feeling that good.

Down the hallway was a pull-down folding staircase that led to an attic room. She reached for the cord and climbed cautiously upward. The attic was a lovely, low-ceilinged room, finished out but unfurnished and empty except for a few storage boxes. Empty and waiting. Perfect for *Family and Children*. Sherry made herself a note to look for a baby toy to hang from the pull-down cord, something so small that Feo wouldn't notice it for months.

She moved to the front porch and sat on the swing. A few elderly neighbors passed by. *Helpful People*, she decided. She gave each of the geezers a friendly half-wave and they waved back but gaped as if she were an orchid sprouting in a field of dandelions.

She studied the unfinished Bagua map. She still needed to assign *Career* and *Reputation* but the only spaces left were the bathroom and the garage out back. That didn't seem right at all.

The weather had warmed and the sun felt good on her bare legs. Sherry put the map aside and before long dozed in the stillness. She heard a mockingbird call and wondered if it nested in the towering live oak in the back. Somewhere down the street, a baby cried.

"Excuse me, ma'am," said a voice. "Are you visiting Feo?"

The voice belonged to one of the geezers. This one wore khaki shorts, a long-sleeved button-down shirt and white socks.

"I live across the street," said the man. He looked amicable, yet distrustful. "Are you visiting Feo?" he repeated. "I'm a friend of his."

Sherry considered the question and thought about restocking Feo's kitchen and about her books resting on his bookshelf. About the way he had made love to her and about the baby toy she planned to hang from the attic pull cord. A smile came to her face like a spasm. "I'm not visiting," she answered. "I live here now."

David

David's stockbroker opened for business at ten. David stumbled in at 9:45 and waited in the lobby. He wanted to make certain that he got his business done before Jack's afternoon press event. The distorted glare of the glass door told him that he had forgotten to shave and had his shirt on wrong side out. At least he had put on pants and socks.

David felt hazy. He had gone to the opera hoping that Miranda's anger would fade and she would let him come home, but she'd maintained a cold fury the entire evening. When the time came to leave, she had driven away without a word.

At the motel, a couple of beers on top of the champagne he'd drunk at the opera helped him relax. Then he took some blue sleeping pills that should have knocked him out but instead induced a kind of dopey halfway state. He'd watched reruns of the *Andy Griffith Show* until the small hours and during the third or fourth episode the events of the evening began to fuse with the scenes on the television screen. Jack Burnam came to him in the genial visage of the young Andy and Miranda appeared as Andy's prim but alluring girlfriend Helen Crump.

"Mr. Sesno?"

David came back to the present. A fellow who looked a dead ringer for Opie said that David's regular broker was on vacation. Opie would be happy to handle David's needs.

"My needs?" said David. "Very simple. I want to buy Conquest stock. A lot of it."

David's Keystone mistake had eaten up most of his and Miranda's rainy day fund, but they still had almost $90,000 of long-term investments. After talking with Jack the night before, he had come up with a surefire way to recover at least a part of what he'd lost.

Opie screwed up his face. "Maybe I should call in my manager. I wasn't expecting..."

"No need for that. I'll sign whatever you need."

More hesitation.

"Look, this is pretty simple," David said. "Conquest took a huge nosedive yesterday. Lots of people think it's a lock to rebound and I'm one of them."

What he didn't tell Opie was what he had overheard shortly before the curtain went up on *The Golden Ass*. At 2 p.m. today, Jack would demonstrate Bluebox to the world and make a complete fool of whoever wrote the *Examiner* story. Conquest's stock price would go screaming upward again and David was determined to go along for the ride.

"Of course," said Opie, with evident skepticism.

David knew exactly what was at stake. With Conquest's stock price near 41, he calculated that he needed to buy about 1,800 shares. When the price bounced back, David would recover his losses on Keystone and maybe have a stake to start day trading again. And he would have shown Miranda that he knew what he was doing after all.

"Not the entire account," David said, trying to sound more reasonable. "Only seventy-five thousand."

Opie studied his computer screen and jotted some notes. "You own mostly high-grade bonds, fourteen different issues. It'll take us a day or so."

"I don't have a day or so. This has to be completed right away. Today."

"Yes, sir," said a wide-eyed Opie. "I'll get to work right now and call you when it's done."

"I'd like to wait."

"You want to wait? Here?"

"This is very important to me. Very..." David was surprised to find himself choking up, unable to finish.

Opie gestured toward the reception area. "Make yourself at home."

David waited and dozed. In a daydream, he saw himself at a Sunday afternoon celebration in Mayberry. Aunt Bee had fixed an enormous fried chicken dinner. Everyone gathered around the dining table, David and Aunt Bee and Opie and Andy and Helen Crump. Barney was there, too, wearing his deputy's uniform with a Glock buckled into his holster.

Oh Christ, *Jane* was there. He looked away, praying that Helen hadn't caught on to anything, but couldn't help looking back at Jane again. *Sweet Jesus*, she looked good. He wondered why no one else had noticed that she wasn't wearing anything except those doll-sized black panties. He reached under the dining table to adjust the front of his pants.

"I think we're all set, Mr. Sesno. Would you like to go over the details?"

Andy's house vanished. Opie the child-stockbroker looked at him expectantly.

"Absolutely," David said. "Let's have a look."

Five minutes later, David, proud new owner of 1,829 shares of Conquest stock, turned to leave. It was 1:15 so he needed to head over the Conquest Plaza for the press announcement. He thought there was something else he had planned for the day, something involving Velotrade, but the haze so enveloped his brain that he wasn't certain what it was.

Opie coughed. "Mr. Sesno, one last thing."

"What is it? I'm running late."

"This is a joint account. Both you and your wife have full authority to execute trades, but for a transaction of this magnitude we strongly recommend contacting the other spouse." He smiled weakly. "For informational purposes. Would you like us to do that for you?"

"No. Don't do that."

For some odd reason, the sound of David's voice echoed off the walls. Opie's eyes widened and the receptionist stared in surprise. It puzzled David that his fists seemed to have clenched themselves and his body had taken a step in Opie's direction.

"There's no need to shout, Mr. Sesno."

Had he shouted? He moved slowly backward and toward the exit. "Of course not," he said. "No need at all."

Jack

Jack strode to the podium, Bluebox in hand. On the blue monitor he could see that Conquest's stock price had steadied. He rubbed his hands together and motioned to silence the audience.

"Let's get right to it, ladies and gentlemen. Yesterday's edition of the Houston Examiner contained an article relating to Conquest, its acquisition of Bluestream, and a new product we call Bluebox. Some of you may have seen this story."

A titter rolled through the room. This crowd had talked of little else for the past twenty-four hours. He spied Lulu Barker. She had no idea, he guessed, that by the end of the press conference her career as a reporter would be cut as short as those outdated mini-skirts she wore.

"The article in question," Jack continued, "consists of nothing more than unsupported conjecture and outright falsehoods. It is so wildly inaccurate as to call into serious question the integrity of the Examiner's editorial process."

He held up the Bluebox prototype for everyone to see. "Contrary to the reckless speculations of the Examiner, this device is a miracle of modern telecommunications technology. It works, and it goes far beyond anything currently available to consumers. Conquest intends to begin mass production immediately and bring Bluebox to market within three months."

A buzz erupted from the audience. While he waited for the noise to subside, Jack checked the monitor. Conquest's stock price had begun to edge upward.

"Now I'd like to introduce Josh Morris of Bluestream. Josh headed up the R&D work on Bluebox."

Josh took the podium and motioned onto the stage with him a group of men and women, each of whom carried a Bluebox prototype. To a person, they looked as if they had enjoyed a front-row seat at the Second Coming.

"Earlier today," Josh said to the crowd, "we chose these ten individuals at random from the media pool and invited them to come in for a sneak preview. For the past hour, they've participated in a more exhaustive version of the presentation you are about to see. This was done to make sure that the press would have ample opportunity to authenticate the capabilities of Bluebox."

Josh moved into a point-by-point demonstration of Bluebox's functions, with its audio wired into the auditorium sound system and its video transmitted to an on-stage screen. At key points, members of the sneak preview group commented and corroborated. Josh invited a few additional volunteers from the audience to come on stage, bear witness and be amazed.

The impact of the presentation was electric. Reporters pushed one another aside for a chance to handle one of the prototypes. The clamor in the room rivaled anything Jack had heard in his entire career.

While Josh responded to questions, Jack scanned the room and saw something odd. There in the front row sat Miranda Sesno's sad sack husband. The guy had cornered him at the Wortham Center the night before and gone off on a tangent every time Jack tried to end the conversation. Jack considered himself a master at giving bores the slip, but he was no match for this one. Daniel? Darrel? No, David. That was it. Jack wondered why in hell David Sesno was sitting up front giving him a double thumbs-up like they were the best of friends. Norah had assured him the guy was fresh out of a job but he sat there grinning like he'd hit the daily double.

Jack saw that Josh had reached the final segment of his demo, which consisted of maps showing a phased rollout of Bluebox throughout the United States. He retook the podium. "There's one thing, and only one thing, that the Examiner was right about. I've staked Conquest's future and my personal future on the success of this product. That's how strongly I believe in it."

A few of the Conquest employees in attendance stood and began to clap. Reporters streamed for the exits to file their stories. Jack once again checked the blue monitor and saw that Conquest's stock price already had taken a jump. Jack had no doubt that within a few days it would recover from the *Examiner* story. And then climb higher.

From the corner of his eye, Jack saw Lulu Barker, glued to her chair and looking dazed. Her skirt had ridden so high he could make out a skein of incipient varicose veins on her upper thigh. He watched until she caught his gaze. Her face tilted upward in his direction and their eyes locked. Then, despite the near-certainty he would appear on the evening news in a stance that hardly befit the powerhouse CEO of a global corporation, he did something he knew that he shouldn't. He simply couldn't resist. Jack gave Lulu his most ingratiating smile and simultaneously extended in her direction his upright middle finger.

Miranda

Norah had invited her to attend the Bluebox show, but Miranda couldn't bear to abandon the privacy of her office. She didn't want Norah or anyone else to see her in her present condition. She told her assistant to hold all calls, went into her office and closed the door. She logged onto her Bloomberg terminal so if anyone asked she would at least have some idea of what happened. Sure enough, Bloomberg already had posted a report.

Bluebox, it seemed, had knocked everyone for a loop. The report quoted commentators who made the device sound like a rock star: *I have seen the future of the Internet and its name is Bluebox.* Clearly, it would be a phenomenon. Miranda wondered how the *Examiner's* reporter could have written a story so far off the mark.

Conquest shares had made an about-face. Once again, Conquest was a market darling. At that very moment, Miranda suspected, half the people in the building were recalculating the value of their options.

Miranda recalled Norah's cryptic prediction when Burnam announced the Bluestream deal three weeks earlier. *Conquest will never be the same.* Miranda hadn't gotten it then, but she did now. Bluebox would generate revenue on a scale far beyond any other line of business in the company's history. Despite her qualms about Norah's hinky accounting methods, she couldn't help feeling excited about the impact of the Bluestream deal and her own role in making it happen. Her misgivings began to recede as she thought about the future. What did dubious accounting gimmicks matter so long as Conquest made a profit, paid its creditors and enriched its shareholders?

"Miranda, I know you told me not to interrupt, but it's Jesse. He's on the phone."

Jesse? He should be at his after-school program.

"Hi Mom." His tone was suspiciously casual. Had he gotten into trouble?

"Jesse, is something wrong?"

"I wanted to talk."

He wanted to talk? With a sinking feeling, Miranda understood where he was headed.

"Mom, when is Dad coming home?"

Miranda inwardly groaned.

"I miss him." Jesse's voice had become small and tremulous.

On Thursday, Miranda had told Jesse that David had gone out of town to visit some friends. Jesse hadn't exactly challenged the story, but she knew he didn't believe it. She didn't know what to tell him.

"Mom, I miss Daddy."

She heard him sniffle and sob. She listened silently until pretty soon she was crying along with him.

"Mom, are you still there?"

Miranda melted. For Jesse's sake, she would have to give David one last chance. Maybe it didn't matter that he didn't have a job. She made enough now for the both of them, hell, for all three of them. She would make him promise to give up day trading. And, as for his Wednesday night disappearance, she knew what her mother would say. *Men can't help themselves.* She pulled herself together long enough to answer Jesse.

"He'll be home soon, honey. Tomorrow, I guess. Maybe Sunday."

Silence. *Maybe Sunday* wasn't going to be good enough.

"Sunday, *for sure*. Really."

They chatted a bit longer, making plans for the weekend, but Miranda sensed that Jesse was ready to end their conversation. He'd heard what he wanted to hear. She hung up the phone, and at least ten minutes passed before she regained control of her emotions. She dried her eyes and checked her face in a mirror. Black streaks. Bleary bloodshot eyes. Her chest hurt as if she had run a marathon, but she had a sense of peace. She had done the right thing for her family. She mentally reclassified David from liability back to asset, albeit one that was nonperforming.

A popup on the Bloomberg home page drew her attention. Another Conquest story, but it wasn't about Bluebox. *SEC to Launch Routine Inquiry of Conquest*, read the headline. The Securities and Exchange Commission, she read, has requested voluntary production of documents pertaining to Conquest's accounting policies and practices for the past three years. The agency described the inquiry as routine in nature and part of its ongoing supervisory activities. The article contained a statement issued by Conquest stating the company's belief that its accounting policies and practices complied with all applicable requirements. Conquest pledged full cooperation with the SEC inquiry. And, at the very end, a link to a related story: *Senator Logan's Office Denies Any Role in SEC Inquiry Into Conquest.*

Her sense of peace evaporated as quickly as it had come and her stomach felt hollow. The deliberately understated tone of the SEC announcement did nothing to stem the tide of alarm rising inside her.

The truth was that she didn't know anything for certain. She had read some files and she didn't agree with some of the accounting treatments, but that was all. She had no proof of wrongdoing. When the SEC investigators came calling, she would keep her suspicions to herself Anything else would be crazy. She didn't really *know* anything.

Feo

Feo stood in Norah's waiting area for the fourth time that day. The first two times she'd been busy helping Mr. Burnam prepare for the press conference and the third time she'd been handling the reporters' follow-up questions. This time the management committee had called her in for a post-mortem.

The assistant gave him a sour look. "I told you before you should leave Mr. Wheeler's materials with me. I don't know why you think you have to see Ms. Needham in person."

Feo surmised that, in this woman's estimation, he ranked somewhere between janitor and mail room employee. She didn't seem to have recovered from the fact that the day before Norah had stepped out of a meeting with Mr. Burnam to take Feo's call. During the day's visits, her attitude toward him had progressed gradually from peevish to surly. He'd taken to calling her—under his breath, of course—*La bruja*. The witch.

"I'll wait," he said, and took a seat.

It troubled him that *La bruja* knew that the file had belonged to Wheeler. Norah had lectured him about secrecy and he didn't see any reason why her nasty secretary should have this information. He didn't intend to give the materials to anyone other than Norah and he didn't intend to leave without telling her that Sherry had agreed to return the money. It wasn't every day that someone in Security saved the company a million bucks. He wanted to deliver the news in person.

On the other hand, it was well past five o'clock and he wanted to get home. As his wait dragged on, the vision of Sherry's morning workout passed through his mind again and again. Not only that, but he could almost taste those macrobiotic tamales. This would be his first day coming home to Sherry and he had no desire to keep her waiting. What the hell, maybe he should leave it with the assistant. He could always talk to Norah about the money tomorrow, like it wasn't that big a deal and he expected to save the company a million dollars every time out. Or he could write her a memo. That's how an executive would do it.

He stood and made ready to hand the files over when a redhead came through the doorway looking as if she'd come from a traffic accident. He could see she'd been crying.

"Is Norah in?" she asked. "It's urgent."

La bruja chortled. "Get in line. Mr. Duarte here thinks he's an urgent case, too."

The redhead became aware of Feo for the first time and turned crimson with embarrassment. Feo watched her struggle to compose her face.

"Mr. Duarte, this is Miranda Sesno," said *La bruja*. "She took over from Wheeler." *La bruja's* tone made it clear to Feo that, unlike him, the redhead was important.

Feo offered his hand and wondered at the flash of apprehension that crossed the Miranda's face at the mention of Wheeler. "Nice to meet you. Please call me Feo."

"Mr. Duarte is the one that tracked down Wheeler in California," said *La bruja*. "Of course, by that time, he was dead." She seemed to think that Wheeler might well have survived had Feo been a bit more on the ball.

"Those are Wheeler's files?" asked Miranda. "But I thought..."

She stopped, but Feo could see that the fact that Wheeler's files still existed hit her pretty hard.

"I've got an idea," said *La bruja*. "If you don't want to give that stuff to me, maybe you'll leave it with Miranda. Otherwise, you're going to have to wait for Ms. Needham to get back and then you're going to have to wait for her and Miranda to finish."

Feo absorbed the humiliating notion that despite his waiting for an hour on his fourth attempt, *La bruja* had bumped him to the back of the line. Meanwhile, Miranda looked as if she'd rather receive Wheeler's dead body than his old files.

La bruja rose from behind her desk, moving pretty briskly for an old crone, and snatched the envelope from his hands.

"Here, Miranda," she said. "Take this. Maybe there's something in there you'll want to know."

Miranda

A half-block from Conquest Plaza stood Antioch Baptist, a modest church of white-painted brick construction and Greek Revivalist design, looking more than a little out of place amid the surrounding skyscrapers. Miranda passed it all the time but until today had never given it a second thought. The church's heavy door gave way at her touch. Inside it was cool and dry and the din of downtown traffic receded into noiselessness. That a place of such repose could exist virtually across the street from her office astonished her.

Initially Miranda thought the church empty, but as her eyes adjusted to the light she saw a man crouched at one side of the altar. He didn't seem to have noticed her. From time to time, he took a tool from a nearby box. When he reached toward the tool box, she saw the tangle of unconnected electrical wires that occupied his attention.

"Excuse me," she said.

The man had the size and build of a professional basketball player and looked down at her from a considerable height. He wore a clerical collar.

"Yes, ma'am?"

"I work nearby, but I've never visited your church before," she said. "It's glorious."

"Thank you." He told her his name. "I'm the pastor." He smiled. "Also the maintenance man."

She didn't respond. She was thinking about the files that she held behind her back, the copy she had printed with nervous dread after racing from Norah's office a half-hour ago.

"May I sit here for a while?" she said finally. "I need a place to think for a few minutes."

"Of course," he said. "We don't get many visitors this time of day. You'll have the place to yourself." He returned to his patch job.

Miranda sat down on a deeply worn high-backed pew. Her hands trembled slightly as she unfolded the printout. Air seemed to enter her lungs only with a conscious effort. She looked down at the document and began to read.

Thirty minutes later, Miranda allowed the papers to fall to her lap. She leaned back against the hard wood of the pew and looked up toward the ceiling. Dust motes drifted unperturbedly through random shafts of light entering through the clerestory. She closed her eyes and wished for sleep.

"Are you okay? You look troubled."

Troubled? Yes. She opened her eyes to find the pastor looking down at her. "A friend of mine has a problem," she said.

The pastor nodded. "A lot of the people I talk to have friends with problems."

"My friend found out something terrible about the company she works for. Something so terrible it might ruin the company if it gets out."

"So your friend isn't sure what to do."

"That's right. Thousands of people work at this company and only a few of them are responsible for the terrible thing. It isn't fair that they should all lose their jobs, is it?"

Miranda suspected that the information on her lap would bring Conquest crashing down, destroying the jobs of all the employees who, like her, had come to work every day for years and given their time and talent to build the company and who, unlike her, hadn't the slightest inkling of Norah's dirty tricks. The release of the information would decimate those same employees' retirement accounts, most of which were over-invested in Conquest shares. It seemed to her that she held in her hands, literally, the livelihoods of thousands of fellow employees and their spouses and children.

"So your friend might keep this information to herself."

"Yes," said Miranda. "She might."

Maybe the information wouldn't hurt anyone. Maybe it wouldn't hurt anyone because maybe on her way home Miranda would toss this stuff into a garbage dumpster.

"Your friend thinks that if she keeps the information to herself," the pastor said, "the company would be able to go on making money and people could keep their jobs."

"Exactly. This company has a new product that might be a huge success. Then they could stop doing the other stuff."

"True. But your friend could get in a lot of trouble if someone else knows about this. And wouldn't your friend would be equally as guilty as the people doing the bad things?"

Miranda believed that what she possessed was a solitary copy. If it disappeared, she'd bet her last pair of pantyhose that Norah had otherwise covered her tracks. But she couldn't be one hundred percent sure. It was conceivable she would lose that bet.

To whom did she owe her loyalty? To Conquest? To the creditors and shareholders who'd been duped? To her fellow employees? To some government investigators she had never met?

The pastor drew himself up as if he had reached a conclusion. When he spoke, his voice was deep and resonant, like a pipe organ. "Your friend has to follow her conscience."

Follow my conscience? That was no help at all.

The pastor returned to the front of the church and completed his repair work. He flicked a switch. Far above the altar, halfway up the interior of the church's three-story bell tower, a blue-and-white neon sign buzzed and hummed and finally lit up, its pale glow barely penetrating the quiet dark of the church. The oddity of a neon sign in a place of worship piqued Miranda's interest. She craned her neck and made out the words on the sign: *Jesus Saves.*

Miranda wasn't a religious person. It had been years since she set foot in a church, but that didn't mean she rejected the church's teachings. As a matter of common sense and good behavior she accepted and strived to abide by many of them. The Ten Commandments, for example. *Thou shalt not bear false witness.* She fixed her eyes on the neon sign.

* * * * *

THE OIL CRASH

HOUSTON, 1983

Life went poorly for Wally Harvey in 1983, beginning with his father's death in mid-January. Less than a year after taking an early-out package, Ernie Harvey had slipped climbing out of the back-yard hot tub the kids gave him as a retirement gift. His head struck the concrete step and he never woke up.

"Twenty-seven years at Monsanto without a scratch," said Wally's mother, "and now this."

In 1947, a freighter exploded in the Ship Channel across from the Monsanto chemical plant, killing more than six hundred people. Wally's mother held the view that lightning could strike twice, and never started dinner until she saw Ernie come through the door. Wally didn't bother to point out that his father, after making it into middle management, had worked in the Admin Building a quarter-mile inland and hadn't been in harm's way for years. Nor did he mention the case of Budweiser empties he found behind the hot tub the day after the accident.

As the eldest, Wally absorbed the brunt of both the funeral arrangements and his mother's grief. Every Sunday for six months he drove his pickup truck the thirty-two-mile round trip from Deer Park, where he and Norah lived in the modest two-bedroom ranch they bought when they got married, to LaPorte, near the coast, where his mother lived. At first, Norah traveled with him every week. Then it became every other week and then once a month. Eventually, she begged off altogether.

"You and your mother need some private time," she'd said.

That his mother never warmed up to Norah surprised Wally because Norah resembled his mother more than any other person he knew. Not physically, of course, because Edna had gone soft and pear-shaped in middle age and Norah was all angles and elbows. The similarity lay in their outlook, the way they feared life more than they enjoyed it.

In those days he had a decent job at the Humble Oil Refinery—the name had changed to Exxon years earlier but the locals still called it Humble, with a silent *H*—where he earned $16,800 a year. He operated a crude oil coking machine and came home most days wearing a layer of coke residue. A monthly paycheck of $1,400 seemed like good money before they bought the house, but then Norah quit her job at the fast-food chicken place to get ready for having a family. Less and less cash remained at the end of each month.

He'd never given the briefest thought to college. Jobs along the Ship Channel had always been plentiful. Men who didn't mind a bit of grime could choose among the companies that lined the Channel from the Turning Basin down to Barbours Cut. Everyone Wally knew found work as a coker, a pumper or a mechanic and anyone with some smarts, like Wally's father, could eventually get a white-shirt job.

During the 1970's when the Arab oil embargo put most of America flat on its ass, Houston barely blinked. Out-of-work men from Cleveland, Detroit and Buffalo flocked to Houston by the hundreds of thousands. They found jobs at Humble and Hughes Tool and Cameron Iron Works and sent word to their wives and kids to give away the snow blowers and come to Texas. So many U-Haul trailers arrived in Houston that for a decade anybody willing to pull one to another state could take it free of charge. Home prices along the Channel shot upward. Traffic jams and lines at the grocery store became the norm.

Like all Houstonians, Wally believed his hometown was immune to the downturns that other cities suffered. America would always need oil, and Houston refined most of the crude produced in Texas and much that came in from other countries. In a nation that collapsed into recession in the face of rising crude prices, Houston found itself in an unspoken economic alliance with Libya, Venezuela and Saudi Arabia.

"Houston ain't like other places," Wally's father had always said, pointing out that not a single Houston bank had failed during the Great Depression. God's blessing upon Houston, and one of its only blessings, was jobs.

So it was that shock reverberated throughout the city when its economy began to wobble in 1982. The next year, when the Crash reached full force, shock gave way to outright panic. Due to big strikes in Mexico and the North Sea, the supply of oil finally caught up to demand. The Texas oil boom that had raged for eighty years came to an end. Crude prices fell and drilling ceased. The companies that exploded in the 1970's began firing men in droves. Shopping centers went dark, grass grew chest-high in unused parking lots and oil service companies stacked vast quantities of unused drilling equipment in empty fields. The Texas banks that had survived the Great Depression went under or sold out to New York banks. Defeatism lay over the city like smog.

In May of that year, Wally got laid off. Norah took a counter job at the chicken place, working the five-to-midnight shift. She brought home enough to cover the utilities and buy groceries, but they had no savings and missed the mortgage payment four months running. Coming home so late, she slept until noon every day and Wally rarely saw her awake. For the first time, they quarreled. His mother said that all married couples have quarrels, but it hadn't happened to him before. Wally hadn't dated much and certainly had never had to cope with a frazzled, unhappy woman who served chicken until midnight every night to pay the bills.

He saw little point in looking for a new job himself. All around him, several hundred thousand men sought work and Wally had nothing better to offer than any of them. The best he could find was occasional day work at Humble loading and unloading empty gas canisters. The foreman had a soft spot for the laid-off guys and tried to bring them in once or twice a month. Minimum wage, but Wally didn't know anyone who wouldn't stand in line through a winter's night to get it.

In November, when the first foreclosure notice arrived in the mail, Wally made a plan. He'd heard of a few other guys that had done it, one at Shell and another at Dow Chemical. One afternoon when Norah was at work he pulled out the accidental death policy that Edna had given Norah as a wedding gift. It cost only a few dollars each month and Edna kept the premiums current when the money got tight. Upon his death by accident, Norah would receive a lump sum benefit of $25,000. Not a fortune, but enough to let her keep the house and the truck and maybe take some college courses at night school. She was smart, he knew that, much smarter than he was, and she might eventually move away from the Ship Channel and get an office job.

The policy didn't cover a suicide, of course, but Wally didn't see that as a problem. In an oil refinery, leaky valves, worn-out seals and flammable gasses abound, lacking only a spark to send a man up in smoke. It was no great trick to provide the spark.

He made ready and on December 22, when the foreman called him in for day work, Wally didn't hesitate. He drove out to Humble and parked the truck at the front of the lot where Norah would easily see it. He rolled up the windows, left the doors unlocked and put the keys in the glove box.

It took him only a few hours to find what he needed. He had loaded a dozen or so empty propane canisters onto his forklift when he came across one that, judging by its weight, remained at least a third full. Not a surprise. Lots of men liked to change canisters at the start of a shift, when they were fresh, so they wouldn't have to do it later when they were tired and more inclined to make a mistake.

As the forklift inched toward the storage shed, tears welled and his jaw clenched. His resolve wavered. He brought the machine to a halt. Then he pictured himself sitting home every night while his wife filled paper bags with chicken and biscuits for strangers. He imagined moving from their two-bedroom house into a crummy little apartment, or worse, moving in with Edna. He put the forklift back in gear.

When he reached the shed, Wally unloaded the canisters from the forklift and lined them up next to a row of empties already in place. He closed the metal door from the inside and stuffed some old newspaper that he'd brought along into the space underneath it. The shed had no windows and it became hard to see, but his eyes gradually adjusted. Wally twisted the valve of the partially-full canister to the full open position and sank to the floor, his back against it, his work boots jammed against a wall. He listened to the hiss of the escaping gas.

His shirt pocket held four Diamond Brand kitchen matches with wood stems and red phosphorus tips. He'd made certain to buy the kind that strikes against any type of surface. When he tested them on the back porch, it had never taken more than four matches to get a good flame, so he had put four matches in his pocket and thrown the matchbox out the truck window. He stood and put his ear close to the canister valve. The hissing noise had stopped. Empty. Feeling nauseous and light-headed, he returned the valve to the closed position and sat back down.

He placed the tip of a match against a small ridge on the hard cement floor of the shed and gave it a sharp flick. The match burst into flame. The flame burned yellow and orange and blue and, finally, purest white.

* * * * *

CHAPTER 14. SATURDAY

MARKET CLOSED

Miranda

Midmorning Saturday found Miranda in gray sweats with a powerful urge to clean house. She swept the floor, unloaded the dishwasher, put away clean dishes and loaded dirty ones. Then she vacuumed.

She had an appointment in ninety minutes with two men from the government. She found their names and contact information by tracking down the agency's letter notifying Conquest about its inquiry into the company's accounting practices. When she called they initially expressed little interest in meeting with her, especially on a Saturday. No surprise there. She supposed that every SEC investigation draws a plague of cranks and disgruntled employees. So she mentioned that she reported directly to Norah Needham, the CFO. Within seconds they had specified a meeting time and given her directions to their location.

Switching off the vacuum, Miranda went back to the laundry room and moved clothes from washer to dryer. She grabbed Windex, Pine-Sol, cleanser and a toilet brush. She hadn't done the bathrooms yet.

She intended to give as little explanation as possible when she handed over Wheeler's files. The files would make everything clear. Booster, Boiler, Blueco. And, most damning of all, that the third-party investors who put in the sliver of outside equity required by the accounting rules consisted of family members, friends, neighbors and employees of Conquest officers, all of whom funded their investments with special grants of stock options. Not a particularly ingenious fraud, Miranda thought, but plenty brash.

Miranda froze, toilet brush in mid-air, as the reason for Wheeler's unaccountable disappearance made itself clear to her. Norah had brought him into the inner circle, as she had done with Miranda, but Wheeler had gone her one better. He'd compiled all this information and blackmailed her. That's why Maggie's investments were worth so much money. But then Wheeler had died before collecting his take. She felt a shiver run through her, then applied a furious scrub to the toilet bowl.

At eleven-thirty Miranda put away the cleaning supplies and returned the vacuum to the closet. She grabbed her purse and the files, which were still in the envelope in which she had received them from the Security guy.

"Jesse," she said, "put on your shoes. Time to go." She was dropping him at a play date on her way to the meeting.

"Mom, I thought you were going to a business meeting."

"That's right, and I'm late. Let's get going."

He shrugged and made a face. "You aren't dressed."

She was still wearing her sweats. Sweet Jesus. In the bathroom she stripped off her sweats, swabbed herself with a damp washcloth and changed into fresh underwear and a black pants suit. Once again, with Jesse in tow and her purse and Wheeler's files in hand, she headed for the car. She dropped Jesse at his play date and drove to the address the government men had given her.

The meeting went well. They took her information, asked her a few basic questions and scheduled another meeting in a few days to ask more questions after they'd reviewed the files. They cautioned her not to speak with anyone else. They briefly explained the whistleblower laws which, in theory, would protect her from retaliation or reprisal by Conquest for her reporting potential violations of federal law. She didn't pay much attention to that part. It was clear to her that her career at Conquest had ended, and she had serious doubts that Conquest would survive as a going concern.

When she got back home, a weariness as heavy as a late August afternoon came over her and she sank into a living room chair. Despite her fatigue, she decided to drive over to Somerset and spend the rest of the afternoon on horseback. She changed into a long-sleeved cotton shirt and her tan riding pants. She smoothed band-aids over the blisters on her feet, then pulled on her socks and riding boots.

Most likely, this would be her last chance to go riding for a long, long time.

David

His suitcase was already packed, although he wouldn't see Miranda and Jesse until the next day. He was desperate to get out of the Motel Six and back to his family, but he faced a dilemma. If he didn't carry his suitcase to the door, Miranda might think he didn't want to return, and nothing could be further from the truth. On the other hand, if he showed up suitcase in hand, she might think him overconfident. She might take offense that he had presumed too much. He wasn't sure what to expect.

She'd been noncommittal on the phone, saying only that Jesse wanted to see him. She hadn't said *Come back* or *Come home*, which would have implied some element of forgiveness. Nor did she say *Come by* or *Come over*, which would have suggested merely a visit. Her voice had sounded ragged, and he was pretty sure she'd been crying.

He had thought long and hard about what conditions she might lay out for their getting back together. Stop day trading. Pay back the money he'd lost. Get a job and hold on to it. Quit the gym. Lose some weight. Spend less money. Do the grocery shopping. Polish her shoes. Whatever it was, he would agree.

The Conquest trade gave him an ace in the hole, but he didn't want to tell her about it yet. When the bell rang on Friday afternoon his shares already were up by more than $11,000. He felt sure they would continue to climb on Monday so he'd carried the position over the weekend. He planned to sell it some time on Monday when his profit reached $15,000. No reason to be greedy. Then he could tell Miranda with the real numbers. She would have to let him off the hook.

Maybe she was going to confront him about the night he didn't come home. He'd thought about that, too. Every guy he'd ever talked to said the same thing: *Never confess to an affair. Never.* Better for all to stay mum. Besides, he hadn't had an *affair*. It was a one-night-stand, and completely unintentional. There was no way Miranda could know about Jane, so he'd made up his mind not to admit anything.

He promised himself he would never again think about those miniscule black panties. Except that he couldn't get them out of his mind. Not Jane, her panties. They were made of a shiny silk material with no lace or other ornamentation whatsoever. And *so* small.

He caught himself. Lately he kept drifting off on the oddest tangents at the oddest times. He wondered what was going on with his mind.

CHAPTER 15. SUNDAY

MARKET CLOSED

Miranda

Miranda watched from the window as David parked in the driveway. It was his own driveway in front of his own house, but he somehow looked like a stranger in a way she couldn't put into words. He got out of the car and headed up the front walk, suitcase in hand. Halfway to the front door he faltered. He put the suitcase back in the car and stood motionless. He seemed not to know what to do next. A cloud passed overhead.

He looked up as Jesse pounded down the front path in his direction.

"Daddy!"

Miranda moved to the doorway and stood with her arms folded against her chest. In the split second before Jesse leapt into his arms she caught David's eyes. He looked exceptionally tired, more tired than she'd ever seen him. She kept her expression noncommittal. For the time being, she gave him nothing.

For the next several hours, David and Jesse enjoyed each other's company. They ran dribbling drills in the driveway and walked down to the playground to shoot baskets. She had pizza delivered for their lunch. They played a card game. Jesse won most of the hands and Miranda couldn't tell if David was letting him win or was so exhausted he couldn't focus. After fourteen or fifteen hands, Jesse yawned and his eyelids drooped. Miranda put a disc in the DVD player and parked him in front of the television.

"I need to talk to your Dad for a little while," she told her son.

Miranda sat down at the kitchen table. David started to take chair on the opposite side, but hesitated. He took a breath and sat in the chair nearest her, his hand within reach of hers.

"I'm so sorry," he said. "I'll do anything you want. I want to come home."

He seemed contrite, not at all full of his customary bluster. She'd been on the fence when he arrived but as she watched him and Jesse together she had begun to lean in his favor. Maybe they could start over and make things work. They would talk. They would make up. She could forgive him for quitting his job and for the money he'd lost and she could ignore the rest.

She'd read a book once that said the secret to a long-lasting marriage was simply to lower your expectations. She could do that, too.

David

"And how long are you staying, Mr. Sesno?"

Back at the Motel Six, David decided to try out one of the extended stay rooms. Queen bed. Kitchenette with dishes. Sitting area with a sofa and coffee table. He'd be snug while he watched his marriage shatter.

"I don't know," he told the desk clerk.

"You get a better rate for two weeks or longer."

Two weeks? Why not? Sitting at the kitchen table with Miranda an hour earlier, they had talked through everything and he thought he would be moving back home. He had reached to take her hands in his when she said, *One more thing*, and the wheels came off. She told him about some files and what they showed and about her meeting with the government investigators. He rose from the table and left the house without saying another word, and judging by the look on her face it could be two weeks or two months or forever. He had no idea.

"Sure," he said. "Put me down for two weeks."

Once in the room, he tossed his suitcase on the bed and began to pace, trying to think of a way to get out of his Conquest shares. He didn't have his broker's home or cell number. The market wouldn't open until Monday morning. He would be at the broker's office at the moment it opened on Monday. In the meantime, there was nothing he could do but wait and pray. With luck, the guys that Miranda had met with would spend Sunday afternoon on the golf course, like normal people, and wouldn't dive into those files until after their Monday morning coffee break.

He stopped pacing and emptied his suitcase onto the bed. Something cold and heavy fell out. The Glock. He'd intended to return the damn thing and ask Buzz for a refund. He'd never loaded the ammunition. Instead he had stuffed it into the bottom of his bag and forgotten about it. Seemed he'd forgotten lots of things lately.

He lifted the Glock and pointed it at a David Hockney print hanging over the bed. He had intended to use it to frighten the Velotrade floor manager, but the truth was that the guy who caused his problems was the guy sitting in a room at the Motel Six pretending to shoot a hole in the wall. With a despairing sigh, he laid the Glock on the coffee table.

He clicked on the television. Whoever watched it last had left it tuned to CNBC, and there was Maria Bartiromo, big as life. The Money Honey herself. At Velotrade, activity among the traders came to a virtual standstill when she came onscreen.

Maria's hair looked damp and her face slightly flushed, as if she had stepped right out of the shower onto the set. Her black eyes glittered with excitement. Something big must have happened to bring her in on a Sunday.

A box opened over Maria's left shoulder. The scene inside the box was an aerial shot of Conquest Plaza. It told him that God, in record time, had eliminated his last desperate hope with a big, fat, *Fuck you, David Sesno.*

He turned up the volume and Maria's euphonious contralto filled the hotel room.

"...and has demanded documents relating to hundreds of questionable transactions allegedly engaged in for the purposes of manipulating earnings and overstating financial results. In addition, the government has issued subpoenas to dozens of senior executives and third parties, including the company's audit firm and legal counsel."

The aerial view of Conquest Plaza dissolved into a live shot of the main entrance to the building. A lone security guard stood in front. Maria paused, mouth half-open, apparently surprised at something she'd heard in her ear bud. "Due to rumors of extensive shredding of files," she continued, "the government has issued a cease-and-desist order. A team of federal marshals is on its way to Conquest headquarters to secure the building."

David's eyes flitted between Maria and the disaster unfolding over her shoulder. Dark blue mini-buses disgorged squads of uniformed men. The posse of feds chased the security guard into the building, leaving several of their own at the entrance.

"We now take you live to Washington," Maria said, "where the SEC enforcement director has begun a press conference."

The screen shifted to a shot of a square-jawed woman facing a phalanx of microphones. Short hair. Power suit. The audio came on in mid-sentence.

"...wherever it may lead. Our commitment to protecting the investing public demands nothing less. Furthermore, we have suspended trading in Conquest stock, effective immediately. We've taken this action based on evidence we have in hand indicating that the information available in the marketplace is so untrustworthy as to make it unfair to allow investors to continue to buy and sell shares in this company."

Maria returned to the screen, but she no longer held David's attention. Instead, the box over her shoulder riveted his attention with footage of Jack Burnam at the Friday press event. In freeze frame, Burnam extended his middle finger, a smile of triumph and derision splitting his face wide open.

David had stood among the crowd and watched as Burnam delivered his obscene gesture to someone on the other side of the room, but it looked different now. The camera angle caught him dead center full face and it now looked as if Burnam was giving the finger to...well, everyone. Including David.

It came to David that the nightmarish situation in which he found himself wasn't entirely his own fault. Someone else was partly to blame. *Burnam.*

David lifted the Glock from the coffee table and aimed it at Burnam's beaming face. He pulled the trigger. *Click.*

CHAPTER 16. TUESDAY TEN DAYS LATER

CQC TRADING SUSPENDED

Norah

The man flashed a badge. "Are you Norah Needham?"

He wore an ordinary business suit, but had two uniformed policemen with him. Both of them carried guns.

He's joking, she thought. The man and his pals had tracked her every move for more than a week. They followed her home at night and back to work in the morning. A female marshal watched her in the ladies room. Her face had appeared on television a hundred times over captions like *Conquest on the Brink.* He certainly knew her name, but it wasn't a joke. He demanded an answer and she had barely finished saying *Yes* when he pulled out a yellow card and began reading a string of legalisms. *You have the right...*

They stood in the lobby of Conquest Plaza. Norah was going to lunch when the man intercepted her. Reporters mingled with Conquest's lunchtime crowd. Their shouted questions decomposed into the cacophony surrounding her. *What are the charges? Who's your lawyer? How do you feel?* Men with bulky cameras shoved them in her face. One of the policemen motioned them back. *For Christ's sake, this is an arrest in progress.*

The throng of employees watched in stupefied silence. Elevator doors opened and closed every minute or so disgorging more people into an already jam-packed space. Conversations broke off as people saw what was happening. The spectacle of the company's Chief Financial Officer doing the *perp walk* transfixed one and all. Most of the faces registered shock and concern, but an uncomfortably large number contorted with hostility and resentment. *Why did you do it?* their faces said. They didn't know the truth. None of them. They didn't know that she had *saved* the company, that she had kept the place afloat for nearly a decade while Jack's acquisition binge brought together the most spectacular agglomeration of duds, flops and washouts in modern business history. In the early days, Norah, like everyone else, found Jack's smooth confidence irresistible. Every new venture promised more profit. Every new product would boost shareholder value. Every new undertaking fit neatly into the jigsaw puzzle of his grand plan.

Jack eventually had given her the coveted assignment of raising cash for his blizzard of purchases. His confidence in her, a woman not that far removed from night school classes in accounting, came as a happy surprise, and she repaid his trust with the ferocious loyalty of a true believer. She bullied the bankers and accountants and lawyers to the breaking point and beyond. Pushing the envelope and blurring the lines of legality bothered her not at all. When all the new revenues that Jack foresaw began hitting the books, their success would so dazzle the markets that no one would notice a few hiccups along the way.

Norah loved making an essential contribution to something huge and, to most observers, hugely successful. She enjoyed watching the reporters fawn and the bankers grovel. Most of all, she reveled in her own indispensability as little by little Jack came to rely on her as he relied on no one else in the company. The heady experience of being needed so badly by someone as important as Jack almost filled the emptiness that she had felt for so long.

"If you cannot afford a lawyer," said the man arresting her, "one will be provided for you at government expense." The crowd snickered. She certainly could afford a lawyer.

Norah couldn't recall precisely when she came to the realization that her bag of financial tricks no longer merely facilitated the company's business but in fact had *become* the company's business. At the start, the center of gravity had rested with a team of people who tracked down new businesses to buy and new products to make and sell, while Norah and her crew of specialists toiled in obscurity devising ways for the company to choke down all the acquisitions. At some point, the balance shifted. As more and more of Jack's ventures fizzled, each quarterly report triggered a scramble for new tricks to make his audacious earnings targets. Time and again, Norah delivered when everyone else failed. Eventually financial artifice took precedence over making things and selling them.

All the while she maintained to herself that Jack someday would stumble across a deal that would turn the place around. If she could hold the company together long enough, lightning would strike. When Bluestream came along, she saw a glimpse of her salvation. Bluebox would bring in revenues the likes of which Conquest had never seen. The newspaper bitch couldn't have been more wrong, but it was too late.

The man motioned for Norah to put her hands behind her back. She did as he said. One of the policemen snapped handcuffs around her wrists. To her mortification, a smattering of applause ran through the crowd. The smattering grew into a steady ovation. In the faces around her she found an appallingly uniform antagonism. They weren't clapping for her. They were cheering the fact of her arrest. Norah choked back tears.

The cops pushed people aside, opening a corridor that led all the way to the street. Norah saw a Ford sedan and two police cruisers parked out front. The man led her outside where one of the cops stood beside the open rear door of the Ford. She felt her knees tremble as he pushed her down to climb into the car. It was awkward with her hands cuffed. She lost her balance and pitched face-first onto the car seat. She burned with embarrassment.

"Careful, ma'am," said the cop.

She couldn't reach his extended hand. Turning onto one side, she lay on the seat with her hands behind her and her knees drawn up to her chest. A draft on her backside told her that the back of her skirt had ripped open. "Close the door," she pleaded.

A motorcycle engine roared to life. The roof lights of the police cruisers blazed.

Norah struggled to right herself and in the process ripped more seams. She made it into a sitting position just in time for a final glance at the building where she had worked for so long. Many of the employees had moved outside, along with the media people, to watch the police take her away. They stood mute and nearly motionless.

The motorcycle pulled away from the curb, followed by the cruisers. As the Ford surged into the caravan, Norah pressed her cheek against the cool glass of the car window. Screaming police sirens filled the air. The procession roared eastward toward the federal courthouse.

Jack

Jack had a special place to go for quiet reflection in times of crisis. A step away from Glenwood Cemetery's main roadway a six-foot wrought-iron fence surrounded the gravesite of Howard Hughes. The plot's modernistic granite wall and bronze torchiéres drew inquisitive stares from passersby, but the three markers within, those of Hughes, his mother and father, lay flat to the ground behind a bank of flowers, unreadable from outside the iron fence. Years earlier Jack had bribed Glenwood's head caretaker for a key to a hidden access gate. Jack inserted that key into the gate's lock and pushed it open, allowing Santo to pass through with a wood-and-canvas folding chair. Santo placed the chair in a grassy spot where a dappling of sunlight filtered through overhanging live oaks. He withdrew, leaving Jack to his thoughts.

Never before had Jack faced a crisis of such magnitude. The Executive Committee had demanded his resignation. *SEC pressure*, they said. *Accounting irregularities. Your CFO is going to jail! We have no choice, old friend.* It was galling. His hand-picked buddies had basked in his reflected glory for years, but now had turned on him like unnerved virgins.

As he saw it, he had helped Houston claw its way back from the economic abyss of the 1980's. He had refashioned Conquest from a worn-out utility into one of America's sleekest conglomerates, and his company's transformation had set the pace for a city feverishly retooling and diversifying its economy. Computers and biotech had replaced derricks and drill bits. Conquest, with Jack at the helm, led Houston into a new age. Christ, instead of forcing him out, they should name a building or a park in his honor.

Those are nice thoughts, Jack. They're crap, but they're nice.

Jack looked around, startled, unsure of his eyes. The apparition before him stood an emaciated six feet tall, with a stringy beard and scraggly hair. A tumor the size of a pecan protruded from a spot above his left ear. Needle marks carpeted his arms. A breeze wafted a cadaverous odor in Jack's direction. Jack couldn't help himself. He gagged and retched into a flowerbed.

"Sorry, Mr. Hughes," he said, and retched again. "Mighty sorry."

Jack had visited the burial plot many times since moving to Houston and had long felt a kinship with the man interred there. It was as if the billionaire aviator had watched over him and inspired his entire career. So there was no reason why his spiritual mentor's appearance in the flesh—or whatever it was—should surprise, particularly at such a critical juncture in Jack's life. What did astonish him was to see Hughes sitting in a white recliner that had materialized from thin air, reading a newspaper. Not only that, but today's paper. The *Examiner*, open to the editorial page.

This is strong stuff, Jack. Blatant manipulation of earnings. False illusions of financial health systematically created by top executives. An unethical culture festering at the highest corporate levels.

Hughes tossed the newspaper aside and fixed Jack with a look of fatherly disappointment. *You screwed the pooch this time.*

"Just some accounting nonsense." Jack allowed his head to hang ever so slightly. "I can't be responsible for every little detail."

Hughes emitted a cackle. *Save it, Jack. Save it for the jury.*

"No, I'm serious," Jack said with a strenuous gesture of denial. He started to explain about the deal approval sheets that bore everyone's signature except his own, and about all the documents that his people shredded before the feds arrived, but decided not to waste Hughes' time with details.

"I have to admit this is a tough time," he said. "It's nice of you to show up."

Hughes smiled, revealing yellowish gums. *Happened to me once, you know.*

"What's that?"

Board asked for my resignation. My own damn company. Can you imagine?

Jack shook his head. "Goddam outrage."

The tax authorities made a little noise and my directors wet their pants.

"What kind of noise?"

Said my medical foundation was a phony charity.

One of Jack's professors in business school had called the Hughes Foundation the most audacious tax shelter in American history. Jack wondered what Hughes would say about it. "Was it?" he asked. "Phony, I mean."

How should I know? I can't be responsible for every little detail.

They shared a laugh that dwindled into a companionable silence. Then Hughes stiffened and seemed restive. *Got any blue bombers?*

Jack reached into a jacket pocket and offered a several Xanax tablets. "Take these." He didn't know exactly what a blue bomber was, but he knew that Hughes when alive had a superhuman capacity for medication. A few Xanax couldn't do a dead Hughes any harm.

"So what do you think?" Jack asked. "Should I fight? I could force a full vote of the Board. I still have plenty of favors I can call in."

Sorry to tell you this, Jack, but you don't have the votes.

"How can you know that?"

Hughes tapped the side of his nose. *Trust me. I know.*

Jack struggled to absorb what Hughes had told him. He couldn't imagine life as anything other than CEO of Conquest. It was as addictive to Jack as the blue bombers were to Hughes.

It came to Jack that he was in the midst of a transcendent moment, perhaps the sole opportunity in a lifetime to seek counsel from one of the most remarkable men of the twentieth century. Hughes had run businesses as diverse as an oil tool company and a Hollywood movie studio. He designed airplanes and undertook secret missions for the CIA. The man surely possessed unparalleled insight into the deepest realms of human striving. He framed his question with utmost care. "Tell me something," he said. "Is it true you slept with more than five hundred women?"

Hughes lip curled and his face took on an expression so lascivious that Jack could almost see the parade of starlets, heiresses and hat check girls sauntering across Hughes' back pages. His voice dropped to a whisper. *That was a long time ago. I lost count.*

A car pulled up and stopped in the road outside the iron fence.

That's my ride, Jack.

He was mistaken. The car window opened and Santo's head emerged. It was Jack's limo come to take him back to Conquest Plaza. Jack turned back toward Hughes to explain but as he did so, his mentor's visage shimmered and faded. He was leaving, it seemed, but then he faded back into view. He had something else to say.

Hughes put a bony finger into Jack's chest. *Take it from me. There's more to life than business.* With that, Hughes, white chair, tumor and all, vanished into the Glenwood shadows.

Hughes' advice resounded in Jack's head like a thunderclap. He was telling Jack to get out while he could and enjoy what was left of his life. Hell, yes. *There's more to life than business.*

Hughes was incontestably right. His time at Conquest was over. That's why Lorelei had entered his life when she did. They would marry and live a life free of the pressures of running a monstrous multinational corporation. He already had more money than he could spend in ten lifetimes.

A tremor ran through Jack. He wondered fleetingly if Lorelei, like his friends on the Board of Directors, had deserted him. He hadn't heard from her since the SEC launched its attack. He missed the sound of her voice. He missed her laugh. He missed her fantastic rack.

He brushed his doubts aside. She wouldn't throw him over because of a little fuss in the media. Doubtless she was lying low until the commotion died down.

Santo called to Jack from the limo, his voice uncharacteristically insistent. "Time to go, Mr. Burnam. They want you downtown."

David

David had no trouble getting into the Conquest auditorium. No employee ID. No press pass. The guy out front gave him a *who-cares-anymore* look and waved him through. Apparently all the feds in the building were busy guarding documents. Despite the crowd, David found the seat he wanted. Right side, center aisle, seven rows from the front. Security seemed as sparse inside the auditorium as outside. The lone guard stood by a door at the right side of the stage. David checked the exits. Two at the front on each side of the stage, two at the sides, four at the rear. He might be able to reach one of the front exits afterwards.

People poured into the auditorium. He listened to the buzz. *He's announcing a bankruptcy filing. No, he's recapitalized the company. No, he's going to resign. No, he's been cleared. No, he sold the company. No...* The media people were giddy with excitement. Conquest employees jostled for seats, with plenty of attitude. Anger. Disbelief. Indignation. A woman in the row behind David sobbed quietly, as if they were in a movie theater watching Bette Davis die at the end of *Dark Victory*.

The lights. Why were the lights so bright? He squinted up at the ceiling. Ordinary fixtures, as far as he could tell, and the brightness wasn't coming from above. It was all around, as if he were standing in the center of a ring of spotlights. He shielded his eyes but the glare got worse. Must be the drex, he thought. He'd wanted some extra energy for what he had planned so this morning he had cracked open a Benzedrex inhaler and swallowed the cotton do-hickey, a trick he had heard about from one of the guys at Velotrade. He had energy now, that was for sure. He might not sleep for weeks.

He wanted to take off his jacket but he couldn't, of course. The Glock. Inside jacket pocket. He patted his chest to make sure he hadn't forgotten the gun. He'd forgotten too many things lately. Had he loaded it? He combed through his memory again. Yes, this morning. Full magazine. Nine rounds. Every day for the past ten he'd taken target practice at the Top Gun indoor range. He wasn't very good but he was good enough for what he had in mind.

Some papers rustled in his pocket on the side opposite the Glock. He pulled them out. Three sheets, legal-size, blue backing. Petition for divorce. Sole legal and physical custody of a child under sixteen. Exclusive use and possession of family home. His life, reduced to a three-page form document.

No point in making a fight. He'd expected it all, except for the curious fact that she didn't claim child support. He could guess what she was thinking—that he would never have the means so she would do it on her own. He would have taken it as an insult except for one thing. She was right.

His eyes flicked back to the right side of the stage, where Burnam would make his entrance. An explosion of crowd noise erupted as the security guard opened the door to signal Burnam's imminent arrival. Applause ratcheted up at his initial appearance and then abated at the sight of his mid-day stubble and the dark circles under his eyes. Burnam motioned for quiet and bowed his head in prayer.

Smug bastard. On the television shows all week he'd veered between piety and outrage, swearing that Conquest remained fully solvent. If the feds would leave him alone, he could stabilize the situation and Conquest would sail through this little rainstorm. David didn't buy a word of it. He expected the company to file for bankruptcy within days, making it a near certainty that he would suffer a near-total loss on his frozen Conquest shares.

"Amen," said Burnam, his moment of reverence at an end. "Ladies and gentlemen," he intoned, "it is with the deepest of regrets that I announce my..."

The thing that burned David was the likelihood that Burnam would get off scot-free. They hadn't arrested him when they arrested Miranda's boss, so they must not have enough evidence. He would skate, David guessed, but no matter. He wasn't about to wait for the government. This was David's chance to set things right. He again felt the reassuring weight of the Glock in his jacket pocket.

Burnam droned. "As CEO, I take full responsibility. Of course, I had no possible way of knowing of the allegedly unlawful actions of others within the company."

Nice trick. He took the blame and denied wrongdoing all in one breath.

"...immeasurable pride in the accomplishments of this great enterprise...a decade of unmatched achievement...worldwide renown..."

David had to hand it to the guy. He made getting sacked for reducing the company to ashes sound like a lifetime achievement award.

"...heartfelt gratitude to the many thousands of dedicated hardworking..."

Enough already. David stood and in a half-crouch moved forward toward the stage. He held Miranda's divorce petition in his left hand, outstretched as if he was delivering some important documents. He'd started at row seven. At row four he let the divorce papers flutter to the floor and reached into his pocket for the gun. A few steps from the stage he shifted to the right for a better angle. The security guard at the side of the stage finally spied David and bolted toward him. Burnam paused in mid-sentence, a look of annoyance on his face. He seemed irritated that someone had interfered with his moment.

David raised the Glock and aimed at Burnam. *Stop him!* a woman screamed. Men cursed. The crowd sucked in its breath as one. The security guard reached the front of the stage and dove off of it, mosh-pit style. A half-smile came to David's face. What was it Buzz had called the Glock? A *fucking hand cannon*. Wait till Buzz heard about this.

Just after he squeezed the trigger, the guard smashed into him and knocked him backwards. He got off only a single shot. The gun's earsplitting report reverberated in the hot air and bright lights. Burnam went down like a Marine ordered to hit the deck for pushups. *Oh dear God*, someone cried.

The guard slammed David to the floor and drove his cheek against the thin auditorium carpet. The carpet abraded his face from forehead to jaw line. He tasted blood. He'd bitten all the way through his tongue. The guard put his full weight on David's arm. David screamed as his wrist bent backward, snapped and then went limp. The Glock dropped to the floor and skittered under a seat.

Pandemonium all around. Hands clutched at David's back. A punch knocked the breath from his chest. He gasped for air. An elbow smacked into his eye. The guard kept him pinned to the carpet but with a supreme effort he wrenched his head toward the stage.

Burnam hadn't gotten up. He remained flat on the floor behind the lectern. Motionless. Someone leaped onto the stage and touched Burnam's shoulder. He didn't respond.

David relaxed. He'd done it. He'd done it. He'd *finall*y done something right. Satisfaction rolled over him like a warm ocean wave.

Jack

Jack studied the polished pine boards of the stage floor. From such a close distance, less than an inch, the knots and whorls reminded him of the solar system. He gave himself a mental once-over. His pulse raced but seemed to have begun a return to normal. His knees and elbows stung like the blazes where he hit the deck. He was drenched in sweat. Uh-oh. That wasn't all sweat.

He wasn't hurt, as far as he could tell. He would have loved to stand up and reassure everyone, but every muscle in his body seemed to have turned to pudding. Besides, if he stood up, the television cameras would make it known to everyone in America that he'd pissed his pants.

So David Sesno was a crazed would-be assassin. Jack hadn't seen that coming. In the instant before the gun sounded, Jack caught a glimpse into David's eyes, but he wouldn't be able to explain what he saw there if he thought about it for the rest of his life. Which he might. Not desperation or hysteria or mania, the things Jack would have expected. Not at all. What he saw was a preternatural self-composure wholly unsuited to a fuckup like Sesno, and a baffling look of self-satisfaction, as if he'd played his all-time best round of golf that day. Jack had thought Sesno strange that night at the opera, but never imagined he would go so completely off the deep end. And he had no clue why he, Jack, would be the target of Sesno's derangement.

Jack had figured out that it was Miranda who tipped the SEC, but he saw no reason to hold it against her. Having Wheeler's files land in her lap must have scared her silly. Jack blamed Wheeler for creating the files in the first place and letting matters get out of control and then dying. And he blamed Norah for a world-class all-around botch job.

All of a sudden, the auditorium was lousy with police. They hoisted Sesno up off the floor and hustled him out a side door. It was weird, Jack thought. The guy looked like he was having a day at the beach.

The security guard who had tackled Sesno got up off the floor, too. He might have saved Jack's life. Jack made a mental note to offer some kind of reward. That would look good.

A forest of legs had grown up around Jack. Someone pushed his shoulder as if to wake him from sleep. Voices babbled. "Mr. Burnam? Can you hear me?" This was getting embarrassing. He tried to lift himself but someone placed a hand on his back.

"Please wait a minute, sir. Please wait until we get the room cleared."

No problem. He would rest a bit longer. He continued studying the patterns in the floor. Mercury. Saturn. Earth.

Jack brought himself up on one knee. He flex-tested each arm and leg. Not too bad. "I'm okay," he repeated, this time sharply enough that the surrounding legs moved back a step or two.

"He's okay," someone shouted. *He's okay!* echoed its way toward and out the exits.

Earth? A brainstorm came to Jack. *Earth!* An adrenaline rush brought a modicum of strength back to his body. He would do what Howard Hughes had done, what they all did when they found themselves in a tight spot. He would create a *charity*, the Jack Burnam Foundation for a Better Earth. He would endow it with a big round number, like a billion dollars. He hoped he still had a billion dollars. With everything going on lately, he'd lost track of his net worth. And he'd get his rich pals to contribute more, lots more.

He congratulated himself on the best idea he'd had in years. This would put the SEC attack dogs back in their kennel. Bringing charges against him would put at risk billions of dollars dedicated to worthy causes. Hauling him into court would be tantamount to snatching food from the mouths of widows and orphans.

He grabbed the ankle of one of his assistants in the group hanging over him. "Get Mrs. Logan on the phone. The Senator's wife." She'd probably seen the press conference on television and would be worried sick.

"I'm okay," he told her. "Don't worry. Crazy bastard missed me."

"Jack..."

"Hey, listen. I've decided to start a foundation. I want you to help me. We'll run it as a team. We can do this together."

As he explained his idea to Lorelei, his enthusiasm grew to mammoth proportions. He would do *good* things, as he'd always intended. As he'd meant to do before Lacey's father turned him in a different direction. By the time he finished, his original motivation of getting the government off his back seemed seamy and shallow, and he pushed it out of his mind. He'd found his true calling.

"*Jack...*"

They would be mega-partners, living in Houston and travelling the world in search of worthy causes. With his money and her visibility and charm, they would become an unstoppable force for global betterment.

"We could put your name on the foundation, too, if you want."

"*Jack!*"

It dawned on him that she hadn't said anything about telling the Senator she was leaving him. It had been over two weeks. What was she waiting for? Moreover, her tone wasn't warm and close. It was brusque. Peremptory, in fact.

"Have you told him yet? Have you told him about us?"

"Told him what? That I'm leaving him for a crook? That I'm running off with a criminal?"

A *criminal*? Coming from her lips, the word stunned him. Maybe his accountants didn't dot all their *i*'s and cross all their *t*'s, but that didn't make him a *criminal*. She'd been around. She should know better than that. Some of his enemies in Washington must have told her bad things. "Who's saying that?" he demanded.

She adopted a blasé tone, as if reading the guest list for a formal dinner. "The Attorney General. The Chairman of the SEC. The Secretary of the Treasury. The Vice President. The..."

Jack cut her off. "Wow." He was torn. On the one hand, he was mortified that she considered him a crook. On the other, it was pretty impressive that his name was on the lips of practically the whole damn Cabinet.

"But you said you would marry me."

"Conjugal visitation wasn't exactly what I had in mind, Jack."

Jack focused on a single word. *Conjugal*. She had wrapped her tongue around it in a way that caused him to go hard as a brick. He simply couldn't lose this woman. He tried everything he could think of to change her mind.

"Stop it, Jack. It's no use."

Jack couldn't believe they'd come to such a miserable end. "So you're going to stay with him?"

"Now you've got it."

Jack pounded a fist against the floor in frustration. His mouth flooded with the sour taste of defeat, but he refused to accept failure. "Listen," he said, preparing for another go at her, but the sudden soundlessness of their cell phone connection told him she was no longer listening. *Call Ended.*

Jack had always preferred the way a land line signals a hang-up. A dial tone tells a man where he stands. A cell phone, on the other hand, simply goes quiet. Unless he happens to glance at the screen, a man might go on talking into empty space for hours. He made a mental note to have someone in his product development group look into the feasibility of a dial tone for cell phones. Someone in marketing could run a test.

Wait a second. He didn't have a product development group. He didn't have a marketing department. He didn't have a company. All he had was a lousy foundation.

Miranda

Miranda climbed the bleachers to her regular seat with the other moms, Rhoda, Betsy and Alice. She smoothed her Levi's and sat down by Rhoda. Betsy waved hello but Alison's focus remained on the tiny screen of her Sony Watchman.

"Oprah has Mel Gibson today," she said without looking up.

The notion that she had a *regular seat* amused Miranda in a bittersweet way. She had attended only two of Jesse's games in the first two months of the season, but she'd seen three in the past nine days. Her current schedule was a blank, other than a few follow-up meetings with the government investigators. With four weeks left in the season, she expected to make every game remaining.

Before, she sat apart from the group, not wanting to get caught up in the chitchat. Now, she joined the mom squad every game.

"Hello TV star," Rhoda greeted her.

Miranda groaned and blushed. The men from the government had promised to keep her name out of the news, but that had lasted for no more than a day or so. She had refused all interviews, but nearly every news story about Conquest featured the same photograph of her leaving the building with a look of absolute desolation on her face. *Conquest Whistleblower*, read the caption. Her fifteen minutes of fame and she looked like she was passing a kidney stone.

A deafening buzzer signaled the start of the game. Jesse's white-shirted teammates raced onto the court and took positions amid the red shirts around the center circle. The referee tossed a ball into the air between the two tallest boys.

"How are things at work?" Rhoda asked. "Must be tough."

"Not really," said Miranda. "An hour after my face showed up on television the head of HR called me. He suggested I take administrative leave. Full pay. *Best for all concerned*, he said. I can't disagree with that."

"So you haven't been back to the office since..."

"I went back to get some personal things." Miranda shook her head. "You can't imagine the looks I got. Half the people in the company think I'm a traitor and the other half think I'm crazy."

"Are you going to look for another job?"

Miranda shrugged. "Eventually, I guess. Everything has happened so fast I don't have a plan yet. Maybe after the fuss dies down."

Miranda was deliberately casual, not ready to share with Rhoda or the others how dire her situation had become. Full pay from Conquest was good, but would last only until the bankruptcy filing, which she expected within the week. When she checked their joint brokerage account, she finally understood what David had done and why he'd gone incommunicado. Instead of $90,000 of nice safe high-grade bonds she found nearly-worthless shares of Conquest stock. Worse, on a credit card statement she found a $977 charge from an online jewelry store called *Bling*, confirming her worst suspicions about the night David didn't come home. By the end of the same day, she had hired a divorce lawyer and by the end of the week the lawyer had served David with papers.

At the end of the first quarter, Jesse's team trailed the red shirts by four points. The moms clapped ferociously as the second period began.

She'd drunk many glasses of cheap Merlot and on most nights, after putting Jesse to bed, cried herself to sleep on the sofa. She cursed David for his absence and alternately prayed for his return. Finally she had stuffed most of his clothes into black plastic trash bags and dropped the whole mess at the Salvation Army. After that, she stopped praying and Jesse stopped asking when Daddy was coming home. Once, waking on the sofa at midnight, she'd found around her shoulders a blanket that she had no recollection of taking from the closet. She was sleepily trying to figure out who put the blanket over her when she saw Jesse asleep on the floor beside the sofa, still in his school clothes.

She'd filed for divorce, her remaining savings would last only another month or so, and before long all of her potential job references would occupy prison cells. She was mentally exhausted and emotionally wrung out. Nevertheless, Miranda felt strangely placid, in fact guardedly optimistic, about her future.

She forced her attention back to the game. The white shirts had narrowed the gap to three points. Jesse received a pass, pivoted and drove for a lay-up. A boy a good four inches taller than Jesse knocked him to the floor so hard that a worried silence descended over the gym. Miranda sprang from her seat and had taken two steps toward the court when Jesse bounced up from the hardwood. His eyes froze her in place. *Mom, don't you dare.* She beat a sheepish retreat, much to the amusement of the other moms.

Alison abruptly shoved her Watchman at Miranda.

"Not now," Miranda said, trying to keep the annoyance out of her voice. She liked Mel Gibson as much as the next woman, but not in the final moments of the game. Her attention remained with Jesse as his team huddled around the coach.

"No, it's about Conquest. They interrupted Oprah."

Miranda took the television but left the sound off and didn't bother to insert the ear bud. *Breaking News*, read a banner over a shot of Norah leaving Conquest Plaza in custody. The shot of Norah gave way to one of Burnam at the podium in the building's auditorium. *Conquest CFO Arrested on Fraud Charges; Burnam Resigns as CEO.*

"Can't say I'm surprised." She handed the television back to Alison. She'd had her fill of Conquest.

"No," said Alison, seeming embarrassed. "There's more."

Miranda looked again. Silent images flashed across the screen in quick succession. Burnam at the podium, only this time there was something odd. He dropped out of camera range and when the camera found him again, he was flat on the floor. Then her own face again. Then Norah once more, in handcuffs.

No, wait. That wasn't Norah. It was a man. They'd made another arrest. She squinted, wondering who it was. A shock of recognition shot through her. The man in cuffs was David. Her husband. Jesse's father.

She fumbled to jam the ear bud into her ear. "In an apparent act of vengeance," said an announcer's voice, "David Sesno, the husband of Conquest whistleblower Miranda Sesno, fired a gun at Jack Burnam today during Burnam's resignation announcement. Burnam was unharmed. Police arrested Sesno and took him to the city jail where he's being held pending psychiatric examination."

Oprah and Mel returned to the screen. The Watchman fell from Miranda's hand onto the bleachers. A plastic cover cracked open and batteries tumbled out and rolled under Miranda's feet. She sat in a trance. All the disappointment and agony of ten years of a failed marriage to this man merged into a single dizzying white pain. David had tried to kill a man.

At mid-court Jesse poked the ball away from a red shirt, snatched it on the dead run and drove to the basket for a breakaway lay-up. He tossed the ball up against the backboard. It bounced off the rim, then rattled through for two points. With seconds left in the game, his team had pulled within a point.

"Miranda, shouldn't you do something?" Rhoda asked.

Miranda broke out of her trance. "I guess you're right," her voice little more than a gasp.

She gathered herself and stood. She watched her son in the game's final seconds and cheered for him. She cheered and cheered until Rhoda and the others stared at her. She cheered until her throat grew raw and her eyes blurred with tears and her heart ached to the point of bursting.

CHAPTER 17. SIX MONTHS LATER

CQC 0.24 ↓↓↓

Sherry

Sherry moved directly from *Needle at Sea Bottom* into *Snake Creeps Low*. None of the Forms she had studied put these two positions in sequence, but she'd felt much more creative since moving to Zihuatanejo.

When she asked for a house on the *huerto de cocos*, the real estate agent laughed out loud, taking her for another crazy gringo. So there wasn't a coconut grove in sight, but otherwise the *hacienda* she found matched to the last detail the vision that had come to her on her trip with Wheeler. White stucco. Red tile roof. A secluded, spacious, high-ceilinged front porch where she practiced the Set. A garden overflowing with hibiscus, palm and bougainvillea. Beyond the garden a small servant's apartment. And a footpath winding through the trees to a deserted stretch of the *Playa Manzanilla*.

She had despaired when the agent told her the place would cost two *million* pesos, but it turned out two million pesos was only about $180,000 in American money. "I'll take it," she said, without the slightest hesitation. That left her with more than $800,000 in the bank, and life in Mexico was so inexpensive she thought that much money might last forever.

But it wasn't as though she was doing nothing. *Apply your body in the service of others*, the Master said. *Work is pleasant and present*. She drove her new used Jeep over to Ixtapa four days a week and taught T'ai Chi to vacationers staying at *Las Brisas*. Word about her classes had gotten around and she'd been approached by a few of the other resorts, too. She worked for herself teaching T'ai Chi, as she'd always hoped. And she had next to no competition in this part of the world.

Taco peeked out from under a pine and wormwood bench that she had gotten for 500 pesos from a man who swore it came from a Buddhist monastery somewhere up in the Sierra Madre. She didn't believe him, but it didn't matter. She had sewn cushions covered with bright Mayan fabric and liked to imagine that she shared the bench with the spirits of some long-dead monks.

Sherry did *Crosses Hands* twice, which brought her impromptu Set to a conclusion. Flushed, she pulled a cord on the overhead fan. The fan's lazy breeze slowly dried the perspiration from her body. She put on the cotton shift that she'd hung over the back of the bench. She sat down to wait. Feo would be back soon.

Feo

His work day at an end, Feo shut off the lights and stepped outside. A pebbled path led from the servant's quarters through the garden to the rear door of the house. He gathered up a score of hibiscus blooms fallen onto the path and added them to a corner mulch pile.

Sherry had insisted that he install his office in the servant's apartment. "It'll give you plenty of privacy," she said, but Feo had come to understand that she wanted his computers, modems and all the other gadgets at a respectable distance so as to minimize the level of electronic radiation in the house. Besides, they didn't need the servant's quarters for a housekeeper or anything like that. They had hired a man who came weekly to keep the garden plants at bay, but Feo intended to take over those chores himself before long. It wouldn't be the same as riding his lawn tractor around his back yard in Houston. It would be better.

After leaving Conquest, he knew he'd had enough of big corporations to last a good long while. When Sherry said she wanted him to sell his house in Montrose so they could move to Mexico, to a place she'd seen in a vision, it seemed crazy. He did sell the house, though, followed in short order by the car and the lawn mower, and within a matter of weeks they had relocated to Zihuatenajo. And he couldn't have been happier.

His consulting business in bilingual information security had been running for three months and already he had as much work as he could handle. He helped Mexican companies starting online marketing operations protect themselves from hackers and phishers, and he wrote security programs for U.S. companies doing business in Mexico.

He still worried about the million dollars Sherry had received from Conquest. He had tried to return it, but when he'd gone into work on the Monday after the cash reached Sherry's account, federal agents prowled the building and the company already had fallen into chaos. No one in the treasurer's office would give him wiring instructions for the money's return. No one wanted to take responsibility for moving money in or out of the company.

It was when he'd asked Sherry to write a check that he could simply leave in the treasurer's office that she began quoting the Master. *The kink in a dog's tail cannot be straightened.* "But what if someone figures out what happened and comes after us?" *Those who practice deception are most easily deceived.*

The final straw came when rumors of a bankruptcy filing and massive employee layoffs began to swirl. It was one thing to return the money to a thriving enterprise that might give him some credit for saving it a million bucks. The logic behind sending the money back to an insolvent outfit about to cut him loose seemed less compelling.

Feo pushed open the back door of the house and entered the kitchen. He took a pitcher of juice from the refrigerator and two glasses from the cupboard. He sprinkled into each glass a half-spoonful of ginkgo biloba, as Sherry had shown him. She swore that it not only improved brain function but stimulated the libido as well. As to the former, Feo hadn't noticed any change. As to the latter, he wouldn't deny feeling pretty frisky, but he didn't think that ginkgo biloba had anything to do with it.

On the front porch he found Sherry sitting on the tile floor lotus-style, eyes closed, facing the ocean. When he sat on the monastery bench she raised her face for a kiss. They sipped papaya in silence as a sangria sun plunged toward the *Bahia de Zihuatenajo*. A sea bird called from somewhere nearby. A mottled lizard scurried onto one corner of the porch and off again. Taco emerged from underneath the bench, aroused by the prospect of a chase. Finding no trace of his prey, he eased onto Feo's lap and resumed his *siesta*.

Lulu

Maria Bartiromo swept onto the set and into her moderator's chair. Nobody, thought Lulu, should look like that and have brains, too. To make matters worse, Maria was pleasant enough, at least as TV people went, always remembering your name and saying hello and all.

"How's that?" asked the makeup assistant.

Lulu checked her face, asked for another dab of powder and then sent him away. This made her fourth appearance on Maria's show. She'd also done Jim Lehrer and Lou Dobbs and given interviews to *Fortune* and *Bloomberg*. They couldn't get enough of the woman who brought Conquest to its knees and ruined Jack Burnam.

"Heads up, everybody," said the director. "Three, two, one, and... we're live."

Maria went smoothly into her opening. "Good evening, ladies and gentlemen. Today scandal engulfed Quanta-Com, the nation's third-largest maker of silicon chips. Sources allege that CEO Barney Linton has utilized hundreds of millions of dollars of corporate funds on personal expenses such as a villa in Crete and an ocean-going yacht. Sources also charge that Quanta-Com has used a variety of accounting tricks to overstate its cash flow by more than four billion dollars."

"Joining us this evening is Lulu Barker," said Maria, "formerly a reporter at the Houston Examiner and recently named by Forbes as a finalist for its Business Journalist of the Year award. Lulu, can you give us your perspective on today's events at Quanta-Com?"

Of course she could. The show wasn't completely scripted, but Lulu didn't need a script to know how they wanted it to go. Maria would give the particulars of the latest CEO misadventure. Next, one or more experts, such as Lulu, would decry the abysmal level to which business ethics had sunk and excoriate the CEO for a lack of moral fiber. Then a lawyer or media flak representing the accused would deny all charges and swear that his client would be fully exonerated when all was said and done. Depending on time remaining to the next commercial, the experts might plead for stepped-up legal enforcement to reign in the cabal of renegade executives that had taken over American business. It was a great gig.

"Certainly, Maria," began Lulu. "It's nice to be here again. You know, it boils down to individual people. Either they're honest or they're dishonest. The CEO sets the tone for the entire company. These days we have far too many dishonest CEO's."

Lulu felt the tiniest stitch of guilt. Everyone now knew her as the reporter who broke the news of a scandal at Conquest. Hardly anyone seemed to recall she had her facts entirely wrong. Bluebox, far from a bust, might have saved Conquest if Lulu's story hadn't sent the stock reeling, which caught the attention of the regulators. That and possibly a nudge from a United States Senator upon whose wife Jack Burnam had launched a hostile takeover bid.

Everything had happened so fast that only Ed, her boss, caught that Lulu's story had been a fabrication. He'd allowed her to resign but made it clear that otherwise he would fire her. No matter. Harcourt had advanced $50,000 against royalties for her forthcoming book and she'd heard a rumor that she had moved to the top of a short list for a regular spot on CNBC.

The director signaled Lulu. He wanted a sound bite for the wrap-up. Lulu looked into the camera, the same way she had looked at Ed the day she sold him on the Bluebox story. "Maria, when a CEO goes into that executive suite, it's like a witness stepping into the witness box. What's required is the truth, the whole truth and nothing but the truth."

Maria smiled her beautiful smile. The director beamed. Lulu saw a CNBC executive producer standing in the wings, watching and nodding his head. He was young and reminded her of Josh. When the red lights went out, Lulu detached her mic and headed to the dressing room to wash off the TV makeup.

The executive producer touched her arm. "Lulu, could we visit a minute?"

"Absolutely. Let me..." She motioned at her face with both hands.

"Whenever you're ready, of course." He gave her a broad smile, indicating that he had good news to deliver.

In the dressing room, Lulu applied soap to her face and considered her good fortune. He was certain to offer her at least six figures. She checked her face. Even at her age, fresh-scrubbed looked good. She opened the door, then retreated in a moment of uncertainty. Maybe his smile hadn't been all that broad.

She unfastened one more button on her blouse. Just in case.

Norah

In her right hand, Norah held plastic tweezers. In her left, an acrylic mirror. She scrutinized her scalp, comparing areas of sparse hair to those where it remained dense, and committed the pattern to memory. She had mapped her scalp into twenty-six sectors. She knew that the average woman has 130,000 hairs on her head. That worked out neatly to five thousand hairs per sector. She hadn't counted them, of course. That would be weird.

According to the schedule she had devised her first week at Federal Prison Camp Bryan, she plucked not more than three hundred hairs per day and not more than fifteen hundred per week. Each week she worked in a different sector so as not to create bald patches. Six months would pass before she returned to an area already plucked, enough time for irritation to heal and hair to re-grow. She'd gotten a supply of Extra-Strength Minoxidil from the camp doctor that would help it grow back faster.

Her eyelashes and eyebrows weren't part of the schedule. For one thing, she had no idea how many hairs were involved. For another, if she pulled hairs from her face, someone might notice. This was her secret. Nor had she yet gone down *below.* There was plenty of hair down there, but she was keeping that in reserve for some future time of crisis.

Her roommate entered their dorm room. Like most of the camp inmates, her roommate had committed some kind of nonviolent drug offense. Norah had encountered only two other pink-collar criminals since she arrived, both of them embezzlers.

"You got a visitor, Norah. I was up front and they asked me to tell you. A Dr. Frost."

Norah slipped the tweezers and mirror back into her locker. So far, Dr. Frost was the only person to visit her at the camp. He'd twice driven the 95 miles from Houston to Bryan in the hope of convincing her to undergo more therapy, but she knew what he was after. Having a notorious patient like Norah Needham wouldn't hurt his practice one bit.

"You'll be in prison quite a while," he'd said. "Might as well put the time to good use."

Her sentence would run for twelve years, but with good behavior she might get out in ten. She was bound to get credit for good behavior. Here she followed all the rules.

She had pled guilty to four counts of fraud and one of conspiracy, a fraction of the boatload of charges the prosecutor brought against her. It wasn't a plea bargain, exactly. She simply saw no point in paying lawyers millions to fight a losing battle. Better to check in at FPC Bryan and get on with it.

In addition to the prison time, the judge levied a fine of $17 million, leaving Norah with a serious cash shortage. She didn't need money in the camp, but she had to pay taxes and upkeep on her home back in Houston. Otherwise, there was no telling what might happen to her belongings. It would cost much less to sell the place and put her things in storage, but Norah couldn't bear the thought of sweaty strangers pawing through her possessions. She wanted every item in its proper place and waiting on her release day. Thinking about it gave her nice, cozy feeling.

"How are you getting on?" asked Dr. Frost when Norah reached the visitation room.

"I'm okay," she answered, and it was true. Other than missing her belongings, life at FPC Bryan wasn't bad. No fences or barbed wire, only a yellow perimeter line and the threat of transfer to medium-security for crossing it. She lived in an open dormitory cubicle with a bunk, a metal locker and a small writing table. She wore camp-issue khakis, tee shirts and white cotton underwear. She worked 40 hours each week baking bread, and otherwise had time to herself. She could exercise, grow vegetables, play board games, watch television, read, or talk on the telephone, and Norah sometimes did some of those things. But mostly, she studied her scalp.

In one way, life at the camp was better than life on the outside. Other than baking bread, she had no responsibilities and never a decision to make. No belligerent employees seeking raises, no blustery board members demanding explanations of this or that. No hotshots like Russ Wheeler with blackmail schemes, and no twits like Miranda Sesno going Girl Scout on her. Most importantly, no Jack, making deals and creating disastrous tangles for her to unsnarl.

"Did you bring it?" she asked Dr. Frost.

He pushed a plastic shopping bag across the table. "This is very significant," he said. "With some work, we could correlate your unresolved feelings about your dead husband to your present-day non-positive affect. We could probe your ongoing bereavement."

"Thank you for bringing these things, Dr. Frost," said Norah. "I'll consider that." A flat-out lie. She wouldn't give it a moment's thought, even if he did drive 95 miles.

Back at her room, Norah spread out the contents of the shopping bag. She placed the truck brochures flat on her writing table, along with the menu from Roznovsky's and the compact disc of Texas Johnny Brown's blues songs. The photograph of Wally's headstone at Glenwood she pinned to the wall. In the picture, the burial plot looked immaculate, better than when she had last seen it. Maybe Dr. Frost had tidied things up before taking the picture.

She would have Wally Day some weekend soon, when she didn't have bakery duty. It would be a pale imitation of her customary ritual, but it would have to do, and it would have to do for the next ten years.

Passing a hand absent-mindedly through her hair, Norah came across one that felt particularly out of place. Too long. Too coarse. She resisted the urge to pluck it. It was in ten, last week's sector. This week was sector eleven.

Norah paused, undecided. A finger ran over the out-of-place hair. She pinched it between thumb and forefinger and couldn't help giving it a slight tug. The hair slipped through her fingers. She tugged again.

The tweezers rested on a shelf in her locker. She reached for them. Seizing the hair squarely at the root, she gave it a sharp yank. The hair popped free with a prick of pain and a ripple of satisfaction. She pressed the pulled hair against her cheek.

She plucked a second hair, and a third. And then another. And another.

David

David awoke to the sound of Miranda's voice. Then the voice's muffled, metallic timbre reminded him of where he was. Jail. A place where he slept on a metal cot and the meals came to him through a slot in a steel door. To be precise, the Federal Detention Center, a holding pen for prisoners awaiting trial, located in downtown Houston not ten blocks from Conquest Plaza.

He opened his eyes. David's cellmate, Jim Ben, a hulking but amiable kid from West Texas awaiting trial on dual charges of armed robbery and indecent exposure, squatted on the aluminum toilet in the corner of the cell. It went without saying that Jim Ben, like every other inmate David had encountered, denied committing any offense whatsoever. Jim Ben chalked up his incarceration to a ferocious run of bad luck.

David again heard the woman's voice. His fellow inmates had told him that he was lucky in his cell block assignment. A favorable acoustic property of the plumbing that connected their block, Four West, to the women's unit in Five West, allowed sounds to pass from one to the other. It wasn't possible to distinguish specific words, but one could make out the higher-pitched tones of female prisoners and sometimes identify a specific woman by the tone of her voice. Some of the men claimed to have known women in Five West on the outside and now carried on sorrowful muted conversations with them.

David considered putting on his headphones and listening to his portable radio, but that would alert Jim Ben that he was awake and he didn't want to interrupt Jim Ben's business. He decided simply to try not to listen. He distracted himself with thoughts of his own upcoming trial. In contrast to the other people here, who almost certainly would suffer convictions for offenses they denied, David expected exoneration for a crime committed in broad daylight and seen by hundreds of eyewitnesses. His court-appointed lawyer promised that no jury would convict him of trying to shoot someone who had become the most unpopular man in Texas. David couldn't use the insanity defense, said the lawyer, because what he had tried to do made too much good sense.

Even if the lawyer was wrong, David wasn't worried. Jack Burnam, in what David viewed as a shameless bid for public sympathy, had announced a sizeable reward to the security guard who had saved his life and simultaneously asked the prosecutor's office to drop the charges against David. The prosecutor declined to grant David a full release, but did reduce the charge from attempted murder to aggravated assault, a mere two-to-ten offense. Between the reduced charge, the lack of any prior criminal record, and the likelihood of a sympathetic jury, David figured his worst case at a few years.

Sadly, he knew that, whenever his release might occur, he would never recover his family. Jesse's picture hung on the inside of his locker door, but jail rules didn't allow visits by children. He didn't want Jesse to see him in this place anyway. He'd rather spend the rest of his life in a cell with Jim Ben. Miranda hadn't visited him since the first week, and he didn't blame her. She should get on with her life.

The worst thing about jail, other than a lack of privacy so absolute that watching and listening to Jim Ben on the toilet several times each day had come to seem normal, was having nothing to do. David tried to keep busy by working on a new trading scheme. He listened to the financial news every day, tracked stocks from daily newspaper reports, kept information in a spiral notebook, and looked for patterns. By the time he got out, he would be ready to go.

He felt his spirits sink. It was a struggle, he had to admit, keeping his equilibrium in the joint. So much empty time. So many mistakes to think about.

Try as he might, he couldn't put the sound of women's voices out of his head. It permeated the cell's musky air like a soft, soothing lullaby. The voice was talking to David and to David alone, only no longer was it the voice of an unseen, unknown woman prisoner in Five West. It had changed. He'd been right the first time. It was Miranda's voice.

Jack

Jack arrived early, anxious to get started. On the room's walls hung several Gainesboroughs. Scattered about were more pieces of antique furniture than he'd ever seen in one place. Through a deep-set window he saw the magnificent parterre garden that surrounded Waddesdon Manor. Hedges. Fountains. A moat, for chrissake. Once a home of some lesser Rothschilds, it survived in the modern era by hosting corporate get-togethers. The evening before, Jack and Maggie had dined in the garden while minstrels in Stuart-era costumes serenaded them on period instruments.

Jack nodded as others began filing into the room. Nice clothes. Expensive shoes. They sat facing each other in sumptuous leather chairs arranged in a circle. Everyone looked at their hands or a wall or down at the floor. No one met anyone else's eyes. Odd, Jack thought, for such a high-powered group. But then again, under the circumstances, maybe not.

He suppressed a sigh. He sure never thought he'd end up in rehab. The program carried an imposing name—*Executive Renaissance*—and they dressed it up like some kind of corporate think session, but rehab was what it was. Getting straight. *ER*, everyone called it.

The past six months had been the worst period of Jack's life. Not only had Conquest collapsed like a thatched hut in a tsunami, but the IRS had quashed his foundation within a few days. Nor had they let him give a reward to the security guard that saved his life, calling it a bribe to a federal officer.

Lorelei had cut him dead. His letters came back unopened and the Senator's campaign committee had returned Jack's contribution with a note from her that read, *Are you kidding?* Worst of all, as if to taunt him, the Senator's campaign speeches invariably named Jack as a prime example of everything wrong with American business. Seeing Lorelei on the dais behind her husband as he nattered on about putting corrupt executives behind bars made Jack want to put his foot through the television screen.

Lacey had filed for divorce. Kick a man when he was down, that's how Jack saw it. She never would have filed if he still had his old job and his nine-figure income. Fortunately, since the government scotched his foundation, his lawyers had plenty of time to do battle with her lawyers. She would have to scrap for every penny of whatever he had left.

Thank God for Maggie. She'd been as loyal as a basset hound. Lacey took the River Oaks house, so Jack had lived with Maggie in her apartment for the past few months. He liked the apartment well enough, but Maggie wanted to start looking for a bigger place as soon as the divorce judge unfroze some of his assets.

The only trouble with Maggie was that their Maserati sex had become something more like an SUV. She still had the orchid tattoo coming up from the crack of her ass and she still catered to his every indecent whim, but something was missing. Last week they were going at it when a blazingly disheartening thought came to mind: neither he nor Maggie had a spouse or anyone else who gave a rat's ass. He'd wilted on the spot. When Maggie turned around to ask him what was the matter he had no words. He just shook his head.

The best news was that the government hadn't indicted him. Thanks to his shredding team, the SEC couldn't find a single incriminating document with his name on it. And Norah, bless her tortured soul, had pled guilty without turning state's evidence. Jack was in the clear.

So much so that he was ready to get back in the game. He might start a company of his own, or maybe he would find an outfit that needed a kick-ass turnaround CEO. All he needed was a new image and a new credential. He'd admit some mistakes. Get a little therapy. In America, everyone deserves a second chance. And if he resurrected his career, if he made a walloping comeback, maybe he would get another shot at Lorelei. Thus, *ER*.

He'd perused the materials the ER people had left in his room. Today's CEO's should be farsighted, tolerant, humane and ethical, the materials said. It reminded Jack of the *core values* meeting he'd attended so many months ago. *Benevolent CEOs. Firms of endearment.* It all made his hair hurt.

A bearded fellow wearing an open-necked shirt and loafers entered the room and called for attention. "Gentlemen, I'm your facilitator Barry. Let me begin by welcoming you to our first session. You've all shown tremendous courage by being here today. So are you ready to begin?" The room went as still as Conquest's stock as they wondered what Barry would say.

"The first step to recovery is admitting that you have a problem."

Miranda

Miranda clamped her thighs against Fanny's flanks, urging the mare toward the jump at center ring. Six strides. Four, three, two, one. She hiked her rear off the saddle into jumping position, but on the final stride Fanny veered away from the cavaletti and skimmed past the right-side standard. For Miranda, however, it was too late to change direction. Her forward momentum carried her out of the saddle and over the cross-pole. She landed on her back and left side, hard, in the dust.

Joyce Dunlap watched her from the fence. "That's pretty good," she called. "Only you're supposed to take the horse with you."

Miranda had made it her project, contrary to Joyce's advice, to make a jumper of Fanny. Joyce thought Fanny, at seven with no prior training in jumping, too old for such a radical change. Miranda thought otherwise. Fanny had made the jump two days before, but seemed to have forgotten all about it.

Miranda had first heard Joyce's voice on the telephone three months earlier. "Miranda Sesno? I saw your picture on television, part of that Conquest thing. I thought maybe I saw you at the stables a few times. That you?"

"The stables?"

"Somerset. I own it. I run it."

"Yeah," Miranda said warily. "That's me." Since becoming semi-famous, she'd kept as low a profile as possible, but still received scores of crackpot calls.

"Brave thing you did." That's what some of the callers said, but most of them, especially former Conquest employees, took a different view and weren't shy about letting her know it.

"Thank you."

"You like to ride? Come on over. Anytime. No charge."

Before she knew it, she'd begun driving to Somerset every morning after dropping Jesse at school. At first, she simply rode for her own pleasure. Then one day she filled in as an instructor when one of Joyce's regulars walked off the job. She started giving lessons to kids, beginners, and before long recovered enough technique that Joyce let her take over some of the intermediates, mostly well-to-do wives taking up horseback riding as a variation on golf and tennis and shopping.

She stood up and brushed the dust from her clothes. "Thanks for the advice," she told Joyce. "I'll try to remember."

Fanny, after circling the ring twice, approached Miranda looking deeply apologetic. Miranda grabbed her reins and gave her a pat. "Let's give it another try," she whispered into Fanny's ear. "What do you say?"

Most days she worked until dusk and took only a few minutes for lunch and a mid-afternoon break to pick up Jesse. On the days when he didn't have baseball or some other after-school activity, he waited for her in the tack room, doing his homework and studying the strange gear hanging on the walls. He'd long since gotten over his fears of seeing his mother on horseback, and he'd learned the difference between a hacking saddle and a jumper and between a snaffle bit and a curb.

Best of all, she spent hours each day in the saddle. In addition to Fanny, she rode Tombo, a spirited Arabian, and Mr. Ed, a lazy Western saddlebred, and eight or ten others, all of them horses whose owners hadn't the time to give the animals daily exercise. It was simple, physically demanding work, but satisfying. At day's end, sleep came easily, her muscles aching and her lungs full of fresh air and the smells of sweat and hay and manure.

She nudged Fanny into a trot.

"Eyes on the trees," called Joyce.

She was right, thought Miranda. A horse can sense a rider that focuses on the jump rather than beyond the jump. She raised her eyes. Four, three, two, *one*. On *one*, Miranda squeezed Fanny's sides as hard as she could, but with no more success than before. At the last instant, Fanny swerved sharply to the side. Miranda managed to stay in the saddle, but only barely.

Working at a barn didn't pay much, but she earned enough to pay the rent on the apartment she and Jesse had moved into when she sold the house. Between the money she got for the house, what she got for David's car and the $15,000 he'd left in their brokerage account, she had a cushion to carry them until she got back on her feet.

Miranda climbed down from the saddle and tethered Fanny at the side of the ring. Joyce watched bemusedly as Miranda reset the jump's cross-pole on the lowest cups, not more than a half-foot from the ground. "Back to basics," she said.

She directed Fanny to the far side of the ring and then approached the jump at a trot. This time Fanny took the jump easily and moved into a canter on the other side.

"That's more like it," Miranda told Fanny. She dismounted and gave the mare a treat from her pocket.

Once or twice each week Miranda swapped her English riding clothes for Western-style gear and led groups, most often local business-people hosting out-of-state clients, on trail rides through the woods. The trail's turnaround opened onto a clearing from which the visitors enjoyed an unobstructed view of Houston's downtown skyline. In nearly every instance, the sight of Conquest Plaza triggered a discussion of the company's downfall. *Biggest fraud in American history. Yeah, but half the companies in America do the same thing, Conquest just got caught. They got caught because somebody blew the whistle. Can you imagine?* Miranda listened but never commented, even when she sensed a glimmer of recognition in the eyes of one of the visitors. To her, it was all impossibly distant. When they finished their chat, she would bring the sightseeing to an end and lead the group back for Mexican food or barbeque.

Had she made the right choice? If she had tossed Wheeler's files into the dumpster, Conquest might have ridden out the storm. Bluebox might have turned the company around. She might be earning more money than she'd ever hoped for and have her favorite seats at the opera. David might not be in prison. Jesse might have a father.

Enough *mights* to haunt her for a lifetime. But she knew one certainty. If she hadn't done what she did, she'd be one of them. She'd be no better than Norah and the rest.

With a sidelong glance at Joyce, Miranda returned the cross-pole to a two-foot height. She remounted and patted Fanny on the neck, whispering encouragement. Fanny, seemingly emboldened by her success at six inches, this time needed no urging. Moving at a canter, she headed forward toward the jump. Her pace and spacing were perfect.

This is it, thought Miranda. Four, three, two, one. Jumping position. She fixed her eyes on the horizon. Fanny gathered herself and leaped.

The End